BREAKAGE

Nia Williams

Gurning Gnome

www.niawilliams.com

Rosalyn. One hundred million volts. Twenty-five years incinerated in one lightning strike.

Or maybe I'm hallucinating. I've been to the cottage, and that always puts me in a strange frame of mind. Even the journey there is surreal. As you approach the turn-off along the old Roman Road, you'd think the village was on fire. A great swirl of black smoke drifts over the trees and the church. Open the car window, and you can hear the villagers' screams. Then you take the turning, start winding down the steep hill towards the churchyard, and the smoke disintegrates into a flap of wings, billowing out and back around the treetops; and the screams of panic broaden into a relentless, rasping call. I don't know why the rooks have picked on this particular corner of nowhere. They've probably been there a lot longer than the people. And the noise never stops. It throbs away from hour to hour, day and night. Even the guns on the firing range don't stop them. Each blast brings a brief aftershock of more frenzied cawing, and then it all settles back down again to the normal, unremitting din.

Getting back to the city is always a relief. I usually call in at Astey's for a drink. It's only a few doors down from the gallery, and the sort of place that suits me down to the ground. Quiet, sophisticated, well thought-out. Bare bricks, light wood, and a couple of glass features from my own collection. One is 'Frozen Flight', a scarlet, tapering wing that forms a ripple of colour against a blank plastered wall. The other is a clinical row of sky-blue lozenges, lining the corridor that leads to the loos. They're perfect for this place. They flatter the customers, make them feel part of a creative, civilised space. People sit themselves under Frozen Flight and settle into appropriate attitudes over their brandy coffees. I approve of that. We should all try and add to the elegance of our surroundings. I once had to stop at a burger place off the motorway, and it was one of the more dispiriting experiences of my life. Foam spewing from the slashed banquettes; congealed leavings and coffee-stains on the tables; filth and litter rimming the floor. No wonder the customers slouched in, dressed like a chain gang, and sat stuffing slaughtered muck into their hamster cheeks, slobbering and belching and eyeing their fuel under drooping lids. We're all defined by our surroundings.

Anyway. I rushed back from the village as soon as I could. Dropped in to Astey's. Had a bland chat with Julio at the bar, read the paper over my Shiraz, then popped down the road, as usual, to check on the gallery before heading home. I generally spend an hour looking round, assessing the displays, making the odd change here and there. It's not that I'm anxious—the security system is faultless. The tightest money can buy. I just go to see the collection.

So here I am, standing in the dark, watching as the city light fingers the curves and rims of the items around me. I'm floating on a starlit sea, trying to shake off the effects of my visit to the sticks.

And there she is. Rosalyn. Hurrying past, eyes fixed ahead, tugging a shopping trolley behind her. Truly. A shopping trolley, on wheels. But it's her, no question. Rosalyn. My body forgets how to function. Breath, pulse, brain, all stunned into stillness. One hundred million volts. I quoted that figure to her the day I first met her, in a factory on the edge of a southern Italian town. The charge hits the earth, I told her; the circuit is complete. Lightning strikes. I remember her eyes, when I was saying it. Looking aside—not at me—listening to what I said. Rosalyn was

4

never one for schmalz; never one to sully the moment with a corny sexual subtext. I remember speaking to her, watching the effect of my words, and thinking: *perfect*.

And look at her now. When my body revives I hurl myself at the door, press my face against the glass to see where she's gone. She's not far—I could easily catch her up, call her name and … What? What then?

'Rosalyn, Good God, I *thought* it was you …'

'I don't believe it, how *are* you?'

'How long is it since—?'

'Oh, don't!'

No. Don't. I can't do it: the shifting feet, the awkward small-talk—just can't. And look at her. Once the first impact has died away I can judge her a little more impartially. Jesus, she's put on weight. Look at the mack, a shapeless, voluminous thing, bellying out behind her, belt flying. And the hair, once thick and sleek with a sheen like polished wood—greying, now, and coiling into corkscrews like springs bursting out of an old sofa. She looks … frumpy. Just another ageing woman rushing home to the semi-detached.

OK. I'm breathing again. My heartbeat is steady. So I saw Rosalyn. It doesn't mean a thing. Let's face it, I know absolutely nothing about her any more. It strikes me, watching her tack round the corner and out of sight, that she might pass the gallery regularly, twice a day. If she works or lives in the area, I'll inevitably bump into her sooner or later. Well, fine. I'll avoid it as long as I can. But if it happens, it happens. I'll be prepared.

5

2

I never pursued anyone else that way. In fact, even at 21 years old, I'd never really pursued anyone at all. I'd never wanted anyone enough. Then I met Rosalyn, and I had to have her. Simple as that.

I've still got photographs of Rosalyn in her prime, framed on the wall of my apartment. Black and white shots. One of her performing, a close-up of that blank and lovely face, the glister of stage-lights sketching her profile, shining in her eyes and on her teeth and lips. The only missing element is the sound of her heartbreaking, yearning voice. The other picture was taken in a café in Florence: Rosalyn lost in thought, or maybe sulking, laced with the smoke of her cigarette. I come home, after seeing her again, and stare at that picture for several minutes. I remember everything about the day that was taken. The day Scott came into our lives. But I don't want to think about that. No. I'm looking at a lovely face, captured by a superb photographer. It's a work of art, an asset, an essential element in the style and order of my home. Never mind what's become of that face. Never mind the expansion of flesh and the greying hair. That's just life.

3

Glass is my world. I've always loved it, and I've got Uncle Don to thank for that. When I was six he took me to a craft display. It was mainly weavers and potters, some woman painting boiled eggs in a tent—that sort of thing. I was bored. I kept pulling his belt to move on, and saying,

'Can I have a candy-floss now?' I'd never had a candy-floss before, but I'd seen someone at a stall, spinning pink clouds onto a stick.

Uncle Don kept promising I could have my candy-floss when we'd seen the crafts.

'Have we seen the crafts now?' I'd ask, after yet another trestle-table of beaded jewellery. 'Is it time for candy-floss?'

'Nearly time, sunshine. One more place to see'.

We went into a low building called the Studios, and as soon as we entered I could feel the warning touch of a great and dangerous heat. There was a barrier. A crowd of us stood behind it and watched as a man dipped a long, thin tube into a furnace. At first, it was the furnace that caught my fancy: the thrill of that white-hot roar, near enough to colour my face. The man was sweating so much, his flesh seemed to be flowing off the bone. And then he put his mouth to that tube, started to spin it, and twist it. It reminded me of the candy-floss man. I craned to see what was emerging from the pipe. More pink sugarwebs? No—it was a soap bubble, wobbling insanely, fluttering, bulging, dancing this way and that, so transparently thin that I thought it must pop any minute. I was mesmerised. I tugged on Uncle Don's belt.

'Is it soap?'

'No.'

After a while I had another idea.

'Is it water?'

'No.'

'Is it air, then?'

'No. It's glass. He's making glass.'

I couldn't make sense of it. Glass was the gleaming tower block where Uncle Don worked, on the very top floor, where my mother would take me sometimes, pointing up and up till my neck hurt, showing me a second sun blazing from the corner of his office. Glass was the panes of Dad's greenhouse, framed with mould, enclosing a crumbly smell of earth and tomato plants. How could glass be these things, and also this liquid magic, pooling and pirouetting to the pipe-blower's tune?

'You like this, don't you, mate?' said Uncle Don.

'Yes.'

'Let's see what we can get you, then,' he said.

After the demonstration we were herded to the little shop, and Uncle Don told me to pick anything I liked. I chose a glass elephant. It was blue and chunky and smooth. Then he said,

'Let's get something for your mum too, shall we?'

So we picked a paperweight, a bloodred pebble of captured swirls and loops, and Uncle Don said,

'There you are, sunshine. Now you can tell your mum you bought her something made with magic.'

Sunshine. Uncle Don always called me that. It's one of the terms he picked up at the police station as a lad, when he was often in trouble. He used to show off about it, about being a bit of a tearaway. He always used terms like 'the beak' and 'the old bill', like some minor character in an Ealing comedy, and he played up his London accent in a way my parents never did. The greater his success, the stronger the accent grew. All part of the Don Cutler legend.

On the way home I nursed the paperweight in one hand and the elephant in the other, noting their weight, feeling with my thumbs how smooth they were, and how strong. I started to look around as we drove, spotting where the glass was. Lampposts. Houses. Wide shop windows, suddenly vulnerable and exposed. I pressed the button and the Daimler's tinted windows rose and fell with a delicious electronic purr, as I played languid hide-and-seek with the outside world. I kept thinking about the bubble flowering from that pipe, and about water, and getting the two things mixed up. I thought about rain on a window, and wondered what separated one from the other. When we got to the house my mother came out to meet us and I launched myself at her with the gift.
'Mum, we saw glass coming out of a water-pipe!'
She kept her grip on me with one arm and took the paperweight with her free hand.
'It's glass!' I was yelling, 'It's glass made out of water!'
and my mother told Don over my head,
'This is beautiful.'

4

It's never really dark here. There are lights burning all night, around my apartment block and strung along the dual carriageway on the horizon. Makes it difficult to tell what time it is, when you've woken for no reason. I can see a grass verge from my window, and a frill of shrubbery through the railings of our communal garden. There's a silver clarity to it all: not daylight yet, then. As I watch, a cat reverses out of the bushes, dragging a dead bird by the neck. It pauses to adjust its grip, then trots away with its catch, accompanied by droplets of distant birdsong. The first notes of the dawn chorus. That wretched bird was probably gearing itself up to sing in the day when it all slammed to an end. A bird has died; a cat lives. The sadness of that swaying little corpse; the sleek fluidity of the cat. Swings and roundabouts.

The dawn chorus is building up to its peak now. Somewhere in the undergrowth that cat is probably feasting itself, down to the birdbones. And the other birds just carry on as usual, which I suppose is all they can do. I don't know what it is that woke me, particularly. The weirdness of seeing Rosalyn, quite possibly. Resentment, that she's assumed a banal reality after all these years of charismatic absence. Could be that. Anyway, the sky's lifting now, and my mind's beginning to clear. The traffic builds, the streetlights go out. On the wall to my left, the mirror is rattling in its white oak frame. I'll have to think about hanging it somewhere else, or adjusting the frame somehow. One of these rush hours, that glass is going to crack.

Swings and roundabouts. That was a game my father taught me when I was very small. It was a distraction technique, really, to divert me from a tantrum about some passing catastrophe. Basically just a convoluted way of counting your blessings. For every cloud, you find a silver lining. That's all. Except that the lining, naturally, has to be directly associated with the cloud. So, for instance, if I was in a sulk because it was raining, I had to come up with something I liked about the rain. It makes puddles I can jump in. That kind of thing. I've got a vivid memory of sitting with him in his shed—so I must have been very young at the time—searching for a silver lining to the model aeroplane I'd accidentally stood on. It was only a flimsy, balsam-wood toy; it didn't even fly. But I'd broken the wing and I was devastated. What I remember is the way he kept me diligently to the rules of the game. So even when I'd recovered sufficiently to offer:

'I suppose I could play football instead?'

—he wouldn't have any of it. The lining had to be connected to the cloud. I can see myself now, weedy little mite, squatting on a wooden stool among the sawdust and tools: mouth still wobbling, tears growing sticky on my face, lost in concentration on that wrecked plane, searching for an advantage.

He helped me out in the end. The answer was: he would make me a better one. And he did—a good, sturdy biplane with propellors that turned. I played with it every day for months. Then Uncle Don bought me a remote controlled one for my birthday, and the biplane was relegated to the toy chest.

These memories come swilling to the surface in the early hours—unexpected, irrelevant. I suddenly hear my mother mocking my father with that sidelong smile: 'Oh, stop mollycoddling the boy, Keith. Tell him the truth for once: every silver lining has a cloud.'

And my father's gentle protest:

'I just want him to look on the bright side.'

I think of that now, and I think of the hours Dad spent making that plane, and the easy way Don trumped him with a fistful of cash … Still, I was a child. I wanted flash toys and Don liked to splash his money around. Dad didn't stand a chance.

11

Uncle Don was more exciting than my Dad in every way. He was tall, good-looking, full of chat, full of swagger. He took me places: the circus, the races, on the ferry to France. The games he played weren't about pros and cons; they were about winning. Even a kickaround in the park could turn into gladiatorial combat. He never let me win, and didn't hesitate to exploit his size and strength—or to cheat, come to that. I remember once, when I'd made a good run at the ball and was about to land a kick, Don just hauled me up by my armpits and swung me out of the way. I yelled and punched and screamed for the non-existent ref, and generally had a whale of a time.

My Dad, now, he was a maker. You might even say a craftsman, though he would have snorted at that.
'I just cobble things together', he used to say. 'Make do and mend.'
He spent hours in the garden, planing and hammering, figuring out the anatomy of hinges and grooves, making things work. Things for the garden, mainly—containers, raised beds, an arbour where my mother could sit and read on summer evenings … I can see him now, pondering some problem over a heap of wood and rusty metal, belly hammocked in his old dungarees, mouth bristling with nails. He grew things too, of course—flowers to please my mother, veg and fruit for himself. By the time I was old enough to register his presence, he'd stopped going to an office. But he never took a day's rest. Dad laboured away from early light to nightfall every single day, until he dropped like a tree into the trench he'd just dug for his early potatoes. He worked the garden, and the garden generated work. His life had closed into a perfect circle.

I could never do it. I was clumsy—'cack-handed', Uncle Don used to say. Dad tried to show me how to whittle wood once. I remember standing in the shed with him, his rough hands closed around my fingers, guiding the pocket knife. I remember his patient voice saying: 'Look for the shape in the wood. It'll show itself, if you give it time ...' The sweet smell of wood-shavings, the mellow, misty warmth of that little shed, the sense of being safe inside but outside at the same time ... and bang! I'd lost control and the pocket knife had leapt off the wood and into Dad's thumb.

'What in god's name are you showing him now?' said my mother, when we went indoors to tend to the cut. And 'Oh don't snivel, Nathan', at me, her scorn instantly halting my tears. 'Whittling wood!' she repeated, with comic incredulity. 'Whatever next—how to chew straw?'

I must have been a disappointment to him. He must have wished for a son who could share tasks with him, discuss the problems and practicalities, or just labour away in companionable silence. But I couldn't do it. And as I grew older, Uncle Don's designer suits and glass office had far more appeal than Dad's shed. As Uncle Don used to say,

'You're better off selling a box than making it, sunshine.'

Nevertheless, part of me has always felt like a fraud. I can tell you anything you want to know about the items in my collection—the techniques, the tools, the history of their creation. But I can't create them myself.

5

I give up on sleep, and go to the gallery early. Gabby's amazed to see me already there when she arrives. I usually make time for brunch at Astey's before putting in an appearance. It's one of the privileges of running your own show.

'Bright and early! Where's the fire?'

She's got a stock of these little phrases. They remind me of those magnetic strips you can buy for the fridge door—compose your own poetry, with a random line on each one.

'Well,' I say, not quite matching her level of chirpiness, 'I'm seeing this new one today, so I thought I'd better be prepared'.

'Ah yes! Pastures new! Fresh blood! A new addition to the fold!'

'We'll see. I'll be in the back room if you need me.'

I can't stand Gabby's sprightliness for long. The customers love her, though. She's done wonders for repeat sales.

The new one is a young artist called Freda Pannage. Background in fine arts, ceramics, stained-glass, blah. What caught my eye were the pictures she sent of her 'glass moods': a series of masks, or pared-down expressions, in smoky, uncertain colours. I've asked her to bring a couple along.

She arrives 10 minutes late, which for an artist is the equivalent of half an hour early. I hear her talking to Gabby out front. A husky, low voice. Saxophone to Gabby's piccolo. Gabby shows her in and as she leaves us, I catch her retreating look, skimming the girl's hips and bottom. Freda must be—what? Mid twenties? She's still got that lightness of line and movement. Her clothes, which should look ridiculous, seem designed with her body in mind. Big belt; a top that looks like Dad's sleeveless vest; some kind of flying jacket. A frenzy of red hair. She stumbles in with her portfolio and her product case, all sweet disorder, insisting we call her Freddie, everyone does.

So we have our meeting, and I ask about her interests and she tells me about her preoccupation with identity, the interplay of the translucent and the opaque, and all sorts of other cobblers, and we make a little more eye contact than is strictly necessary, and then she puts the product case on the table and unlocks it, clears away a great wad of bubblewrap, and there they are. Three emotions in a row. A quizzical fragment of face in slate-blue: forehead, eyes, the outer line of a nose. A satisfied smile with just a sliver of one eye, in green. Lying between them, a whole head, in mottled glass: this is the one she takes out first, easing her long hands around it, burying them into the foam that protects it, lifting it as tenderly as a mother. Its expression is inscrutable. Freddie says,

'I was aiming for serenity, but he sort of took over'.

Well, I've heard that one before: it usually means things went wrong. But this time I can quite believe the glass man set his own agenda. The lips seem about to open, to say something; the curve of his eyelids suggests he's had second thoughts.

'I love it' I say.

'Cool.' she says. 'He's my fave—Alfie.'

Apparently *What's It All About, Alfie* was on the radio when she was at work on it. I ask if she's willing to let him go.

'Oh, yeah. Much as I love him, I've got to eat.'

We clinch the deal, and I offer to buy her brunch.

'I didn't get my fix of eggs benedict this morning' I explain. 'I'm getting withdrawal symptoms.'

'Cool' she says automatically, and I realise she's more nervous than she lets on.

Over brunch she chatters on about her work, and the Mini Clubman she inherited from her aunt and immediately crashed, and about falling through a plate glass window when she was 10.

'Funny thing was', she rattles on, through mouthfuls of eggs benedict, 'I didn't have a scratch on me, but my brother came leaping after me like a hero, and his arse was torn to shreds. I used to call him Scar-butt for years after that.'

'Children can be very cruel' I say, watching the delicate way she balances her fork between fingers and thumb.

'Whereas, me—not a scratch. Even at the time, I remember thinking how spooky that was. I guess that's when I started being hung up about glass' she says. I look at her face, then, and see the spark of response, and think: yes, OK, wouldn't mind at all.

As we're saying goodbye outside the bar, I'm aware of someone watching us from across the road. My breathing quickens. I kiss Freddie on both cheeks and she canters off, and I try to turn back towards the gallery without looking that way. But the observer is waving, now, and dodging the traffic, and there's no sense pretending I can't hear her calling my name.

'Nathan! I *thought* it was you! I thought, bloody hell, it can't be …'

'Rosalyn! Good god! I don't believe it!'

Still in that terrible mack, but no trolley today, praise be. We gape at each other for a minute, then do the awkward half-embrace, and she tells me what a long time it's been, and neither of us mentions the fact that, when we last met, she was crying hysterically, and screeching: *Why are you so fucking cold?*

'My gallery's just round the corner' I say, for want of anything else. I back away a couple of steps, implying the urgency of business.

'That's incredible' says Rosalyn, and her face is as open and guileless as a flower.

'Bryn's office is just up there.' She swings an arm vaguely behind her. 'I've just come from there, now.'

I raise an eyebrow.

'My husband' she adds.

We stand there, unable to move the conversation any further. I say,

'Well, I really …'

And she interrupts, as if a miraculous thought has occurred:

'You should come round! Come and see us—we're not far from here. Look! I'll jot it down …' She's fumbling with an enormous handbag, ignoring my protests. 'See … it's really straightforward, you probably know it …' —scribbling an address on a till receipt, leaning on her own thigh and putting the pen through the flimsy paper a couple of times— 'Come tonight! Come on, it's usually open house with us, anyway, people trooping in and out at all hours …' She flings the paper at me, nearly dropping the contents of her bag into the gutter.

'I'll do what I can' I mumble, with no intention of doing anything at all, and then she says,

'Go on, Nathan, do something spontaneous, break the habit of a lifetime!'

I stare at her and she blushes deeply. It's such a bizarre thing to say, at any level, and she knows it is. I mean, all else apart, how would Rosalyn know whether I'm spontaneous or not? I've had no part in her life since she slammed the door behind her on the 27th of January, 1995. She giggles and shrugs, and I feel sorry for her. Besides which, there's no denying a certain curiosity—about Bryn, and the house in (I glance at the receipt) Trenter Avenue, and the life Rosalyn made after the front door slammed. So I allow myself a teasing look, and say,

'Spontaneity is the next item on the list',

and promise to call round as soon as I've finished the day's work.

6

When I grew older and found less to say to my Dad, I would shuck off his attempts to assuage my moods with swings and roundabouts. I found it unbearably irritating and smug, and as soon as Dad saw that, he dropped it. But I find myself playing the game to this day. Even driving to Rosalyn and Mr Rosalyn's house in Trenter bloody Avenue, I sit at the wheel of my car thinking:

Con: At least an hour of my evening wasted in a dreary corner of pebbledash city, drinking herbal tea, no doubt, in a hideous house stifled with flowery furniture.

Pro: I'll have a chance to snoop at her life and possessions, and to congratulate myself on a lucky escape.

Nevertheless, even as I park on the pavement and turn off the engine, I'm tempted to make my getaway. I really am dreading this. I've got to find something to say to a woman who used to be the centre of my life; a woman who's now turned from sexy principal boy to panto dame. As I'm checking the number of the house I see a movement at the window and it's too late. She's knocking at the pane and gurning, and the next minute she's opening the door, hurling her greeting down the path in the voice that used to touch my soul.

Actually, the house isn't too bad inside. Messy, yes, and shabby, but peppered with quite interesting odds and ends—an antique crimping iron, some old pewter serving plates, a couple of rather good oil paintings—one of Rosalyn, I'm intrigued to see, in younger days. She's been fussing with the kettle and comes in to the living room behind me while I'm peering at it.

'When was this?' I ask, without meaning to sound so abrupt.

'Oh, years ago' she says. 'When I was expecting my eldest.'

I turn away sharply, and have to master my expression. I hadn't factored in children. Stupid of me, of course. She was only in her 30s when she left. Why shouldn't she have gone on to have a family? She smiles at my surprise.

'Yes,' she says, 'it was a bit of a shock at the time, but a very nice one.' She goes to a sideboard and opens a drawer, bringing out a sheaf of photos. 'Here … That's Josh … That's him at his graduation, did very well, a two-one in Chemistry … and here's Poppy … she's in Canada now …' —dealing me shots of a curly-haired, broad-shouldered young man, a rather plain girl with bad skin … 'And … oh, well, this is Delyth. She's Bryn's daughter, actually … We've sort of lost touch.'

I study the picture of a stern face, masked with thick glasses. A girl with thoughts of her own. Judging by the quality of the photograph it was taken quite a long time ago. Maybe when Rosalyn and I were still together, who knows? I'm reeling slightly from this avalanche of new personalities and untold sorrows. I make the right noises, look from the pictures to Rosalyn and back to the portrait on the wall.

'It's good' I say. 'Who did it?'

'Bryn!' She's pleased. 'I keep telling him he should take it more seriously. But it's just a hobby to him …' The kettle clunks in the kitchen and she flaps off to make coffee. She returns apologetically with a mug of something bog-coloured.

'I know you like *proper* coffee' she says, 'but I'm afraid we're too lazy for all that …'

I take a minimal sip. It's disgusting. I make a polite face before slipping the mug onto a bookshelf. I recognise some of the spines. *The Story of Opera. Vocal Exercises. An Anthology of Italian Song.*

'You're still singing, then?' I say and she snorts.

'Not really. Not since the kids. Lost the time, lost the muscle, lost the urge.'

Tacitly I curse Mr Rosalyn for inflicting the shock brood.

'That's a pity' I say. 'You had a fine voice.'

'No I didn't.' She's brusque and embarrassed. It threatens to become an uncomfortable moment, but just in time there's a commotion at the front door and she goes into a dance of welcome for the homecoming husband.

He's older—much older; I'd say early 70s. And shorter than Rosalyn. She kisses the top of his bald head. Something about him, about the inquiring stoop and the eager button eyes, seems familiar.

'Bo' she says, 'this is him, this is Nathan.'

She ushers him forward and he pumps my hand affably.

'Aha! The glamorous ex!' He performs a snarl, then laughs uproariously.

'Ah, well,' I say, adopting the same tone, 'the best man won.'

Rosalyn is hopping around, getting girlish.

'Stop that, you two!' she squeaks. 'I'll have to run away and hide!'

God. I really am in a house of strangers.

We settle down and Bryn pours me a brandy—thankfully nobody's mentioned the abandoned coffee—and I tell them about the gallery, and about our bright new talent, and wish to God I was in a restaurant with Freddie now, making her nervous and playing it by ear. Then Bryn starts on about his work, something to do with the law, immigration, asylum rights, but I'm not really paying attention because I've suddenly put two and two together and realised where I've seen him before. I sit forward, with an effort, on the sofa, and fix him with a look.

'Tell me,' I say, 'did you used to come and hear Rosalyn perform?'

They exchange a smirk.

'You see' says Rosalyn, 'I *knew* he'd remember. Nathan is like an elephant, he never forgets.'

Good god, yes, I remember. We used to call him The Boffin. Always turning up at Rosalyn's concerts, hanging around afterwards to shake her hand and proffer musical advice.

'Knows all there is to know about music. Couldn't produce a note of it to save his life'—that's what she used to say. She was withering. I have a flashback of her at yet another freezing church hall, peering through the vestry door to check out the audience and muttering, 'Look out, The Boffin's here …' And look at her now. Mrs Boffin, the lady wife, the other half. And clearly the insult has become an affectionate in-joke. She's calling him Bo for short. You couldn't make it up.

As a matter of fact I can see, however grudgingly, that he's a good partner for Rosalyn. He has a sense of calm benevolence about him. And apparently he was desperate for Rosalyn to revive her singing career—so I was wrong about that as well. They bait each other gently:

'She's always underestimated her talent', he says; 'I told her, there are ways and means; you don't have to be a slave to motherhood …'

'Bo doesn't understand, you can't live two lives at once …'

'Nonsense, we could have found a way—I would have been all too happy to step in …'

'He was just jealous of my quality time with the kids …'

'They would have been proud to have a diva for a mother …'

And so on, to and fro, while I sit and watch like a Wimbledon spectator. I wonder whether it's too early to make my excuses, and too late to give Freddie a ring.

Then I'm saved by the doorbell. Bryn goes to answer it: he seems to know it'll be for him. I'm hoisting myself and my excuses off the sofa when Rosalyn says, softly,

'Was that your daughter?'

'Sorry?'

'When I saw you earlier on, in the street. Your daughter, was it? She's very lovely.'

21

I'm ridiculously flustered.

'Oh! Oh, God, no! No, that was the new artist I was telling you about …'

She's equally thrown. Her hands flail around.

'Oh, sorry! I thought—you know …'

Yes, I know. She thought: middle-aged man, slim young girl—what else could it possibly be? I get to my feet and see my reflection in the mirror over her fake-coal gas fire. She notices, of course.

'You put me to shame, you really do, Nathan. You seem to have grown younger. How do you do it? It's so unfair!'

Is she being kind? I've always sworn to myself I'll know when to bow out gracefully, before the segue from Attractively Mature to Silly Old Fool. I wince at my reflection, allowing myself a quick check. No, she's not being kind. OK, I'm no Johnny Depp, but she's right, I've kept myself in trim. It's amazing what clever dress-sense and a knowing haircut can do. I'm reassured. Definitely worth giving Freddie Pannage a ring.

It's impossible to get out while Bryn and his visitor are clogging up the hall. They're out there talking in sombre, quick tones, as if some crisis has occurred. Rosalyn is urging me to stay and have something to eat; I'm muttering something about an appointment, and searching inside my jacket for my phone. I feel I might be entombed in this place forever. Then Bryn reappears, mouthing a message to Rosalyn. He turns to me and speaks brightly:

'Nathan, we're going to have a quick snack in the kitchen—please, come and join us. Come and meet Anna, she'd love to meet you.'

We're all bundled in a big knot from the living room into a surprisingly spacious kitchen, where we unravel around a pine table, and Rosalyn starts fussing with a loaf of bread. I touch her elbow.

'Not for me, really, I'm meeting someone for—'

'Oh, that's all right, I'll just make a big batch and people can take it or leave it.'
She's obviously accustomed to this—unexpected visitors, overlap of guests and refreshments … As she said, it's a bit of an open house.

Bryn introduces me to Anna.

'Anna' he explains 'hasn't been over here very long.'

He doesn't tell me where she's from or how she got here; maybe that's a standard precaution. I shake Anna's hand and she looks past my face. She has the empty eyes of someone who's seen the worst. No pressure from the hand, no smile, no animation. This woman has been crushed.

Bryn says,

'Anna's had quite a difficult time—'

I shift in my seat with alarm. Surely he's not going to start recounting her experiences? Torture, rape, god alone knows what other atrocities, over cheese and pickle sandwiches?

'—finding her feet' he goes on. 'We've been giving her a helping hand with the, er …'

'—formalities' adds Rosalyn, placing a hill of sandwiches on the table.

Now or never. I stand up and give them my most gracious smile.

'That's great', I say. I fumble for the phone again. 'I don't mean to be rude, but I'm afraid I really have got to go—someone's waiting for me …'

I catch Rosalyn's inquisitive glance. I've managed to get away without telling her anything of note about my life. Satisfying. That goes down as a Pro. I shake Anna's hand again, and say,

'Good luck with everything.' And this time Anna smiles—a brief but glorious smile, doused in an instant. I'm moved, despite myself, and give a moment's more pressure to her hand. To have seen the worst of humanity, and smile like that at a stranger … 'Good luck' I say again, and take my hasty leave.

Rosalyn sees me to the door.

'Well, we must keep in touch,' she says, 'now that we're …'

'Yes, yes' I say, and give her a businesslike kiss on the cheek. She's still holding the door open as I get into the car and wave to the rearview mirror. I drive to the next street so that I can stop and find Freddie's number, and make that call.

Yes, Freddie is free, and we have a pleasant enough meal at Puccini's. But my heart's not in it. I keep thinking of that alien world I've just left: Rosalyn and Bo, the house, the children. And then something else keeps intruding too: Anna, her vacant eyes, the brutality that's chased her out of one country and will probably frogmarch her out of another. It's disturbing. Probably easier for Rosalyn and her husband—they're *doing* something. Trying to help, however futile that help might be. I'm just not made that way. It's not that I close my eyes to these things: I watch the news, I give to charities, I abhor cruelty and war. But there's nothing I can do about it, except encourage the best of us: the art. The beauty.

Still, the mood is spoiled. I apologise to Freddie and see her home early, pleading pressure of work. She can sense I've got something on my mind, and I can tell that's doing me no harm. She thinks I'm complicated. Troubled. I play it cannily, kiss her only a little more than socially, and walk away from her without looking back. No doubt about it, Freddie will be the first to call.

7

I grew tired of Dad's gentle games. But there was one game I never tired of playing, well into my teens—a rainy-day game I played with my mother, at first, and later on my own, with obsessive teenage solemnity. I couldn't play it just once: it had to be over and over again, getting quicker and quicker every time. In the early years my mother would eventually hold up her hand and make that humorous, pained look, and say:

'Enough, Nathan. Even this thrill can pall by repetition.'

In the teen years she just left me to it.

The game was called Pairs. It was simple enough. It involved laying rows of picture-cards face down on the floor, in random order. Every card had its exact pair. Players took turns to flip two cards face up. If they matched, that scored a point. If not, the cards were turned down again. Essentially, it was a memory test. I always used to beat my mother, and I don't think she was letting me win. She was just no good at anything systematic. Life was a fairground ride to her, careering from one experience to the next; if that experience happened to be unpleasant she simply averted her eyes and waited for the next good thing to come along.

I find her difficult to describe. She was lovely: everyone agreed about that. But her loveliness was in the animation of her face, the light beneath her skin, the knowing humour of her eyes. Photographs never did her justice. Look at the snaps of her now, and you see a cheerful woman, blonde or, in later years, greying, quite pretty but nothing special. There's no clearer refutation of that old myth about the camera's truth. She had a kind of haze around her; she had a particular scent … at the risk of being crass, I have to say she was like a spring day. Think of the way you feel when the air softens and the trees start to bud: that's the effect my mother had on everyone who came her way.

Snapshots are all I have of her now. She couldn't be bothered with anything else. When I once tried to persuade her to pose for a picture, she waved me away. 'Nathan,' she said, 'you set too much store by appearances. And at this stage in life I do not want my appearance stored, thank you very much.' Only Scott Carter was ever allowed to take a portrait shot—and that didn't turn out for the best. But in any case, happy snaps are the closest approximation to her character. She's virtually never still in them: always a blur of laughter and fair hair, a glance over the shoulder, a moment that's passed.

We had a drawer full of photographs at home. Mother chucked them there carelessly, but I used to spend hours taking them out and replacing them in neat chronological order. I pored over each one, comparing features and colouring and build. I had no brothers or sisters, so I was intrigued by family likenesses. Not envious, though. I never longed for a sibling to bully or adore. I was a self-contained child, always content with my own company and my collections.

There were lots of childhood photos of the three of them—Mother, Don, Dad. One in particular held my attention. Dad and Uncle Don standing side by side in a back yard. You can see a fence behind them, one panel askew at the join; an upturned pail; a football. Dad and Don are both in baggy shorts, shirts and identical knitted tank-tops. Dad short and stocky, looking askance, grinning uncertainly. Don about a foot taller, rangy, smiling straight at the lens. Both have the flop of black hair, the dark eyes and straight eyebrows. They stand close, Don leaning slightly towards Dad as if someone's told him to move into the frame. It looks as if they might be holding hands. I remember asking my mother whether they were.

26

'Doubt it' she said.

'How old are they there?'

'Ooh, hard to say. Older than you are now. Not exactly sure.'

'Where is this?'

'Looks like the back yard of our house. Or next door's. Hard to tell, from that ...'

A mine of information, my mother.

Was I an odd child? It's hard to say. Hard to see myself from this distance, from outside. At this stage in life you can turn everything upside-down, and define your childhood quirks by the identity you forge as an adult. I'm a collector: nothing odd about that. And from the standpoint of a collector—a very successful, very well respected collector, at that—it's easy to explain away a child's preoccupation with order and pattern, his compulsion to tidy life into categories and index the world around him, laying claim to the best items on the inventory, the beautiful and the correct. There I am, Nathan Hill, maybe 10 years old, kneeling in a corner of the living room surrounded by photographs ready to be rearranged. And there's 14-year-old Nathan, taller and spottier, flipping those cards up with machine-gun rapidity, gaining useless points to store away in secret. And my mother, standing at the mirror over the mantelpiece, done up to the nines in a dress that shows off her slim figure and long legs, inspecting her lipstick, putting on her earrings, exuding that delicious scent, a mix of shampoo and eau-de-cologne and make-up, the scent of parties and dances and a whole strange universe closed off to me. The doorbell rings, and my mother calls to my father:

'Keith, the driver's here. I'm off. Don't wait up'. She's throwing a wrap around her shoulders, and an instruction at me: 'Have fun, sweetheart.' And she's gone. *Have fun*. Was it sarcasm? I can't tell from here. I can just hear the clap of the front door and the smooth revving of an expensive car. A car sent by Don and driven by a stranger. The car drives away, the house resettles, the pairing game resumes. After a while the living room door opens and Dad is there, irritating the air, asking stupid questions:

'Everything OK, son?'

—retreating into the kitchen to cook supper, which we'll eat on trays, letting the telly fill the silence till it's time for bed.

God, I longed to get into that car with my mother. To be wafted away to one of Don's jollies, as he called them, to stand at my mother's sweet-scented side and watch her laugh and flirt and captivate everyone around her. At about 15 I made a decision. I decided I couldn't possibly be Keith Hill's son. I must be Uncle Don's child, product of an illicit affair between my mother and the one true love of her life. By that time I was going to a school that boarded during the week. I've got a feeling I would have been packed off all term if that option had been available. But as it was, I spent sullen weekends at home, folded into a corner with my cards, or doing prep, or reading about glass. I didn't have many friends, but I didn't have any trouble either. Don saw to that, coming to collect me at the end of every term in his Daimler, impressing the other boys with his Cockney big-talk and slipping them the odd fiver. Rumours went round: Don had gangster contacts, that sort of thing, and just enough of his dodgy glory rubbed off on me to see me safely through each term.

One holiday I was in Don's office, swivelling around in the big leather chair he kept for guests. He was remarkably tolerant that way. He'd let me examine the big wooden globe that was really a drinks container, or play with the calculator on his desk, while he carried on with his phone calls. Sometimes he'd go off to a meeting, forgetting I was there, and I'd wait at the window till he came back, watching the silent traffic below.

This particular day he was in a talkative mood. One of his employees had just
delivered a report and when he'd gone Uncle Don commented:

'Now, there's a man who'll never climb out of his rut.'

'How do you mean?' I asked.

Uncle Don explained, as he scanned the report, flicking the pages over impatiently,
'People are scared of change, mate, you'll find that. Love status and money.
Whinge on about it all the time. Won't change so much as their underpants to get
it.' As I launched the chair into its next circuit I caught sight of him looking up
from the report to point in my direction: 'Never be afraid to change, sunshine,
that's what I'm telling you.'

'Change what?' I called as the office door spun past.

'Anything, lad. Anything you bloody well like.'

'What did *you* change?' I screwed my eyes shut against the dizziness.

'Changed my name, for starters.'

I let my leg crash into the bookcase to bring the chair to a halt. Despite my
obsession with patterns, I'd never really untangled the exact relationships between
Don and my parents. They'd all grown up together, I knew that; and I had an idea
they all lived in the same house for at least part of their youth. But I'd never
gleaned any more than that, and my parents weren't exactly chatty about their past.

'Changed your name to what?' I demanded, suddenly alert.

'Well, to Don, first off—instead of Donald. Didn't like Donald. Kids at school
called me Duckie. So I chopped it in half. Then I thought, in for a penny ... so I
changed my surname an' all. Called myself Don Cutler. Got a ring to it, innit? Don
Cutler. Thought it sounded like an American detective. Kept it ever since.'

I mulled that one over. Yes, Don Cutler did have a better ring to it, and it set him apart, as it should, from Keith Hill, who could never be anything more than a bloke in a garden shed.

I began to feed the rumours among my contemporaries, and I added a few more hints of my own. Yes, Don and Mother were very close. They always had been. She spent more time, to be honest, with Don Cutler than she did with her own husband. And Don was particularly fond of me … I let them draw their own conclusions, without actually slandering anyone. And thank god for that, in hindsight. I could have caused all manner of scandal, if I'd been more specific. When I finally realised the truth I felt a thundering idiot, but nothing worse than that.

I found out in a ludicrously casual way. I was 16 or so, home for the weekend and too bored and listless even to attend to my obsessions. It was one of those wet, dreary Sunday afternoons. My mother was standing by the window that looked onto a small courtyard to the side of the house. Dad was out there, in his raincoat, fussing around with pots.

'God almighty' said my mother, 'I sometimes think he'll put down roots out there and start shedding leaves every winter.' I grunted, and she went on talking, mainly to herself. 'His father' she said 'was just the same. Potting up and bloody pricking out—that's all you ever heard about. No wonder she made a break for it.'

'Who?' I asked, and she started. She may have forgotten I was there.

'Your grandmother' she said. 'You've never met her—she took off when your Dad was a child.' She gave me a sharp look. 'You knew that.'

'No I didn't. I thought she died.'

My mother turned back to the window. Her voice grew artificially blithe. She knew she'd put her foot in it.

'No, she's alive and kicking somewhere in Scotland, as far as I know. Miserable woman, I always thought, but then I suppose she was stuck with his father, so ...'
She waved a dismissive hand. I unravelled my legs and sat up.
'So I've got a grandmother I never knew I had!'
'Oh, don't be melodramatic. *Nobody's* clapped eyes on the woman since she did her runner. Buggered off in the middle of the night. Cut off all communication with your dad from that moment on.'
'And what about Uncle Don? Did she stay in touch with him?'
She wrinkled her forehead at me in that mocking way of hers.
'Why would she do that?'
'I don't know, because he's the older brother, maybe—'
I can see the expression on her face as if she's standing before me now— caught between horror and hilarity.
'*Brother?* Uncle Don and Dad aren't *brothers*. What on earth put that into your head?'
I opened my mouth but couldn't speak. I felt winded. She made the most of it.
'Haven't you ever noticed they've got different surnames?'
'Of course I have. Uncle Don changed his name' I countered, triumphantly.
'Yes, but not from *Hill*. From *Harris*. They used to call him Hairy-Arse at school. That's why he changed it.'
'He said it was because they called him Duckie.'
'Yes, well, name-calling wasn't rationed, where we came from.'
A slow tide of humiliation crept up my neck to my face. I said,
'Harris is your maiden name.'
She was laughing openly by now. My foolishness had really brightened her day.
'Bingo!' she cried. 'Give this boy a prize!'
Her laughter softened into affection and she came across to ruffle my hair. I tried

to writhe away but she gathered a handful of hair and held it loosely, smiling down into my face.

'You great oaf!' she said. 'Don isn't Keith's brother—he's *mine.*'

She gave my head a couple of gentle shakes, then left me to my embarrassment and returned to the window. She rapped on it and gestured to my Dad, mouthing an exaggerated version of her stage whisper: 'Keith! Get indoors, you idiot! It's *pissing* down!'

I dug out the family photographs again, and studied them in this new light. When I'd recovered from my mortification, I pestered my mother into going through them with me, assigning names and dates. She dealt through them impatiently— 'My parents … Don and his pet dog … your father …'—then a pause—'oh, that's me on my first day at school …' and so on. She didn't really tell me anything at all.

'Is there a picture of Dad's mother?' I asked.

'I shouldn't think so. I imagine his father chucked them all in the bin. If he could summon the energy.'

'What did she look like?'

My mother lowered a shot she'd been studying of herself on a seafront somewhere, laughing out of a spin that had made her skirt circle out and show her knickers.

'Nathan' she said wearily, 'don't start building this into a drama. It's just a woman who left, that's all.'

'But' I persevered 'it must have been horrible for Dad.'

'Yes' she conceded, 'it probably was. But he got over it. Look at me in this one, showing off. Don took this at Southend.'

Once I'd had a chance to think about it, I decided this new information was all for the best. This new pairing may not have had the romance of an affair, but it did, at least, extricate glamorous Don from any connection with my father. Of course, it all made sense, now: Mother and Don. Two peas from the same pod. They belonged together, naturally, and left me only the question of how in the name of glory my lovely mother had ended up marrying dungareed Dad.

The following weekend I went to see Uncle Don in his office. He still let me hang around there, though I had less and less to say for myself with every passing year. 'Wotcher, sunshine' he said as Taff, his secretary, ushered me in. 'At a loose end? Not on the run, are you?'—then, with a nod to Taff—'Nah, this one keeps his nose clean, he's not a little thug like I was at that age …'
'Good for him' said Taff, winking at me as she shut the door. I liked Taff. She'd been there forever, and was one of the few who answered him back.
I sat in the swivelling chair and started swinging it back and forth out of habit.
'How's the knick-knacks then, sunshine?' said Don.
'All right.'
'Can't fathom it, myself. Hoarding stuff like a bloody magpie. Then again, there's big money in it, I know that, if you play it right. Long as you keep a level head and don't get weird about it.'
'I thought you were Dad's brother.' I blurted it out like an accusation of fraud.
'Yeah, she told me.'
I bet she did. They probably had fun with that one. But to give him credit, Don let the joke go by.
'Daft bugger, got your head in the clouds is your trouble.' That was all he said. Then: 'Listen, you can sit there and pick your nose as long as you like, but I'm taking a call from Bangkok any minute so you'll have to keep your trap shut, I can never understand a sodding word he says at the best of times.'
'I didn't know Dad's mother ran away.'

33

'Yeah, sorry business, that was.' He was preoccupied, swotting up on notes for the call. 'Ran off with a plasterer, was it? Something like that.'

I mulled over this new snippet of information, then decided to clear up the last remaining puzzle.

'Why did Mother marry Dad?'

Uncle Don lifted his head sharply, and halted my swivelling with a look.

'Why wouldn't she?' he snapped. I shrugged and he levelled his index finger at me like a pistol. 'Keith Hill is a good bloke, sunshine. Just you remember that. She couldn't have done better. Me and your Dad might not have been brothers for real, but we were good as twins, growing up. And that's what matters, innit?'

I was stung. In a bid to regain his favour, I assumed a new tone of innocent enquiry.

'Did you all go to school together?'

'Sright. Well—when I bothered. Them two was the scholars. But we was always a team. The three musketeers, we were.'

'And Dad fell in love with Mother.' I put the statement between us as a feasible explanation.

'Course he did' he said, returning to his notes. 'Everyone with a blood supply was in love with your mother. She was the school sex-bomb.'

I was losing his attention. I became reckless.

'I thought *you* might be my father.'

That did it. Uncle Don looked up at me with a loud laugh.

'Don't be a prat!' he said, but I could tell he was pleased. 'I tell you what, if you were my son, you'd be finding a good price for those trinkets by now, not ferreting them away in a secret hidey-hole. That's pure Keith Hill, that is. You're the original chip off the old block.'

8

The three musketeers. I was in that office, swivelling that chair, every chance I got after that—no longer brooding and picking my nose, as Don would have it, but pestering him for stories of their youth. He was a busy man, but he rarely sent me packing. He liked telling his tale, drawing his own character, and I couldn't get enough of it.

Mother and Don grew up in a two-up, two-down on a street of identical houses. Dad lived a few doors down. Then his mother ran off with a plasterer and his father gave up on life, and the Harrises more or less took Dad in as their own. The neighbourhood suffered badly in the blitz. Don and Mother were sent to their Auntie Del in Abergele, and Keith Hill tagged along too. While the children were away, Mr and Mrs Harris went to see *Pimpernel Smith* at a local cinema, and the roof fell in.

'Shouldn't have been open at all' said Don. 'Weakened by a raid. But there was money to be made, plenty of bums on seats for the flicks in them days, getting away from all the crap going on outside. Old bugger who ran it kept it going, never mind what. Can't blame him. I'd have done the same. Matinée showing of Leslie Howard—brought the house down. Literally. The old folks copped it in the ninepenny stalls.'

Auntie Del offered to take in Dad and Mother. Keith Hill was a quiet, well-behaved boy, and Mother knew how to pretend. But Don was another matter. Always a handful; always stopping out, getting into tight spots with the local youth. Once nicked the postie's bike, for a laugh. After his parents were killed, by his own account, he 'went a bit nuts'. Stole from Auntie Del's own purse. Set fire to an empty barn near Pensarn. She wouldn't take him on, and the three musketeers wouldn't be parted. So they went home, all three of them, to be minded— ostensibly—by Dad's father.

'But he didn't mind about anything much, poor old git,' remarked Don, 'except how soon he could get another drink down his neck.'

So the three of them went back to the Harrises' empty house.

'I'd like to say the neighbours kept an eye out' said Don, taking a thin cigar from a wooden box. 'But believe me, sunshine, you don't wanna believe all that bollocks. Time of need, all pull together—load of cobblers. All too busy trying to stay fed and stay alive to bother with a bunch of big kids like us. Got back in that house, and it was like the Marie Bloody Celeste in there. Coal in the grate, tea leaves ready in the pot, half a mouldy loaf out waiting … The folks always liked a cuppa after going to the flicks …'

His head dipped over the cigar and I wondered whether Uncle Don might actually be trying not to cry. I watched from my swivel-chair, fascinated. After a moment or two there was a red gleam and puffs of smoke punctuated the air. Just getting the cigar going, after all.

'How did you manage, on your own?' I asked, with something like envy. 'What about money and things?'

'Money' said Don drily 'was the least of the worry.'

They weren't little children, after all, he reminded me, with that sharp look that meant *not spoilt little brats like you*. They all added a couple of years to their age when anyone asked—'well, look at it this way, we wasn't about to be sitting in a classroom learning long division.' Keith Hill, already a sturdy, square boy who was good with his hands, got himself a job as a carpenter's apprentice, patching and shoring up those tottering buildings that might still serve a purpose after a hit. At the end of the working day he kept his carpenter's apron on and cooked for them all.

'Regular little mother, he was,' said Don, with as much admiration as scorn. 'Saved our bacon, did Keith Hill.'

As for the two Harrises, they seemed to live the high life, if I could take Uncle Don at his word.

'Your mother, now—always a popular gel. Even then. Fluttered the eyelashes, flashed the smile and hey presto, extra bit of butter or a lamb chop slipped under the counter. And when the Yanks come over, well, what can I tell you? Every swaggering cowboy wanted 'Eartbreak 'Arris for his sweetheart.'

Lashes, smiles, sweethearts … The language of romance. Of innocence. If there was more between the lines, I didn't choose to read it. It's hard to know exactly how old my mother was—so much adding of years in her childhood and subtracting later on, and never a certificate or a passport that I could trace. But I doubt she was any older than 15 when the war dragged to its end. She and Don can't have been more than a couple of years apart, but by VE Day Don had already established himself as one of the local spivs—'Suspected Persons and Itinerant Vagrants, sunshine. Or VIPs the wrong way round, to you and me.' Already tall and handsome before he turned 14, all hair-oil and cuff-shooting, a cut above the kipper ties and pencil moustaches of yer common or garden crooks. But he dealt in the same dodgy trade.

'Lifting here, flogging there—you know the sort of thing.' I didn't, but I was flattered by the assumption. 'Thought I was the dog's bollocks at the time. Look back at it now and I was just a cocky little bastard, chasing my tail like a fleabitten stray. Would have gone on from bad to worse, probably ended up cooling my heels at Her Majesty's pleasure. But Keith Hill got me in hand.'

My father salvaged chunks of wood from the bomb sites, and brought them home to whittle on. The whittling grew into something grander, and before long he was making cigarette boxes, filigreed with curls and flourishes. Don saw the potential. 'Flogged one to a desk sergeant for half a crown, and gave your dad sixpence to make me another.'

As he counted out the cash, Don knew this was far stronger and better than the rush he got from passing on knicker-elastic and bottles of whisky out the back of a van. He was more than a delivery boy now: he was a capitalist. Don the Spiv had become Don the Boss. This marked the beginning of his transformation from Ducky 'Hairy-Arse' Harris, orphan tearaway, to Don Cutler, king of the quick buck.

That's not to say he developed a greater appreciation of the goods. OK, Don and I are both sellers, not makers; but that's where the comparison ends. Unlike me, Don didn't give a monkey's *what* he was selling, as long as it paid its way. He started with a market stall selling Dad's boxes; then moved on to the rag trade, then to remainder books, then he got his big break with a brand of cheap cosmetics called Glimmer. It was sold in corner shops and flea markets before Uncle Don got his hands on it. He jazzed up the packaging, splashed out on advertising, changed the name from Glimmer to Shimmer and before long the same old industrial sludge and beetle-mash was being daubed over teenage faces from one end of the country to the other.

'Remember this, sunshine—most people want to feel good and look good, and they want someone else to tell them how to do it.' He peppered his accounts with these little homilies. 'Never underestimate the power of snobbery'—that was another one. And 'an ego flattered is a deal done.' Jabbing his cigar to underline the message, delivering each syllable with a spasm of smoke.

'Anything goes, in this life,' he told me once. 'Anything. People will say you can't, it's a joke, it'll never happen … You just plough on, my son. People might whinge about it, might stamp their feet and wag their fingers, but you plough on and eventually they'll just give up and join the party.'

He claimed Shimmer was used by the top Hollywood make-up artists. He claimed it improved skin texture and reduced wrinkles. People seemed to buy his lies—and whether they did or not, they still bought the goods.

Shimmer went international, sponsored a dire teen soap in the US, and made a fortune when it was launched on the stock market, all in the space of a very few years. Uncle Don was still a young man. By the time I came on the scene, his transformation was complete. I couldn't remember a time when he hadn't been filthy rich.

9

Keith Hill. The bloke in the garden shed. I've been thinking about him a lot just lately. Thinking that I would have liked to know him better. I suppose that's an old, old story, isn't it? While they're around, every day, in the corner of your eye, in the back of your mind, their routines and noises and clothes forming the landscape of your life—you just wish they'd go away and leave you alone. And then, before you know it—too late.

I was already a collector. I had a home-made catalogue, intricately organised and regularly updated. Dad had put up shelves in my room and they were crowded with glass orbs, flutes, bowls and discs, all retro stuff, even then, and mostly picked up from junk shops and flea-markets. I loved the stalled quality of these pieces—the sense of a movement trapped: bubbles, twists and turns of impulse made solid and permanent. I read about the craft, I took a deep, almost reverential interest in the manufacturing process. However unassuming the item, however poky and miserable the factory where it was produced, I regarded everyone concerned with its creation as an Artist. But Dad, who could whip up a toy biplane or a cigarette box, adding a little beauty to a shattered world—no. I could never see him in that light.

'What does your father do?' asked one of my peers at school. We were sitting on our desks, waiting for the notoriously unreliable Physics teacher. The others had been killing time in vicarious competition about their parents' wealth and status. We'd gone through all the 'my-dad's-a-QC, my-dad's-got-a-jag' routine (mums never got a look-in), and I'd even chipped in with a few comments about Don's motor. But I couldn't dodge the straight question, and an expectant silence fell as I searched for an acceptable reply.

'He's … he sort of works from home' I managed. Miraculously, one of the others, son of a financier, came to my rescue.

'Consultant, you mean,' he nodded sagely. 'Yeah, my dad's going to do that. He reckons that's where the money is, and then he can retire early and do what he bloody well likes.'

It hadn't really occurred to me till then that Dad should be doing something other than pottering about in his shed. I put it to my mother the following weekend.

'Do? What does he *do*? You mean other than tend to his King Edwards? Good question, dear boy.'

She was curled up in an armchair with a Sunday supplement and a G&T, but the irony didn't strike either of us at the time.

'Did he take early retirement?' I offered, and she gave a yap of laughter.

'Excellent answer! Yes, that'll do nicely. Early retirement—smacks of slippers and cardigans and nice mugs of Horlicks, don't you think? Yup, that fits your father to a tee.'

I did well in my 'A' levels and yearned to study fine art and design, but I couldn't bring myself to admit it to anyone. So I did a History degree instead, to prove my academic gravitas. I wrote the required essays and seminar papers, attended all the lectures and tutorials, joined the cinema club, carried on trawling the junk shops at weekends. There were no philosophical discussions late into the night. Most of my fellow students seemed more intent on getting as pissed and as laid as humanly possible in the space of three years. Personally I didn't have that kind of despair. At the risk of sounding smug, I never had a problem attracting girls, once I was free of that school and its bizarre atmosphere, half monastery, half rugby club. If I hadn't been put right on the paternity score, I would have grown even more convinced that Don was my father as the years went by. I wasn't as tall, but I did have his slim build, his dark sweep of hair and an arrangement that seems to trigger all manner of emotion: black eyelashes, blue eyes. So there were always plenty of confident blondes winding their brown arms through mine or slipping notes onto my desk in the lecture rooms. And I went out with the quieter, more serious girls from time to time. But I wasn't really that interested. Without trying, I seemed to cultivate an image of poetic isolation, which did me no harm at all from that point of view, but by the final year I found myself mantled in my solitude, unable or unwilling to cast it off and become a fully signed-up citizen of the wider world.

I did realise pretty quickly, though, that my connection with Don was no longer a clear advantage. I twigged that, right from the first day of the first term. He and Mother dropped me off (Dad had said his goodbyes at the house, handing me a home-made wooden pencil-case, much to my embarrassment). Don did his usual proprietorial tour of inspection, hands in pockets, a sneer on his handsome face, slagging off the hall of residence and offering to buy me a nice bang-up flat with all mod cons instead. And all at once, I felt the sea-change. Don's cockernee act and rich-man swagger had worked perfectly well with the barristers' boys and minor gentry at school. But here his moneyed manner told against him, and by a curious paradox, his accent was considered a joke. I suppose snobbery is like water, it just fills all the gaps available. As usual, Mother was my saving grace; her beauty and humour won everyone over, and before the end of that first afternoon she was sharing tea and Jaffa Cakes with three of the students with rooms on the same floor.

When I graduated, Uncle Don took the family out for 'a swanky feed up west'. We went to the Monarch, an impossibly stuffy place where jowly businessmen and ageing politicians chewed the cud in corners, and the menu was heavy with red meat. I was quite looking forward to it as I inspected myself in the bedroom mirror—the chauffer-driven glide through a glistening city, the good-looking threesome handed out by a liveried doorman … The doorbell rang and I cantered downstairs, only to see Dad in the hall, dressed in a suit that can't have seen the light of day since before my birth.

'Are you coming with us?' I asked. I hope, now, that I managed to keep the dismay from my voice.

'Not every day your only son gets certified' he quipped, shrugging to settle his jacket. I was startled to see that, far from bulging out of an ill-fitting off-the-peg, he was wearing a well-cut, expensive suit—and wearing it well. My mother emerged from the living room, her silver earrings chattering softly, and said with more approval than I was used to hearing,

'Still scrub up pretty well, don't you, Keith?'

When we got to the Monarch, I had to admit that my father looked like a man who was used to restaurants. He put on his glasses to consult the menu and even explained to me, quietly and without condescension, what some of the more obscure items were.

Don ordered a syrupy red wine without asking anyone else; then made fun of Dad's measured cat-sips.

'Go on, Keith, lad' he taunted, 'it won't poison you. Pretend it's a beer, knock it back, old son. Might as well enjoy it, at this price.'

Dad just smiled, a little private, wrinkle-eyed smile, and said nothing. With that particular arrogance of youth, I kept an eye on him during the meal, to make sure he used the right cutlery. I needn't have worried. He seemed completely at home. While Don and Mother ordered another bottle of wine and became giggly and shrill, Dad looked on indulgently from his calm plateau. I began to see how they had operated, these three, in the wild years after *Pimpernel Smith.*

After a second glass Dad loosened his tie and undid the top button of his shirt. It was the gesture of a man at ease, not a man who was out of his element. Don noticed and said—

'Must be the first time in eons you've had to put on your whistle, mate.'

'First and last time,' said Dad, 'if it's up to me.'

But he spoke as if it really were a matter of choice. Apparently my father had once been part of this privileged world, and had left it of his own free will. With an effort eased by my own inebriation, I turned to ask him a question.

'Dad—what did you do, before you retired?'

At the word 'retired' there was a conspiratorial snorting from the other two.

'Do?' he repeated.

'For a living.'

'Oh …' he poured himself a big glass of water. '… I shuffled paper, mainly. You know—office work. But it was never really my kind of thing.'

Don leaned forward with his mouth full of game:

'Don't know if you've noticed, but someone's doing an interview over there with Omar Sharif.'

I ignored him and continued my slurred interrogation.

'What do you mean, though—shuffled paper?'

My mother cut in.

'Your father was a *middle manager.* Isn't that what it was called?'

'Something like that' muttered Dad.

Don reached across my father's shoulders, still holding his bloodied knife.

'Told you before, sunshine—your old dad set me up in business, didn't he? His handiwork, my brain …'

'But, you mean, you were both in business, *together*?'

In my imagination Dad had always been in a corner somewhere, whittling.

'Couldn't split us apart with a jemmy, son. Me and my shadow.'

My mother raised her glass of wine in a toast. Don winked at me and added:

'Always a place for Keith Hill on my payroll.'

Dad smiled that contained smile and said,

'I was never very good at the desk jobs.'

'But fair play', said Mother, really quite drunk by now: 'Don was always happy to find a place for Keith's paper-shuffling talents. And then, when it turned out your father didn't actually have any, he found a place for him in the garden shed.'

Uncle Don's chauffeur took us home. Don himself rarely set foot in our house. When I craned dizzily through the car's back window to watch him sauntering off down the wet city road, I assumed he was going back to his office. He had houses in Richmond and France and an apartment in New York, but he rarely seemed to be going home.

'Bit of business to see out the day'—that's what he used to say. 'There's always money on the run somewhere on this planet, if you take the time to hunt it down.' So off he went, apparently not much the worse for a few bottles of posh goo. My mother snuggled against me and kneaded my thigh. She was always more affectionate after a few drinks. I was still trying to make sense of everything through the smog of alcohol and family history.

'What did you mean' I mumbled into the citrus scent of her hair, 'about the garden shed?'

'Oh, Nathan stop worrying at the past. You're like a dog at a bone. You concentrate on living your own life, sweet boy. No need to fret about anything else. Everything's fine—' her arm launched itself up and out; her bracelet hit the window like a gunshot. 'Everything—is—*fine*' she repeated, with careful placement, 'as long as Don pays the bills, and Keith keeps us all in potatoes.'

10

Part of the appeal, for me, is the mystery. Glass is like fire: we use it, we refine it,
but we don't really know how it all began. Presumably someone—some quiet,
observant soul, probably ostracised and mocked by the rest of the tribe—noted the
effect of lightning on sand. Imagine that: imagine the sorcery of it, the crack of
hellfire, the blinding rift in a wild, black sky; the ferocious touch of alchemy. And
there, when the darkness lifts, is the strange jewel, discoloured, misshapen, solid
and alien and new. The quiet soul crouches over it, reaches out to make sure of it,
recalls the flash, the blast that tore into the beach last night, during his clifftop vigil.
He thinks about it. This is what makes him different from the rest of them. He
doesn't run from it, or thank a god for it, or see it as a harbinger of fortune, good or
bad. He just squats in the sand and turns the fragile cylinder in his hands, and
thinks about the flame that created it.

Well, that's how I picture it, anyway. There has to be a romance to it. The vicious
storm, the swirling clouds, the pounding surf and the sudden scream of fire
… There can't be anything prosaic about a substance like glass.

I've got some pieces of lightning glass in the collection. Fulgurites, to give them
their proper name. They don't look like much at first glance: crusty, hollow tubes,
a translucent brownish colour. But they hold captive within them an instant of time
and motion. The paths of the lightning-rod can be seen quite clearly, spreading like
the roots of a tree. All that speed and power, seized and mapped forever. They're
some of my most prized items, and they'll never go on sale.

Kept under lock and key with the fulgurites are a number of other pieces without a price. The blue elephant is there; and the bloodred paperweight, which came back to me after my mother's death. These two pieces have historical weight as well as emotional resonance. I consider them to be the start of my collection, although originally they were just possessions, and of course the paperweight wasn't mine at all. After I presented it to my mother, on that momentous day of the craft fair, it vanished into her bedroom along with all the other gifts. Some from me, maybe even some from Dad, who knows?—but most from Uncle Don. These last would emerge from time to time: her amber earrings, her velvet scarf, her silver necklace—all fine and graceful things, complements to her beauty. But as far as I knew at the time, the rest were lost or thrown away. I didn't realise she'd kept that paperweight until after her death, and by then Uncle Don had sold off every other trace of her life.

I'm preparing an exhibition for one of my favourite artists. Peta Krantz calls herself a scavenger. She uses odds and ends to inspire her work: bits of rubbish from the gutter or the beach, stuff that's thrown out. Sometimes they form part of the work itself. A vase with an old key embedded in the base. A froth of coloured glass incorporating bus receipts and sweet papers. She likes to forage round for cullet—bits of broken glass chucked away—and to meld new jigsaws of old patterns and shades. She's been ticked off more than once for going along her street on bin day, rummaging through the recycling boxes. Gabby calls her Great Uncle Bulgaria, which is actually quite witty for Gabby—not just because of the rubbish-picking, or because she goes around in a big duffel coat, but because Peta Krantz is half Serbian, which as far as Gabby's concerned is more or less the same as Bulgarian. Peta came to the UK in a hurry when things turned nasty in the '90s. I always remember her saying, the first time we met,

'How is it possible that I am a refugee? I'm *normal.*'

Anyway, Peta is showing some of her new stuff, based on rock formation and using 'modern geology'—chunks of concrete, pebble-dash, clutter from building sites, all captured in her wedges of glass, like flies in amber. After that there's an on-site exhibition of Byron Black's architectural work, in the atrium of the Chaise building. Uncle Don's company used to occupy the Chaise building. I've been there already to see the work in progress—a strange experience, to be sure, as it was the first time I'd set foot in the place since the collapse. I was quite nervous, walking that old, familiar route past polished façades and vast, mirror-dark walls. But as soon as I entered the atrium, any twinges of nostalgia or regret were blotted out by the thrill of Black's majestic pieces: tiers of smoky glass dripping down an entire wall; a mushroom-cloud chandelier; a lifesize group of glass office workers heading for the lifts. Very exciting, very dynamic. A complete transformation.

Lots to do, then, and as luck would have it I've got another early start. That's the silver lining to my nights of disturbing dreams and churning memories. All side-effects of my unsettling encounter with Rosalyn, no doubt. So once more I beat Gabby to it, and am already in the office and in the zone when she arrives at the gallery, singing tunelessly to herself. She has the sense to leave me to it for an hour, but just as I'm deep in thought about an e-mail there's a rap at the door and there she is, hovering in her infuriating way.

'Someone's trying to get hold of you' she ventures, and winces at my stony look. 'They rang the gallery because they can't get through to your mobile ...'

'They can't get through to my mobile' I growl 'because I switched my mobile OFF.'

Rosalyn. So it's starting up already. I *knew* it was a mistake. Never try and mend an old fracture. But did I give her my mobile number? Surely not? Gabby is shrinking into a hairline crack as she closes the door.

'I thought you'd want to know' she pipes before disappearing altogether. 'You and Freda seemed to hit it off so well ...'

Of course. I'd forgotten about Freddie. When Gabby's shut herself out I switch on the mobile. Three missed calls and a text:

Hope u r OK XX

I switch it off again and settle back to my e-mail in higher spirits. My hunch was right. I'll let it stew for a while and then give her a call.

12

'I like it. It's sort of … stark.'

Freddie runs her hand along Suki Mezler's tubular wall display, letting her fingers drag in a rather desperately suggestive way.

'Yes, stark is Suki's style' I say, handing her a glass of wine. 'She's interested in absences, negatives, vacuums, that kind of thing.'

Freddie is nodding fervently, trying to look as if she knows all this already. I can't resist teasing her a little.

'What do you think of Suki's work?' I ask, and watch her colour mount.

'Er …' she drinks her wine, playing for time, and turns back to the piece. 'Well—I like this one. But to be honest with you, it's the only one I've seen.'

Clever girl, not going for the bluff—and what's more, she's managed to put me on the back foot somewhat, hinting that it's rather passé to know about Suki Mezler; that the new generation is looking elsewhere. I decide it might be politic to like Freddie, despite some of her gratingly young traits.

'Feel free to look around' I tell her. 'I'll just check the sauce and I'll be right with you.'

'Smells awesome' she says, and drifts after me into the kitchen area. She's fingering the granite worktop, now. All this touching and stroking—maybe she read it in a teen magazine. *How To Attract Your Man.*

'I just can't believe this place' she says. 'It's amazing. And the view—' She looks across the apartment to the windows overlooking the old factories. 'Unbelievable.'

'They used to make shoes in that factory nearest us' I tell her. 'And beyond that you can just about see the gasworks. They've turned the whole complex into an industrial heritage site, but there's always some developer on the horizon, threatening to pull them down and build a Waitrose. I hope they don't. I'd rather see a genuine industrial roofscape than some dreadful identikit shopping complex, wouldn't you?'

'God, yeah' says Freddie, but she's lost interest in the view already. She's got her eye on me again. I'm wearing a chef's apron and slicing a couple of extra chillies for the sauce. I've put my reading glasses on though strictly speaking I don't need them. I reckon the vaguely camp, secure-in-middle-age look will do me no harm with this one. She's probably wondering right now whether I'm gay. All adds to the mystery and keeps her on her toes.

Set the sauce to simmer, whip the apron off, and resume the apartment tour. She asks about this item and that, glances at the pictures of Rosalyn more than once, then sees the signature on the corner of the Florence shot.

'Scott.' she says. 'Is that your son?'

Why is everyone so intent on giving me offspring?

'No, he was a friend.'

'Oh.' She's startled by the past tense, and too young to know what else to say.

'He was a professional photographer', I add.

'Cool' she says, and stares too hard at the picture. 'Really … really atmospheric.'

'Yes, it certainly captures a mood. So, Freddie, we should talk about the best way to launch your work on an unsuspecting public …'

Poor Freddie. Although she talks with energy about her work, and listens keenly to my suggestions for display and promotion, I can see those green eyes flitting from my face to the photograph on the wall behind me. Who is that woman? she's thinking. Is she still around? What does she mean to him? Well, keep her guessing. That's the effect Rosalyn's image *should* have. It's the effect she always used to have, and it's what first brought Scott into our lives.

Rosalyn was the sort of woman people felt they should recognise. When she walked down a street, people turned and whispered, trying to remember where they'd seen her before. A film? On the telly? They hadn't, of course—she never made it beyond the church concerts and minor roles—but something in her profile, something in the way she carried herself, made her seem to occupy a higher level of life than everyone else. So it wasn't that surprising that, one damp morning in the via dello Sprone, a striking young man came up to our pavement table and asked if he could take her picture. He took a couple of shots there and then; I've got those too, hidden away in an album. One of Rosalyn glaring straight at his lens; one of the two of us, facing in opposite directions. He didn't ask us to do that. We'd just had a row, and were both wallowing in our sulks. Then he asked if she'd mind sitting indoors for a moment, so that he could use the slices of light through the café window. She said,

'My pleasure. I can have a smoke, without being lectured about it.'

And there she is, on my wall two decades later, huffily silting up her lungs, while I wait for her outside the café, outside the frame.

None of that was particularly remarkable. But when Scott had finished, and came back out of the café alone, I looked up at him and saw Rosalyn's face. Same arrow-straight nose, same high cheekbones, same dark, long eyes and dark, long hair … Even the eyebrows had that casual, swift look, as if they'd been painted with single brush-strokes. He gave me his card, and I watched his clumsy progress down the road, hung with cameras and bags. When Rosalyn emerged I said, 'Nice time with your doppelganger?'—with an edge of jealousy. I was still in a mood.

And she pouted and shrugged and said,

'Don't be so daft. Just the same colouring, that's all.'

Then she was chattering again as she took her seat, telling me how he'd rearranged the tables, charmed his way through the café owner's objections, told her not to strike a pose, not to change a thing … She'd come back to me, shucked off the sulk and forgotten it in her usual sweet-natured way, as I never could. I always had to have the last word, the *right* word. In many ways her inability to continue a stand-off was a victory in itself: I was left looking silly and infantile, abandoned on the high ground. My mother was the only other person who could do that—sail her way through, as the sulk evaporated around her. But with Mother it was calculated and canny. With Rosalyn, it was innocence that won. She had a purity I've never seen in any other living soul.

Freddie enjoys her food. I like that. We sit at the table in the window alcove, and eat as the sky deepens. As I serve the linguine onto her dish I can see her straightening her spine, preparing to restrain herself, and the first few mouthfuls are a delicate attempt to avoid slurping. Then I say,
'Go on, Freddie, pitch in',
and she goes at it like a pig at a trough. Wolfs it down, and accepts a second helping without a fight. I'm delighted. I've never taken to those women who treat their fuel with caution.
She watches as the city lights begin to pierce the dark.
'No curtains!' she suddenly says. 'Don't you feel exposed?'
'I'm too high up to worry' I say. 'No-one can see in on this side. You can romp around in the buff if you like and nobody's any the wiser.'
'Might take you up on that' she says, and blushes fiercely. The wine is loosening her tongue. Yes, maybe tonight, I think; wait and see.

Three hours later I'm nursing a brandy on the sofa, listening to Ravel's string quartet and waiting for Freddie to regain consciousness. She's sprawled all over the parquet, head on a cushion, skirt rucked up to show a very agreeable expanse of pink thigh above her knee-high green socks. I suppose I could stir up an interest. But her mouth's hanging open, she's about to dribble over the silk cushion-cover, and besides, that meal is playing havoc with my digestion. It's all I can do to retain my dignity; I thank god she's too drunk and comatose to register the occasional roaring of my gut.

A rivulet of saliva worms along her cheek and I prod her leg gently with my foot. 'Come on then, Freddie, wakey-wakey, rise and shine—I'm going to call you a cab.'

I heave myself to my feet and go to find my phone, giving her time to come to her senses. As I finish the call she appears at my elbow, swaying slightly and kneading the bridge of her nose.

'Christ, Nathan, I'm so sorry. I don't know what's wrong with me. I've been working so hard lately ...'

I put my arm around her and give her a fatherly hug.

'Don't worry about it—I was out for the count too' I lie. 'It's the end of a long week. It's been nice to relax.'

Then I take her chin in my hand—checking that she's mopped herself up—and give her a very unfatherly kiss. Might as well derive some reward from the evening. She's sagging towards me, starting to fiddle with my shirt, and I grasp her by the shoulders and prop her up.

'OK, don't start me off' I say, and kiss the tip of her nose. 'What we both need is a good night's rest. But we'll get together again soon.'

'Yes' she whines, still craning in the hope of another kiss. 'Yes, let's definitely do that, Nathan. I'd *like* to.'

OK, OK, I get the message.

Luckily the cab firm I use is just round the corner and very quick off the mark. By the time I've helped her into her jacket and retrieved her bag and shoes, the driver's ringing the buzzer. Before she leaves she takes my hand and kisses the fingers.

'You're amazing' she says.

I feel like the Pope.

I watch her staggering to the lift; she turns her heel in a perfect Dick Emery move, and swears. I can't help smiling. Yes, as long as she doesn't get too clingy, Freddie is going to be fun.

13

I was 21. Only just out of university, teaching English to businessmen and trying to learn Italian in return. I had no clear idea of a career in mind, and no field of particular interest except my collection. But Uncle Don had arranged things, the way he generally did—big talk about hard work and initiative and finding my own way in life, followed up by the whole package of cash and contacts, signed, sealed and delivered by him. So although to all appearances I was a hard-up teacher trying to get by, I'd actually been presented, on a plate, a small, spotless flat in Santoribio, a Fiat, the TEFL position and the promise of a managerial job when the planned Shimmer offshoot was launched in Rome.

I loved Italy. Loved the ease and the chaos of the place, the operatic street-corner conversations, the food, the peeling, fading, crumbling echoes of an age when the arts exploded like a new sun. In my spare time I wandered through galleries and churches, of course, but also started to sniff out the shabbier corners, forgotten alleys, dull streets where tiny shops and workrooms sold a lot of rubbish and occasional glorious gems of retro glass. My heart would thud as I veered off the main drag like a sex tourist finding the red light area. On the day I met Rosalyn I'd ventured further afield, driving to the scrubby outskirts. I'd seen a flyer advertising guided tours of a glass factory called Zenada. I say 'flyer'—it was little more than a photocopy, really, with a few lines in bad English to try and lure the tourists out of their comfort zone. It struck me, as I parked on a weed-riven forecourt, that few people were likely to negotiate the bumpy bus trip and 10-minute walk required to reach a place like this. Nevertheless, there were five of us standing about in the reception area when Carlo the guide arrived to welcome us. And I already had eyes for only one.

'This family Zenada is making glass for more than 350 years', intoned Carlo as we plodded along a corridor in his wake. He narrowed the vowels in an attempt at an English accent. 'Giovanni Zenada move here from Venice and teach the craft in 1635.'

There was an elderly couple, German, I think; an American woman who stayed at Carlo's elbow, drinking in every word and badgering him with supplementary questions; and then there was Rosalyn. I slowed my pace to fall back level with her, then let her go ahead, so that I could absorb her perfect grace.

'All through war times, Zenada still in business, still making glass bowls and goblins and other pretty things …'

'Goblets' said the American woman.

'Yes, this is what I say', replied Carlo. 'Still making good business from goblins and all the other, even during very furious wars.'

'That's quite surprising, isn't it?' put in the American woman. 'You'd have thought, you know, luxury items—they'd be the first to go in a conflict. Wouldn't you say?'

Carlo gave her a dip of the head that conveyed gallantry and disdain at the same time.

'In war time', he said, 'rich people want to show everything still OK, everything still the same; for long time they ask more of everything. More parties, more clothes, more jewels, more glass.'

On we went, grateful for the cool of a building on a hot September day, dutifully pausing from time to time at some niche in the wall where an unremarkable glass object had been placed. There was nothing much to see here, and it soon became clear that the 'exhibition' was just a way of funneling us into the shop. I would have counted it a waste of an afternoon, if it hadn't been for Rosalyn.

It's a fatuous exercise, trying to explain an attraction. Vast industries are built on the premise that appearance is the key: forests-worth of magazine advice, factories and shops pumping out creams and potions and lotions and fashions and scents and powders and paints, armies of makeover artists and marketing officers and research lab staff, all those gyms, diets, beauty spas, hair salons … all pointless. You may as well pay people to fold and unfold napkins, or dig holes and fill them in again. Humans are meat and bone and water; no geometrical symmetry or mathematical formula will ever grant them the beauty of a well-crafted artefact. Until that September day, I took that to mean that no human could ever have the appeal of a work of art. But I hadn't bargained for the mystery of connection: a certain slender lightness, a certain natural, easy movement, a shade of hair, a humorous expression—some indefinable trigger, combined, maybe, with the secret workings of biological chemistry—that grips the heart and steals the breath and sets life on an entirely new course.

'Do you …' I had to pause and regain control over my voice. 'Do you like glass?' What an imbecilic question. She didn't laugh or raise an ironic eyebrow. She just said,
'Not really. I mean, not particularly. I was at a loose end and this was somewhere to go.'
The voice was huskier than I'd expected. I noticed the tiny upsweep at the ends of her lips, a kind of smile-in-waiting.
'Funny place to be at a loose end!' I said, aiming for a knowing breeziness, but fearing I sounded nosy and critical. She gave me a full, guileless, slightly toothy smile. My chest seemed to fill with bubbles.
'I know', she said. 'We're staying in a guesthouse right on the edge of town and

I've got to be back by 4, so I didn't have time to get to the centre.'

The clues and hints packed into that reply made me dizzy, but overriding everything was the First Person Calamitously Plural. I couldn't find a way of tackling it without sounding like an out-and-out creep, so I stalled, and pretended to turn my attention back to Carlo's commentary.

'…always a family business' he was saying, picking up his speed of pace and narrative as we drew nearer the shop, 'and still in the family of Zenada today …'

I was starting to panic. Evidently there wasn't much time before we were all ushered towards the till and then out into the infinite outside world. Frantically, I searched for a question or a comment that would snare her, if only for a moment or two.

'I love glass' I gasped. Idiotic. I tried again. 'I collect it.' Better. Maybe I didn't sound quite as manic as I felt. She said,

'Do you?' with apparently genuine curiosity.

I started to babble, even though Carlo was still winding up his talk just ahead. I found myself telling her about fulgurites, about my fantasy of discovery, the beach, the lightning-strike, a miracle of nature refined by Man. When I dared to come up for breath I found her gazing at me with a childlike air that made me light in the head. I calmed down as we entered the wider space of the Zenada shop; I settled into my theme, showing off, imparting the knowledge I'd acquired without effort, without even considering it 'knowledge' till then. Carlo thanked us; we searched our pockets and bags for tips; the other three browsed the trinkets and goblins on the shelves. I hung on to her attention like a drowning man, rattling out details of style and period, snippets of history and technique. She showed no anxiety to get away. But neither did she have that coy look I knew well from the confident blondes at college. She said,

'I never realised there was so much to know. I never really thought about glass before.'

I put my hand out, flat on the air, only just controlling its tremor, to show her the ring on my little finger.

'It's set with Roman glass' I explained. 'My mother bought it at a market, without knowing what it was.'

Rosalyn took my hand naturally, without any weight of suggestion. She just grasped the fingers and brought them closer for inspection.

'Roman?' she asked. 'You mean, as in Ancient Rome?'

'That's right' I said. I could feel her breath on my knuckles. She studied the ring for a moment, and I studied her face. The shallow curve of her cheek. The straight nose. The graceful line from lower lip to chin.

'That's amazing', she said, more to herself than to me. Then suddenly she dropped my fingers, checked her watch, shot her hand up to her mouth.

'Oh my god, is that the time? I'll miss the run-through. They'll kill me if I'm late *again*!'

Manna from heaven. Naturally, I offered her a lift—to a tiny church, as it turned out, squeezed into a packed suburban street and serving that night as a performance venue. We bowled and clattered along the potholed roads; I did my best to drive like an Italian, one-handed, gesticulating into the open air as we talked. I had never been happier in my life.

To thank me, Rosalyn sneaked me a complimentary ticket—though given the sparse audience, her group could probably have done with any *lire* going. With a sort of instinctive choreography, those few of us there dispersed ourselves evenly, leaving equal portions of space between us. I sat in the second row, towards the side, as nervous as though I were about to sing an aria myself.

The piece was billed as a semi-staged opera, written by some earnest youth who accompanied it on the piano. The music was tedious and forgettable, and the story involved a woman accused of matricide. Rosalyn was one of the Three Witnesses. They sang a trio, and she had a few lines to sing alone. She wore a long, lime-green shift and a stovepipe hat—it was that sort of production—and I hardly gave anyone else a passing glance. Part of me dreaded the first sound of her voice: would it be the kind of cranked-up wobble that put me off so many operas? My god—I needn't have worried. When she sang, every cell in my body seemed to vibrate in response. It wasn't a big voice (to her own consternation), or a particularly pure sound. You could hear the effort in it—unlike the other two Witnesses, who sang with casual ease. Rosalyn had told me in the car that she couldn't act, and in a way that was true. But it all added to her appeal. There were the other two, running through their portfolios of expression, all arching eyebrows and engaging eyes, while they poured out a stream of vanilla-yoghurt sound. And there was Rosalyn, impassive as a sculpture, wrenching that voice from some dark region of the soul. When I went to congratulate her afterwards, she was a little taken aback to find me red-eyed and breathless.

'Did you *really* like it?' she asked, examining my expression like a scientist. I asked her to dinner, but she said she was shattered and going back to her digs. There was no hiding my anguish: the whole experience had stripped away all emotional veneer. She held me with that open gaze of hers for a moment, taking it all in. Then she took my hand, which was still clutching the typed one-sheet programme, and turned it so that I could see the list of forthcoming venues on the back.

'That's where we'll be' she said softly. 'Come and see us again if you can.'
Just the memory of it makes my blood flow faster.

She troubled my dreams that night: her marble features, her anguished voice. The following morning I phoned work and told them I had flu. Then I packed a bag and followed the production to its five remaining venues. I bought front-row seats, hung around afterwards, ignored the smirks and comments of her fellow performers, and took her out for dinner every night. By the third night she was letting me kiss her goodbye. On the last night she stayed at my hotel. She was beautiful, soft, sweet, everything I could have hoped for. And yet, in a way, that night marked the end of a chapter, rather than the beginning. I might well have been better off as Dante to Rosalyn's Beatrice: an ardent but hopeless devotee. For all the ecstasy of knowing she returned my feelings, there was also an infinitesimal sense of loss.

She had a couple of days free after finishing the tour and came back with me to my flat. It was high time I got over my 'flu' and went back to work, but the thought of slogging on with that daily routine while Rosalyn went back to the UK was unbearable. I'm not sure it was the prospect of separation itself that appalled me—there was something to be said for striking a soulful pose, staring miserably into my espresso against a shabbily romantic Italian backdrop. But the idea that Rosalyn had a life back home, had friends and favourite places and histories and memories that didn't include me in any way at all … that was the torment. I handed in my resignation as soon as we got back to the city.

Before I followed Rosalyn home, I decided on a big gesture to mark our last Italian day. I drove her back to the Zenada factory, intending to buy her something expensive or meaningful as a lifelong reminder of our first meeting. When we pulled into the forecourt I had to brake sharply to avoid hitting a stack of boxes. As we got out of the car Carlo the guide emerged from the building carrying another load, fag dangling from his lips. He looked astonished to see us, dumped the boxes and approached, whipping the cigarette from his mouth and sketching a figure-of-eight in smoke as his hands danced to his words.

'Ah, I am sorry, I am sorry, no more tours, tours is finished now!'

More employees were following him out, all carrying boxes, some empty, some evidently full of stock. Carlo's hands described the scene.

'All finished now' he said. 'Zenada—all finished. Pfff!' He blew on the fagless hand and fanned out the fingers to illustrate the vanishing of a business and all their jobs. 'Sad, sad, sad' he added, shaking his head. The other workers carried on with their task, setting down their loads, returning for more, avoiding each other's eyes.

'Oh, no! What happened?' said Rosalyn, already welling up. Carlo gave the sort of shrug that only an Italian can give—one swift movement that speaks of fate and injustice and resignation and human suffering and forebearance across the ages.

'The family, she run out of money. Zenada family. *Incredibile*. This family is making glass for more than 350 years.' He reverted to his tour-guide script with a crackle of sadness in his voice. Rosalyn reached out and squeezed his arm.

'I'm so sorry, so sorry' she said, and looked at me with round, swimming eyes. 'Isn't that terrible, Nathan?'

I wanted to be a hero. I wanted to show her that I could banish anything that caused her pain. I was sorry for the Zenada staff, of course, and their uncertain futures, and I was troubled by the prospect of one less glass factory in operation. But above all I wanted to prove that Rosalyn could rely on me to put everything right.

'Who's organising the sale of the business?' I asked, in as clipped and confident a way as I could muster. Another shrug from Carlo, more workaday this time. I stepped forward like a gladiator into the ring.

'I'd like you to find out for me now, please', I said. 'I'd like to discuss a proposition.'

14

It's a strange thing about memory: there are scenes that always rise to the surface—clear, self-contained. Bubbles in the stream. They stay with you, strung along the course of the past as bright and vivid as Chinese lanterns.

Here's one: four of us in a café round the corner from Don's office. Don, Mother, me and Rosalyn. I don't know where Dad is—probably not invited. I can't remember getting there, or any of the small talk that must, surely, have taken place. But I can see this scene as clearly as I see myself, now, in the mirror with the white oak frame. We're in a quick-stop café, the sort of place that makes sandwiches for city workers, but it's a quiet period and we're the only customers apart from an old man sitting in a far corner, reading a paper and still wearing his hat. The owners are a Portuguese couple who know Don by name. We're at one of those tables that juts out from the wall, fixed in place. We're sitting in silence. Looking at each other. It's the first meeting.

Mother, of course, was scrutinising Rosalyn from the second they met. My vivacious mother shaking hands with perfect, innocent Rosalyn: it was like the spark of two fuses touching. I could tell Mother was drinking her in, processing every detail of her appearance, her voice, her way of moving and responding and drinking her coffee … *So this is the woman my son has chosen*. That disturbance beneath the civility, the hint of rivalry, possessiveness—I revelled in it. Don was charm itself, in his brusque, loud way. He too gave Rosalyn the assessing eye, but it had more of the dealer about it: *is this a long-term investment?*

There wasn't a lot of room for small talk in that meeting. Poor Rosalyn—I can see her doe eyes sliding from one to the other of us, as we went through the awkward business on hand. First I had to apologise to Don for walking away from the teaching job, the great opportunity he'd bought for me, and sit nodding, shamefaced, while he delivered a little lecture about stamina and loyalty and seeing things through. Rosalyn squeezed my hand under the table, but she needn't have worried. It was all an act. I'd already gabbled my new scheme down a bad line to Mother, and she had clearly relayed it to Uncle Don. So when he sat back after finishing his rebuke and said,

'So, what now, sunshine?'

he was really feeding me a cue. I gave them my spiel about Zenada, what a great future it could have, what a waste it would be to let the business go to the ground. Don listened, betraying no sign of having done his own homework on the venture. Then he said, with flat-voiced scorn,

'And you reckon you're the bloke to save the sinking ship, do you?'

He looked at Rosalyn as he spoke. 'Suddenly gone all Superman have you? Nipped into a phone box and whipped some Y-fronts over your Lionel Blairs?'

Rosalyn blushed and smiled, and Mother said,

'Don't encourage him, Rosalyn'.

Don was enjoying himself. Taking a long, long breath in, letting his chest swell, pretending to turn the whole idea over in his mind. We sat in silence. The silence of settling thoughts and impressions, of decisions being made. A city silence, touched with distant traffic, passing footsteps, the rustle of the old man's paper, the quiet activity of the café-owner behind the bar.

After a small eternity Don tapped an impatient rhythm on the table and passed his judgement.

'I should tan your hide, you spoilt brat' he said. I felt Rosalyn tensing up beside me. He went on, 'But it looks like you might finally have grown some balls out there.'

He winked at Rosalyn.

'Really, Don' said my mother, smiling. 'You have such a charming turn of phrase.' Another silence. Then Don reached into his inside jacket pocket and brought out a folded document, tied with ribbon like some medieval edict. He slapped it onto the table between us.

'That', he said, imperiously, 'is your factory. From now on, sunshine, it's up to you.' He jabbed a finger towards Rosalyn. 'And *you*, sweetheart, better make sure he does a good job of it. 'Cause he's only doing it to show you he's cock of the heap.'

He held her in a solemn stare, then crinkled into a smile. Rosalyn gave a little laugh.

'Well!' said Mother. 'Now we've got that settled, is it too early for a drink?'

Rosalyn was off on tour with another tin-pot production—to Scotland this time. I had to go back to Italy and face the consequences of my recklessness, and Rosalyn was going to join me there when she was done. We'd planned to go out for a meal before parting ways and were trying to decide which restaurant to book. I happened to mention that Mother and Don were out that night, at some posh do.

'Won't your father be all on his own, then?' said Rosalyn. 'Shall we ask him to join us?'

I groaned at the thought and belted her waist tight with my arms.

'Oh, have a heart. Can't I have you to myself this once?'

She was kneading my earlobe, nuzzling my neck.

'Afterwards, of course you can. But your poor Dad ... he's the only one I haven't met ...'

'He doesn't like restaurants', I moped.

'That's OK. I'll come to your house and cook for you both.'

I couldn't deny there was something appealing about that idea. In the end, though, Dad ended up cooking us all bangers and mash. He and Rosalyn hit it off straight away. It was a nice, relaxed evening, and Rosalyn even sang something at Dad's insistence. He sat and listened to her, then had to fumble for a hanky and blow his nose. I was amazed. I'd never seen him like that before. Then Rosalyn said, 'Nathan told me you're a craftsman', and Dad and I glanced at each other, both equally stunned. 'He said you're always making things in your workroom' she went on. I could see that Dad was touched, and I didn't point out that my exact words had been *whittling in his shed*. The upshot was that Rosalyn and Dad retreated to the garden shed to drink tea from cracked mugs, while he bashfully showed her his latest creations. And later, when Rosalyn and I were lying in my bed, clutching each other as if one of us might float away, she said in that low, lovely voice,

'I really like your Dad.'

And suddenly, so did I.

15

I was scared witless. When I greeted the factory manager I had to grip his hand violently to control the shaking. He and the shop manager, the glassblowers, the guide—they all greeted me as a conquering hero. I'd saved Zenada, saved their jobs, handed them a future. Except that I had no future to offer. Uncle Don's cash didn't change the fact that everyone wanted light, sturdy plastic tumblers. Glass had become a curiosity, an archaeological artefact. I'd been given this factory as an experiment, and when it failed I'd throw it away and stroll off to do something else.

The guide, Carlo, insisted on speaking English, despite my eagerness to practise my Italian. He gave me the whole tour again, more or less, and trotted out the family history even though I knew it year for year.
'This family is making glass for more than 350 years', he said, and,
'Si, si, lo sai' I said.
'Giovanni Zenada move here from Venice and teach the craft in 1635, and all through war times, Zenada still in business, still making glass bowls and goblins and other pretty things …'
'Goblets' I said, automatically.
'Yes, this is what I say', replied Carlo, as he always did.
As he progressed through his script I recalled the American tourist who'd challenged him with questions: why would people buy luxury items in wartime? Wouldn't they be hiding those precious things away, putting them into storage? And Carlo's withering reply:
'In war time, rich people want to show everything still OK. They ask more of everything.'
Carlo's cadences rose and fell as we made our ceremonial way through the

building to the furnace-room. And I thought about war and calamity, and how long people could go on surrounding themselves with beauty, and pretending the bad stuff was all happening elsewhere. I'd stopped shaking. My stomach had settled. My thoughts were untangling themselves. I was beginning to see what we might do in our crumbling little glassworks. Never mind goblins and paperweights and blue chunky elephants. We were going to create a civilisation.

When we reached the office the entire staff had gathered there and greeted me with a round of applause. Some of them had tears in their eyes. I cleared my throat, and stood on a small bench.

'My friends', I said, 'I have big plans for this little factory.' At my side, Carlo translated, and there was a murmur of anticipation.

'I intend to make Zenada a byword for style, for class, for the highest quality design.'

The world is changing, I told them. New industries, new money, new people calling the shots. In the city of my birth, derelict warehouses were being stripped bare and turned into loft-lives for young market bucks. Terraced houses, two-up, two-downs, were being gutted and stretched and transformed into chic urban nests. I paused and looked at my workforce. They were confused, wondering where this might be heading. Dread and resentment flickered in their shadowed eyes. I was meant to be resurrecting their hope, not topping it off with a headstone.

'You think I'm talking to you about an alien life', I said. 'You think this world I'm describing has nothing to do with you, is a threat to everything you know. Not true. *Not true.* You, people like you, the people who design and make and handle and sell real and beautiful things—*you* are the nobles of this new world. It *cannot* exist without you. All those money-makers, all those dealers and gamblers in stocks and shares, figures and trends—what do they want? What is it all for?'

Carlo's translation, now frayed with uncertainty, echoed over stony faces. I took a moment, gathered my thoughts, battled with them, as my soundless audience waited.

'Money', I finally resumed. 'What is it? Nothing. It's nothing. It's a promise. Nothing else'. In a moment of inspiration I dug into my back pocket and pulled out a 50 lire note. I handed it to Carlo. There was a faint mumbling of amusement as he hesitated, then took it from me, still translating.

'This is my IOU, my promise to give you a lump of shiny metal' I said. 'Would you like a lump of shiny metal, Carlo?'

As he repeated his own name, then shrugged and shook his head, the mumbling rose to a chuckle.

'No,' I continued, 'I didn't think so. And it's just as well, because I haven't got a lump of shiny metal. In fact, it doesn't actually exist.' I took the note back and Carlo played along with a mime of operatic disappointment. I had to wait for the laughter to subside before carrying on.

'Money is just an idea. A number. A means to an end' I said. 'And all those traders and dealers who grow it like fungus … they need to translate it into something, if they want us to see their success. What makes them superior, what gives them status, isn't the numbers. It's the *things*. Things that they can buy, but don't know how to make. That's why they. Need. *You*.'

One or two heads tilted ambivalently from side to side. There was a half-hearted smattering of applause. Still some puzzled frowns, some sceptically pursed lips. I started painting my vision in clearer colours. Those converted lofts, those gentrified terraces, I reminded them—they were good for nothing without sleek furniture and beautiful adornments. I started to furnish them with wood and steel and slate and great, shining acres of glass. '*Italian* glass' I emphasised, and waited to hear Carlo's proud translation. 'Traditionally blown, hand-crafted, specially

71

imported Italian glass. The only glass that will meet the exacting standards of a new generation of design.' Another pause to let Carlo catch up before I spread my arms to conclude: 'The best glass in the world. *Zenada Glass.*'

Even before Carlo had finished translating, they gave me a thundering reception. I was helped off my bench into a storm of slaps on the back, and their handshakes hauled me towards the exit. They believed in me, and as I picked my way out of that factory, between half-packed crates and broken rejects, I believed in myself.

Uncle Don had agreed to keep the place going for three years while I built the business up, and then it was down to me. They were three exhausting years, rushing between Italy and the UK, expanding the factory, bringing in designers and craftsmen, pumping Don's money into promotional material, exhibiting at trade fairs, glad-handing and string-pulling everywhere I could. Confidence, I discovered, was the key. Not spin, not big talk, not sales pitch—that's where people so often get it wrong. It's about striking that balance between enthusiasm for the product and contempt for the client. If they don't understand how classy your goods are, well, that's their problem. That's the sort of confidence you cannot fake. You can't act it. And I didn't have to. I had a genuine, sensual love for every bevelled table-top, every calligraphic vase, every geometric lampshade we produced, and that shone through. After three years of flogging myself to the bone I had an order sheet beyond our means, and we had to start looking for new premises.

I've kept some of the first items we produced in our new lines. My favourites are four goblets—or goblins, if you prefer—loosely curved into fat commas. Stylish. Original. I drink from one of them every night, and toast the artists who put all those long hours of sweat, skill and faith into a droplet of light.

16

Freddie comes in to the gallery for a launch strategy meeting. She's excited about everything I suggest, and hasn't an inkling of how pitiful a budget I've set aside. Freddie's work is good, but not that good. Not yet. We spend a pleasant hour or so poring over dates and display plans and catering, occasionally letting the tips of our fingers touch on the table, smirking at the faintest whiff of a double entendre, and generally behaving like besotted teens. She plays her part well—no explicit references, no open affection; she keeps up the professional front, and we actually get a lot of work done. It strikes me that Freddie may have played this game before. She's not a child, after all, though I've developed a habit of casting her as an ingénue. Who knows how many times she's been round the block? But she's at the starting line of her career. I'd lay odds her lovers have all been nobodies till now— spotty schoolboys, hairy students … Yes. That'll be the extent of it thus far. I'll be the first grown-up, the turning point, the Svengali who leads her into artistic and sexual maturity. I like the sound of that.

We're winding down the meeting. Freddie's packing up her promo shots and starting to drift round the table in my direction. Tight, hipster jeans, today, and a lacy little blouse that shows half an inch of soft midriff. I'm about to touch that waist, blot it out with my hand, when a rifle shot at the door hurls us a yard apart. Gabby comes in immediately after her warning volley.
'Visitor for you, Nathan. Mrs Rathbone?'
I shake my head, helplessly, and then a familiar voice calls from behind her,
'—or Rosalyn, to you!'
Rosalyn Rathbone. So she took the Boffin's name too. The name, the brood, the charitable activity—she really did it: stepped out of the old life, slammed the door

and headed in the opposite direction.

I emerge from the office with my smarmiest grin.

'Rosalyn Rathbone! How deliciously alliterative!'

'Oh shut up, Nathan.'

We fall into our roles as easily as that: fond ex-lovers. She stands in the gallery, still in that godawful mack, not a scraping of make-up, hair shoved into some extraordinary woolly hat. We embrace—warmly, this time. In fact, it's rather nice hugging Rosalyn now that she's put this extra weight on. She smells of soap, and of the sea, as she always did. I find it difficult to release my hold, and then she pulls away and says,

'Oh, I'm sorry—I didn't reālise—'

And here's Freddie, smiling too brightly behind me, and I introduce Rosalyn as 'an old … friend', and let my hand linger on Rosalyn's arm, and think: I might enjoy this.

Gabby goes for coffee from the takeout place on the corner, and I show Rosalyn the gallery displays. She studies every piece with that same open wonder she showed in the factory some three decades ago. I talk her smoothly through the chronology, the artists' themes, the use of colour, form, technique … She sighs at Emmett Gray's 'ice cap' jewellery series; she chuckles at the bus tickets in a Peta Krantz cube. I watch her reactions, see the ripples of movement in her loosened neck, the bulge of flesh above and below her eyes; I see her moving her lips like a child who's just learning to read. And suddenly my throat closes. If I try and speak, I know I'm going to sob. She turns to me.

'Are you all right?'

Gabby's back with the coffees and Freddie is fussing around, helping her detach them from their cardboard tray. For a moment Rosalyn and I are free to look at each other, at our shared past. Then I master the impulse, give a dry cough, and say,

'Sorry—frog in my throat. Where's that coffee?'

We all focus on the takeouts, and Gabby hops about offering sugar, and we sip at the tiny holes in the plastic lids and say how hot it is, and how *nice* it is, and I thank god I didn't cry.

Freddie is the tonic I need. Fresh and firm and watchful, manic in her efforts to disguise her jealousy. We stand in a circle with our coffees, and I make the most of it.

'Rosalyn and I met in a glass factory. It was *my* glass factory, eventually. The original Zenada Glass.'

'Are you an artist?' twitters Gabby to Rosalyn.

'God, no. I'm as cack-handed as they come. I was just a tourist.'

Freddie flicks her hair back in an unconscious movement of victory. An overweight, middle-aged woman in a comic hat, who calls herself a tourist. How much of a threat can *that* be?

'Freddie' I tell Rosalyn 'is one of our bright new talents. We've been planning a launch for her first collection.'

'Well,' adds Freddie, 'not exactly my first ...'

'Gosh' says Rosalyn, 'that's impressive. Is there anything of yours in here? I'd love to see ...'

'The pieces aren't out yet' I explain, 'but Freddie's got some great shots in her bag, haven't you, Fred?'

I touch Freddie's back. I've never called her 'Fred' before. The intimacy reels her in from a sulk and she becomes condescendingly friendly, taking out the photographs and laying them on the floor for Rosalyn to see.

Rosalyn half crouches over them, and is so genuine in her interest and admiration that Freddie's defences crumble. She becomes girlish again, and self-effacing, and tells Rosalyn little details about the way she achieved certain effects. She looks up to monitor Rosalyn's response, and after a while straightens her back to get a better view, and says,

'Oh! Are you the person in the photograph?'

This should be fun.

'The photograph?' asks Rosalyn, nonplussed.

'On the wall in Nathan's apartment.' Freddie blushes. Rosalyn blushes back. They both look at me. I laugh, and look at Gabby, whose eyebrows have disappeared into her scalp.

'If any customers come in now' I say, 'they'll wonder what the hell is going on. Shall we get these pictures put away? And we'll go and sit in the office, Gabby, and leave you in peace.'

Poor Freddie. She makes her coffee last as long as she possibly can, turning from me to Rosalyn, from Rosalyn to me, red hair swishing, eyes searching for clues. But then she has to go.

'So … shall I …?'

She hovers at my chair, slim hip almost touching my shoulder.

'I'll give you a ring' I say, resisting the urge to launch her into movement with a slap on the buttock.

'Cool.' Still hovering. 'Good to meet you, Rosalyn.'

'Lovely to meet you too. You're *very* talented. Best of luck with the launch.'

Freddie recalls herself at the door.

'Well, you should come! Yeah'—with a tentative glance at me—'you should definitely come. See you.'

As the door shuts Rosalyn is levelling a questioning look at me. In fact, if this weren't Rosalyn, I'd suspect her of laughing at me.

'Sweet girl' I comment.

'Mmmm …' She sucks at the plastic lid.

'Meaning?'

'No, nothing!' She's beaming at me, now. She still smiles in that same generous way, despite the frown that's embedded itself permanently between her brows.

'She obviously thinks the world of you.'

'Maybe she sees me as a *father* figure' I say, pointedly. Rosalyn laughs.

'Sorry about that. A natural mistake, though, you must admit …'

Outside, the gallery phone rings and we hear Gabby's voice peaking and swooping. Rosalyn says,

'I shouldn't take up your time … I really came to ask a favour …'

'No hurry' I say. 'It's a quiet day today.'

There's a silence. We can hear the drone of traffic, and a brief blast of car horn. Rosalyn is turning her empty cardboard cup, pretending to read the brand name, turning and turning it again. This is what I dreaded: this undertow of history, pulling us away from the present. I rouse myself and break its grip.

'How's Bryn? Did he manage to get something sorted out for … the, er, your friend …'

'Anna! Oh …' She straightens in her chair. 'Well, it's tricky … She's been treated with such cruelty, you know, Nathan, and I don't just mean in her own country …'

I nod sympathetically, and Rosalyn talks on about Anna's family, and the accident of birth and geography that dumped them in disputed territory, persecuted and tormented by rival militia groups.

'They took her husband' Rosalyn says, and her voice hardens in a way I've never heard before. 'They killed him, and made her watch.'

'Dear god.'

'It's how they operate: through fear. They make their money from drugs, and anyone who gets in the way of that … Well. To them, it's business.'

'Barbaric.'

'And then, after she's been through seven kinds of hell and finally made it over here, she finds herself being interviewed on a lie detector.'

'Jesus.'

I'm appalled. Genuinely appalled. But all the time Rosalyn is talking, and mauling that cardboard cup, I'm thinking about her, noting the changes, the scribbles of grey, the quiver of jowls, and wondering what it is about her that prevails—that makes her Rosalyn, still, overriding all the superficial detail.

'Actually, that's sort of what I wanted to ask you about' she's saying.

It seems Bryn is planning an event of some kind, to publicise a campaign, and he's already sniffed me out as a useful sponsor.

'I don't want to push my luck', she adds, with a flirty, sideways look. 'I remember how cross you used to get when people hassled you for funding …'

'Nonsense.' I'm affronted. 'The only thing that bugged me was being used as a connection to Uncle Don.'

She grows serious again.

'Poor Don. That was so awful …'

'Yes', I say.

She focuses on the crumpled cup.

'It was all so horrible, wasn't it? I mean … everything.'

She almost sounds as if it's her fault. I don't know how to answer. In the end I just say,

'Yes, it was pretty horrible. But … you know. It's over and done with now. Life goes on.'

'I suppose so.'

Another silence. Eventually I scrape my chair back and she leaps up in response—

'Anyway, Nathan, I mustn't hog your time, but if you do think you could help us out at all, let me give you Bo's e-mail and we'll fix something up …'

And then, while she's dithering over another scrap of paper, she lobs a casual grenade:

'I'm so sorry about Scott, too, Nathan. I should have said before.' My jaw locks. I can't reply. She pushes the scrawled e-mail address across the table at me. 'It must have been so traumatic, I'm so sorry …'

'Well …' I manage. Then I meet her eye and see the message there:

I understand.

And I realise she doesn't understand at all. I know what she thinks. It's what everyone thought. Why I should have expected Rosalyn, of all people, to grasp the truth about me and Scott, I don't know. But she wallops me with that look of empathy, and I know Rosalyn's had it all wrong for over 20 years.

When she's gone I drop into my chair and sit staring into space for half an hour. Then I retrieve Bo's e-mail address and switch on my laptop and start keying in a message:

Hi Bryn, Rosalyn has told me about your proposed fund-raiser and I'd be delighted to help. Let's talk. I'm free on Thursday morning if that suits you …

17

We were sitting on the tiny balcony of my flat, in the merciful cool of a summer evening. I'd managed to get home from the factory before dark, for once, and Rosalyn had one of her long and frequent spells without any bookings. She'd started taking on singing pupils, though I pointed out that she needn't bother—by this time Zenada was more than capable of supporting us both. But she said she wanted the human contact, and it was good for her voice, and for her Italian. On this particular evening we'd both finished for the day, and were enjoying a glass of ice-cold Soave while the sky faded from blue to rose to violet. I'd been bringing a few items from my collection over, every time I returned from my UK trips. I wouldn't have them shipped—too risky. My latest arrival was a Roman perfume bottle—an *unguentarium*—made to be placed in a grave. I was showing it to Rosalyn, letting her touch it, though she was nervous of its great age, and seemed to think her slim hands would spoil it in some way. She ran a tentative finger over the handles and the lip, and I told her they'd probably been shaped by slaves. 'Potters' I explained 'from Asia Minor, taken from their families and carried off to Rome to mass-produce grave goods.'

Rosalyn frowned.

'That's awful', she said. 'Just imagine it. Torn away from your home'—she was already getting teary at the thought of it—'and forced to do all that work, day after day after day—just to see it chucked into a grave.'

I considered this for a moment, then said:

'They probably didn't see it like that. They probably thought it was a great honour. All their work would be seen by the gods.'

She mulled this over, still caressing the tiny bottle. I poured more wine and treated her to one of my little lectures. She was such a good audience. I told her about the boom of the Roman glass industry in Augustan times, about the advantages of transparency, which allowed consumers to see how full their perfume and wine flasks were, even when the stoppers were sealed in place. All the time, Rosalyn skimmed the bottle's contours, still wary, respectful. Eventually she asked:

'How long would it take, then, to make something like this?'

'Couple of minutes' I said. 'No more than that.'

'And they all went into graves? *All* of them?'

'Dozens at a time. So there was plenty of demand.'

She shook her head.

'I can't imagine it. Making the same thing, over and over again, just to see it buried with the dead.'

'But … as I said …' I was irritated that she hadn't taken on board my comment about the gods. She took no notice; her mind was on a different course.

'Come to think of it' she said, with a little pout of self-pity, 'that pretty much sums up *my* career, doesn't it?'

'What do you mean?'

'Waste of time. Doing my warm-ups every day, practising and perfecting, singing into the air, with no one to hear it …'

I made a squeaky noise of incredulity. She bowed her head over her wine.

'That's nonsense!' I said. 'Bookings will pick up soon. This is how it is in your business, that's all. Peaks and troughs.'

'My *business*!' she scoffed.

'Well—that's what it is. Isn't it?'

She looked away, staring into the dusty twilight. 'That's not what your Uncle Don thinks.'

'Oh, come on!' I topped up her wine. I knew I'd put my foot in it, by telling her what Don had said on my last trip to the UK. *What about the songbird then? Made it to Lar soddin' Scarlar yet has she?* I'd said it to make her laugh. But she knew very well how Don felt about anything involving the arts: load of bollocks. He couldn't fathom why an intelligent, fully functioning adult would choose a pursuit that lost more money than it made. He had no time for the honour of the gods, or the elevation of the soul.

'He didn't mean it', I coaxed her. 'He always takes an interest, always asks after you, how you're doing ...'

And I always tried to make her few performances sound more impressive than the tuppence-ha'penny affairs they actually were. But I didn't mention that. I said, 'He wants you to do well. Wants to help. *If she wants to make it big, sunshine, she just wants to put herself about a bit. Give me the word and I'll sort it out for you. Nothing easier!*'

My panto impression of Don did the trick: she was smiling again.

'Fair play', she conceded. 'He means well.'

'Yes, and that's because he thinks the world of you' I said. I rubbed my bare foot against her calf. 'And who can blame him?'

She closed her eyes and sat back, and the mood had passed. She said,

'I love this time of day. I want to stay here with you for*ever.*'

So I took a risk, and said: 'Why don't we let him lend a hand? It's peanuts to him. He can book a few venues, pay for a bit of publicity ... lunchtime recitals. How about that? There's plenty of call for it ...' Her eyes stayed closed but her smile faded. I hurried on: 'And if we time it for one of my UK schmoozing trips—that means you can come with me, without feeling like a spare part.'

18

So Uncle Don sorted it. Two weeks of midday recitals in various country churches and village halls, advertised with glossy flyers and a couple of features in local newspapers. He paid for an accompanist to rehearse with her, covered all the travel and accommodation, and generally did everything she refused ever to let me do. I didn't mind: Rosalyn was getting excited about her work again, chattering on about Fauré and Schubert and some new song cycle she'd like to try. I was taken up with Zenada business most of the fortnight, of course, but I managed to make it to a couple of the concerts, and they were pretty well attended. My first encounter with Bryn was in a little church in Hampshire. Rosalyn was using the vestry as her green room, but as it was tiny, freezing and cluttered, she came back into the main hall after the performance, to shake hands and accept praise as the audience filed out. One chap captured her hand and cornered her for quarter of an hour, talking earnestly an inch from her face.

'Who was that?' I asked when we'd finally shut the church door and she was changing back into her jeans. The accompanist, packing up her music in the corner, gave a knowing laugh and the two of them shared a look.

'Ammiratore …' she sang softly. *Admirer*. Rosalyn coloured.

'He came to the first concert,' she told me, 'and then the one after that … I think this is his fourth?'

She checked with the pianist, who circled her eyes and made a swooping sound without opening her lips.

'What a creep' I said, hoping I didn't sound troubled.

'Oh, he's OK, just a bit lonely, I think. He does get on my nerves, though—doling out advice like he's doing me a favour.'

'Advice? What sort of advice?' I couldn't control the snap in my voice.

'You name it. Vocal technique, choice of music … apparently I should be more ambitious in my programming.'

I was outraged.

'Who the hell *is* he, then? A musician?'

She looked up at me, laughing, stooping to lace her trainers and showing her sweet, T-shirted cleavage. Her hair was escaping from its chignon, and hung in thick strands over her face.

'No, of course not! He's the kind of bloke who knows opera libretti off by heart. Couldn't produce a note of it to save his life.'

So that was the Boffin. Rosalyn was never bitchy about anyone, but she came close, talking about Bryn and his ilk.

'Snobs' she told me, taking my arm as we left the church. 'That's what these people are. They don't really care about *music*, just the *notion* of it. They talk the talk, but they can't walk the walk.'

'Well, then, who does he think he is, telling you what to sing?'

She squeezed my arm reassuringly.

'People need to feel important, don't they? And anyway,' she eyed me mischievously, still buzzing from her success, 'isn't that what you do? Telling the glassblowers what to make? When you can barely make a mess? Who do you think you—aaaaAAAGH!'

She screeched and giggled and twisted about as I released my arm and attacked her ribs. She was as ticklish as a child.

19

As soon as we returned to Italy, I collared Zenada's master-blower, Dino, and offered him a fat bonus to teach me how to make glass. Dino was doubtful. He was the old hand of the factory—he'd been there since he was 14, and had the look of a man fired by the furnace: tough, with a permanent glaze over his skin. He tried to talk me out of it.

'There's no need' he said. 'You're the boss, not the worker.'

He spun his words through a strong accent, and I always had to ask him to slow down, although my Italian was pretty sound by then.

'I want to know what's involved' I said. 'I'm not trying to take your job!'

He laughed, and as usual the laugh disintegrated into a fearsome smoker's cough.

'You wouldn't want my job!' he crackled. 'One day of this and you'll be scuttling off back to your desk!'

'Is that a challenge?' I asked, and held out my hand. He shrugged. It was extra money, for a couple of hours whenever I was in town. What the hell. His shovel-hand engulfed my own. Despite the hellfire of his workplace, it wasn't a clammy hand: it was dry and rough and strong. It reminded me of my Dad's.

We met in the early morning or late at night, and Dino showed me how to dip the blowpipe into the fire and gather the right amount of molten crystal. He was working on a full-lead batch at the time—top quality, high-end stuff, 33 per cent lead crystal to produce that classy sparkle. Dino had spent a year in Ireland, learning to work this stuff. It's softer and more wayward than regular glass, splashing around impossibly at the end of the iron.

'Your bad luck' Dino told me 'that we use the best.'

He tried to teach me to blow the gather into a ball. It was hopeless. I could barely hold the blowpipe, let alone spin it, and my breath seemed to peter out an inch from my mouth. Dino and his team found my efforts hilarious. He wasn't a natural teacher. After a few minutes of my lame attempts he'd lose patience, order one of his minions to clear up my mess, and say 'let me show you'—and he'd be off, like a circus performer, turning and turning, blowing and blowing, using all that energy and dexterity to give a steady, calm symmetry to the bowl at the other end of the blowpipe. I was reminded of the propellors on a plane: the faster they turn, the smoother the action. This part of the job was usually done by Dino's juniors. So even the basics were beyond my capabilities. When he progressed to the grand finale, using his wooden paddles and pincers to tease the bowl into new forms, pinching here, patting there, I quickly concluded that he was right: this was something I would never be able to do.

When I told Rosalyn about my lessons, she said,
'You should go to someone else. You need someone who'll teach you the steps. Dino's forgotten how to do that. He can only do the dance.'
I said, no, it wasn't that: it was my lack of skill that was the problem. And Rosalyn held a hand up to block the excuse.
'Doesn't matter how good you are, Nathe. If you *really* want to do it … if you really *need* to do it—you put the work in. Hour after hour after hour. Like Dino must have done, once upon a time.'
'Ah well, but Dino's lucky. He's got the knack.'
She rolled her eyes.
'That's what everyone says' she pointed out 'when they can't be arsed to learn the knack themselves.'

In 1985 a Serb farmer in Yugoslavia was treated for wounds inflicted by a broken glass bottle, which had been rammed up his rectum. He said he'd been attacked by his Albanian workers. After a three-hour interview with the army, he changed his story and said he'd done it to himself, in a failed attempt at sexual gratification. Later he returned to the original claim. It was said the Albanians had set on him simply because he was a Serb. The press raged. Poets harked back to the days of Ottoman impalings. The lid on Yugoslavia's emnities was rattling. It didn't look good.

The suburb that edged and crumbled towards our factory housed a substantial number of Albanian immigrants. Most of them were out of work and spoke little if any Italian. In the church hall where I'd first heard Rosalyn sing, a group of volunteers set up a drop-in centre and held informal classes: language, basic computer skills, whatever anyone could offer. Rosalyn heard about it at the hairdresser's, and in her boredom decided to offer her services.
'As what, exactly?' I asked. I didn't much like the idea.
'As a singing teacher. Everyone deserves a chance to sing, Nathan. Even if they've got nothing else.'
Fat lot of good that'll do them, I thought, but I was aware of sounding like Don, and kept my mouth shut.
She went to see the volunteers the following weekend and met me afterwards for a coffee. She arrived breathy with adrenaline and success and fell into her seat clutching her bag and notebook.
'I'm starting a choir!' I hadn't seen her so happy in a long time. 'We're going to do a weekly session. Italian songs, Albanian songs, pop, classical—whatever people enjoy, really, but I've got a whole list of ideas, and …'
Off she went, chattering on about her plans. When she finally calmed down long enough to sip her coffee, she looked up at me in a way that made my heart sink.

'You know, Nathan, there were some lovely young lads at the hall, asking about work. Really eager, really willing to please … And the volunteers are desperate for support …'

I sighed.

'Go on, then, out with it. What have you promised?'

So Dino earned another bonus, as did a couple of his colleagues, and the Zenada training scheme got underway, teaching immigrant youngsters the art of making glass. As time went on, some of them found employment in our Italian or British factories, others elsewhere. Two brothers even started up their own business in Sicily. Uncle Don claimed not to approve.

'If you want to do good on your days *off*, that's up to you,' he said, when I delivered my next swivel-chair update. 'Business is business, son—it's about making money, not making you feel warm and fluffy.'

'But this *does* make money,' I insisted. 'Indirectly, anyway. These kids work bloody hard—they'll happily put in twice as many hours as the old guard, and for half the pay.'

He couldn't really argue with that. He nodded slowly, pushing out his lower lip, mulling it over.

'Well,' he concluded at last, 'your baby, your decision. Just keep an eye on the I-ties, is all I'll say. If what you say is true, they won't like it one little bit.'

20

My mother found Dad face down in the potato bed. He'd had a massive heart attack.

'All that bloody digging' she said afterwards. 'And what for? I kept telling him, they sell them clean and packed in the supermarket, you oaf.'

It was all done and dusted by the time I got there. Dad had been put away in some hospital fridge, and Uncle Don was in our back room, keeping my mother's brandy topped up. I wasn't used to seeing him at our house—though I suppose, strictly speaking, it was *his* house, along with all the others. Nevertheless, he seemed out of place: too tall, too extrovert, as if he'd come to visit the pixies.

My mother was in shock—I see that now. She was already half drunk when I arrived, and relating the whole episode for the umpteenth time.

'He had earth in his mouth', she kept saying. 'He must have breathed some in. All over his tongue, on his face, in his eye, everywhere. *Filthy bastard.*' She spat the words out in a little shower of brandy. 'Always bloody digging, always planting and potting and harvesting and messing around with those bloody bits of wood …'

Don had folded his leg onto the arm of her chair, trying to adjust to the smaller scale of our world. He poured more brandy and said,

'That was Keith, love. That's how he was.'

I'd never heard him call her 'love' before. They seemed like a couple, discussing a nuisance relative. She regarded me with contrived, half-pissed geniality, lidding her eyes like a cat. She said,

'Poor Nathan … you and your father never quite clicked, did you?'

'Yes, we did' I said, too defensively, and she curled her bare feet under her, and purred over her drink.

'Funny, really' she mused, leaning her head against Don's waist, 'given that Keith did all the baby-work, all the nappy-changing … I was always such a dead loss at all that. If he could have whipped up a couple of boobies in that shed of his, he'd have done the feeds as well.'

They both vibrated with wheezy laughter. Don's free hand had somehow worked itself behind her and he was massaging the curve from her neck to her shoulder. He lifted the brandy-bottle to offer me some and I shook my head.

'Never much of a drinker, were you, sunshine?' he said, as if *I* were the dear departed. 'Always been a good lad, intcha—sober. Moderate. Never a scallywag like me.' He gave my mother's shoulder a sharp shake.

'You know feller-me-lad here thought I might be his dad, dontcha?'

She found that hysterically funny, and spilt brandy over her lap.

'Good god, Nathan,' she slurred, 'you don't think I'd have married Keith if he *hadn't* been your father?'

I went out into the garden. The potato bed was rucked into neat trenches, interrupted halfway along by a splattered cavity. I stood over it and stared at the muddy imprint of my father's fall. After a few moments I heard my mother calling from the back door:

'Don't go out there, Nathan, it's so *morbid*. Come in here and have a drink with us.'

Rosalyn was in Stockholm at the time, taking some minor trouser role. I called her later that day, when my mother had dissolved into oblivion on the chair, jaw hanging out of joint.

'I can't cope with her' I told Rosalyn. 'She's being so … *spiteful*. So *angry*.'

Rosalyn's voice was small and distant. 'She's just frightened, Nathan', she told me.

'It's as if she *hated* him.'

'She hates the fact that he died.'

I remember her saying that, so calmly, so sensibly, and feeling comforted, even though I couldn't really believe it was true. As the line fizzled out and I finished the call, Uncle Don loomed up behind me.

'Listen, sunshine' he said in an undertone, 'I don't think it's doing your mother much good being here. When she comes round I'm going to take her to my place, for a good meal and a rest.'

'She can have a good meal and a rest here', I said, without lowering my voice. 'I'll cook for her.'

He gripped my shoulder and shook it amiably. 'You have some time to yourself, son. Gather your thoughts, and that. I'll take care of your mum.'

The next time I saw her was at the funeral.

Uncle Don had insisted I should go back to work.

'No sense in you moping round an empty house' he pointed out. 'You get on and make the best of your time. Meet and greet. Press some flesh. I don't want to be harsh, mate, but business waits for no man, dead or alive. Men are carried off, but money carries on. That's life. You can leave all the formalities to me and your mum. She prefers it that way.'

All I had to do was turn up at the church.

Rosalyn managed to fix an understudy for a couple of days and flew back for the service. I'd suggested at one point that she might offer to sing at the funeral, but she said,

'Oh, no, Nathan, don't make me do that. I'll cry.'

So she didn't sing, but sure enough she did cry—from the moment we entered the church and waded into a swell of organ music. She sat next to me in the front pew, hanging on to my arm and struggling to control the spasms and gulps. Then the coffin arrived, balanced on four of Uncle Don's employees. He'd refused my offer to be a pall-bearer.

'These are stonking lads', he explained, 'and you might cause a dip.'

Behind the coffin came my mother, escorted by Uncle Don. It seems bizarre, now, that I was placed in the audience to watch their entrance; but at the time I didn't question it. This was Don's choreography, and in truth I'd been grateful enough to leave it all to someone else.

As the pall-bearers brought their load down the aisle, Rosalyn's crying threatened to break into loud sobs. Then she twisted round to get a clearer view of my mother, and the tears abruptly stopped.

'Oh my god' she breathed.

The coffin was parked, and my mother and Uncle Don slid into their places at the end of our pew. Rosalyn could barely take her eyes off Mother. I could see why. Usually Mother's skin had a fresh, vivacious glow. The last time I'd seen her, even under the most trying circumstances, her colour had been heightened by drink, and until she passed out her eyes were lustrous, if a little unfocused. Now, she seemed to have no blood. Her face, her neck, her arms and hands, were the colour of dough. In 10 days her laughing features had undergone a landslide. No energy resisted the downward pull of her mouth, her cheeks, her brows. When she turned to me, it was with utterly vacant eyes.

Rosalyn put her mouth against my ear.

'She's taken it very badly' she whispered.

I nodded, but I couldn't quite accept that this was just grief. Even when she was sitting down, Uncle Don kept a supporting arm under hers. If he removed it, her body might deflate altogether. With an effort, I turned my attention to the vicar's address.

92

'Today, we say goodbye to Keith Hill, who departed this earthly life while tending to the garden that he loved …'

All the same, I said to myself, glancing at the coffin, I'll bet he looks in better shape than Mother.

Uncle Don had hired The Ballroom in a nearby hotel for the post-funeral gathering. When Rosalyn and I arrived, ahead of the others, we stared across an acreage of parquet floor at three long tables heaped with food. Uniformed catering staff stood to attention.

'Blimey' said Rosalyn. 'How many people do you think will come?'

'We'll be lucky to get a dozen', I said. 'The church wasn't exactly bursting at the seams.'

Don was next to arrive, striding in like a ringmaster, rubbing his hands and throwing unnecessary instructions at the staff.

'Your mother's on her way' he said, answering my worried look. 'Just gone to powder her nose …'

Rosalyn started for the door. 'I'll go and see if she's …'

'No, that's all right, love'—Don's arm was around her waist in a flash, guiding her back to the banquet—'She'll be along, just needs a minute to herself.'

'Uncle Don' I whined, hating the quaver in my voice, 'why are we doing all this? It's not as if Dad had an army of friends …'

He lowered his voice and his head, and gathered us both towards him.

'I know, son, I know—but that's what your mother wanted. She insisted. So if she wants to send your old dad off with a knees-up and a decent feed, who are we to refuse? Let's say goodbye to old Keith in style. Even if it's only us.'

Rosalyn seemed touched, and went to forage at the buffet. I had no appetite, so I stayed by the door to watch for my mother. Presently I saw her pegging along the corridor from the Ladies, a zombie in high heels, concentrating hard on staying upright. She gave no sign of noticing me there, but as she passed me at the door, she muttered,

'I'm fine Nathan. Don't fuss. I just need a drink.'

And she was right. After downing a large glass of fizz, she came to life, just in time to welcome the eight or so stunned arrivals. The arms reached out to them, the smile was switched on for them, and she was the picture of chic mourning in her well-cut black two-piece.

'Your mother' said Rosalyn softly 'is amazing.'

Mother thanked the guests for their support, and told a sweet anecdote about Dad making me a cradle. She held court in the middle of that vast, bare room as if she were playing to a full house, then ushered the awkward guests towards the open sandwiches and hors d'oeuvres. A couple of them made their excuses, and escaped under the envious eyes of the half-dozen who were left. I wondered how long we'd have to keep up this farce before we could decently leave the staff to clear up. Rosalyn had piled her plate and was answering polite questions about her singing career from my parents' next-door neighbour. I spotted Uncle Don nipping out of The Ballroom and heading in the direction of the hotel reception. When he came back a few minutes later he tapped my arm and whispered,

'Sit tight, sunshine, the cavalry's on its way.'

Ten minutes later The Ballroom door swung open and in came a stream of sober-suited men and women, each one pausing to shake hands and murmur condolences to Uncle Don, to me, to Rosalyn and to Mother, before forming an orderly queue at the buffet. The place began to thrum with respectful conversation. The staff were suddenly busy, serving the salads, pouring the drinks, and my mother could be heard laughing at somebody's quip. As I moved among small groups of strangers, I caught threads of conversation:

'We need to have a chat about that New Delhi account …'

'… I'll set it all out at the sales meeting …'

I found Rosalyn helping herself to seconds.

'You know what he's done, don't you?' I hissed. 'Uncle Don—he's just summoned his workforce. These are all people from his office. Basically he's hired the mourners.'

Rosalyn paused in the act of manoeuvring a large wedge of cheese onto her plate. She looked around and I could see from her expression that she knew it was true. None of our emergency guests had the foggiest idea who Keith Hill might have been. Her gaze settled back on my face.

'Well,' she said, in a chivvying way, 'does it really matter that much, Nathe? At least it's a proper wake, now, and a decent send-off for your dad. And look—your mother really appreciates it, you can tell. Come on—come and have something to eat. These cheeses are delicious.'

After Dad's funeral Don spirited my mother away to his suburban villa, and there she stayed, lounging on the white leather sofas, presumably, or opening the remote-controlled curtains to survey the lions rampant on the gateposts. Our old house was sold up; I was given a week to salvage anything of value before the clearance people came and flogged the lot. I took some photographs, some of my childhood treasures—the blue elephant, the wooden bi-plane my father made … I searched for the paperweight, too, but it had already gone, along with Mother's clothes and jewellery. Evidently, she'd forced herself to return to the family home for one last visit. Or perhaps she sent staff.

21

It was after Dad's death that Don really started to meddle. I don't know why that was: maybe Keith Hill had quietly been restraining him all along. Anyway, in the months following the wake, Don made it his business to 'lend a hand', as he put it, with Rosalyn's singing career, without bothering to consult her or anyone else. Out of the blue, we'd get a call in Italy from some entirely inappropriate agent in London, saying he'd been tipped the wink by Mr Cutler about a cracking new talent with a belting pair of lungs. Rosalyn pretended to find it funny at first. As she pointed out, there was no problem putting them off.

'I tell them it's opera. Then I tell them my age. That settles that.'

She was in her 30s, maybe at her most beautiful. I stared at her flawless profile, her brown arms, and I said:

'Uncle Don might have a point, though. You can't hang around, in your business, can you? If you're going to get anywhere—'

'Nathan', she said, gently, but conclusively, 'I'm not interested in *getting* anywhere. I'm here. I'm doing what I love to do. That's enough.'

Art for art's sake. I understood that, of course; it's what I'm all about. But I've got enough Don Cutler in me to keep an eye on the earnings too. I savoured my wine for a moment, enjoyed the breeze from the river, then said,

'That's fair enough. As long as Zenada can pay the bills.'

She was rattled. Upset, even, though she tried not to let it show. At a later stage of our relationship she would have answered back. She'd have pointed out that she never *asked* to live off my business, that she'd been happy to slum it with her other struggling-artiste friends, doing a bit of teaching and a bit of shop work to keep body and soul together; she'd have told me in no uncertain terms that this was her choice, her vocation. Money was all well and good but, in the end, for Rosalyn, it wasn't the point.

Yes, I heard all that from Rosalyn many times, when everything was going downhill. But at this stage, when we were still calm and happy together, she preferred not to provoke any arguments. She just bit her lip and turned aside, feeling chastised. Guilty. And next time Don 'lent a hand' she accepted it, and did as she was told.

He bought a session at a recording studio. Set up a cringeingly embarrassing lunch with a music critic from The Telegraph. He hired some swanky concert venues for her song recitals—but even Don couldn't fill them. He was constantly summoning her back to Britain for more 'promo' as he called it. Rosalyn and I both began to get tetchy.

'Don says I should think about singing more popular stuff' she reported after one of his phone calls. I was preparing our supper, enjoying the sensuality of the fresh ingredients—tomatoes, glistening olives, crisp garlic, and the heavenly scent of basil. I didn't want to think about Uncle Don and his good advice. I growled some half reply and carried on with my task.

'And he says I should get some better head shots' she added, wretchedly.

'Something *peppier*, that's what he said. He reckons my old ones are too poncey.'

We exchanged a look. I said,

'Your head shots are beautiful. They couldn't be anything else.'

She came to stand behind me, wrapped her arms round my waist and leant against my back.

'He's found some photographer and he wants me to go over there again—'

'*Again?*'

I dropped the chopping knife and twisted my head to try and see her.

'I told him it was tricky. I mean, Auntie Monica doesn't mind me staying but it's getting a bit—'

'And Don said, Why are you staying with your auntie anyway when he can put you up in a five-star hotel. Am I right?'

'Sort of'. Her voice almost disappeared into my shirt. 'He said if I was that bothered I could stay at the villa.' Suddenly she was loud and clear again, craning round to plead with me, eye to eye: 'Nathan, I don't want to go to the villa. Your mother doesn't want me there—no, Nathe, it's true, she doesn't like me. I can tell.'

I could hardly argue the point. While Don made it his mission to 'solve' Rosalyn's career, Mother remained notably absent. When the two women did meet, Mother was unfailingly polite. But there was an edge to the atmosphere—I felt it too. I was afraid Rosalyn might be right. Mother didn't approve. I reached my arms behind me to clasp her in a backwards embrace. I said,

'Look, don't worry. I'll talk to Don. I'll tell him you've got to stay here for—I don't know, I'll think of something—'

'But this photographer, he's booked some session and he says—'

Panic was creeping in. Don had a way of inspiring that kind of fear. I tightened my arms, squeezing her ribs and making her yelp.

'It's OK' I said. 'It's fine. I'll put him off. You leave it to me. It's none of Don's concern, anyway. He's not your manager, is he?'

'No …' She didn't sound too sure about that, and who could blame her? After all, Don and his money had been managing pretty much every aspect of our relationship, from my first sight of Rosalyn's exquisite profile on that tour of a failing little factory. I wouldn't have been there at all, if Don hadn't set me up with a job and a home and a car. I'd have been at home, or maybe renting a damp room in a shared house behind the Poundland in some dismal town, slogging through accountancy exams, or offering assistance to the walking dead of Homebase. I couldn't have jacked in my job to chase after Rosalyn's opera group, without the certainty of a thick, soft bed of money to break my fall. I wasn't brash or confident or foolhardy or clever enough to create a new business without that faith in an ocean-deep cushion of wealth. And now that business, as I had cruelly pointed out to Rosalyn, was putting food on her plate, allowing her the luxury of long hours of vocal practice, and voluntary musical do-gooding for immigrants. If Don was suddenly so keen to devote his business savvy and his fathomless riches to improving Rosalyn's professional lot—who were we to say no? Nobody. That's who. Of *course* he was Rosalyn's manager, and mine, and everybody else's, if they took his fancy. Don paid the bills, Don pulled the strings.

So instead of phoning Don and telling him to mind his own business and let us sort things out our way, I called my mother.

'The thing is,' I explained, in a pointlessly confidential tone, 'Rosalyn doesn't want to seem ungrateful. She doesn't want to hurt Uncle Don's feelings ...'

'NooOOoo ...' My mother sang the word sympathetically down the line. Without seeing her face, I couldn't quite tell how sarcastic she was being. 'I'm sure she only wants the best for Don.' Oh. *Very* sarcastic, then. I pressed on.

'And I don't really want her to be travelling back and fore quite so much ...'

There was a silence. I knew what my mother was thinking, and I let her think it for a moment, before adding, 'I mean, it's just unsettling. That's all I mean.'

'Ah. Well, yes, I can see that.'

'But apparently he's arranged some sort of photo shoot ...'

'Don't worry, sweet boy', she said, magnanimous in her relief that grandparenthood wasn't on the cards just yet. 'You leave Don to me. You're absolutely right, the poor child should be there, with you, resting while she can. There'll be plenty of time for travel when the bookings start flooding in ...'

99

Well. I could forgive a touch of waspishness, in return for mother's diplomatic skills. We didn't hear another word from Don about his photographer, and a few months later, we found one of our own.

22

I've persuaded Peta Krantz to create a piece for auction, in aid of Bryn's campaign. 'Wonderful idea!' Her voice scrapes through the phone. 'Of course, I'm happy to help a fellow refugee.'

She's changed her tune. Now that she's settled in a smart house in Crouch End with three dogs, she's all too willing to play that 'refugee' card. But I can't complain—it gets me what I want, and when I meet Bryn at Astey's on Thursday morning I present him with a stylish and generous offer.

'A one-off Krantz creation' I explain, 'produced free of charge, and auctioned to the highest bidder at an event which I will host at the gallery.'

Bryn is beside himself.

'Well!' he says, stirring his coffee with vigour, 'Well! This is far, far more than I'd hoped for!'

'It's the least I can do', I say, adding, for the hell of it, 'For old times' sake.'

He doesn't seem the least bit perturbed.

'Very good of you,' he says. 'Rosalyn will be over the moon.'

'Rosalyn not joining us today?' I ask, nonchalantly.

'No, Rosie's gone to visit our boy Josh.'

Rosie. For heaven's sake. *Rosie Rathbone.* It gets more Saturday Night Variety at every turn. Absently, he slurps a spoonful of coffee. I search for signs of discomfiture, but he's completely at ease with me. I imagine he's a sort of father-figure, really; sexual tension would never have played much part in this marriage. I waffle on about the auction idea for a while, tell him Peta's initial thoughts: a glass key, inset with a penknife, perhaps, or a bullet. He nods, frowning:

'Mmm … sounds very, um … to be honest, I'm rather a muttonhead about this. Music is more my speciality …'

Speciality, my arse. I toy with the idea of relaying Rosalyn's first, scathing opinions about the Boffin and his specialities. But I don't suppose it makes a blind bit of difference. The man has a rhino hide.

'It's such a pity' I say, innocently, 'that Rosalyn stopped singing—don't you think?'

He spreads his hands. 'I did everything I could to persuade her, but … Of course, she was never the same after the Edinburgh fiasco, and as soon as our first child was on the way, that was it. Her get-out, you might say.'

'The Edinburgh fiasco …' I flatten my inflection, hoping to prompt elaboration without sounding completely at sea.

'She didn't tell you? Ah … maybe I shouldn't have … Rosie probably didn't want you to know … She has such respect for your opinion. I expect she was a little ashamed.'

I coax him a little; it doesn't take much. For a man so used to dealing with delicate situations, Bryn turns out to have a pleasing streak of indiscretion.

Apparently the Edinburgh Fiasco occurred six months after Rosalyn walked out on me. She was singing at a concert, an opera-pops sort of affair—'not my kind of thing at all, really' confides Bryn, 'but I happened to be in town and saw her name on the poster. And as you know, I was a great admirer of Rosie's voice.'

(Yes, I think, you lecherous old stalker: maybe not such a father figure after all.)

Well, Rosalyn opened the second half with Dvorak's Song to the Moon; and halfway through it she went to pieces.

'Oh, it was terrible … ' Bryn's hand flutters across his forehead at the memory.

'What happened?'

'She just stopped singing. Her voice cracked, she stood there like a rabbit in the headlights, and then she burst into tears and left the stage.'

An electric current washes over my skin. He gabbles on, telling me how he rushed backstage to see her, how he comforted her, how she couldn't stop crying, and kept saying over and over again that she'd had enough of it all, that she just wanted to run away. And good old Bryn was on hand to escort her into his car and drive her to her B&B, and because she didn't want to be alone, whaddyaknow, Bo stays all night, squashed into the smelly bedroom armchair, while Rosalyn sobs into her pillow. All heart, that man.

When he's finished his account he slurps in another spoonful of coffee and says,
'Listen, please don't tell Rosie I spilled the beans. She'd be *furious.*'
After an uneasy silence, I say,
'I don't remember her ever having stagefright before.'
Bryn gives me a strange look.
'Well, she was going through a tricky period of her life ...'
A tricky period. So, basically, the old bugger stepped in after our break-up and did a spot of looting.
'That's all water under the bridge' Bryn says, brightly. 'Rosie was happy enough to concentrate on family life. And that's how it's been ever since. As a matter of fact ...' By his sheepish expression I guess he's about to let slip another secret. '... as a matter of fact, there'll be more family to concentrate on before long. That's why she's gone to see Josh. He's expecting. Or rather his girlfriend is. So Rosie's over there making a fuss of the poor girl. Can't blame her, really. First grandchild—big event ...'
Granny Rathbone. I find I really don't want to dwell on this prospect, and I shift the subject hastily back to the auction. But before Bo leaves I make sure I've asked him for Rosalyn's mobile number. He doesn't seem to mind.

Freddie's launch is fixed for September the sixth. Coincidentally, that's Rosalyn's birthday. Maybe she'll be celebrating it with her new grandchild—who knows? I didn't ask about the timing. I should give her a birthday present. Yes—that would be nice. To mark our renewed friendship. I consider the gallery displays. Something particularly lovely, particularly pricey. There's a kingfisher by Trent Hope—a flash of cobalt blue, rising into a dusting of gold. Gabby's always loved it, always jokes that she guides the punters away from that shelf. That would probably go down well, and I'm sure Bryn wouldn't think it inappropriate. It's an adult, sophisticated thing to do: a symbol of new beginnings, tinged with nostalgia and sadness; a gesture of goodwill for the future ... As he said, Bo the Boffin doesn't really do symbolism. He'd just think it was a pretty present. But Rosalyn would understand.

It's a busy afternoon at the gallery, so I come back late at night and enjoy the richness of that kingfisher blue. It's a cloudy night, but every so often the moon shrugs off its shadows and floods the gallery floor. I turn away from the exhibits and lean against the door for a moment, thinking of the story Bo told me, of Rosalyn and her serenade, pushing out that ascending octave with the force of lamentation—'Moonlight ... far above ... shining ...' And then the crack of glass.

23

'Moonlight ... far above ... shining ...'

Rosalyn, barefoot, in a light kaftan she used to wear after a bath. Standing in the centre of our cool, uncarpeted apartment, facing the open windows, her hair and kaftan wavering in the breeze. Rosalyn, soft and young and smelling of lavender soap. Rosalyn, singing to the moon with the sunlight on her face. Standing there, feet planted firmly on the tiled floor, arms at her side, slightly bent at the elbows, as if some unseen force had started to draw her towards the light, and she was just beginning to resist. That face. That voice. Lost to me, now. Gone. You go through the days, the nights, you find that years have passed and somewhere in your deepest, most irrational being, you believe, you really believe, that things will go back to the way they were. That the past, and your younger selves, are all there, waiting for your return. Even now that I've seen her, and the evidence of a different life—even now, I can't shake off the certainty that I will open the door of our apartment and see her standing there, hear that heartbreaking plea to the moon.

'Nobody has the right to beat you!' Slobodan Milosevic told a crowd of Serbian demonstrators in 1987. They'd clashed with police in Kosovo Polje. A fracas. A brouhaha. But those words were later described as the end of Yugoslavia. Kosovo Polije was just a name on a map to us, but it was far more than that to his followers. It was here, in 1389, that Serb defenders were crushed by Ottoman invaders. Both armies were virtually wiped out. That carnage paved the way for the Ottoman conquest. In 1989, Milosevic descended into Kosovo Polje in his helicopter, stirring up six centuries of resentment. By then, over half the Kosovan population were Albanian.

I'll be honest, I always found the whole Yugoslav situation baffling and boring. Every week Rosalyn brought back from her singing sessions sorry tales of neighbours turning on each other, children steered away from their friends, windows smashed and punches thrown—she couldn't really grasp the details behind it all, and the truth was, neither could most of her Albanian friends, or the Serb neighbours they'd left behind. Whatever their language or their gods or their songs, all anyone really understood was that sooner or later, people find any excuse for hatred.

In late 1989 we sat in our living rooms and watched people scaling the Berlin Wall, hacking away at the stone, partying, dancing, roaring their euphoria, as this most visible of borders was chipped and jeered into rubble. Of course, the borders themselves don't disappear, just because walls are brought down. That's why I've always found the whole notion of building walls or raising fences a bit of a farce. As Scott always said, the only insurmountable borders are in our heads, and they might be there forever. Well, be that as it may, this latest scattering and re-shuffling of the political cards brought another wave of immigrants, and a spate of discussions and articles in the Press. We'd been approached by a glossy news magazine, a short-lived venture called *La Settimana*. They were doing a big feature on immigrant communities in Italy and wanted to include something about the Zenada training programme, get some pictures of the trainees at work, do a few interviews. The journalist arrived early one Friday morning with a photographer in tow. I recognised Scott straight away, though he blocked my laugh of recognition with blank eyes.

'You came up to our café table, in Florence,' I prompted him, still shaking his hand. 'I bought the prints, eventually. Remember? You asked Rosalyn to go and sit indoors, where the shadows were more interesting ...'

'Oh, *her*!' His face cleared and he nodded. 'Yes, I remember *her*. One of those faces that loves the lens, without trying.' But his attention was already wandering, claimed by the glow of the kiln, the play of light on the idle blowpipes, the spangle of dust in the air. 'Can we get one of your trainees in to start making something?' Our two current trainees, Mergim and Arber, were summoned to show off their new skills, while Scott hopped and bobbed around, getting the best angles. The journalist interviewed them briefly (their Italian was stilted); spoke to Dino; spoke to me. I said all the right things about skill potential and fresh starts and opportunities, and was cleverly equivocal, I reckoned, when she brought up the touchy issue of pay, and local sensibilities.

'Generally, the feeling hereabouts is positive and friendly' I said, animating my eyebrows in a positive and friendly way. The journalist—I've forgotten her name—was 30ish, I'd say, quite attractive; padded shoulders, short leather skirt, good legs. Our sightlines met and sizzled now and then in a pleasant way. She was taking notes, in shorthand, I remember, but had a little tape cassette as well, 'just for checking purposes', she'd assured me. I suppose we still worried about things like recording speech, in those days, although I should have worried far more about the story her skipping pencil might be telling.

'And you've really encountered no opposition at all?' she asked, glancing up from her notebook with a smile that had nothing to do with the question. 'This isn't an affluent area, after all—people must feel threatened?'

'I really don't get that impression' I assured her, giving her earnest eyes. 'There's been a lot of effort, locally, to make our new friends feel welcome.' (I liked that 'new friends'. I said it again, to make sure she had it down somewhere in her hieroglyphs.) 'There are several projects to integrate our new friends into the wider community, and share their cultural knowledge, and ours. My wife is running one of them, in fact.'

107

Did I really say 'my wife'? That's what the journalist wrote, anyway, and Rosalyn teased me about it, said I was 'so *conventional*!' and referred to herself as the Little Woman for a while. Maybe I was delivering some kind of message to the leggy journo: *I'd love to, but* ... Or, more likely, she made assumptions and misquoted me. Anyway, I told her about Rosalyn's choir, and she was quite intrigued, would have liked to see a rehearsal, but wasn't available that coming weekend, and her deadline was looming. Scott had overheard, though, and suddenly he was all interest and charm.

'Well, I'm free on Sunday—why don't I pop over, take some shots, and you can get a couple of quotes by phone?'

The journalist was happy with that. Did I think my wife would mind? No, I didn't. And all at once, a neat solution to Uncle Don had presented itself.

'While I think of it, Scott,' I added, 'do you ever do publicity headshots?'

Rosalyn wore a smart dress and jacket for the choir shoot, made herself up, pinned up her hair, even though she usually led the sessions in her sweater and jeans.

'I want to look professional' she explained. 'I want people to know I take this as seriously as the rest of my work.'

I didn't point out that precious few people would even look at the feature, far less speculate about Rosalyn's other work. The magazine was always a niche product and folded completely after five years. Anyway, she looked lovely, and when she and Scott returned to the apartment for the headshots, she had the flush of adrenaline, the shine in her eyes, that always made me want to smother and possess her when she stepped off stage after a good performance. So I was taken aback when Scott, unloading all his equipment, pacing around our apartment, pacing around Rosalyn, issued his first instructions:

'OK, let's get shot of all *that*'—his hand pirhouetting to indicate Rosalyn's clothes and hair—'and get back to reality. Wash off the make-up, take a bath, and put on the simplest dress you've got.'

Rosalyn and I looked at each other, but neither of us put up an argument. You didn't, with Scott. In matters of photography, he was in charge.

While Rosalyn followed her orders I watched Scott gauging the environment and preparing his gear. I'd been right about the physical likeness. They could have been twins. The difference was all in their bearing. Rosalyn was calm, still, gentle; Scott was a lizard—lithe, quick, darting here and there, twitching with nervous energy. When Rosalyn emerged, unpinned, unpainted, as beautiful as I'd ever seen her, Scott stood before her, assessing her with a professional eye, and I stood in the shadow and went on watching with a strange, uneasy curiosity. Patterns. Similarities. Compelling, to any collector worthy of the name.

'OK' he said at last. 'Face the light, and sing.'

'Sing what?' asked Rosalyn, at a loss.

'Anything. First thing that comes to mind. But make it something you love.'

She gathered herself in, the way singers do, found that higher plane, steeled the muscle, adjusted the stance, summoned the sound on a column of air and cast it out across the room, into the air, over the city.

'Moonlight ... far above ... shining ...'

And Scott went to work. Click, click, click, click ...

'Tell me, oh, where is my dear loved one ...'

That's the picture I should have on my wall. But I didn't keep those shots. I can deal with the Florence photograph—that was a passing mood, and Scott just a passer-by. But some works of art are too significant, too sullied by association. The results of that photo shoot were glorious. They captured Rosalyn at her loveliest; you could almost hear her voice. There came a time when I simply couldn't bear to see her, in her prime, at the zenith of her beauty, caught and summed up by the man who eventually drove her out of my life.

24

Rosalyn and Scott. Two lightning strikes. One inspiring, illuminating, glorious; the other—catastrophic. Only three weeks after that photo shoot, Zenada was hit by a thunderbolt of its own. I can't blame Scott for that, of course. If I'm going to blame anyone, it should really be the leggy journalist, or her sub-editor. Not that I was unhappy with her feature; it put us in a good light, and she even included one of our own marketing shots of a decorative piece made by a former trainee. I did comment to Rosalyn that she hadn't drawn a very clear line between our legit programme, for registered immigrants, and some of the shadier employers who didn't ask to see the paperwork. But Rosalyn shrugged and said,
'People need jobs. They need to live, whether they've got the right papers or not.'
Anyway, the blame game is a waste of time. It was probably just sheer bad luck.
After all, as I said before, not that many people were going to buy the magazine.
Those who did buy it were scanning the pages on their commute to a nice, cosy desk job, or discussing world affairs over a quick macchiato. Not at all the kind of people who assembled in Piazza dell'Amicizia on the 4th of September, screams in their bullfrog throats, righteousness bulging in their temples.

Any anti-immigration rally would be a provocation; a rally in Piazza dell'Amicizia was like the infantry's opening volley. There's nothing remarkable about that particular square—it's just a dusty quadrangle of tired and anonymous office buildings, known to locals just as 'Amici', where a second-hand clothes market used to set up once a month. But it's slap bang in the middle of the immigrant community. A crowd of young Albanians, bolstered by local students, came out to greet the rally. There was a football match going on at the other end of town that afternoon, so the police were more stretched than usual. For a few hours, according to subsequent reports, the event was nothing more than a shout-off. Name-calling, banner-waving, a bit of chest-thumping and the occasional surge-and-retreat posturing. But as we all know, it only takes one idiot, one temper snapping into action, one hand to fling a missile … and even as the bottle traces its soaring arc, turning in the air, before it cracks itself and its victim's face open, it's too late. One spasm of movement is all it takes to turn protest into war.

It was a workshop demonstration day. We'd reinstated Zenada's public tours, but made it a much more stylish and confined affair, guiding visitors into the viewing gallery to watch Zenada craftsmen at work, before letting them leave, of their own free will, via the shop—which now looked more like a tastefully arranged foyer. Leather tub-chairs here and there, a discreet presence in a suit, making notes at a counter, a small selection of exquisite Zenada *objets* locked and underlit in cabinets. And strictly no price tags.

Scott was due to deliver the publicity pictures. Overdue, in fact. We'd already had an earful from Uncle Don: why didn't we listen to him, why did we have to go for some poncey clown with fancy ideas when we could have had everything up and running a fortnight back?—and so on and so on. But Scott, as ever, was in no hurry to please anyone else. He'd promised to bring them round three days running, and I told Rosalyn, before setting out to work, that if he didn't come up with the goods this time I'd personally go and tear the bloody things from his camera. She kissed me and patted my chest and said,
'Don't try and sound like Don Cutler, Nathe. It doesn't suit you.'

Anyway, I was glad to be in the factory. I still got a thrill from demos, all those years after the momentous craft fair day. I slipped in with the spectators and sat in a corner of the gallery. The children were manoeuvred to the front so that they could lean on the wooden barrier for a close-up view. Carlo the guide had been moved to Sales, and replaced by Selina the interpreter, a former actress, who made the most of the dangers in the workplace.

'Now, the furnaces and the glory holes are burning at over *two thousand* degrees Fahrenheit. Can you *imagine* how it would feel if you sucked in that much heat, instead of blowing?' (Squeals of ecstatic horror from the front row.) 'Luckily our craftsmen are highly skilled and using the best and safest equipment and protection … And by the way, the reason they're wearing these goggles is to stop them going blind from the ultraviolet light … Because behind those furnace doors is, effectively, a little sun, which could *sizzle your eyeballs* if you looked at it too long …'

And so on, cleverly using our health and safety assurances to frighten the tourists out of their wits. She paused as a yowl of sirens expanded outside, then receded.

'Sounds like trouble' commented a man sitting next to me.

'Some protest going on' said his companion.

Selina resumed her spiel.

'When the furnace is fully charged, we can get about 500 kilos of molten glass in there. In a minute we'll see how some of that glass is scooped out to make our smaller pieces—like getting honey onto a dipper, but much, much more scary! …'

She had to raise her voice above another blossoming of sirens. They sounded closer than before. A few of the adults at the back of the group started murmuring quizzically. These days the mobiles would have been out, checking for updates, but nobody had them then. In any case, the noise passed, heading elsewhere, and the demonstration carried on.

The show was about to end. Selina rounded off her thanks to Dino and his crew, and the visitors applauded and gathered themselves up, reaching for their bags and jackets. There'd been a smattering of shouts from outside, mollified by the factory walls—but in Italy there was nothing unusual about that. Suddenly, those shouts fanfared into a deafening cacophony. Everyone stopped, looked in the general direction of the reception area; one or two smiled in anticipation of some contrived entertainment.

It was only afterwards that the news reports tidied all those individual morsels of sound and fury into a clear narrative. The anti-immigration rally had ruptured into violence. Some people—possibly to get away from the fighting, possibly following a predetermined plan—had broken away from the square and marched through the smattering of streets leading to the factory, hurling chants at the hastily closed curtains and bolted doors. When their opponents realised what was happening, they gave chase. All that frenzy of aggression was funnelled through the neighbourhood and eventually splayed out into the factory forecourt. Some of the crowd were armed with metal pipes. It's not clear whether they were already planning to attack us, or whether we simply lay in the path of the battle. Whatever the case, the police caught up and let loose with tear gas, and that was a splash of petrol on the fire.

Breaking glass is the worst sound in the world. A cataclysmic sound. The first impact, a smack, like a body hitting water. Then the shiver of fallout. Arpeggios of shards and nuggets and lethal dust, twinkling over the screams and the bellowing and choking. Trails of tear gas chased the intruders into the building. They burst through the workshop doors, followed by the retching receptionist. I saw Dino wielding his punty rod like a warrior—not brandishing it, but aiming its heat away from his crew. I saw him yelling, saw the square of his mouth and his missing front tooth: he was ordering them out, off the workshop floor, out of its infernal danger.

The spectators had made a rush for the exit into the shop and plugged the door; the protestors and Carlotta, our receptionist, were writhing, stumbling towards us. Then the gas arrived—and we understood why. It was like the claw of death, that gas, embedding itself in the skull, piercing the eyeballs, wringing the throat. Abruptly the level of panic rocketed. Children were trampled underfoot. I launched myself into the mass of bodies with no other thought than escaping that gas. Behind me, I heard the clang of steel and stone, the crunching and the splintering, and a shriek of pain that blanketed everything else.

In the space of five minutes, all the glass in the factory shop was broken. The cases, the products, even the lamp on the counter, all cracked or pulverised in the stampede, when the logjam of people finally erupted under its own pressure through the exit. That sound, the sound of everything breaking, is what wakes me at night, sometimes, even now. In my nightmares, there is no boundary, no distinction, between that and Dino's animal scream. They're the same. Before them, there is order. Stillness. A balance of heat and air and liquid, spun and stretched with the skill of millennia, cooled into a fragile stasis. A window, an ornament, a bowl: precious and civilised and sane. And then the screaming, the shattering of everything that's safe and beautiful. Smashing the barrier between routine and a savage and random world.

25

I got away lightly. Effects of the gas, and minor cuts from the glass: that was all. I called Rosalyn from the hospital. Between her cries of horror and my reassurances I could hear another voice, like an echo, heard the crescendo of interest and anticipation.

'Who's that?' I demanded.

'Scott Carter. He brought the photos—Nathe, are you sure you're OK? I'm on my way now.'

We finished the conversation but I could still hear Scott firing questions at her, as he sensed the promise of disaster.

She got to the hospital with Scott in tow, wielding one of his less complicated cameras.

'What's *he* doing here?' I whispered.

'He insisted.' She touched my jaw with the tips of her fingers and studied me with concern. 'Are you *sure* you're not hurt?'

There was a minor commotion behind us. Scott was being hustled out by a couple of orderlies after taking pictures of one of the walking wounded. Rosalyn tutted.

'He's a strange one' she commented. 'But I have to say the pictures are amazing.'

I spotted a doctor who'd been seeing to Dino and trotted after him for news. It wasn't good. One side of Dino's face and one arm were badly burned. They were particularly worried about his lips. The medic illustrated his words by brushing his own mouth with his fingers, wrongly assuming, from my blasted expression, that I didn't understand what he was saying.

We were lucky no-one was killed. I don't know what the casualty rate was among the rioters. The worst injury from those inside the factory, apart from Dino's, was a broken arm: one of the children who slipped under the stampede and was trodden on. I saw him hours later, in the hospital, proudly exhibiting his plaster cast and telling his mother,

'Mamma, when the man stood on it, I heard it go snap.'

The press began to arrive. I didn't want to be buttonholed so I pleaded dizziness and was taken to a side room and given some water. Sitting there, alone in a corner, was our receptionist Carlotta. She looked up as I came in, but said nothing. Her eyes were wary, red-rimmed; for some reason, they reminded me of cattle in a field—the way they watch as you pass, take you in, then turn away. She drew her hair back and tucked it over her ear, revealing a scree of lesions spattering across her cheek and forehead. Rosalyn went over and dropped to her haunches, looking up into the poor cow's face.

'Are you all right?' she asked. When Rosalyn spoke Italian it was like hearing her sing a lullaby. 'Can I get you anything?'

The girl shook her head slowly, then leaned forward and spoke in a confidential tone.

'All those lovely things on my desk, the pen holder, the swirly ashtray … all smashed.'

'I know,' cooed Rosalyn, 'I know…'

'But you know …' —the voice dropped even further— '… when we were quiet and the phone wasn't ringing, I used to pick them up, and they were so lovely, I almost wanted to smash them myself.'

Rosalyn cast me a look. In English I said,

'Shall I fetch someone?'

But Carlotta was whispering on:

'Do you ever wonder if you could make things happen, just by thinking about it?'

117

Rosalyn took her hand and said something reassuring. Then she got to her feet and drew me to the other side of the room.

'I think it's shock' she murmured. 'I mean, look at her poor face. I think she's gone a little bit mad.'

Just before midnight, I was discharged. I wanted to go straight to the factory, but Rosalyn insisted on returning to the apartment.

'There'll be plenty of time for thinking and doing,' she said. 'For now, just be glad we're still here. And *rest*.'

We got into the rickety old lift. It creaked and clunked its way up three floors, and Rosalyn clamped her arms around me till my ribs squeaked.

'Thank god you're all right', she kept saying. 'Thank god, thank god.'

The lift doors rattled open and there was Scott, sitting on the floor outside our door.

'There you are!' he cried, leaping to his feet. I felt Rosalyn's arms loosen in dismay, then saw her mustering her good nature.

'I'm so sorry,' she started, 'you need your equipment, don't you, and we just need to settle up—'

'No, no, no,' Scott was chirruping, hopping from one foot to the other in his impatience as we unlocked the door, 'never mind all that—who's been hurt? What's the damage? I couldn't get any more from the police, and the hospital kicked me out.'

Automatically, I began to relate the incident, told him about Dino, about the unhinged receptionist ... Rosalyn had gone very quiet. She shot me a look I didn't understand. Presently she drew herself up in the centre of our main room, almost barring Scott's way, and said,

'Thanks for everything, Scott. If you want to collect your stuff—you'll understand Nathan needs a little peace and quiet now.'

'Yes yes yes'—he buzzed round the room, packing up his things, then paused and fixed me with his dark stare. 'So you're Don Cutler's nephew?' he said. I could feel Rosalyn's impatience ruffling the air.

'Seriously, Scott. Not now. Please.'

He put up his hands in defeat.

'Sure, sure, I'll leave you in peace. Just one last thing, Nathan—I need your permission to visit the factory tomorrow. First light. Before anything's been tidied away.'

26

Dino had to have plastic surgery. Rosalyn badgered me into visiting him at the hospital, though I found the prospect appalling. I was quite relieved, when I got there, to find him still bandaged up out of view. He was unable to speak, of course, but his wife was there, gripping his good hand for all she was worth. She stood when I came in, but kept a hold of that hand.

'Mr Hill' she said—*Signor Eel*—'tell him, please—he'll be back to work again, when they've put it all right, won't he?'

'Of course, Signora' I said. 'Nothing to worry about on that score. We couldn't manage without Dino.'

I'd never realised what a smooth liar I could be.

After nearly a year, we'd made no progress on the factory refit. My plan had been to make something positive out of this catastrophe, to rebuild our little factory as a state-of-the-art workplace, as befitting the home and origin of our expanding business. I sent reassuring letters to the workforce. I visited the site with teams of men in hard hats, who drew visions in the air across our actual view of a stunted brick shell—all that was left after it had been made safe. But the whole thing was sucking up money like a whirlpool. We claimed third party damage (which was covered by insurance); our insurers hammed it up as an act of terrorism (which wasn't). I had British lawyers on the case, and was flying to and fro for meetings on a weekly basis. After one particularly frustrating session I retreated to Uncle Don's office, to sit in his swivel chair and hear his words of wisdom. Taff was still guarding the sanctum, still treating Don like a wayward schoolboy. She greeted me like a long-lost son, hugging me then holding me away by the arms, looking me up and down with wonder.

'Any minute now' I told her, 'you're going to tell me how I've grown.'

She gave me a little shake, and said,

'It may seem daft to you, my love, but to me it's only five minutes since you were a little mite, come to play in your uncle's den.'

She gazed at me, examining my features, then reached up to flick a strand of hair from my eyes.

'You've got *such* a look of him, you know. Couple of inches taller and broader, you'd be the living spit.'

But Uncle Don was still the bigger man, and I still felt like a novice and a fool when I slumped into the chair and recited my woes. Don lit a cigar, squinted through the smoke as he listened, then threw his head back to whistle out a blue stream. He levelled a long look at me, till I had to drop my eyes, and then he said: 'You know what to do. Get rid.'

I swung the chair from side to side, tempted to launch into a circuit but holding back for dignity's sake.

'I've told them their jobs are safe' I whined.

'Well, you'll have to tell them you was wrong. Won't be pretty, but it can't be helped. You done a good job with that business. Don't chuck it down the toilet now.'

'The whole *point* of that business' I protested 'was saving the factory. The *original* factory. Zenada Glass.'

Don shrugged and put out his cigar.

'No point saving the factory if it kills the company, is there, sunshine? It's tough titties, but that's the way of it. They're not kids and you're not their dad. Get rid.'

To be fair, he left it at that. No 'I told you so'. It was a problem to be solved, not a point to be proved.

'Now,' he went on, sitting up straight to signal a change of subject. 'I've had a request from that happy snapper friend of yours. Wants to take pictures of me, for some magazine, something about self-made men. Understandable, of course, I'm a good-lookin' geezer though I say so meself. So what do you reckon? Should I say yes?'

Before the move back to Britain I had to break the news to the Italian workforce. I was dreading it. At least the demolition of the factory made it impossible to gather them together for a farewell speech—a negative version of my triumphant introduction, all those years ago. At least we were all spared that. We had to do it by letter. I made sure I added two handwritten lines to each one—at the beginning, so that my own hand formed the employee's name; and at the end, giving my best hopes and wishes for the future and finishing with my signature, so that nobody could accuse me of rubber-stamping.

'I'm going to write the whole letter to Dino,' I told Rosalyn, as she stood behind my chair and kneaded my shoulder. 'Something more personal. Put it in with the official one.'

'I think that's a lovely idea,' said Rosalyn. 'And Carlo, too. He brought us together, after all.'

She stooped to rest her head briefly on mine, then straightened with a new thought: 'Actually, we should probably go and see them. Don't you think, Nathe? They've been there so long, and they supported you so much …'

'Oh … I don't know …' I pushed my chair back from the writing bureau and ran my fingers along its carved flourishes. I was stung by Rosalyn's suggestion. 'I don't think they'd appreciate it, necessarily … it seems a bit … you know, visiting the estates, before turfing out the tenants …'

I was babbling, and she knew it. She held fast to my shoulders despite my fidgeting. 'Well, all right, maybe not Carlo' she conceded. Maybe a letter and a gift for him.

His wife's got a decent job, anyway, and he should get something soon enough, with his English and everything.' Rosalyn seemed to know about all my employees' home lives.

'I'll give him a spectacular reference' I said, eager with relief. 'All of them. I'll give them all the best references possible—I mean, they *are* the best. They *all* are.' I was becoming quite emotional. I could almost have wished for that farewell speech after all.

'But Dino ...' said Rosalyn, and my eyes dried. 'Poor man. He'll probably never work again.' She gave my shoulders one decisive squeeze. 'I think you should go and see him. He's at home, now'—I mean, how did she *know* these things?—'so you don't have to sit in a horrible hospital ward or anything. Just a visit to him and Fortuna, quietly, at home, to break the news.' As if that made it *better*! I twisted in my seat to glare at her. I was horrified.

'But he's not well! He's not going to want me crashing into his house with bad news ...'

'You won't be *crashing into his house*. You'll be paying a visit. Out of respect. Out of decency. I'll come with you, if you like.'

'It's not as if he won't get compensated' I pouted. 'They'll all get a helping hand.'

'I know, Nathe. But sometimes a handshake means more than a cheque.'

So we drove to the smallholding where Dino and his wife, Fortuna, lived, a few miles out of town in scrubby countryside. Fortuna's father had once farmed the land there; now she grew tomatoes and fruit and sometimes rented the one remaining outhouse to holidaymakers. *Fortuna*. Luck. Cruel joke. She looked far older than her years, far older than Dino—than the way he'd looked before the incident, at any rate. As she ushered us in to the cool back room, taking Rosalyn's arm, clucking over her, already treating her like a daughter, I held back and cast my eyes over the heavy furniture, the stone floor, the crucifix on the wall. I sensed Dino's presence before seeing him. He sat in the corner, in shadow; his face was still partially bandaged, a pallid, one-eyed moon. Rosalyn advanced on him, softening and brightening the room with her voice and her scent and her sweet compassion. Then Fortuna drew me forward, taking my wrist in her woodbark hand.

'*Signor Eel*' she told her husband, '*è così gentile ...*'

So kind. So kind that I could hardly meet his eyes. He thanked us for coming and assured us that he was on the mend. Fortuna echoed his words in a rapid undertone—he had difficulty speaking because of the damage to his mouth.

We drank sweetened fruit juice, and Dino sat straightbacked in his chair, clutching one wooden arm, staring ahead and saying little. Fortuna and Rosalyn kept up a stream of conversation. Within a heartbeat, Fortuna was baring her soul, unburdening her worries about their wayward son, who'd gone to Rome to make his millions and fallen in with the wrong crowd.

'He's too trusting,' she cried, as Rosalyn nodded, nodded, and gripped her hands. 'Too ready to make friends. He gets led astray ...'

'He's an idiot. A druggie' growled Dino, without looking any of us in the eye. Fortuna gazed into Rosalyn's sympathetic face. 'He needs *help,*' she said. 'He needs to come home. But Dino won't have him back. He stole from us, Signora. He can't help himself ...'

'No, of course,' murmured Rosalyn. *Signora*, I thought. Mrs Hill. I wanted to catch her eye and share the joke, but it would have been inappropriate. Dino covered his eyes with his good hand.

'He's young,' offered Rosalyn, and Fortuna nodded extravagantly. 'Young and headstrong. It must be so difficult for you all.'

There was a pause, marked by a few whimpers from Fortuna and soothing noises from Rosalyn. This wasn't the *mis-en-scène* I'd have chosen, but I had to get on with it sooner or later. I cleared my throat.

'I'm afraid,' I said, 'the news about the factory isn't … isn't as good as I'd hoped …'

I'd prepared my speech, of course, with Rosalyn's help, and they listened to it patiently. Fortuna nodded as I spoke, though she looked confused, and I wasn't at all sure that she was grasping my meaning. She kept hold of Rosalyn's hand throughout. Dino said nothing. When I'd finished we just sat there for a while. A broad-shouldered clock on the mantelpiece tallied the silence. Then Fortuna said, 'Well … we knew how it might be. How can he do his job—the way he is now? So. It's a shame for all the others. But we knew, for Dino, this might be the end.'

So she had been following, after all.

When we left I took her hand and apologised again.

'I feel I've let you down' I said. Fortuna patted my arm. She said,

'No, Signor Eel, this isn't your fault. This is just life.'

She looked up at me with the face of a previous age: that sun-hardened, furrowed skin, the wary eyes, the neck bowed by effort and distress. I found myself thinking: *Scott Carter would make the most of that face.*

27

In later years—the jealous years—I became a master at the art of replaying and reinterpreting my memories. I practised the art, just like a craftsman: persevering, focusing, refining my recollections. I reached a point of control which allowed me to step into a memory, freeze it and take a look around, studying expressions and tones of voice, checking surreptitious touches and glances that I'd missed the first time round. Using this painstaking technique, I built a new narrative of my own life. The narrative of suspicion. Some of it may have been right, or none of it; I doubt, now, that it all was. What a waste of time and skill, what a waste of *me*. But still, that's the way it was. I told myself a story, and that story always began one early autumn evening in 1991.

Demolition work on the shell of the factory was well underway. The site was still mine, at this point, but there were developers slavering over the kill. I couldn't fail to profit. Rosalyn and I were having a break from all the stress: we'd promised ourselves a quiet evening together, read, share a meal, maybe listen to a little music (Italian telly was depressingly bad), then an early night. We had the french windows open; russet reflections of sky were quartered and framed in their panes. Occasional, solitary sounds floated up from the street: a child's call, a dog's sudden patter of barks, a flare of engine. Rosalyn had just got up to head for the kitchen, stroking my head as she passed, and I heard her humming as she started to gather ingredients from the cupboards. I was reading the paper, trying half-heartedly to get my head around the pandemonium of new states and old quarrels that seemed to be turning Eastern Europe into a fireworks display. The Soviet Union was dissolving like the blob of milk on my macchiato—state after state bubbling off into its own, independent sphere. Estonia, Latvia, Lithuania, Ukraine,

Belarus, Moldova, Azerbaijan, Kyrgyzstan, Uzbekistan … in my head they were all in that pompous old imperial lettering, on antique maps of an antique world. Now, here they were, coming back to life, complicating the news and our minds. Yugoslavia continued its meltdown. Words had taken form as shells, artillery, mortar fire, tanks. The term 'Serbo-Croat', unremarkable and lacking in irony as far as I'd been aware until then, now snapped at the hyphen. The handsome, multi-ethnic riverside town of Vukovar was being reinvented as a battle ground. Within a couple of months the place would be annihilated: every building a wreck, dead people and animals rotting in the streets, survivors starving and shell-shocked. That particular September evening, it was just another name, another conflict, to puzzle over before turning a page and rustling the sweet silence. The rhythm of that name reminded me of an old pop song, *Reet Petite*. *'Vukovar, Vukovar,'* I sang absent-mindedly to myself, as I sought more cheering stories: *'Vukovar, Vukovar, oo-oo-ooh wee!'* I was reading about the discovery of a mummified prehistoric man in the Ötztal Alps, when a gunfire rapping at the door made me curse with shock.

Rosalyn came out of the kitchen, pepper in one hand, knife in the other, giving her little questioning frown.

'I'll send them away' I promised, expecting some new crisis about the sale. When I opened the door to see Scott there, unusually relaxed and cameraless, I was lost for words. I heard Rosalyn, behind me, supplying the good manners.

'Scott, hello! What a nice surprise, come in!'

I stepped aside and held the door open like a butler. He hardly looked in my direction, but took his grin straight past me, indicating the pepper in Rosalyn's hand.

'Looks delicious, don't mind if I do!'

So then, of course, she had to invite him to join us, and then, of course, he settled in for the duration and we had to open a second bottle of wine, and she was all for letting him sleep on the couch—did her best, in fact, to persuade him, even though he kept reminding us that he was staying in a friend-of-a-friend's room in town, that he didn't even have a car, that he wasn't drunk or incapable. (I spent many a future hour trying to remember whether there'd been a suggestive look with that phrase, whether Rosalyn had met his eyes, laughed, looked embarrassed, ignored it altogether?) They certainly seemed to get on well, that evening—better than they had during the photo shoot, though that was probably because Scott was more laid-back when he wasn't working. He chatted away with us amiably over dinner—about his work and his ambitions, gossip about the magazine journalist, my relationship with Uncle Don, my plans for the factory. But the main purpose of Scott's visit was to ask a favour. Even in my later, green-eyed narrative, I had no doubt about that. Scott's first priority was *always* his photography. He wanted to showcase his work in an exhibition, and his suggestion was what he called a Valedictory: a farewell to Zenada, set up as a temporary installation on the demolition site.

'Invite all the workers,' he pretty much instructed me; 'make it into an event for them, have music—'

'My choir could sing!' yapped Rosalyn, who was fairly tipsy by that stage. 'I think that would be fitting, Nathe—no, really, seriously—it's like saying: we're still here, we're still singing: whatever you throw at us, you can't win.'

'Exactly' chimed in Scott, holding up a hand that may have been to interrupt her or to underline her point. 'You don't want to slink away from a ruined factory and hand a victory to the racists, do you?'

'No ...' I clutched my wine glass in defence against the two of them, both leaning across the little table at me with their alcoholic zeal. 'I certainly don't want that, but ...'

'This show,' announced Scott, and he actually slapped the table and made the plates rattle, 'will be called *Broken Glass*. It's about beauty and ugliness, destruction and creation … it's about the state of the world today. It'll be *relevant*, and *powerful* … it'll be *magnificent*.' I smirked, but his self-assurance was irresistible. All that hyperbole sat between us as statements of fact. And I ended up agreeing that, yes, a Valedictory would be a fine idea, and, certainly, I should fund and organise the erection of a Portakabin, the catering, some of the publicity … and I even thanked Scott for taking care of everything else.

After he'd left, at about 2 in the morning, Rosalyn complained that he'd never asked about *her* work. This was true. He showed no interest in Rosalyn's singing, and directed most of his conversation either to me or to us both, as a pair. It was only in the jealous years that I invested his indifference with cunning, and decided he'd been putting me off the scent. At the time, I yawned, I tutted at Rosalyn, I turned off the light, I said,
'Don't be so sensitive,' and I wrapped my arms around her warmth.

28

The photograph Scott chose to advertise *Broken Glass* was a cleverly angled view
of a glass pane, one of the few in the factory doors that survived the onslaught.
Some small object had obviously hit it hard, and had left a gouge right in the centre,
from which two jagged gashes travelled in opposite directions, like electric charges.
The heavy, late afternoon light had created a deep and vivid reflection in the rest of
the pane, showing remnants of the previous day's violence: a shoe, an abandoned
punty rod, a snowscape of shattered glass in drifts and banks, and one distant and
solitary figure—maybe a policeman—walking away from the scene. The reflection
is so clear that, when you look at the photograph, it seems as if that gouge and
those long, spiny cracks are actually on your own eyeball.

Scott had made good use of my dazed authorisation, that day. Armed with my
permission (which I don't think was ever checked) and his Press pass, he somehow
charmed his way through the cordon and roamed around the chaotic factory site all
day. It was a dangerous place: he cut his leg quite badly before he was done, and
had to get a few stitches. (When he came to dinner he showed us the fading scar.)
In Scott's opinion—and in the critics'—it was well worth it. The Valedictory
gallery glimmered with images of glass in all its possible forms—sublime and
lethal. A heap of it, crushed to crumbs, sparkling with the arrogance of diamonds.
The menacing remains of a glass sheet, its fangs smeared with blood, hair and flesh.
The disastrous workshop floor, strewn about with discarded irons like lances on a
battlefield, the glory hole gaping and cold.

It wasn't just glass—though the theme ran through all his pictures. He called it the
'golden thread'. He explained it to me as I followed him round the temporary

gallery, watching him choose and place his images with infinite patience and care. 'I always need a theme' he told me. 'It forces me to focus, to make decisions and edit things out. Otherwise I'd want to show everything. *Everything*. All the details,'—holding up a shot of the amputated neck of a bottle to try the effect—'all the patterns, all the random, surreal shit and all the bland nothing stuff—all of it. If I pick a theme, I can still go all over the place … yeah. This one …'—choosing a portrait instead—'I can really go off on a tangent, but it has to have the *golden thread*. Has to justify itself, fit the title. Then I can use up all those thoughts, all those ideas, package them up, put them aside, move on to the next one.'

They were installing stand mics for the choir. Every now and then we heard a boom of voice, followed by muffled discussions and the rasp of ducktape. He edged along, judging, measuring, marking up, handing me the tape measure, demanding the pencil. He insisted on hanging his own pictures, and I was glad to tag along as his assistant. Despite all the clearing up, and despite the flooring we'd had put down, every step still produced a faint scrunching sound, as though all that glass had been swallowed by the ground, had become a part of it. Everyone who came to peck at me with questions was accompanied by this vaguely comic sound effect, like approaching villains in a pantomime. And there were a lot of questions, of course. Being in charge is largely a matter of answering questions, while other people get things done. They already *know* the answers. It's not wisdom they want from me, it's permission. The skill is in gauging which answer they want, and providing it.

'Signor Eel, will the choir need more than two microphones? Two should be enough to give the right balance, but if you want more …'

'Two mics will be fine.'

'Signor Eel, are you certain that the bar should be so close to the door? Our girls will be there to hand out drinks as the guests arrive, so if we have the main bar area towards the back instead …'

'Let's have the bar at the back, as long as the space works.'

'Excellent idea, Signor Eel, thank you.'

I handed out the required replies, and at the same time responded to Scott's commands, handing over and taking back like a nurse in an operating theatre. I was fascinated to watch him at his work; I soaked up all his theories and musings as if they were the art itself.

'There have to be people' he told me. 'Human figures, human faces. Whatever else I show, they have to be in there—for the show, and for me. A landscape can be awe-inspiring, thought-provoking, majestic, heart-breaking. A face … I don't know. That makes it a *story*. You know?'

The portrait he'd chosen was of Carlotta, our former receptionist. Despite the stark hospital lighting, Scott had found a way to give all those tiny wounds on her ravaged face the texture of a filigreed veil. It was a profoundly humane portrait. Her eyes were sad and baffled. Viewers would stand for a while at that photograph, thinking about fate and suffering.

He included some shots of the immigrant district: a family in its cramped room in a shared house, children caught mid-squabble, mother young and exhausted, turning baleful eyes away from the lens; a window pane in the background missing a chunk in one corner, as if someone had bitten it out, and inadequately stuffed with rags. Some of the young bucks, clustered on a corner under a cracked lamplight, two of them stooping over a cigarette, others laughing at the camera, striking that peacock pose that you see in young men of all nationalities, everywhere. There were a couple of the pictures he'd taken of our trainees at work, and a loving detail of one of our finished products that never made it into the magazine feature—a glorious crescent-edge, and the pearly sheen of a bubble trapped inside the glass.

Scott had taken no pictures of the protest, of course—and that was *our* fault, as he made quite plain to me.

'Farting around delivering headshots' he grumbled, 'when there was a, a *symphony* of *incident* going on just across town.' He would have given his eye teeth to capture that gliding bottle, the first shot of the hostilities. He wanted to trap the savage wrath, the tide of aggression, the impact. He had to make do with some photographs he'd taken of a demonstration in Rome a few years back. There was a very powerful one of two adversaries, forehead to forehead, frozen mid-scream, their spittle reflecting the light like crystals.

Broken Glass was well attended and well reviewed. Our workforce were offered complimentary tickets, but not many took up the offer. I had touching letters of apology from Dino (or, rather, Fortuna) and from Carlo; I had one letter that was pretty abusive; a few simply returned the tickets with no comment. Some of them did turn up to the launch, dutifully took their free drink and shuffled around the exhibition looking puzzled, or amused, or just blank. Mergim and Arber came along, and stood awkwardly in a corner, watching the drifting shoals of artistes, critics and hangers-on—with more derision, I suspect, than awe. They were stranded there until Rosalyn's choir had finished, and she made a beeline for them. She ushered them towards the pictures of them both at work, and encouraged the bystanders to applaud and fuss over them for a moment or two.

Rosalyn's choir sang exceptionally well. I'd underestimated their skill, and hers in coaxing and organising such a haunting, heartfelt sound. Even Scott was impressed, though he'd spent a good deal of the evening lurking outside the gallery, smoking and avoiding what he called the 'wordspew':

But, between you and me, don't you think the narrative is somewhat lost in this hang?

Oh, to my mind, the whole haphazard air says something in itself—something about the arbitrary workings of fate, you don't think?

I'd say it's all a trifle obvious. But quite arresting, nonetheless.

The exhibition was open to the public for a month. Scott was listed among the 'Names to Watch' in a British Sunday supplement, and given a few name-checks in the Italian arts press. I sent out another letter to my ex-employees after the launch, making it clear that the comps would be admissible throughout the month. But nobody else from Zenada came along. I wasn't surprised. I'd seen Mergim and Arber and the others; I'd seen them standing before those framed views of their obliterated careers, and the desolate way they stared and shook their heads. Every one of them took the time to congratulate Scott and to thank me with immaculate politeness, before crunching out into the night.

29

Don was childishly excited about having his photograph taken. I was surprised. It wasn't as if he was new to the whole thing: his handsome, self-assured face had brooded from any number of glossy corporate brochures and business articles. They were all the same kind of thing: Don leaning back in his office chair, cigar in hand, apparently weighing up the lens prior to challenging it to a fight; or Don half-sitting on the edge of his desk, considering a smile, one eyebrow Roger Moorishly raised. This time it was different, and presumably that's what had piqued his interest. Scott wanted take his pictures at the villa: Don Cutler at home, among his personal possessions.

'I want to show the human being' Scott had said, 'not the boss.'

Don was a show-off. A vain man. He liked his big, expensive house, his cars, his gadgets, he liked having gardeners, cleaners, staff. The thought of catching and consolidating all this in shiny cropped rectangles, in publications bound and multiplied and distributed to the world—it fed the legend. As he was always saying himself, 'An ego flattered is a deal done'. He couldn't resist.

So Scott Carter arrived at the villa and went about his business, and Don moved around his house in his pricily casual tailoring and held forth, bragging about his remote-controlled curtains and his acreage of lawn. Rosalyn and I were there that day. We were in the course of moving back to Britain and establishing Zenada's new UK base. And in later years I recalled, by careful mental effort, that Rosalyn had wanted to go over and watch the shoot. Why? *Why?* I would demand rhetorically, going back over it all yet again. She didn't like the villa. She didn't get on with my mother. Why would she have the least interest in seeing Scott take pictures of my uncle? Oh, I thought I knew very well why. And a moment later, I had no idea, and I needed to take myself through it all one more time. Jealousy and doubt are joined at the hip.

Anyway, we were there, and we watched Don exulting in his success, snapping his orders for drinks while dancing to Scott's tune. I'm sure there were monochrome icons parading through his imagination: Cary Grant, Paul Newman, Gregory Peck … Don Cutler would be next in line: framed and preserved in all his power and glamour, by a Name to Watch.

Scott arranged and adjusted his gear on the white marble floor, conducted his forensic study of reflections, shadows, light; and Mother watched him for a while, then fixed Rosalyn with a quizzical look.

'Not related, by any chance?' she murmured. She was the only other person who'd picked up on their physical resemblance. But I could tell, right from the off, that—unlike Rosalyn—Scott had won her favour. For one thing, he was utterly impervious to her charm. That was just his way. He didn't bother with all the hand-pumping, eye-wrinkling niceties of life. His work was all that mattered. Both Mother and Don were accustomed to people who fawned and fluttered, who obeyed and adored. Scott was a strange beast, to them.

When the shoot was done, Don tried to persuade Scott to stay for a drink. Scott didn't even pretend to be tempted. Mother chimed in:

'Oh, please, do stay, Scott. I'd be *so* interested to hear about your work'—fixing him with the humorous, intelligent, particular gaze that never usually failed. Rosalyn didn't try and talk him round. But did she monitor his response with special, concentrated interest? I could never be sure. Whatever the case, Scott was adamant.

'I've got work to do before I lose the twilight' he said, and left without further ceremony.

136

'What an extraordinary little creature' said my mother, when he'd gone. She was clearly stunned. She wasn't used to men who preferred to leave.

There was no interview to go with the photos. They turned out to be part of a weird piece of musing by a pseudo-philosopher and 'social commentator', whatever that might be, in a pretentious monthly called *Edge*. The text wittered on about 'success types': The Invisible Leader, The Micro Manager, and so on. Don was pictured as an example of The Doer and Dealer—I have no notion what that meant and no recollection of what manner of bullshit had been written, but Don was perfectly satisfied. I think he'd have enjoyed being cited as *any* success type, however uncomplimentary; and in fact there was nothing disparaging in any of the descriptions. It was just waffle with pictures, something to fill another month's issue, something to be sold and bought and half-read and forgotten on a train-ride to work. Don's ego was flattered; Scott's bills were paid.

But naturally, Scott hadn't just taken those pictures to pay his bills. He retained the rights to everything he took, and saved the best for his *real* work—the shows. While the Doer and Dealer was chucked in litter bins or pulped or rolled up and aimed at a daddy-long-legs—Scott scrutinised and stored his contact sheets, and weighed up the real results. Oblique shots of Don's profile, twinned with their watery echoes in floor or column. Off-centre, sidelong views of Don looking elsewhere, thinking about something else, mid-sentence, distracted … apparently out of place among his own expensive possessions. Even if Don had seen all those unpublished shots, he would still have seen a success story, a winner, a man at the top of his game. But when I eventually saw them, along with everyone else, as part of a story, attached by the golden thread—I saw Donald Hairy-Arse Harris: spiv, loudmouth, fool. And I began to understand Scott Carter's eye for weakness.

30

Dinner at Freddie's place. Personally, I'd be happy to avoid the whole bohemian squalor thing, but it makes sense to go to hers, as she stores several of her finished pieces there and we can lay them out to plan the launch.

'Plus' as she says, breathlessly, 'I owe you one.'

The flat is half an attic in a row of old railway cottages. The buildings have been messed around in various ways over the decades and now house, on the lower floor, a charity shop, a women's advice centre and a store selling model soldiers.

Freddie's flat is reached via an external stairway, added in the 1930s, I'd guess, and slowly succumbing to the elements. Freddie leads the way, chattering, and edges past a row of dead plants in pots, one on each step.

'Someone from the shop put those out' she explains 'to pep things up a bit, but they only last five minutes and then the pollution gets them …'

She fiddles with the key, already apologising, and leads me into a long, narrow room with a low ceiling. Her clothes are heaped on a couch in one corner; sketch pads and tools and magazines and notes are strewn everywhere.

'Basically' she says 'it's just this and a bathroom … sorry it's such a tip …'

'No, no,' I assure her, 'it's charming, it's … well, it's an artist's garret, really, isn't it?'

'Garret is right' she says, and half-heartedly starts shifting her mess from one place to another. 'Apparently there used to be some sort of factory up here, before they divided it up. Shirts, I think, something like that …'

God almighty, I think, picking my way into the middle of the room. How can she work in here, in this murky light?

'I'm no cook' she says, 'not like you, but I can do risotto. It's my signature dish …'

She shuffles over to a recess, which turns out to be the kitchen: an old squat cooker with eye-level grill, a sink fringed with mold and a storage area of sorts, hidden by a grimy curtain. For heaven's sake, I could have taken us to a restaurant … But there's a point to all this: it's an exhibit, a show of youth and poverty and dedication to her art. The disorder, the humble meal, the leaking sink—all as much a part of her seduction as the firm thighs and smooth neck.

'Where do you keep your work?' I ask, with a tinge of horror.

'Ah—that's in my secret hideaway.'

She goes to the opposite wall and opens what I took to be a cupboard door. Then she climbs in, stooping to clear the lintel, and summons me to follow. I clamber through and find myself climbing stairs, barely a person's width, between the external and internal walls.

'This is what decided me to move in' she's calling. Her neat buttocks swivel above my head. 'I think it's where they stored the factory goods.'

We emerge into a cramped loft, crouching until we reach the middle, where the roofline allows us to straighten up at last.

'Your attic has an attic' I say.

'It's just bloody perfect, for me' says Freddie, and I can see what she means. She's lined the area with her pieces, mainly faces, glowering at us in a spectrum of shades, softening the air with their sheen.

'That one' I say immediately, 'is coming to the launch. Centre stage.' I point at a head that's different from all the rest, leaning back in a distorted scream, pushing its skull into glass folds.

'Yeah, that was, like, an experiment?' she says, but I can tell from the scratch in her voice that she's not really concentrating on the launch, now. Not *that* launch, anyway. Sure enough, when I turn back she's standing as close as possible without actually touching. I can smell her hair, and some musky perfume. It's a grainy scent, dusty like her surroundings—nothing like Rosalyn's brackish, clean skin. *Not now*, part of me is thinking. *Not yet. I'm starving.* Besides, once it's done, I don't really want to hang around, playing out the post-coital cosiness. There's work to be done. But her hands are on my ribs, now, and searching for the hem of my shirt. It seems the decision's been made. Might as well get on with it, I suppose.

And we do, performing right there, in the round, to our glass onlookers; and Freddie insists on being on top (to show her experience, maybe, or because the child imagines this is some radical new departure for me). So I'm left thrashing on that grubby wooden floor, and get a splinter in my buttock. And afterwards, when all I want to do is grab my jacket and get the hell out of there, she drapes herself across my chest and lifts her hand to make the dust sway in a chink of light from a loose rooftile. Her glass creations watch and wait, and the experimental head howls at the rafters. I stroke her slim back, and all I can think of is Rosalyn; how she would feel, now, after all these years; how she would have recoiled from the very idea of sex in a filthy attic; how she used to knead my earlobe after we'd made love and call me her poor, lost boy. In my dozy state I start to develop a fantasy around the present-day, matronly Rosalyn Rathbone. I place her in my apartment, confused by my presence, by a desire she thought she'd long since sealed away. Her middle-aged bulk takes on a Rubenesque sensuality; I picture her constrained and hoisted by a corset, then released and generous and soft; the fantasy takes on its own momentum, and Freddie murmurs,
'Bloody hell, Nathan, there's no stopping you.'
Oh, no, I think: not again, not on this floor. I quench the fantasy and sit up.
'I'll have to resist you this time' I say, adding chivalrously, 'at least until I've sampled your signature dish. I'm ravenous.'
She says, 'We'll save it for pudding, then …' and kisses me, and as we disentangle

she says, with a coquettish tilt of her head,

'Do you reckon we could get some telly coverage for my launch?'

I hadn't planned a visit to the gallery, but the after-effects of Freddie's meal have made me restless. I felt my age in that place. Not because of the sex—that's never been a problem, despite long periods when I haven't bothered. It seems to be an instinctive skill, perhaps because I take such pleasure in the aesthetics. The curve of a waist, the brittle elegance of a collarbone, the silver-blue latticework of veins at a wrist. Once I've chosen my lover I take my time to appreciate her finer points. A girl of Freddie's age may not be used to that degree of patience and control. So the sex is still good. No, it was the rest of it that made me feel old. Her earnest babbling, still edged with that hint of hysteria that doesn't really wear off till after 30. And the sheer bloody discomfort of that flat. We couldn't even park ourselves in proper chairs to eat; it had to be bean bags, which slithered and shifted with the slightest movement and threatened to upend me and my flavourless risotto. She sat prettily enough in her place, legs crossed, colour high in her face, eyes sparkling and darting as she prattled on about her work. But I was all too aware of my trousers rucking up to show my socks, my struggle to keep the food on my plate, the incongruity of my presence among the sheddings and strewings of a post-student life.

I'm glad to be out of there, glad to be in the fresh air, walking through streets dark and washed by recent rain, guided by the lights still shining in commercial windows, for security or, here and there, in places that stay open for the drifters and night-workers. A greasy spoon where truckers and party animals feed; a laundromat, where one sorry soul stares at his circling underwear; a taxi office, where a short queue of drunken youths is scattering to avoid an eruption of vomit. I

141

walk all the way to the gallery, safely through the dodgy areas and into the chilling quiet of the smart streets, where danger is bolted behind heavy doors. I hurry my pace to cross the square and skirt the block where Rosalyn called my name. Round the corner, out with the key, and I'm in, alone among the fairylight reflections of my treasures.

I take down the kingfisher and stroke its undulating lines: head, throat, wing, belly. Trent Hope told me she sketched it in one unbroken pencil line, and that's what the glassblower has reproduced, to perfection. All that heat and sweat and physical effort and careful turning, pulling, coaxing, refining—all to recreate one easy swing of a charcoal line. I think of Dino, of the years of study and failure and perseverance and passion that went into his craft. Because, make no mistake, it was a passion for Dino too. For all the banter and swaggering nonchalance of that furnace room, they were artists at their work. Included in my private collection is the last complete piece Dino ever created. It's a vase designed to take one rose: a perfect crystal teardrop. There was a letter with it, written in English by his niece. She took Fortuna in to live with her, after Dino died and the farmhouse and vegetable garden were sold. She said her aunt wanted me to have a memento of Dino's work, which had made him so proud.

I decide to package up the kingfisher—take it off sale and out of temptation's way. I'll put in a birthday card, of course, but there's plenty of time to think about that. I'll word it carefully—nothing too intimate or sentimental to embarrass Rosalyn or arouse Bo's suspicions; but something significant, all the same, something poignant, to show her that I remember, and that I care.

As I'm ferreting around in the office for the right box I think again about Rosalyn's parting words.

I'm so sorry about Scott.

She didn't mention my mother. I suppose it's quite possible that she doesn't know. After all, it was Uncle Don who made the headlines. My mother wasn't news. So that's something else I need to tell Rosalyn about. I find the box and start cushioning Trent's kingfisher in a froth of tissue. It's soothing to focus on this task, in the quiet of the gallery at night. It clears my mind, and I resolve to call Rosalyn tomorrow, make an excuse about this charity function, and arrange to meet her, without Bo tagging along. It's curious, this need to see her, to talk to her, considering how much I dreaded our encounter at first. But maybe this is exactly what I was afraid of: the bursting of the dam.

31

'I haven't seen any children around, have you?'

Rosalyn stood at the window looking out across the grass, the dual carriageway, the redundant gasworks.

'Children?' I came to stand behind her and drank in the view. I caught a fleeting sight of figures on the factory roofline. 'There you go', I said, pointing towards them. 'If you're looking for kids—there's a whole bunch of them arsing around on that roof.'

She sighed. 'I suppose there's nowhere else much for them to go' she murmured. Two of the figures returned; I thought I could see arms waving. Then they disappeared. From their vantage point, they could probably see us, full length through our wall of glass. I made a mental note to contact someone about tightening up security at the gasworks site.

'Anyway', I said, going back to my sorting, 'you don't really buy into this place if you're planning a huge brood, I shouldn't think. It's a place for grown-ups. And all the better for that, if you ask me.'

Look at me, lobbing that comment over my shoulder with the pin out. Then turning back to my collection of glass-cutting tools, arranging them in their cabinet drawers with contented absorption. Paying no heed to the sad silence shrouding my poor lover, as she gazes from her new home like Rapunzel in the tower. So many times, I've rewound that scene, stilled it, examined that beautiful, melancholy face, and drawn the wrong conclusion. Yearning—yes, I could see that, looking back: yearning for something, somebody … and Scott Carter was the name that filled every blank, in those days of my private insanity. And now I view it again, across 25 years, and it's so fucking obvious. I am three times a fool: insensitive then;

hyper-sensitive later; and now … now, finally accepting the simple truth, that she was trapped and lonely and wanted a child … now—I'm just too late.

I was exultant when we bought this apartment, and I took it for granted that Rosalyn felt the same. For once in my life I'd withstood Don's 'help' and Mother's cool sarcasm, refused all suggestions of turreted manor houses in the Cotswolds or mock-Spanish haciendas in the Home Counties, and found my perfect place: sleek, clever, stylish, unusual—a dwelling which was also a work of art. We'd only just moved in, and the floors were still stifled with crates and stacked furniture, but I already had a clear vision of our life there together: the two of us, playing our part among my exquisite belongings, living on fine food and wine, surrounded by the best music, art and literature … I really did feel we'd come home.

As soon as we'd got the place straightened out I hosted a celebratory dinner. Just the four of us: me and Rosalyn, Don and Mother. We stood at the window in the twilight and raised our champagne flutes to the new UK business and our new UK home. The glasses met and kissed; the champagne glowed and fizzed. Don clapped me on the back.

'Fair play, sunshine. You might be a bit of a ponce, but when it comes to trade, you know how to take good advice.'

'Graciously put, Don', said Mother, adding, 'He's actually rather proud of you, Nathan; it just gets lost in translation.' She raised an eyebrow towards the view. 'Your choice of property defeats me, but there we are, I'm just an East End philistine. I'm sure it'll suit you both down to the ground.'

Then she strafed Rosalyn with a look that immediately denied her words. I thought it was just one of her little digs at the songbird, for her own amusement. Now I wonder whether Mother understood far better than I did that, to Rosalyn, this was no home. Well, if she did, she kept her counsel. Maybe she was counting the days until the songbird flew.

We'd been here for about four months when Scott showed up. I opened the door and there he was, perched on a large metal case, camera slung round his neck.

'Wotcher' he said. 'Been kicked out of my studio. OK if I park some gear?'

Rosalyn was in the kitchen area. He greeted her with a cursory wave as he started lugging in his equipment.

'Nice place' he commented, barely giving it a glance. 'Knew you'd have room to spare, hope you don't mind.'

He'd been living in a shared studio for about five years.

'Camp bed, sink, Baby Belling. Does the job. Means I can spend my money on the kit and the travel, and not worry about … you know …'—his eyes gave our home a swift appraisal—'the trivia …'

He said he was planning to share out his possessions between his contacts and friends, until he could get another base. Together we shifted his equipment into a spare room where we were keeping a couple of unpacked boxes. I had no hesitation about offering the storage. I was bewitched by the idea of a nomad artist, living on charity and his art—almost a monastic existence, I thought, but in the service of something I actually believed in. Rosalyn said nothing about it: she just made us all tea and toast. Later, I had two explanations for this. One: she was cross with him for showing up and putting their secret connection at risk. Two: she'd expected him, and it was all part of a long-term plan to push me out of my own life. As I said, I did go a little insane, and insanity has its own remorseless logic. But it was a phase, and it passed.

'Why were you chucked out?' I asked him, as we eased some mysterious metal poles under the spare bed.

'Oh, I broke some cretinous rule … People are *infatuated* with rules, Nathan. They clutch at them like drowning men at a rope, and they don't care what they are or where they came from …'

'And what was the cretinous rule?'

He mumbled something about 'snorting a line', then grew more voluble in his justifications: 'Jesus Christ, it was just a gram, I had a couple of friends there, we were being sociable, I could have necked a crate of wine, and nobody would have turned a hair, but … Anyway …' His voice dropped to its normal pitch again. 'I don't suppose I could doss down here for a couple of nights? I won't get in your way.'

That night in bed, Rosalyn and I argued in whispers.

'It won't be for long' I insisted. 'We've got the space and the means, and he just wants to get on with his work. He said he wouldn't get in our way …'

'I think Scott is the kind of person who does what he likes.' (*Scott is the kind of person … How well did she already know him?* I would ask myself in a later life.)

'I think he'll stay until we actually throw him out. And Nathan, I don't want anyone using drugs in our—'

Suddenly she'd propped herself on one elbow and was listening. I heard it too: rapid, soft footsteps from the spare room. An opening door. More movement, fast and muffled, like a passing ghost. She shuddered.

'What's he doing *now*?'

'Just going for a pee, I expect' I whispered. I pulled her close and she snuggled up, laid her head on my chest.

'Don't worry,' I assured her, 'he'll be here a couple of nights—and then he'll find somewhere more interesting to go.'

32

Rosalyn was hardly trying for work by this time, but sometimes work found her. She was offered another Cherubino in the Lake District, and took it more from duty than pleasure.

'Maybe it won't sell' she said miserably, as she packed her suitcase. 'Maybe it'll close early.'

I took her chin in my hand and kissed her mouth.

'By the time you come home' I promised 'we'll have the place to ourselves.'

It had been pouring like a punishment all day. I took Rosalyn to the station then came back determined to give Scott his marching orders. When I got in he was sitting at the window with his camera, watching the vertical rain.

'Scott. We need to talk' I said.

'Sure' he said, absently. 'Just as soon as it's happened.'

'What's happened?' I approached him grumpily, and tried to see what he could see in the malevolent weather.

'I don't know yet', he muttered, experimenting with his viewfinder. 'Something that tells me what the rain is.'

I was intrigued despite myself. I never could resist seeing an artist at work. But I held my ground and snapped sarcastically,

'It's hot air rising to meet cold air. So now you know. Let's talk.'

'Ah, but you don't really *believe* that, Nathan,' he said, never shifting his attention from the view. 'Not in your gut. Not even the most rational scientist believes, in the most superstitious, most obstinate part of his being, that when rain falls it's got nothing to do with *us*.'

'What do you mean?'

He grinned up at me briefly, before turning quickly back in case he missed a trick.

'I mean, we might know with our *heads* that the weather's not there for *us* … and if it never stops raining, we'll all drown, and that's that, and there's nobody left to care … let's face it, Nathan, we don't *really believe* that, not in our hearts, do we? We think *we* cause the rain.'

We watched as it hissed and drummed at the window. From here and there we could hear slower, fatter drips from the building's nooks and gutterings. I tried to rekindle my righteous indignation, but now I was eager to see what he was after. He showed no sign of impatience. I think he would have waited there all night if necessary. A fresh tide of rain lashed the glass and he said:

'Jesus, Nathan, you must have done some very wicked things to cause this—HA!' Suddenly he was sitting forward, adjusting the zoom, clicking away, imprisoning a passing moment. The curtain of weather had been drawn momentarily aside, clearing the view for half a mile and revealing a canopy of black cloud, dragging another shower across the horizon, while a shaft of incongruous sunlight hit the gasworks from the side. I stood holding my breath while Scott concentrated on his task, utterly oblivious to everything else. A minute later, it was all over. The curtain closed again, Scott sat back, and the ordinary world reassembled itself around him. He looked at me.

'So. You wanted to talk.'

'Yes', I said, failing to rouse much spirit. 'About you. And where you're planning to live.'

An expression between boredom and confusion passed across his face.

'Because' I continued, trying to stoke my temper, 'you can't stay here, Scott. Not indefinitely.'

He shrugged. 'You're right. It's too bloody perfect round here, anyway. No soul.'

I shouldn't have risen to the bait.

'What do you mean, no soul? This is my *home* you're talking about. Mine and

Rosalyn's. And it's quite soulful enough for *us*, thanks very much.'

I sounded like a flouncing girl. Scott smirked at his camera.

'Yeah, well …'

'Meaning?' I actually planted my hands on my hips. I could feel the colour mounting in my face.

'Meaning, you've got no idea, mate. No idea at all. You think you're all about art, and look at you. Both of you. Sitting pretty. Safe in your cotton-wool world of pretty songs and pretty things …'

'That is not—' I started, but he was already on his feet, gathering his things and issuing a challenge.

'I'll clear out, Nathan, don't you worry. Just need a couple more nights to go hunting, then I'm done. Tell you what—come with me. Tonight. You'll see what I'm on about.'

33

He wasn't ready to set off till midnight. The rain had cleared, thank god, but
nevertheless, I desperately wanted to stay put. Sit in my warm apartment, sipping a
brandy, listening to music before turning in. But I had something to prove.
'You don't have to come' he said, amused, waiting at the door. 'I'll be quicker on
my own.'
'No, no,' I said, zipping up my jacket. 'I said I'd tag along and I will. Let's get it
over with.'

He walked so fast I could hardly keep up. We sped through the familiar streets of
bistros and bijoux gift shops, out into a no-man's land of betting shops, boarded
windows, delapidated houses, and suddenly he was slipping into a lane so dark and
narrow I hadn't realised it was there at all. I hesitated. Every instinct I had rebelled
against going after him. But then I took a couple of steps into the lane, and it was
too late: turning back was more frightening than keeping Scott in sight. At the end
of the lane we emerged into a wider area, some sort of yard between the backs of
buildings, lit by the dull beam of a security lamp. A row of bulky industrial bins
took up half the space; between them were smaller heaps, a couple of which stirred
as Scott approached. The smell of rotting food from the bins competed with a
thicker, richer stink of human beings. I nuzzled into my coat collar and fought the
urge to gag. Scott had brought cigarettes and a flask, and without a word he
squatted to offer them round. I stood behind him, at a distance, occasionally
checking that black tunnel between me and the road. Someone started coughing, a
hideous, tearing cough, and soon I could hear low voices, as Scott's subjects began
to talk. I moved closer. He was already using his camera. This was much smaller
and quieter than the equipment I'd seen him use before. Its tutting was little more

than a soft punctuation as Scott kept the questions coming. No flash that I could detect disturbed the grimy light. He was focusing on one man, who sat wedged between the bins, swathed in a filthy blanket, sucking away at the fag Scott had given him, and talking between puffs in a young, articulate voice. I heard the words 'done my time'; I soon gathered that he wasn't talking about prison. He'd been in the army, until, as he put it, 'I freaked'. His eyes flickered and he pulled hard on the cigarette. Scott's gentle voice tethered him to the images he was trying to lose:

'You must have seen some pretty bad things …'

'Bad shit. Bad. Bad shit' said the man, and the camera puttered sympathetically.

'What did you see?'

Scott's tender, ruthless persistence made me uneasy. Any minute, his questions might trigger an explosion. I watched as the man's eyes flickered even faster; then suddenly they were open, steady, fixed on a scene we couldn't see. Scott shuffled a little closer and the camera chattered excitedly.

'Christ, Scott' I whispered; a minimal tightening of his shoulders told me to shut up. The soldier watched the unknown horror unravelling for a moment, then Scott said, with the quiet chill of authority:

'Look at me.'

Slowly, the man turned his suffering to face Scott's ecstatic camera. The perfect shot.

To be fair to Scott, he didn't just up and leave. He lingered for a while, offered the flask and more fags, and instead of erupting into the frenzy of violence I'd feared, the soldier simply floated back to his present-day misery. He talked about his return home from active service, and about his subsequent struggles: flashbacks, insomnia, obsessive washing and checking that confined him to his flat for hours at

152

a time, the brief periods of respite he found in drugs and drink.

'In the end' he said 'I just walked.'

The camera was silent now. Scott had what he needed. I took fifty quid from my wallet. A hand emerged from the soldier's blanket, snatched it, and disappeared again. I said,

'Will you be OK?'

Stupid question. The soldier said,

'I'll live.'

I was expecting to head home after that, but Scott had only just begun.

'This is the best time' he told me as we emerged from the yard and strode on in the worst direction. 'It's like a forest, everything interesting comes to life at night.'

He spoke to huddles of girls on the game, some of whom couldn't have been more than 14. He spoke to an illegal immigrant who'd packaged himself into soggy cardboard boxes and whose whole body was shivering violently.

'Can't work' he kept saying, 'Can't eat. Can you help me, sir?'

He complained of coughing blood. Scott gave him cigarettes and I gave him money, but the light was no good and Scott beckoned me away. As we were leaving the man called,

'This is not my life!'

It was about 3am. Scott showed no sign of tiring.

'You should go home' he announced as we picked our way further into the no-go web of streets. 'I'll be a good hour yet.'

I was exhausted. Nauseous. But I was also charged with excitement. I hadn't felt this way since hearing Rosalyn sing for the first time. And Scott was nothing like Rosalyn. She loved her music, of course, but it was just one part of her, something that could and should be set aside for family, love, children. *Pretty songs and pretty things.* Scott wasn't like that. People were fodder to him: good or bad subjects, nothing more. His art was pivotal. Crucial. I quickened my pace to keep up.

'I'm fine', I said. 'Where next?'

'First The Nav,' he announced, 'then The Cut. Any time you want to bail out, be my guest.'

The Navigator was boarded up, but still trading. It's gone now—demolished to make way for a Tesco. The whole area's been targeted for regeneration: old terraces and council houses being spruced up, the stretch of canal at the back being cleared and made navigable again. God alone knows what happens to the residents of the old Locks estate—let alone the druggies and the drunks and the wild-eyed kids who used to plague the streets like poltergeists. When The Navigator was first built, it must have ruled the roost, overlooking a junction of major routes in and out of the city, feeding and watering the travellers and traders and navvies from the canal. Then they opened the motorway and slammed down a flyover, just a few hundred yards from the pub car park, slicing through the neighbourhood, skimming gutters and pounding past bedroom windows. The junction became a patch of tarmac leading nowhere, except to a vaulted concrete space under the traffic, where teenagers went to drink and drape their names around the pillars in garish code.

Scott led me round the back of the pub and rapped on a smeared window. Licensing laws were tighter in those days, but lock-ins were frequent. A misty face loomed up in the glass to check us, then the back door opened quickly, swallowed us up and was bolted again. We filed through a kitchen into the main bar. Scott chatted to the barman—he obviously knew him quite well—and two whiskies appeared.

'I won't be long' Scott assured his friend, and he started to move around the bar, assessing his models through the blue trails of cigarette smoke. Small groups of men were propped around tables and against the bar, as rumpled as their clothes. The long mirror behind the bar was a reflection of darkness. A smell of alcohol drenched the air and squelched in the carpet underfoot. I hung back, conscious of the difference in my skin and my hair, in the material of my shirt and jeans. A man leaning over his drink nearby wheezed a sodden comment. I didn't understand it, but I smiled tightly and he repeated the noise, swaying and sloshing like a sea-creature, exuding that liqeous stench from his pores and his yellow eyeballs. Scott's camera murmured; I braced myself for the bite of whisky, and waited.

From The Nav we crossed into an estate of houses. An amplified beat was thunking from somewhere like a headache. At the end of the estate, a lane ran between the backs of the houses; from halfway it petered out into a muddy slope, slithering past a scrap yard and down to a rubbish-choked bank, and the canal. This was The Cut. The last house before the scrap yard was gagged and blinded with steel shutters. Painted across one of them in huge, red figures was the number '90'. I could see no way in. As I stepped forward, my foot slid on something slithery: a condom. Another step crackled onto plastic. There was a rustling at the side of the house and a girl appeared. She was half my height and so thin she might shatter any moment. Her hair hung in despondent tails; she stumbled forward on bow-legs like a newborn foal, until the sight of me brought her to a halt. Her skull threatened to break through the skin. She was ageless, until her mouth dropped open and revealed uneven, schoolgirl teeth. *Dear God*, I thought. *She's a child.* I heard Scott's camera coming to life. The child seemed unsure which way to go, and incapable of going far in any direction. Scott finished taking pictures and said, 'I'm looking for Mack.'

Her knees buckled and she grabbed the wire fence that ran alongside the house.
'Mack' he repeated, more loudly. 'Where's Mack?'
One fleshless arm wafted towards the back of the house. I caught a glimpse of a
purple rash, punctuated with fresh sores.

We pushed past the wraith and fought our way through dusty buddleia bushes. In
contrast to the clamped façade, the back of the house was open to the elements.
Any door that once existed had long since been kicked or hacked out of existence,
and someone, somehow, had wrenched off the lower-floor shutters to reveal a gape
of glassless windows. We entered what had once been a kitchen, now hummocked
with the detritus of weather and humanity—packets and plates, bottles and
syringes, leaves and leavings, a laceless shoe, a torn photograph. I followed Scott
through the house. Bodies were curled and slumped on mattresses, in sleeping
bags; the whole place stank of old vomit and putrefaction. In the front room
someone was slouching his way slowly towards the shutter's pinprick lights.
'Mack?' asked Scott. A voice from the pit of the room said,
'Upstairs.'
We made for the stairs. They must have been quite a stately feature of the house,
once upon a time. Scott looked into a room at the top of the landing: the smallest
bedroom. Damp had eaten up most of the wallpaper. The fragment that survived,
running round the upper half of the room, showed faded clowns, balloons and
smiling suns. A nursery. At first sight there seemed to be no-one there. Then a pile
of dirty sheets behind the door moved, and I had to clamp my hand to my nose.
'Christ' I said, and the sheets moved again, revealing a shaven, stubbled head.
Even in the solitary bulb's dim light I could make out the scabs and sores on his
scalp. He screwed up his eyes as if the light were blazing.
'Hi' said Scott, and the camera tutted. 'Seen Mack anywhere?'—as casually as a

neighbour chatting over the fence. The creature roused himself, and began to get to his feet in the same dreamy slow-motion I'd seen in the girl outside. I felt like an alien traveller, on a planet where time moved to a lazier speed. The sheet was rising with him like a spectre, clinging to his arm and back. Dark stains covered the sheet and formed a ragged map across the mattress. He made it to his feet and leaned against the wall. He was shaking, hugging the sheet to himself. Still the camera puttered away. The poor wretch began to slide back down the wall. He made a guttural noise, and a deeper spasm shook his body. Then a new noise made me start. A slow, steady thudding of evacuation. The blossoming of an even fiercer stench made me back away, retching. There was a change in the air, a sinking of pressure, as if someone had left. The man's enormous eyes swivelled up into his skull. Scott pulled the door closed between us. I waited, trembling. Presently Scott appeared, edging around the door and shutting it quickly behind him. He looked pale, a little shaken, but he made no comment about the fate of that creature, and I asked no questions. After fumbling with his camera for a moment, Scott muttered, 'Won't be long. Just need to find someone. See you outside.'

I didn't argue. I floundered down the stairs, back through the wreckage and the shrubbery and out into the lane. The Cut was deserted. Even the spirit-girl had gone. I went down on my haunches, expecting to vomit, but produced nothing except a gloop of phlegm. I was still there when Scott emerged, apparently fired with fresh energy. He stooped to slap me on the shoulder.

'All right Nathan? Seen enough? Let's get you back to your safe haven.'

We walked quickly through the estate and across The Nav's car park. A group of youths had gathered there—some of them no more than 10 or 11. A loud argument was about to escalate into a fight. As we scuttled for the exit onto the road I turned and saw the contraction of terror on a small boy's face.

'Shouldn't we *do* something?' I hissed at Scott as I cantered along in his wake.

'What do you suggest?' came the mocking reply over his shoulder.

'I—I don't know, *something*. How can you see all this and not want to *do* something?'

I could hardly get the words out: he was striding like an athlete, almost skimming the ground. He said,

'I *am* doing something, Nathan. I'm bearing witness.'

34

When Rosalyn came home, Scott was still in residence. I'd put off telling her; I planned to warn her on the way back from the station, but she caught an earlier train to surprise me, and arrived at the apartment door an hour before I was due to set off. I was delighted to see her, of course. I took her suitcase from her hand, put my free arm around her waist, and felt her flinch as she caught sight of his prone figure, lounging on my Le Corbusier chaise longue.

'Hello, Scott' was all she said.

'Hello, Rosalyn. I'm still here.'

He hardly sounded apologetic. She said,

'So I see'—then, pushing me gently away—'Shall we get the kettle on? I'm shattered.'

No trace of dismay or displeasure: just the dignity and kindness that was built into her soul. In fact, when we all gathered round with our tea and she started relating all the standard anecdotes of fluffed lines and rehearsal quips, the atmosphere was relaxed and friendly. But then, Scott was different with her: no sarcasm, no mockery. I think, now, that he respected her—plain and simple. Later, I heard him talking to her in the kitchen area, and he was the sweet victim, fringe flopping across his earnest eyes, slim, quick hands brushing it aside:

'I don't want to outstay my welcome', he was saying: 'I can doss down in my mate's garage, until I fix myself up again, that'll do me fine …'

I watched them with a frisson of excitement—my twin artists, high cheekbones, dark hair, dark eyes …

'Nonsense, Scott', Rosalyn was saying, 'It's not as if we haven't got the room, is it? You concentrate on your work and don't worry about the rest. Are you still hungry? Shall I make more sandwiches?'

In later years, that scene replayed with a sinister underscore. My twin artists became twin conspirators, revelling in their triumph, spinning out their lines for my benefit, as I smiled my idiot smile. Easy prey. Cuckold. Dupe.

I told Scott to find himself an appropriate studio space, and I would fund it. He thanked me, but without surprise or emotion: he took it as his due. I had the money—why wouldn't I spend it on such talent? Finding him somewhere to live was a more complicated matter. Scott would happily have set up another camp bed in the studio, but Rosalyn and I wouldn't hear of it. So we carried on as we were, a strange *ménage-à-trois*. And now, if I heard him moving around the place at the dead of night, I had to suppress the urge to leap out of bed calling 'wait for me!'. That long night's 'hunting' had left me disturbed, sickened—and more excited than I ever remembered being in my life. When I described the whole episode to Rosalyn she was appalled.

'How can we let people live like that?' she said, shaking her head. 'We just shove them into the back alleys and hope they'll go away.'

'But listen,' I said, and she took in my quickened breath and shining eyes with a frown of alarm. 'Listen, Rosalyn, it was—it was *vital*. You know? It was like, like treading a line between madness and sanity. Between life and death. Like falling off a cliff. Terrifying, but, but—*thrilling.*'

The look she gave me then made me burn with shame. But it didn't change the way I felt. I was hooked. I did go out with Scott on a few more of his nocturnal trips, though I'm sure he could have done without my presence. He always dismissed me after a couple of hours and went off to fulfil some private engagement. And I'd get home tired but aroused, slip into bed, inhaling Rosalyn's scent of sleep, and I'd pull myself up against her and caress her until she woke. She always turned to me eventually, always accepted me, despite knowing where I'd been, and despite her disgust.

35

Scott was making a real name for himself. He won a minor award. A trendy gallery in Soho offered him space for an exhibition called *Underclass*—mainly a selection of shots taken on his night wanderings. There was a meths-drinker trying to clamber into a skip. A dead-eyed single mother in her rotting kitchen. Two hooded shadows, stooping to pass some illicit item from hand to hand. Then there were other shots, ordinary and bleak: an over-furnished sitting room, where a woman squatted to spoonfeed her senile father. A man with greasy hair and a hunted look, drinking tea at a drop-in centre. Two heavily veiled women sitting at a vandalised bus stop.

This launch had some C-list celebrities on the guest list, all keen to be seen expressing sombre admiration and concern about the state of the nation. Scott had also invited Uncle Don and Mother—I don't really know why. Possibly for his own amusement. I didn't really expect them to turn up, but Don clearly knew the value of a little cultural kudos. In he swept, with my mother on his arm. She looked amazing. Her hair was up and she wore a figure-hugging dress with a little Audrey Hepburn jacket. She moved through the hee-hawing crowd with her usual charm, laughing, remembering names she had no reason to know, touching elbows and hands. She was lovelier, sexier, more magnetic than I'd ever seen her before in my life.

'You'd think it was *her* party, wouldn't you!' murmured Rosalyn in my ear, not bitterly, but with her usual guileless honesty.

Mother approached a corner of the gallery where Scott was trapped by an arts correspondent, answering ludicrous questions. Was it my imagination, or did her performance start to acquire a tinge of desperation? I didn't want to think about it.

I turned to scrutinise the spoonfeeding woman and her father. In the background of the photograph was a mantelpiece, stacked with indistinct notes and pictures, and flanked by china dogs.

'Look at those Staffordshire spaniels, aren't they hideous!' I said to Rosalyn, but it was Uncle Don who replied:

'Worth a few bob now, though, sunshine. Chummy should have told her, while he was happy-snapping away: flog them two, and you can put the old man in a home for the rest of 'is natural.'

I turned towards him, catching my breath like an infatuated teen. I could smell his aftershave, mingled as always with the sweetness of cigar smoke. Even with the shrivelling of time, Don was tall and impressive. His black hair was washed with snow-white, and as thick and as luxurious as ever. He blazed with confidence. He chucked one arm across my shoulders, the other across Rosalyn's.

'Your mother' he said to me 'is on form tonight.' He affected a very bad American accent: 'That dame is a real pipperoo.'

The thought crossed my mind, as I glanced towards my mother and her admirers, that maybe she was better off living with Uncle Don after all. I found it hard to reconcile this scene with my memories of our family house, Dad in his shed, Mother moving through the small spaces of her life like a bird in a cage. A great shout of laughter went up at some witticism she'd thrown out.

'What do you reckon to the piccies, then, darling?' Don asked Rosalyn, then, without waiting for an answer, 'Nathan's mother reckons he's a genius. Won't hear a bad word said. Me, I prefer to look at something pretty at the end of a working day, but there's no accounting for taste.'

'He's a great talent' I announced, rather primly. 'A seriously great—'

'Yeah, well, whatever you say, sunshine.'

Then, in one deft move, he'd somehow given Rosalyn a little nudge in the back so that she was momentarily out of earshot, and had pulled me up close, using his arm as a vice.

'Watch that boy' he said, and I could feel the movement of his lips against my ear. I wriggled like a child.

'What are you *talking*—'

'I'm just saying', said Don, his voice low and firm, 'don't stuff up your life for that ponce. He's trouble.'

Then he released me, turned his attention to Rosalyn, and was all smiles again.

'Right then, my gob's as dry as granny's fanny—where's that fizz?'

Underclass was a critical success. *The Independent* called it 'an uncompromising tour of humanity's leftovers'. *The Guardian* said Scott had 'an eye for truth, an instinct for the brutish reality of societal breakdown'. The *Daily Mail* said it was 'miserable and pretentious'—and that was the quote Scott had printed on his business card.

36

My mother's voice crackled through the speakerphone by Don's front gate. 'Children!' she cried. 'Come in and play!'

The gate hummed open and Scott, Rosalyn and I trudged into Uncle Don's dismally formal front drive.

'I'm not staying long' warned Scott. 'I've got work to do.'

'It's only tea' I reminded him. 'You can leave as soon as you've drained your second cup.'

I was stung, but not by Scott's indifference; I was used to that. It wasn't his attitude that irked me—it was my mother's. This visit was her idea, and it was clear that Rosalyn and I were only invited as adjuncts. If she'd had her way it would have been a full-scale four-course meal for two, by candlelight no doubt, but on Scott's insistence we'd compromised with afternoon tea.

Pippa the lackey let us in but Mother was already there at her heels, opening her arms to us.

'Here you all are! What a treat! Don's stuck at the office, of course, but who needs him with such a gathering of gorgeousness?'

She clutched Scott's arm, leaving me and Rosalyn to follow through the faux-Mediterranean vestibule. Rosalyn was snatching a conversation with Pippa, asking after her mother's health, but my own mother's voice sliced across their exchange: 'Tea for four please, Pippa!'

—and Pippa scurried off, knowing her place.

'We'll sit in the breakfast room, it's sunnier in there' announced Mother. She was still hanging on to Scott, and started gushing about his work. I glanced at Rosalyn, and I saw that she was equally unnerved. Mother was like a 14-year-old with a crush. I'd never seen the like.

Pippa hurried in with a tray of tea things and hurried out again, and Mother went into hostess mode, directing and pouring and serving. She looked more at home in Don's mansion than she ever had in our little house. She handed out the china cups and saucers.

'Well,' said Scott, slumping into his seat, 'this is all very Jane Austen.'

For a split second my mother looked embarrassed, and I wanted to break his jaw. Rosalyn went into action, asking about the tea-set, the garden, anything that came to mind, frantically trying to keep the show on the road. Mother answered her questions in the usual way: with a sort of polite boredom. As soon as Rosalyn ran out of breath, Mother's eyes were on Scott again. He was making no attempt to hide his impatience, swinging his leg from side to side, glaring through the windows at the professionally manicured lawn.

'Scott, dear,' said my mother, 'you've left your engine running.' She addressed me without shifting her focus. 'Where does he get all that energy, Nathan? All that running around after dark in the wrong parts of town—how on earth does he keep going? Such a cheerful *Charlie*.'

She seemed to place that word before him, along with a plate of miniature sandwiches. Suddenly Scott's leg was still and he looked straight at Mother. You could almost hear their vision collide. Her face lit up in a radiant smile. She said, in that same teasing way,

'Really, you're as quick as a whippet, aren't you, Scottie-dog!'

Scott took a long mouthful of tea then held his cup out for a refill, staring at Mother the whole time. Beside me, I heard Rosalyn's faint voice:

'Gosh, this weather's holding out well, isn't it?'

As Mother poured his tea Scott said,

'You know, I'd really like to take your photograph.'

I gawped. The last time I'd heard Scott ask to photograph a lovely face was outside that café in Florence. I sensed a shifting, a sighing next to me: Rosalyn was surely thinking the same thing. My mother locked eyes with him for a long moment, then finally looked down, and shook her head, still smiling.

'You're very sweet, Scottie-dog, but I don't think so.'

'No, Mother, you really should let him!' I blurted out. Rosalyn's cup rattled tetchily in its saucer. 'This is an opportunity you shouldn't pass up!' I was already picturing the perfect, soul-capturing shot of Mother, larger than life and framed on our mezzanine wall.

'Nathan,' said Mother, finally giving me her attention, 'you set too much store by appearances. And at this stage in life I do not want my appearance stored, thank you very much.'

As the villa gates purred shut behind us, I urged Scott to persevere about the portrait.

'She'll give in eventually' I said, 'if you stick at it. She likes you a lot.'

Behind us, Rosalyn protested weakly:

'If she doesn't want to, Nathan ...'

'I'll pay,' I continued. 'It could be her birthday present. I know she goes on about getting old but she's not daft, she's well aware of her beauty ...'

Scott snorted. As ever, I almost had to sprint to keep up with him, and Rosalyn had already been left behind. Scott said,

'Nathan, come on. You know I'm not interested in *beauty.*'

He said it like a dirty word. I was puzzled: why offer to photograph Mother, then? Was he humouring her, or maybe—more feasibly—making fun? None of us realised, then, that Scott's X-ray vision had caught something we'd all missed: her fragility. The rot had set in, and Scott, with his merciless eye for decay, had detected it. He saw a sickness festering beneath her flesh, behind her lively eyes, which was nothing to do with the gradual decline of age.

37

Well, that plan misfired. Instead of a private tête-à-tête with Rosalyn, I get a meeting with the pair of them at Bo's office. Maybe he's picked up on something, and doesn't want to leave me alone with his wife. At any rate, Bo is there when I arrive and doesn't so much as go for a pee until I leave. In fact when I get there and open the office door immediately after knocking, I catch them hastily disengaging hands. How sweet.

We meet in a small, windowless room with an old-fashioned desk, on the top floor of an architect's office. The lower two floors are peopled in the usual way by employees in shirt sleeves, exuding stress and sweat. I can see them at their computers and drafting boards, as I step out of the lift on the second floor and take to the fire stairs—the only means of access to the third. As I open the fire door at the top of the stairs, I enter another world. Apart from loos and what looks like a kitchen, the upper floor seems to be devoted to architects' models, set out on tables the length of the room. I have to walk past them to get to Bo's office door at the other end. Tiny people walk from their miniature parked cars up swirling ramps to their doll's-house offices. Children no bigger than a thumbnail play under pygmy trees outside immaculate shopping centres. No takeout boxes or beer cans underfoot, no barking dogs, no exhaust fumes or screeching teenagers. I sidle past a silent school and a silent hospital; I pause to peer in to a silent block of apartments. Sure enough, there are two silent figures in the furnished flat, one standing at a breakfast bar, the other sitting in an inch-high armchair.

'Wow', I say, shaking hands with Bo and air-kissing Rosalyn. 'This is an interesting place. I felt like Gulliver, marching through there.'

Rosalyn folds her hands and smiles at Bo like a proud mother.

'All his work' she says.

'Not *all*' corrects Bo. 'But a fair bit of it, I suppose.'

'You're an architect?' I'm surprised. Somehow I thought Bo was just a professional do-gooder and part-time boffin.

'Well, I trained as an architect. But model-making was always my main interest. I worked for this lot' he jerks his thumb vaguely to imply the rest of the building 'for about a hundred years. I was what you might call their pet model man. That's why they've been letting me hide out in here, since I retired. I expect they'll kick me out as soon as they've found a better use for it.'

I turn to take another look at his creations, and he says,

'Come on, if you're interested—I'll give you the guided tour.'

So Bryn the Boffin takes us around his dwarf empire, pointing out this feature and that, telling me about the particular difficulties of a brief, pointing out the projects that came to nothing and those that are now part of someone's landscape, trampled and scuffed by lifesize feet, worn by real weather, leaking from gutters blocked by real leaves from real trees.

'It's all done by computers nowadays' he says. 'Well, most of it, anyway. But actually I've been told some of the clients still prefer the real thing. They like to poke the doors open, walk their fingers up the ramps, that sort of thing. Gives them a sense of control, I suppose.'

'And of mystery' says Rosalyn. 'It's much more exciting, wondering what's inside a real building, than floating through someone's software.' She gives me that direct, open gaze and smiles broadly. I imagine us both as tiny fugitives, hiding in one of those tiny apartment beds, while a giant Bo searches in vain through tiny windows.

'It's all very impressive' I tell Bo, and I mean it. I find it hard to picture his chubby hands fashioning these delicate scenes. He snuffles modestly.

'Oh, it was a living, you know. Now, compared with *real* talent—' he doubles his chin at Rosalyn '—a brilliant voice, for example ...'

Rosalyn slaps a hand impatiently on her thigh. She seems really cross.

'I have *never* had a brilliant voice' she says, and holds up the hand against our protests: 'Never *brilliant*. That's just a word people use about something they can't do themselves.'

Bo waggles his eyebrows at me and leans forward conspiratorially.

'She's very harsh, you know, about us proles ...'

'Merciless' I agree, playing my part, while thinking: *don't tell me what she's like. I know what Rosalyn is like. And she's not harsh.*

'Anyway', says Bo, dropping the act, 'I lost interest in the models in latter years. The work I'm doing now seems far more important.'

I nod solemnly. With my head, I know that's true. Helping a human being in profound distress is, of course, infinitely more important than making a model of a school that never gets built. But in my heart of hearts, I have more respect for Bo the model-maker than for Bo the Good Samaritan.

We go back into his office to discuss the charity auction. I feel like a character from a Damon Runyan novel, sitting in my wooden chair-on-wheels at Bo's leather-topped desk. His office door has a milky glass panel etched with the word 'Supplies'; it should say 'Bo Rathbone, Private Eye', and Rosalyn should be squeezed into stays and an hourglass dress. I cross my legs quickly and press my fingernails into my palm.

'It's very good of you to give us your time like this' says Bo. 'I can't tell you how glad I am you and Rosie ran into each other again.'

Are you sure about that? I think. Rosalyn takes a flask and some camping cups from a carrier bag.

'I'm sorry it's not very fancy' she says, 'but the water here is horrible, so I always give Bo a flask of tea to take to work.'

We drink our plastic-tasting tea and I ask after Rosalyn's pregnant daughter-in-law. 'Oh, did Bo tell you that?'

He shoots me a stern look and I clamp my hand to my mouth. I can tell he's not really miffed. He's a pretty laid-back sort. Rosalyn is flushed pink.

'I'm looking forward to having a grandchild, I really am' she insists. 'It's just the thought of being a granny that's …'

'No-one would believe it' I assure her. 'You're the most glamorous granny I've ever met.'

She hesitates, then says,

'What about you? How are your family? I should have asked before …'

Your family. That's a neat way out of a corner.

'Well, mother passed away …'

She sits forward, nearly spilling her tea, and the colour sinks from her face as quickly as it rose.

'Oh, Nathan! I'm so very sorry …' She turns to Bo. 'Nathan's mother was such a … just such a beautiful woman.'

She's really quite upset, I can see. I say,

'It was a while ago, now. She had a condition, a problem with her lungs …'

'I never knew that!' Her voice is hushed with shock.

'No, none of us did …' I don't really want to dwell on this subject, but Rosalyn seems unable to set it aside.

'Was it …' She looks doubtfully at Bo, as if to check whether she's overstepping the line. 'Was it after all that … business? With your Uncle Don?'

'No, it was before all the … fuss.'

'Ah … well, she was spared that, in any case' says Rosalyn. Typical of her to search for a positive note. She and Dad really were two of a kind in many ways. *Cloud: she kicked the bucket. Silver lining: she was spared a scandal.* Some day I'll tell Rosalyn how it really was, but not today. Not here in the private eye's office, with all those mute mannikins listening from the other side of that door.

38

It hadn't been my plan to sell off Zenada, but an offer was made and it warranted a discussion, at the very least. So I was in the London office, embroiled in speculative talks, when the call came from Scott.

'What is it?' I snapped, expecting him to ask for money. 'I've just been pulled out of a meeting so this had better be *really* urgent …'

'Rosalyn's bleeding like a stuck pig and the ambulance is on its way' he said, calm as you like. 'I don't know how that rates on your priority list, but I thought I'd keep you posted.'

She was curtained off on a ward when I got there, one arm sprouting tubes, the other flung over her face. She was weeping, quietly, keeping it down so as not to disturb the other patients.

'For Christ's sake', I blustered, almost flinging myself over the bed. 'Let's get you out of here and into a decent hospital—'

'Nathan' she whimpered, revealing her grey, tearstained face as she hooked her arm around my neck. 'Don't fuss. They've been amazing. I don't want to go to some snotty private place, I don't want to …'

She sounded like a child. I pressed my face against hers.

'OK, OK, whatever you want, baby, whatever you want …'

We stayed there for a while, me half lying across the bed, Rosalyn slowly stroking my hair as though *I* were the patient. Finally, though I didn't want to hear the answer, I forced myself to ask:

'What was it? Do they know what happened?'

Then she released her hold, closed her eyes and seemed to search for her last reserves of strength.

'Nathan, I'm sorry,' she whispered, and a whirlpool of dread sucked at my innards. She took a long breath, then went on: 'I was pregnant. But I'm not any more.'

I sat up straight. Relief and fury crashed around my head. I glowered.

'What the fuck … What do you mean? You're on the pill. Are you saying it didn't work? Dear god, I'll sue them dry …'

She waved her arm feebly before dropping it back across her face, so that I could hardly understand what she said.

'No, Nathan, no—I missed a couple … I must have … forgotten …'

Beyond the curtain, the din of the ward went on regardless. Hard footsteps hurrying past. Someone calling for a nurse. The clatter of a trolley. Within our little veiled space, Rosalyn and I were silent, except for her subdued spasms of grief. Eventually I spoke, and I couldn't keep the whine of indignation from my voice. 'I thought you were *seriously ill*. I thought—' I let the rest of the sentence wither, then said accusingly, 'You "*must have forgotten*"?'.

I waited for her contrition, her tearful pleas and apologies, promising myself I would be kind, already beginning to anticipate the sweetness of comforting and forgiving my foolish girl. But after a while Rosalyn gave a conclusive sniff, wiped her eyes and addressed me in a steelier tone than I'd ever heard her use before.

'I'd like you to go now, Nathan', she said. 'Go home. Scott stayed at the flat to finish clearing up. Go and help.'

I didn't move, stunned both by her sudden frostiness and by the prospect of the blood and mess contaminating my home. She met my eyes, then, with something like contempt, and added, 'He was probably going to take photographs.'

175

39

There's a stink from the cottage that hits me before I reach the door. I take a moment to control my stomach, and turn my back on the place, watching the rooks and the high trees sway and creak together. I'm right at the edge of the village. Beyond this little patch there's a confusion of brambles and ferns, a muddy stream and then the swath of woodland that marks the boundary of an agroinudstrial estate where they produce rapeseed oil. In season the rape forms a glut of yellow as far as the horizon, and its fat scent stifles the air. A stray clump of trees and a tumult of wild hawthorn and briars combine to screen the cottage from its access lane. My car is tucked deep under an overgrown hedge, entirely out of sight. But there's no-one to see it anyway. You don't see anyone down at this end of the village. The other houses are all clustered along the A-road, in the shadow of the bypass. Pub, bus stop, primary school, Spar. There used to be a post office, I think. But I never venture up there. I sneak in by the scenic route, snake round behind the church and slip out again, generally without setting eyes on another living soul. Well, that's the whole point. That's why he's here.

Today I wonder whether he *is* still here. It strikes me that this may be the stink of decomposition. It's certainly got a hint of bad meat about it. Maybe all I'll find today is a pile of clothes, squirming with maggots. Maybe someone got in to the cottage. He's not strong; it wouldn't take much to snuff him out. And to some people, taking a life is as easy as refusing a kindness.

I stand there, adjusting to the smell, bracing myself for discovery, and listening to the slow spin of rooks. If he is dead, I have to decide what to do. I run through the options, rejecting them one by one. Bury him in the woods? Preposterous.

Anonymous 999 call? Pointless, really. Better to let him rot down completely, and spare them this reek of change. When it's done, when he's reduced to rags and clean bone, and the flies and worms have finished and retreated back through their chinks and crevices into darkness—then perhaps I could risk leaving a message and a false name from the phone box by the pub. Until then, I could just walk away, turn on my exquisitely quiet car engine, pull out discreetly into the unclassified road, and disappear.

The sky flinches to a distant thump of artillery; the rooksong surges and settles. A worse possibility crosses my mind. Maybe he's injured, but still alive. Lying in the blood and pus of an untreated wound, watching the creep of green along his torso. I've heard that gangrene smells like death. God almighty, what would I do then? I turn sharply to face the cottage door and something skitters into the bushes. I listen for the moan of distress. Nothing. He might be unconscious. I suppose the same plan would apply: call for an ambulance, leave no name, vanish before it arrives. Should I try and ease his pain before I go? Clean the wound? Jesus … with what? The thought of it makes me gag again. I can't simply walk away, though the temptation to do so is an almost physical force. Am I capable of seeing him, speaking to him, hearing his cries of agony? Then what? Walk out, securing the door behind me? Can I do that? It's not as if I'd be leaving him to die: I'd make that call as soon as feasible. But then, I can't be entirely sure of his sanity these days. He'd be out of my control, as soon as those paramedics knelt beside him and asked his name. Even if he refused to give it, or made something up, there are ways and means of tracking down the truth, nowadays. A scraping of cells can tell the world your history.

I start to hyperventilate, and it's nothing to do with that stench. My mind is

177

careering through rational solutions. Let him lie there, and forget to make the call. Or put him out of his misery here and now. It's astounding how quickly, in extremis, we can shed our personalities. One minute it's inconceivable that I should abandon a wounded man; the next I'm running through a mental inventory of the blunt instruments in the cottage, and contracting my biceps as I picture the act of caving in a human skull.

40

A gun thuds. The cawing swells. I put my hand to the door-handle and it dips
before I've touched it. I hear a grunt:

'Shut the fuck up!' Then: 'Oh, it's you. I was just coming out to chuck a brick at
the vultures.'

He turns back in to the cottage and I follow, complaining about the stench.

'It's the pan', he says. 'Been blocked for three days. Just can't shift it. Had to go in
the bushes today.'

I double up, retching; it's much worse in here. He seems to be leading me through
the cottage to the outside toilet itself, but I stand my ground, and assume a wholly
false tone of confidence:

'I expect it'll sort itself out. I'll give you your supplies and go. I can't stay, I've got
a meeting in town.'

'But what'll I do?' he cries. The sudden despair takes me aback. I suppose I've
been telling myself he's used to all this now—the filth, the squalor, doing without.
But that's what we always tell ourselves about people who are suffering: they're
OK. They're used to it. They're not like me.

'I've tried poking it with a branch' he says. 'Just can't clear it.' His eyes brim with
tears. I'm not used to seeing him like this. I shrug helplessly. Does he really expect
me to roll up my sleeves and pitch in? Pummel away at three days' worth of
someone else's excrement? I look at him, standing by the back door, weak as a
child. The flesh and muscles on his neck and arms are pale and withered, and half
his face is covered in greasy stubble. There are cuts and scabs on his cheeks and
chin, where he's tried to shave with a blunt razor. The man's a wreck.

'What if I call someone?' I say. 'A plumber? Or someone?'

His eyes widen in panic.

179

'What, get someone in? You can't do that!'

The horror of that blocked bowl propels me into a plan.

'Yes, I can—I'll get an emergency plumber, pay him in cash, no names—'

'And what about me?'

He squeaks with panic, and I worry that he might soil himself.

'That's OK—you can just lie low while he's here. In the woods. Just don't show your face. I'll say I've only just bought the place to do it up, and some tramp's been using it …'

My plan takes on a logic of its own and I start fumbling in my pocket for my phone.

'I'll see if I can get a signal, find someone local—hang on, I'll be right back.'

Typical bloody benighted backwoods, out of the loop, off the radar … I'm cursing every rural community in the country as I toil up the hill, jabbing pointlessly at my phone. No signal. No signal. The cawing of the rooks becomes the sound of obscurity. This place is out of reach, out of shouting distance, cast away beyond a vacancy of fields, muffled by woods and weather. Could be the Middle bloody Ages. I've almost reached the pub before my phone cooperates. I lurk near the village green, waiting for the search results to wheeze onto the screen. I give my phone an angry little shake, as if that will hurry it up.

There's no-one around. But I know what these places are like. The houses have eyes. The back gardens are incorrigible gossips. My presence will have been noted. I debate whether to make the call from the phone box on the other side of the green. I can't even be sure it actually functions: I suspect it might be some kind of museum piece, preserved with the aid of an English Heritage grant to kid the villagers that life doesn't change.

A man with a Spar carrier clinks up behind me and nearly makes me jump out of my skin.

'Managed to make contact?' he asks cheerfully. 'Not easy to reach the outside world from hereabouts.'

'Yes, I'm OK, thanks' I assure him. I can see a couple of whisky bottles poking out of his grocery haul.

'All right, are you?' he persists. 'Lost your bearings?'

God, the peasants are a nosy bunch. Nothing else to keep them interested, I suppose.

'No, no, I'm fine. Just stopped to stretch my legs ... comfort break, as they say ...' I start to enjoy my ad libbing. 'Don't suppose there are any public conveniences round here?'

He makes a 'no chance' face and shakes his head. 'Pop into the local' he advises. 'Bernie won't mind.'

I thank him and saunter towards the pub. I can sense him watching my progress across the green. Maybe he's wondering where I've parked my car. Maybe ... oh, get a grip. That's the trouble with paranoia: it's catching.

41

'It must have been a terrible blow' Rosalyn is saying. 'It's so hard to believe …
She was so—so *lively*, wasn't she?'

I nod, admiring Rosalyn's endless generosity. My mother was icily polite to her at
best; at worst, only just short of bitchy. She really doesn't deserve such grief. I try
and steer us off the topic.

'But, you know, it was a good while ago now …'

Rosalyn rounds her eyes in wonder at the passage of years.

'Yes, … so … she can't have been very old …'

Honestly, there's no shifting her. For some reason my mother's demise seems to
have shaken her to the core. Maybe it's brought home to her the world of time
we've been apart, lost time, the need to make up for it. I hope so.

'Not very old' I agree. 'It was pretty grim at the time.'

She nods, looking at her feet. We're standing between a miniature office block and
a miniature multistorey car park. There's not much space between these displays,
and she has to stand quite close. I can see the parting of her hair, with a margin of
grey extending into a darker, more artificial shade. So she's been getting some
colour put in, after all. But—typically—she's been careless about it, and let it grow
out.

'You've had a rough time of it' she comments, balancing the tip of her finger on a
tiny pedestrian. 'What with your mother, and Don, and, and …'

I take in a sharp breath. *And you*, I'm thinking. *And you, slamming that door,
walking out of my life.*

'Well,' I say, 'that's how it goes …'

I reach for her hand and balance it lightly in my own. She's disconcerted. She says,
'How, er, how did Uncle Don take it?'

'Take what?'

'You know. Your mother. They were very close, weren't they?'

'Oh … yes. Very close. He took it pretty badly.'

She squeezes my hand briefly—maternally—then takes her hand away. 'Shall we get some fresh air? Don't tell Bo, but I find this place a bit creepy.'

Bo has been unexpectedly detained and can't make our second meeting. Something about a call from a Minister.

'A politician, I presume, not a cleric' I said, too jovially, when Rosalyn arrived with his apologies. I couldn't hide my delight. I hadn't even tried to get her alone this time, and fate stepped in on my behalf. Serendipity. I say the word to myself as we edge out of the dwarf connurbation, and Rosalyn looks back and says, 'What?'

'Nothing. Talking to myself—I didn't realise.'

'That's the first sign of madness, you know' she jokes. I watch her back and hips as she manoeuvres her way to the door, and have to clench my fists to stop myself wrapping my arms around her.

There's a small, dusty park in the next square. We go for a stroll, and get tea from a kiosk at the gate. I ask all the right questions about her daughter-in-law, about being a grandmother, about the children. Her whole face is a smile when she talks about them, and she waves her hands so vigorously that she spills tea on her dress. We sit on a bench and I hold her cup while she dabs at herself with a tissue.

'You've always got tissues to hand' I remark. 'I bet that was a useful trick when the kids were small.'

The kids. As if I'm a part of it all. But she's pleased, and laughs.

'Yes, there was always a good deal of mopping and wiping to do.' Then, after a pause, she goes on, in a worried way: 'Josh is so young to be a father. It was all a bit of a … well, you know. Unexpected. They're hardly more than children themselves, to me.'

'I'm sure they'll be just fine,' I say, as if I had the remotest idea about that sort of thing. 'They've got you and Bo to support them—how can they fail?'

She looks straight at me, grateful, her eyes moistening. I'm perched there, cup of hot tea in each hand, unable to cradle her face and kiss her mouth, and I'm battling not to say 'I love you'. Because I know full well it's just a moment, a memory, a passing mood. So instead I say,

'You must be a terrific mum.'

She looks sad. Wistful. She says, in a small, apologetic voice,

'It's what I always wanted.'

I change the subject quickly:

'Better take this tea now. It's starting to scald my hand.'

42

I should have been kinder. That's probably something we could all say, every one of us, looking back at our various pasts. Apart from the saints and freaks, the Mother Teresas of this world, most of us blunder through life in a dense wadding of selfishness, never bothering to imagine how the world looks to other eyes. In the raw honesty of the early hours, I see how badly I behaved, what a child I was, and I have to get up, move around, to escape the conclusion that I preferred to ignore Rosalyn's misery than to compete with a baby for her love.

When she came home from hospital she was fragile, easily tired, probably depressed. And listen, I took care of her—I'm not some out-and-out thug, after all. I tempted her with carefully thought-out meals; I brought her books and newspapers; I held her hand and stroked her hair and stayed in with her watching mild rubbish on the telly, rather than go out with Scott on his hunting trips. But we never spoke to each other of the miscarriage again. In fact I was reluctant even to load the incident with such a portentous name. On the day she returned, weak and teary, from the hospital, and went straight to bed even though it was still light, Scott asked:

'Is she going to be OK?'

I patted his shoulder and shook my head, not as a 'no' but to shake the question away.

'Yeah, yeah, fine, she just needs rest' I assured him. 'It wasn't too far gone, thank god. More a heavy period than anything else, they said.'

I didn't specify who 'they' were, and in fact nobody had said anything of the sort. But the phrase consoled me as if it had come from an expert mouth, and as far as I was concerned that was the end of that. Rosalyn was going to be all right. She was home. A little pampering, a little TLC, and everything would be back to normal.

Yes, I should have been kinder. OK, I didn't want children, and that wasn't going to change. I was happy with my life, my routine, my possessions; I was satisfied with Nathan Hill, and had no inclination to slip further down the cast list as 'father of' anyone else. If my nights were going to be disturbed, I preferred it to be by Scott's pursuit of a goal, a subject, a moment immortalised, than by screams and shit. So you could say that it was always going to be a deal-breaker; that my stubborn refusal to broach the issue was actually a way of prolonging our relationship. You could say that. But then again, maybe if I'd talked to her about it, made the effort to understand her feelings, shown an interest, for God's sake … maybe I could have persuaded her that we already had everything we needed. Well, there you go, I didn't. We didn't discuss it, and we could possibly have continued as we were, maintaining a diplomatic silence, for years and years. Forever. People do, don't they? They live with all kinds of silences, unasked questions, unnamed resentments … It's a way of coping. Repression, I always think, is underrated. We could have gone on avoiding the subject together—if it hadn't been for Scott. He was the one who dragged everything into the open— Scott the truth-teller, the witness, fascinated by everything, incapable of hypocrisy, whatever the cost. Scott was the one who forced her into a choice.

43

I spent all my working hours in offices, in those days. Zenada had done well from the slimming strategy and, as always happens with great commercial success, the name had detached itself from the product and taken on a life of its own. We had battalions of staff in several countries (but not Italy, not any more) who'd never laid eyes on a glassworks. Some of them barely knew what we actually produced—they didn't need to know. Their skill was in manipulating figures, negotiating clauses, managing teams of other employees who knew nothing about glass. We'd built a whole planet from that molten core, and its population was spinning and spinning around an invisible fire. That was why I accepted the offer to buy the business. Not because I would be richer than Uncle Don for the rest of my life; but because I'd ended up so far from the beauty, the point of it all.

The offer had come from a multinational conglomerate, Mendel, which was bucking the trend at the time and continuing to gobble up diverse operations, while others were shedding theirs all around and retreating back to basics. Mendel had been more canny than most, though, pacing themselves carefully and keeping view of their own 'golden thread', a theme of sorts that ran through all their concerns. They'd started in 1906 as Mendel Bros, a tiny local carpentry business run by three German brothers. Even 90 years later, their DIY stores, tiling companies, garden centres and white goods could all be linked with the word 'home', and Zenada would fit neatly into their family.

So it was a good deal, and I had no regrets, but the whole process was taking far more time than I'd hoped. Mendel's lawyers were being tricky, haggling over details, and I was beginning to worry that they had some other agenda, that the sale

might not be all it was cracked up to be. After one particularly tiring session—
many fruitless hours squinting through the fine print—I staggered out of the HQ
lift into the underground car park and heard my name—

'Signor Eel!'

A vision of Dino flashed into my mind, but this was a younger voice and a
different accent—and of course, Dino was beyond speech and travel by this time.
A young man in janitor's overalls was approaching between the Jags and Mazdas,
a mop in one hand and a bucket in the other. It took me a minute to recognise him.
I pressed my forehead, trying to squeeze his name into my memory. He put down
the bucket and extended his hand, helping me out:

'Arber' he said, with an uneven grin. 'You give me training in Santoribio.'

'Arber, of course, of course, how are—' I shook his hand vigorously, taking in the
clothes, the cleaning equipment … he laughed at my confusion and spread his arms,
tilting the broom like a dancer with a cane.

'I have different job now!'

'You're not making glass, Arber?'

He shrugged. 'I was. I come here to make glass. But …' He made a face to indicate
bad luck, a bad turn: 'No job for me making glass. They say, We got other jobs,
maybe start there.' He leant towards me with a self-deprecating wink: 'I say to
them, I know the boss! Signor Eel, we are like—' and he held up his hand and
crossed his fingers. 'But—pff! No job making glass for me. But it's OK. Still in
Zenada. Still in a job. One day …' He raised the broom-handle to his mouth like a
pipe, then his hand wafted away, tracing imaginary curves and bowls. His friend's
name suddenly popped into my head.

'And Mergim?' I asked, rather pleased with myself. 'Is he still making glass?'

For the first time, he looked dejected. Mergim, it turned out, had gone back to
Kosovo. There'd been attacks on the Serbian police there, claimed by the Kosovan

Liberation Army. Arber reckoned Mergim had gone to join the KLA, though he couldn't, or wouldn't, say for sure. A short silence fell between us. A car door opened and shut; an engine started. The noise bounced around the concrete pillars. Then Arber sighed and his smile was back.

'I miss the glass' he said.

I patted his shoulder.

'So do I, Arber,' I said. 'You take care of yourself, now.'

44

I could hear Scott's voice as I opened the apartment door. I was exhausted after the day's legal wranglings, and for some reason the encounter with Arber had put me even further out of sorts. I just wanted to enjoy the space and stillness of my home. All the way there, sitting in traffic, nursing a vague headache, I'd been picturing the evening ahead: brandy first, that was for sure; I could already taste it at the back of my tongue. A Brandenburg for background, or maybe Corelli—yes, Corelli, cello sonata, that would be just the job, flowing through the room like a soft-voiced manservant transforming all life's complications into elegance. I opened the door, and 'Don't be ridiculous!'—Scott's voice was irritating the air, interrupted by Rosalyn's high, indignant protest. They were in the living area, Rosalyn in a big towelling dressing-gown, nesting among cushions on the sofa, hugging her knees; Scott sprawled over the chaise longue, and our exquisite expanse of oak-block floor was swamped in photography magazines, used plates and cups and glasses, notepads, phone book … I shut my eyes and steadied my breath. They didn't miss a beat, tugging me into their argument.

'There's no point slogging on if the work's not there—and God knows I've tried, haven't I Nathan? Nathan knows how long and how—'

'Bollocks. You could get it if you really wanted it. That's the trouble, Rosalyn— you *don't* want it, does she, Nathan? You've only got half a mind on the job …'

I was on the verge of turning right round and going out again. If I had—if I'd left there and then, walked round the block, gone to the wine bar for an hour—who knows how different my life might have been. But instead I waded through the detritus, intent on getting that brandy, muttering about the mess and accusing them of being like a pair of bloody students.

'Listen' Scott was saying, like a teacher bringing the class to order. 'The point is this: you're either a singer, or a mother. You can't be both, Rosalyn. You'd be torn in two.'

I paused in the act of pouring my drink and shot a look at her. She avoided my eye; her voice dropped, sounded guilty:

'I'm not talking about *me*, Scott, I'm just saying, as a general—'

'Oh, do me a favour. Who *else* are we talking about?'

'Just generally' she insisted, and I knew she was eyeing me, now that I'd turned back to the task in hand. 'Just generally, I'm saying, people do it all the time.'

'It's one thing or the other' said Scott conclusively. 'You make your choice and you stick to it.' He heaved himself to his feet and started gathering up his magazines. 'Come on, Rosalyn,' he added genially, 'I can't see you going down the buying-in-child-care route. Once you start having babies that's it. The word "maternal" was invented for the likes of you.'

He went off to his room and I took his place on the chaise, facing her, nursing my drink, saying nothing.

'How was the meeting? You look wrecked' she said. 'Shall I get you …' The offer petered out, defeated by my silence. I drank some of my brandy. She said, 'The trouble with Scott, he's so—'

'He's committed to his work' I said. 'He has a talent, and he's making the most of it. Dedicating his life to it. I don't find that odd at all. Do you?'

She started to snuffle and fished in the dressing-gown pockets for her ever-ready tissues. She'd been particularly prone to tears since the episode.

'Well, I'm sorry I can't live up to your expectations, Nathan,' she quavered. 'I know I'm not as talented as—'

'It's the *work*, Rosalyn, not the *talent*.' It had been a long day. My apartment was in a filthy mess. I was harsher than I meant to be. But once I'd started I couldn't rein it in. 'The talent is incidental. Accidental. An accident of birth. There's any number of accountants and teachers and till operators and bin men with "a talent". Could have been, should have been, if only I'd had the breaks … It's not the talent, it's not the breaks—god alive, you of all people know this. It's the hard graft. The tedious, daily grind, the practice, the failure, the starting again, the refusal to be beaten, the, the—'

'Oh, what the fuck would *you* know?' she suddenly shouted. The expletive was unexpected and ugly on her lips. 'You've had it on a plate from day one. *Daily grind, failure and starting again*?' I wasn't used to this loud sarcasm from Rosalyn. My colour rose. 'When did you ever know *failure and starting again*?' she went on. 'More like *failure and go to Uncle Don for a bail-out*. You haven't got the first idea what it's—'

'If I could do what you do'—I was shouting, myself, now—'I wouldn't be sitting around on my backside living off someone else's money and whingeing about my tough breaks. I'd be working. Learning. Refining. Perfecting.'

'What does that mean, "living off someone else's money"?' She'd risen to a shriek, now. Tearing at that throat, that precious voice. She flung her arm in the direction of the spare room. 'What the hell is *he* doing, your pet bloody "artiste", if it's not living off—'

'At least Scott knows what he's doing with his life' I roared, sitting forward so that the brandy sloshed in its glass. 'Not just wafting from one day to the next, "forgetting" to take the pill in the hope that a future will foist itself on you and save you the bother of deciding for yourself!'

We sat there, both stunned by my ferocity. You could virtually hear my accusation rebounding off the walls and ceiling, diminishing, vanishing, but undeniable. For a moment the entire city seemed to have paused. Then Rosalyn broke from her bundled position, leapt to her feet, tightening the dressing-gown around her, and hurtled towards the bedroom. The door slammed. I sank back, careful not to spill my drink, relieved, in truth, to be left in peace. I regretted my outburst, of course I did. But I had no doubt that it would all blow over, she'd have a good cry, Scott would diplomatically go out hunting, and all would be well in the end.

45

Rosalyn has taken her tea back and is watching a child on the park lawn, throwing sticks for a terrier. The dog springs around its owner's feet, panting, then powers after the stick to the edge of the grass, retrieves it and turns in one seamless move. Rosalyn's eyes follow it to and fro. But when she talks we're back to thorny matters.

'I know you think I sort of gave up' she says. 'But my heart was never in the singing.'

All right, then. OK. If she wants to tackle the past, let's do it. I shuffle myself backwards on the bench. We're nearly touching now.

'All I wanted' I say 'was for you to be your best. To show what you could do.' I give her a lingering, affectionate look. 'I was so proud of you.'

'Well,' she says bluntly, 'that's not how it felt. It felt as if I was never good enough.'

Now, I tell myself. Time to sort this out—now. I clear my throat.

'I didn't … I didn't treat you very well, did I?'

She blinks rapidly.

'It was the situation. That's all. I think …' She looks at me quickly, then away again. 'We just weren't right for each other, in the end.'

I'm disappointed. Which soap did she get that from? It's just a phrase, it has no meaning or resonance. For a while I'm so annoyed that I just ignore her, sipping my tea, watching the dog's antics. Then she says, softly,

'Don't be cross, Nathan.' She sounds quite upset. I don't know what I was expecting, but this is worse, far worse. The sound of her voice, in its small intimacy, threatens to break everything down. I have to work hard to continue the conversation, just to sit up straight and function in a human way.

'I'm not cross' I mumble, eventually. 'I'm just sorry.'

'You know … It wasn't about, about children. You know that.' I don't know anything. I can't form words or thoughts at this point. She waits, then carries on. 'We were both so *angry* all the time,' she says, and suddenly the words spit out at her:

'So which is it, then? Make your mind up!' Her tea spills again. She moves her knees apart deftly and it splashes onto the path. I don't want this at all—barking at her, behaving like a wounded animal. It's not how I want to come across, and it's not even true, for Christ's sake. That's all over, all finished, I'm genuinely contented with my life, but how will she ever believe that now? I sound weak, and no-one is seduced by a weak man. But still, I go on; the words keep coming like a cough, inexorable: 'Which reason did you land on in the end? I wouldn't give you a baby, you were never good enough for me, I wouldn't chuck Scott out, we were angry, we weren't right … and I was just *so fucking cold!* …'

The words run out. What a disaster. It was all set up so well—no Bo, a stroll in the park, a chat about old times, a sparking of latent passion … Perfect. And I behave like a madman, and ruin it all. Again. To cap it all, a drop of snot escapes my nose before I can sniff it back in, and splats onto the path next to Rosalyn's puddle of tea. Silently, she hands me one of her tissues, and I mop up. She sets her take-out mug down with caution, so that she can give me her full attention. I feel like a client on a psychiatrist's couch.

'Sorry,' I say, finally. 'I don't know where that came from.'

I'm expecting her to say something wise, or kind, or sentimental. But the silence goes on. The boy throws calls of encouragement with the stick; the dog yaps and runs. *Say something*, I find myself thinking. *Say something. Touch me.* After an age, she does say something:

'I wrote you a letter.'

195

'What? When?'

'After I stormed out, that time. I didn't want to … It was a horrible way to end it all. I hadn't *expected* it to end it all.'

My chest is heaving as if I've been chasing that bloody stick. I can't seem to calm my breathing down.

'But—' and now my tongue feels twice its normal size—'you didn't come back. You never came back. Except to clear out your things.'

'No …' She sits back, mulling it over—her version of events. Her story. 'But at the time, I just thought it was another fight. We were fighting all the time by then, Nathe.' *Nathe.* 'After, you know … my hormones were all over the place. And it didn't help that Scott was there. We'd been quiet, before he turned up, just the two of us. Quiet and happy. *I* thought.'

I don't want to talk about Scott. So I say, sullenly,

'I never had a letter.'

'No. I never sent it, in the end. I wanted to make it up with you. I wanted to apologise, and come home. But as I was writing it, I realised …'

'What? Realised what?'

She sighs deeply, leans forward to retrieve her tea, sips at it, then says:

'I realised that I *did* want to make peace with you, I *did* want to apologise; but I didn't want to come home. I couldn't face it. I didn't belong there any more.'

I hide my eyes with my hand. My mouth is twisting in a strange, cartoonish way that I can't control. My voice comes out in a whisper:

'*You're so fucking cold.* That's what you left me with. That's how you left me.'

The pressure of her hand on my arm makes me twitch with shock, but she doesn't take it away.

'I'm sorry' she says. 'I should have sent that letter. When I read it through, it sounded so *final*. I suppose I was too scared of closing all the doors. I still thought

196

it might all get better. And your mother was right, you know—you *were* happier without me, in the end.'

I look down at her hand, still resting on my arm. Rucked skin, emphatic knuckles. The other hand is cradling the polystyrene mug. She takes another sip and wrinkles her nose:

'Too strong. I shouldn't have left the bag in.'

I give a little laugh and look her in the eyes. She holds me in her brown gaze, just that instant too long. So maybe I haven't wrecked everything, after all.

'Thirteen years,' I say, and my voice cracks. 'It's a long time.'

She nods, and her hand slips off my arm.

'Yes. But that was another life. I've been with Bo for over 20, now. I've got two children. One stepdaughter. A grandchild on the way. There's no point digging through ancient history.'

I'm not even listening, now. I straighten up and my voice is clear as a bell.

'What do you mean, "my mother was right"?'

She looks surprised, then puzzled. I go on:

'You said just now: *your mother was right*. What did—'

'Oh!' Her face clears. 'When she came to see me. At Auntie Monica's. You knew about that,' she insists, amused at my stupefied expression. 'She said she was your messenger. I remember her saying those words, in that way of hers. *I'm here as Nathan's messenger.* She looked like an alien from outer space, sitting there on the flowery couch. She wouldn't take her coat off. Had the collar of it up round her chin as if ...' The sentence dissolves as she watches the rise of heat from my jaw to my forehead.

The boy on the grass has grown bored of the game and throws the stick towards the park exit, following the dog after it this time.

'So, I'm guessing that was a lie, then ...' concludes Rosalyn, 'About being a messenger. Well, that's no great surprise, really.' She squeezes my hand quickly, and is gathering herself, preparing for departure, now.

'And your Auntie Monica must have lied to me,' I point out, with the rising of old resentments in my voice. 'I must have called her a dozen times to ask where you were. She always said she didn't know. Every time.'

'That was my fault, not hers.' She's standing up, checking the buttons on her coat. 'I told her I didn't want to talk to you.' I can't look at her. She's so *calm*. 'I needed to make the break,' she says. 'I couldn't let myself ... go back to it all. I'm sorry, Nathan. It was a very long time ago.' As if that wipes everything away ...

But she's right. It's hard to remember, from this distance: all the tangles and eddies of blame and emotion, all the injustices and you-saids and I-saids ... there's no way of straightening it out into a narrative with a crime and a solution. It's just *mess*. Reluctantly, I follow her lead and get up from the bench. We walk side by side towards the park gate in silence. Then she suddenly stops, touches my arm, and says,

'It made no difference, Nathan. What your mother said. It was true, and I already knew it was.'

'What *did* she say?'

'That you were better off without me. She wasn't unkind about it. In fact, in a funny way, I think she was being kind to *me*. Sort of giving me permission, to move on.'

46

We part on friendly terms. I agree to come for 'a proper meal' with her and Bo at some unspecified future date. She looks at her watch, says she has things to do, and we say our goodbyes at the gate, with an affectionate hug. That hug lasts just a few seconds longer than friendship. And I realise that I've been wrong: she's not calm at all. I can feel the tremor in her arms. When she's left, I pretend to search for something in my pockets, so that I can observe her progress back past Bo's former office building, over the pedestrian crossing ... her broad back in that stone-coloured mack, her hand unconsciously pushing back the nest of hair ... until finally she vanishes around a corner. I don't want to go home, or back to the gallery. I don't want to think about unsent letters, or lying mothers, or what might have been. Not now. I decide to take my mind off it all, and pay a call on Freddie.

An hour later I'm knocking on Freddie's blistered front door with my bare knuckles, because the doorbell is hanging out of its case on a frayed wire. There's a scuffling, and a thud of feet, very close; she must be running down those secret stairs. The door barely opens and a fraction of Freddie's face appears.
'Oh! Nathan!' She opens the door wider. 'A surprise visit!' she cries with unnecessary volume. 'Sweet!'
I can't quite tell whether she's in her underwear or her normal clothes. She's wearing something that looks like a slip, with a fluffy shrug over her shoulders. She's all legs and tousled hair. I kiss her hand.
'You're a sight for sore eyes' I say.
'Ah, bless ...' says Freddie. I move forward to embrace her, then realise there's someone else emerging from the hidden stairs. Freddie clutches the edges of my jacket and tugs me towards her other guest. 'Nathan, I'm rapt that you've come,

'coz now you can meet one of my bestest mates in the whole wide world …'

A boy's face, embellished with a goatee that's fooling nobody. A wing of fair hair that he flicks from his forehead in a compulsive, gauche movement, averting his eyes from mine. He shambles up, holding his hand out, and mumbles a greeting. His jeans concertina at his bare feet, and show a width of underpants above the waistband. He's wearing some form of string vest.

'I've been showing Kit the works-in-progress, upstairs' simpers Freddie, still hanging on to my jacket, so that Kit and I have to shake hands around her. The boy's arm muscles clench, and I notice a tattoo of a bluebird on his right bicep. Poor kid—he's doing everything he can to contradict those childish features.

Freddie leans her head on my chest. Her hair smells of henna. Nothing is what it seems.

'Kit' she says in a grating, infantile voice, 'thinks I'm a genius.'

'Well,' I say, 'Kit is evidently a man of discerning taste.'

She flutters. The age gap yawns, dark and deep. Now she's reaching for Kit's hand and for mine, trying in vain to create a connection.

'This' she says, 'is so cool. My two all-time favourite guys.'

Kit grunts.

'Wonderful,' I say. 'But I'm going to be a party-pooper, I'm afraid. I only came by to confirm a few details about the launch.' I'm extemporising furiously. Freddie starts bouncing on her toes.

'The launch!' she squeals. I really can't stand much more of this. I chunter through a few improvised details, throwing in plenty of 'if possible' and 'ideally' so as not to paint myself into a corner. I even lob in a mention of TV, which sends her into a ballerina spin and produces Kit's only coherent syllable of the entire occasion: 'Sick.'

Then I make my excuses and leave, despite Freddie's wails of protest. I have to reverse out of the flat, with Freddie grasping my lapels and spoiling the line of my jacket. As soon as I'm out on that semi-derelict walkway and the door is half-shut behind her, she pulls me into a slow kiss. *Damn*, I think. *Damn her bestest mate in the whole wide world.* She looks a treat in that slip. Never mind. At least my suit is spared the grime of the storeroom floor.

47

This is the trouble: this is why I didn't want to start it all up again. Lying here, in the dark, trying to imagine that instant—and there must have been an instant—when Bo turned from genial boffin to potential lover. What did he say? Did he, maybe, touch the back of her hand, push her hair from her eyes, look up—it must be *up*, from his perspective—into those eyes, with a purposeful, suggestive look? I cannot picture it. And yet I go on trying, as if there might actually be a way to tune into their conversation, to break through time and space and witness it all. When I got back from Freddie's last night I watched an old movie, *The Swan*. Grace Kelly falls for her tutor, Louis Jourdan, but is destined to marry prince Alec Guinness, the older and wiser man. I've seen it before—with Rosalyn. I remember commenting that there was something creepy about the storyline. And Rosalyn saying,

'Well, Alec Guinness is a better catch anyway. He's charming. *Interesting*. Louis Jourdan is just *wet*.'

It's the film that's flicked this switch in my mind. The scene where Guinness gives Grace Kelly's hand an experimental tap, before settling on it like a bird. Now I can't get away from the image, re-cast with Bo and Rosalyn. As for the way things developed from there—NO! I hurl myself around in bed to escape my own visions, but they're relentless. Because it must have happened! Those children are a flesh-and-blood rebuttal of my preferred theory: that it's a platonic relationship, almost father-and-daughter, affectionate but entirely asexual. Clearly not. At least, not on two occasions. So there must have been the build-up, the mounting desire, the tightening embrace, that moment when passion pushes you together and lifts you away from each other at the same time, takes on its own momentum ... STOP. I just can't bear it. I know the next stage will be the wedding—that public performance of love and intention, the fond speeches, the in-jokes, the weepy guests ... I referred to her as my wife, when I was flirting with that journalist in Santoribio; and Rosalyn laughed at me. She was never my wife.

You see, this is how I am. And this is why I should have pretended not to hear her call me as she crossed the road, should have turned and run, gone back to the calm, new life I've made for myself. Jealousy is a disease. It takes years to conquer. I don't ever want to have to fight it off again.

48

There's a theory that men deal with break-ups very differently from women. Men, so this theory goes, are more likely to find distraction, avoid the pain, shut off the triggers and associations that bring the love object to mind. Women, on the other hand, will think obsessively about the love object, wonder what they're doing, question their words and actions, rerun scenes and seek reasons. Those who adhere to this theory don't suggest that the pain is any less for one sex than for the other. It's just that they have different ways of dealing with it.

Well, I'm sorry, theorists, but as Uncle Don might say, that's cobblers. In the months after Rosalyn left I found no instinctive psychological escape routes. I didn't lose myself in work or drink; I didn't sleep with a different woman every night, or go traipsing the night streets with Scott. Instead I surrendered myself to a kind of fever, a churning mental stew of hope and despondency, indignation and self-loathing, misery and rage. I let the Zenada sale go through on their terms and was probably a good couple of million the poorer as a result. I put aside my project of opening a glass gallery and sat at home all day, positioning myself needlessly at the window: not seeing the gasworks or the dual carriageway, but thinking of Rosalyn, her Greek profile, her blank singing face, her animated home face, the smell and touch of her skin ... I drew up inventories of her words and actions over the years, as though pursuing some valid scientific account of our relationship. In one column, her affectionate nicknames for me, small, silly gifts she'd bought me, words she'd whispered in the early hours, the absent-minded, soft way she'd take my hand in the street. In the other column, her lack of enthusiasm for our home, her awkwardness with my family, the angry, resentful accusations and wailing regrets that had characterised our recent arguments—arguments which had increased in frequency and escalated in bitterness in the weeks that followed that first, Scott-fuelled falling-out. At night, after she'd gone, I'd wake to find her ghost in bed with me: her presence, her scent, the essence of her there, beside me, until my mind readjusted itself to the facts. Scott would leave the flat in the morning—glad to get away, I imagine—and return in the early evening to find me in exactly the same place. Hours would have passed, hours which, for me, had been an exhausting marathon of relived scenes, spasms of grief, unblinking surveillance of the apartment-block lawn and her probable route back into the building, should she return.

'Jesus, man, get a grip', I remember him saying. 'You're turning self-pity into an art form.'

I knew he was right. But I was a junkie, now, in thrall to my addiction, and reason had no say in the matter. Besides, I believed—faithfully and wholly believed—that she'd be back, and all this angst would resolve itself in smug, magnanimous victory, when she came weeping for my forgiveness.

49

I'm so sorry about Scott.

Rosalyn's words sing through my brain, competing with the first growl of the ring road. Yes. Me, too. I'm so sorry about Scott. I'm sorry about the course life took, and I do wonder, sometimes, whether I could have steered it in a different direction. In the early chill, staring at the vaulted brick ceiling above my bed, I push my mind away from Mr and Mrs Rathbone, and test different scenarios, taking each alternative storyline as far as I logically can, to see whether it reaches a happier destination. But I know it's a fool's errand. What's done is done.

I need to ask Rosalyn *exactly when* Mother turned up on her Auntie Monica's doorstep in a high-collar coat. I wonder whether it was the same day she called at the apartment. Maybe she was on a mission, doing the rounds, stamping out the dregs of a relationship she'd never liked. A good day's work. Certainly, it wasn't just a casual visit: she didn't do casual visits. It was highly unusual to see her or Uncle Don anywhere near my home. The first thing she said, after embracing me and ruffling my hair, was:

'Scottie-dog at home?'

He wasn't. I couldn't tell whether that suited her plans or wrecked them. Possibly it wasn't me she'd come to see at all. But she accepted my offer of a drink, arranged herself elegantly in a chair, crossed her still sexy legs, and launched into her speech.

'I'm sorry for you, Nathan, darling. You look ... *crushed.* That girl has *crushed* you ...'

'Mother,' I said, and stopped pouring her drink, 'please don't come here sneering at Rosalyn ...'

'I wouldn't *dream* of sneering!' Her eyes and mouth widened indignantly. 'I'm simply stating a fact. I'm not casting blame—in fact, I doubt very much whether the poor child is to blame for *anything*. But the fact remains that she—all right, then, *this relationship*—has crushed you. I'm worried about you, sweetheart. And Don says—Well. Whatever Don says, we're both worried about you.' She'd opened her coat around her, and slid out of its arms before accepting her drink, then surveyed the view as she sipped. 'It is a strangely compelling view, I have to admit. I'll never understand why you want to look at old factories, but ...'

'What does Uncle Don say?' I snapped. I was standing over her, hands on my hips, probably looking, as she'd pointed out, a wreck. Grey-faced, greasy-haired, dressed in whatever was to hand. Instead of answering my question she looked me up and down and said, softly,

'Really, Nathan, one has to ask, what would you do if you weren't a rich man? You'd *have* to pull yourself together, or end up in a shop doorway somewhere, no doubt starring in one of Scottie-dog's productions.'

'Well,' I said, 'I *am* a rich man. What does Uncle Don say?'

I knew very well what Uncle Don said, or what sort of thing, at any rate. Two's company, three's a crowd. Always had him down as a nancy. Not surprised the songbird flew when there's a cuckoo in the nest. All Mother said was,

'Uncle Don thinks you and Scott are, let's say, a little too close for comfort.'

'Uncle Don is an arsehole' I said, and turned to fix myself a drink. Behind me, I heard her voice, edged with amusement:

'You're becoming quite coarse in your old age, dear.'

Scott was not my lover. But that's about the only unequivocal statement I can make about our relationship. I don't know what we were to each other. Friends? Funny sort of friendship. He thought nothing of searching my jacket pockets for cash, or simply lifting my wallet, when he needed funds. Brothers? That might be closer to the mark. More than that, though. The mane of black hair, the slight frame, the feminine face … I suppose there's no denying it, his physical presence had a more than brotherly appeal. And in those terrible, lost months after the door slammed, I needed him there, I needed his echo of her features, as a starving man needs to eat. He was like a watered-down version of my drug of choice, a Rosalyn-lite. On the worst nights, he'd come back from his hunting trips to find me wild-eyed, pacing the apartment. Scott would put aside his gear, take a couple of steps towards me and open his arms. Just to touch someone, to feel the contact of a human body—that's enough, sometimes, to save us from insanity. And Scott always returned from his adventures thrumming with life and energy: holding him was like being recharged. He would endure my desperate embrace, let me sob into his shoulder. Then he'd start to struggle, say,

'Come on, Nathan, let's sit, let's talk …'

—wriggling from my grasp, guiding me to the sofa by my arms, which stuck insistently to him like magnets, as I wept into the space where his shoulder had been.

I've grown so used to casting Scott as the enemy—still, even now, blaming him for the break-up, from habit, you might say. But he did save me, in those terrible months. He was patient, strong … yes, for all his flaws, and for all mine, I do think Scott Carter was a friend. He let me rail against her, reminisce about our better times, analyse the worse times, while the sky grew lighter and the traffic grew louder.

'I just can't believe she would leave it there. Not a word. No phone call. Nothing. It's so *cruel* …' I whined. 'And she's not a cruel person … which makes me wonder, what if something's *happened*?'

'Nathan, nothing's happened,' said Scott. His leg was jiggling up and down. *Scott,*

208

dear, you've left your engine running. He was twisting his cuff round and round his fingers. I knew he wanted a cigarette, but I had never let anyone smoke in the apartment, even Rosalyn. 'Nothing's happened,' he assured me, and his voice was a lot calmer than his body. 'She's just left. She's gone. And you're wrong about her, you know, mate—she *is* cruel.'

'What?' I stared at him, feeling the weight of my haggard, tear-streaked face.

'She doesn't mean to be,' he conceded. 'But it's two sides of the coin, innit, Nathe?' Like Don, Scott used to affect an unnatural accent. In his case, it was the kind of half-hearted estuary English that suggested he'd been to private school (though I had no idea what his background was, and he always shrugged off any attempts to find out). 'Rosalyn's like a child,' he went on. 'One side of the coin is innocent, natural, spontaneous, kind. She's all that, no question.' I nodded eagerly, wallowing in the compliments, and blew my nose. 'The other side of the coin is that childlike cruelty. You know—throw a tantrum, then something else distracts you, and it's done. Out of sight, out of mind.'

'No,' I said, 'no. No.' I just refused to accept it. And something in me, the seed of my later jealousy, I suppose, resented Scott for grasping her character—its weaknesses as well as its marvels—more profoundly than I ever had.

'Well, OK,' he said in the end. 'But you can stop worrying that something *happened*. What happened is, Rosalyn dumped you, and she did it like men usually do—quick and final. Like the guillotine. That was invented to make killing *kinder*, you know? So maybe she is being kind, after all. Whatever—' He leapt up and yawned luxuriously—'All you've got to know is, the blade has dropped, mate.'

'And where does that leave *me*?' I mumbled, suddenly overcome with tiredness.

'Just a head in a basket.'

'You've got to be someone else, now,' he said over his shoulder, as he headed to the kitchen to put the kettle on. 'Reinvent yourself. Forget the *feelings*. They're a colossal waste of energy. *Work*, Nathe. That's what'll pull you out of this. *Work.* That's all that matters in the end.'

One day—it must have been a good few months after I lost Rosalyn, because I'd managed to leave the building for a few hours—I came back to find all her belongings gone. In truth, there weren't all that many. Most of our possessions had been my choice and my purchases. But the wardrobe had been emptied of her clothes: my shirts floated in unaccustomed space. Her music books and letters and photographs—gone, except for the two that still hang on my walls. That night, Scott found me crouching in the middle of the floor, caging my head in my arms. He didn't say anything, but very tenderly, he lifted me to my feet; took my face in his hands and kissed my mouth; and held me, for a long, still time. But we were never lovers. It was always Rosalyn I wanted. Never anybody else.

50

On days like this I appreciate it all. Everything around me. The charm and pleasure of a city life laid on for the affluent to enjoy. It's something to do with the weather: that lighthearted flirtiness of a perfect British day. All my senses are heightened; everything I see, smell and hear carries extra resonance. An overheard exchange between a busker and a passer-by ('On your own, today, mate?'—'Just waiting for the rest of the orchestra!') ... a trail of laughter on cigarette-smoke ... small children reciting a rhyme in elastic unison as they skip behind their mother. I relish the scent of lilies in the floral arrangements along the windows of Astey's, and then of coffee brewing inside, where the sunlight is veiled with cool strips of shadow. I take in every detail. I imagine how Scott might divide all this with his photographer's eye; how Rosalyn's voice would soar into that clean blue sky. I sit at my favourite table, with the breeze from a half-open window touching my neck. There's a sound like soft rainfall as the only other two customers tap away at their laptops. On days like this, enjoying the first sting of a strong coffee, I can shut that door fast in my mind and sweep away the rubbish of the past. Outside, someone's whistling as he passes the window: *Daisy, Daisy* ... . I open my paper and settle more comfortably in my seat.

I haven't yet reached the arts pages when I'm aware of a warmth and a musky fragrance beside me.

'Freddie!' I peer at her over my glasses and automatically tauten my face muscles. 'Where did you spring from?'

She looks different today—less frivolous. She's gone for Parisian elegance, I think: tight, cream-coloured Chinos, flat pumps, a peppermint-green vest-top. The hair has been tamed into a bun on the nape of her neck. She looks older, more professional. It suits her.

'I tried the gallery first' she says, sliding onto the bench opposite. 'Gabby said you'd be here. She said you like some "you-time" before going in.'

So why the hell, I think, resentfully, *are you barging into it?*

'I hope you don't mind me barging in' she says, insincerely, and misinterprets my flicker of a smile. 'I knew you'd be OK with it' she adds. She casts a wistful look towards the counter. Oh, well. It couldn't last. I fold the paper, and order her a coffee.

'Are you all right?' I ask. 'You look peaky.'

God, could I sound more like her father?

She says, 'Well, I am a bit stressed, to be honest. I think it's the launch, it's doing my head in …'

And off we go, into the usual mire of insecurity and self-regard that afflicts every artist before every show. I reassure her; tell her she's a great talent and will go a long way. And she is; and she will. But she's not experienced enough to realise, yet, that she's the only one who cares.

'I'm sorry to go on' she keeps saying.

'No,' I say, 'it's good that you take it seriously.'

She takes my hand across the table and plays with each finger in turn.

'You've been so fantastic to me' she says. 'It's amazing to find someone who really *believes* in me, you know? You've helped me so much …'

I lift her hand and kiss it, partly to stop that infernal fidgeting with my fingers. Interesting: as I put my lips to her knuckles, her arm stiffens, almost pulls away. If I didn't know better I'd think that was disgust. But then she relaxes, leans further towards me, takes charge of my hand again and puts the tip of my little finger into her mouth. Her tongue ferrets around the cuticles. I notice one of the customers clocking the scene over the open lid of his laptop. The sickly light of his screen is reflected in his glasses, hiding the expression in his eyes. Embarrassment, maybe.

212

Disapproval. I twitch my eyebrows towards him and he ducks back to his work.

'Ow!' I yap, as Freddie gives my finger a playful bite. She grins, puts my hand back on the table and covers it with both of her own.

'The other thing I was wondering' she says, returning to her main menu, 'is whether the space is, you know, big enough ...'

'Big enough?' I'm puzzled. 'Well, I'm devoting the whole of that front section to your pieces; that's what people will see as soon as they come through the door ...'

She does her kittenish mugging at me, all rosebud mouth and big eyes.

'I know, I know, it's awesome, I'm really rapt about it, really ... It's just ...' Her fingers start to explore my wrist, creep under my watch-strap, fiddle with my cufflinks. 'I guess I'm just worried that they won't have ... you know ... like, space to breathe ... am I being really selfish?'

Yes, you are.

'No, you're not, of course you're not. I understand what you're saying. But I'm not sure I can do anything about it, Freddie, love. I can't clear the entire gallery for a launch like this.'

'You've done it before, though, haven't you?' she asks, sweetly, tilting her head to one side.

'Well, yes, but rarely. Only for the really big ... I mean, the really *established* names. Peta Krantz, for her first British-made collection. That was a big event. And Suki Mezler—when she came over from the States ...'

She's stung by that. The fingers stop their teasing. She'd never even heard of Suki Mezler until she saw her work at my apartment. *You're a kid;* that's what I'm telling her. *You're a kid, you know nothing, and you should be thankful for what you get.*

'It's a funny thing about Suki Mezler', she says. 'I've been looking at her stuff on your website, and ... I don't know ...'

213

'Overrated?' I suggest. She notes my amusement and drops my hand, pushing herself into the back of the bench.

'No, I'm not saying that—I mean—it's brilliant, God, I wish I could come up with … I just mean, her pieces are so, like, *airy*, and so, like, *non* whatever … you know, I think if they had too much display space they could sort of *disappear* …'

Fair play to the girl. She's no fool. I remember one of the critics who came to Suki's launch saying it was almost like walking into an empty gallery. He meant it as a compliment to the limpid, feathery quality of her glasswork, but still …

'You could be right' I concede. 'But to be honest, Freddie, that's just another argument for *not* removing all the other stock during a launch.'

'My work's nothing like Suki Mezler's' she snaps back, sugaring her words immediately with a simper and: 'I mean, God, if *only* …'

'No, it's not' I agree. 'But I still can't give you the whole gallery, Fred. I wish I could. But the harsh fact is, you're not enough of a draw, yet, to justify taking down pieces that will sell.'

She nods, but the mouth has shrunk into a thin, short line.

'*Yet*', I add, and jab the air to underline my words: 'Not *yet*. But *you will be*. Very soon. I'd lay my reputation on it.'

She's mollified; her feet hug my calves under the table. But I can tell she still wants her way, and thinks she can get it. Freddie's a much tougher cookie than I'd bargained for.

51

Peta Krantz is coming to the gallery office to show her designs for the auction piece. She's running late, naturally. Gabby puts her head round the door to let me know.

'Peta rang to say things have got ahead of her—'

'Whatever that means' I mutter, looking at my watch.

'But she's on her way. Mrs Rathbone is here.'

I try and jump up from my chair, catch my leg against it and nearly smash my jaw on the table. I hear Rosalyn's voice from the gallery, saying,

'I wish you'd call me Rosie. "Mrs Rathbone" sounds so *old...*'

They trill at each other, as women do, and Gabby witters on about some people calling her Gabrielle and making her feel so snotty, d'you know what I mean? Rosalyn touches her elbow and says yes, she knows what she means, and I watch them perform their counterpoint of offering and acceptance, suggestion and concurrence, knitting their bond of conformity. Rosie. Gabby. Why on earth do adult, intelligent women diminish their names that way?

'Hello, Rosalyn,' I say, stubbornly, leading her in by both hands. Gabby announces that she'll get the coffees, remembers how Rosalyn takes hers and says, 'I won't risk getting one for Peta yet—it'll be stone cold by the time she gets here.'

'Oh dear,' Rosalyn says to me, without any trace of real dismay, 'has our artist been delayed?'

'Is the Pope Catholic? It's part of the job description, I'm afraid. No Bo again? Is it something I said?'

'He's very sorry' says Rosalyn, and starts taking off her mack. 'He really hated letting you down again—it's just that he's so busy at the moment ... I'm his sort of spokesperson, I hope you don't mind ...'

I don't answer. I'm mesmerised by the change in her. As she releases her hair from the mack collar, I can see that it's been expertly styled: the grey has softened into a light auburn, and it's been cut and layered into a new, younger jauntiness. She's discarded her frumpy blouse and pleated skirt, and is wearing a wrap dress in a fashionable print, which hugs her curves and reveals a flatteringly bolstered cleavage.

'Rosalyn!' I say, 'You look sensational!'

She smiles at me, and I realise she's wearing make-up.

'Well,' she blusters, 'I thought it was time for a bit of an MOT. Nothing like impending grannydom to kick you into gear …'

I hold her gaze until she looks away. *This*, I tell myself smugly, *is nothing to do with grannydom.*

Gabby pops in with our coffee.

'Wow! Mrs—Rosie, you look *fab*!'

Off they go into the obligatory inventory: which hairdresser did exactly what, where the dress was bought, the doubts and resolutions involved in finding the right size and colour … I wait for them to finish, and enjoy the way Rosalyn's body moves in that dress. I'm awash with a love and desire that's enriched by memory and time. I could never feel this way for someone like Freddie Pannage. Sitting in my office, watching my ex-lover's expressive face and full figure, I revel in an emotion I can only describe as bliss.

Before Gabby's wrapped up her admiration of Rosalyn's new look, there's a small tornado at the gallery door and Peta Krantz is here. Five feet tall, with a stubbling of orange hair and clashing scarlet lipstick, she flaps about like a parrot in her multicoloured hand-woven cape, and forces our attention back to the auction, and the worthy cause. She shows us her draft designs. One is a globe, etched with continents and containing a pair of shackles. Another is a half-open eye, with rolls of glass to represent the eyelids and a splash of colour for the eyeball; inside this one is a key.

'I am torn between them' she tells Rosalyn, diving over the drawings to speak into her face.

'I'm not surprised' says Rosalyn. 'They're both so wonderful.'

She looks happy and beautiful. I can hardly drag my eyes to the designs spread out before us.

'I have a thought' says Peta in her strange, tinny voice, 'to attach the two and make them one piece. To have the eye as a moon, a satellite, you take my meaning?'

'Amazing' says Rosalyn. Then, 'I suppose my only worry is that it's going to be so delicate—I'll be scared to touch it, I'm such a butterfingers …'

I think about the kingfisher, snug in its box in the cupboard at the back. I think of her opening it, timidly touching the pool of blue, with this same expression of delight and awe. Peta says,

'Ach! Don't worry. Glass can be as tough as brass if it needs to be.'

The way she says that word, 'brass', with the exaggerated 'r' and the harsh vowel, makes it sound like a trumpet-blast. I catch Rosalyn's eye as she suppresses a giggle. I wish Peta would put away her drawings and go. But of course Rosalyn gets her talking, not just about the glass but about her childhood, her family, the turn of events that brought her here. Peta is more than happy to oblige. She's so garrulous that I wonder how she copes with an occupation that's essentially so solitary. Maybe she saves it all up for these occasions, when she bursts back into the populated world. She certainly seems to be unloading several years' worth of reminiscences. Her narrative is like her work—a scavenging of scraps and rags, corners of memory, a jumble of associations: it's impossible to step in and round things off at the end of a phrase, because no phrase has an end.

217

'…and my poor mother, who was always a peaceable woman' she's saying, 'and who always tried to get on with everyone, even my uncle, who was a short-tempered man—ah, well, my uncle, you see he was crazy at that time, coming round, threatening our neighbour, who was a very kind old man who made leather sandals, in fact some of my designs are my tribute to him, Hassan, and the times I played there with his daughter …'

And so it goes on, and Rosalyn is soaking it in, apparently enthralled with it all. Only I can sense the other thoughts tugging at her attention.

'You cannot understand the craziness of it all' Peta is saying, 'How friendship can turn into hatred like this—' and she flips her gnarled old hand palm-upward on the sketches— 'from nothing, from nothing … You know, it is as if you suddenly started to smash your neighbours' windows and go after them with guns, because they were Scottish, or Welsh…'

'Well,' I say, hoping to cut it short, 'if they were *Welsh*, fair enough …' and I shrug comically, but the joke falls flat. Rosalyn gives me a thunderous glare and Peta just looks baffled.

'Nathan', says Rosalyn, 'that's not funny.'

'Sorry …' I give her my best naughty-boy look, then turn to Peta. 'Sorry, Peta, that was crass. I was just being silly.'

Peta is quite thrown. She says, 'Yes, yes, I understand' and starts to shuffle her drawings. Her colour is rising, and she flinches when Rosalyn touches her arm.

'Honestly, Peta, take no notice' Rosalyn says. 'It's just stupid schoolboy humour. He doesn't mean it.'

'I know' says Peta, and throws a smile somewhere to the left of me. 'I do understand. We made jokes like this too. My uncle had this sense of humour.'

I can see that I'm about to lose Rosalyn's sympathy altogether. I turn my chair to face Peta directly.

'Peta', I say, 'I'm a bloody idiot. Honestly, I hardly knew what I was saying. It's a kind of default. I'm half Welsh myself ...'

'That's not really the point' says Rosalyn through gritted teeth.

'Please forgive me' I plead, bending almost double to try and see Peta's lowered face. 'I really didn't mean to make light of your experience.'

Eventually she looks at me, with a glint in her eye.

'There is nothing to forgive' she says. 'It isn't your fault that you are such a pampered generation.'

Suddenly Rosalyn says,

'Nathan's friend was in Kosovo, did you know? Taking photographs—I mean, serious ones, documenting events ...' This is a jolt. I can't gather my thoughts for a moment, and she chunters on: 'They were shocking ... *searing*. I went to his exhibition ...'

Peta is putting away her drawings now, grim-faced; she doesn't want to hear about photographs and exhibitions. But I'm holding my breath. I can't move. Is this being said for my benefit? Peta might as well be on another planet. So Rosalyn came to see *Aftermath*. That was three years after she'd left. She must have known she was likely to bump into me there—or at any rate Scott, who would have spoken to her, reopened channels of communication ...

'Well,' Peta is saying, 'I have chattered on so much, as I always do, and I must rush now ...'

And Rosalyn starts gushing about the designs again, and telling Peta how brilliant she is, and what a tremendous boost this will be to the campaign, and how impatient she is to see the finished product—she says all this, because I can't speak at all. I'm too busy arranging the events of the past few weeks, since Rosalyn's casual reappearance, into a new story. Rosalyn just happening to pass the gallery with her shopping trolley? Rosalyn walking down the road, just by chance, when I was emerging from Astey's with Freddie? All coincidence, or the culmination of long years of stealthy monitoring? I'm in a kind of fog, a kind of madness. I have to get rid of Peta.

With a mammoth effort I snap out of it and make a gracious parting speech, congratulating Peta on her superb work, thanking her for her generosity of time and creativity, etc, etc. She seems to have got over my little quip, and even stretches up to give my chin a playful pinch.

'You have great charm' she announces, and winks. 'You know how to win a woman's heart—doesn't he?' she adds to Rosalyn, whose blush spreads delightfully over her arms and chest and face.

Peta leaves, and I shut the office door. We can hear her voice and Gabby's spiralling upwards in competition, but in here, all is silent, and charged. I turn to Rosalyn, who's smoothing her dress, and making a half-hearted move towards her coat and bag. That wraparound does nothing to hide her quickening breath. Eventually, she says,

'Well ...'

I open my mouth to challenge her: *so you went to Scott's show?* But some connection between my brain and my voice has been snipped clean in two. And I've lectured myself over and again since that conversation in the park—don't rake it over. No questions. No demands. It'll only drive her away again. So I can't trust myself to speak—because there's so much I *do* want to ask, and demand. After a moment, my continued silence forces her to look at me. Then, finally, I find one meaningless word to fill the air:

'Well.'

I take a step forward. We're almost touching now. I prolong this exquisite anticipation, and Rosalyn's eyes slide away. When I judge her to be on the verge of taking flight, I reach for her wrists. She gives a little nervous laugh, but doesn't step away. I move my hands to her waist, and after an instant, pull her close. I don't kiss her yet. I lay my cheek against hers, breathe in her scent, move my arms to lock her against me. I think about the time that's passed, count the years, and my arms tighten until she gives a small sound from her throat, half resistance, half relief. Then I kiss her. Her arms are limp at first, but I go on kissing her until they find their way to my shoulders, then wind around my neck, and we're so firmly clamped together that it seems we can never be prised apart.

52

Three years after Rosalyn.

I couldn't understand how those years had passed, how I'd lived through them. How can you measure absence? How do you gauge a loss? There's nothing there to gauge. But I began to notice that time had elbowed its way into my grief and my stubborn, stupid hope. I might stare through the window for an hour, without seeing her; then I'd find myself back there after attending to some task or taking a phone call, and three more hours had sneaked by, with no Rosalyn. The time between one thought of her and the next was starting to expand. That didn't mean that I ever marked off the slamming of the door, the screaming of abuse, as a final event. Even when she'd taken her things, I hadn't drawn a line under our story, not at all. But she was becoming a soft hum in my mind, rather than a shout of despair: a background to the rest of my life, like the traffic on the dual carriageway. I'd started applying myself to finding a suitable site for my gallery. The search, the purchase, the conversion of the site, all provided useful clutter to fill the hours. I supervised everything, down to the last detail, annoying the builders with my constant badgering presence. They hammered and scraped and buzzed and puzzled over plans, and I stood at the centre of it all, breathing in sweet sawdust, avoiding cables, measuring the exact distance required between shelves, the best lighting, shade of paint, placing of furniture … Always, at the back of my mind, envisaging the moment she would open the door and see this little galaxy I'd created in her honour. And at the end of the day I'd go home to my personal collection, to my favourite, private pieces of glass, and I'd caress their smooth, unchanging surfaces; and then I'd go to the cabinet to study the fulgurites, trace their ancient veins with my eyes alone, knowing one touch of my hand could turn those fragile miracles to dust. When 1997 passed into 1998, I hardly noticed. As 1998 turned to 1999, I made a resolution: to ration my thoughts of Rosalyn, to save them up as a promise after a day's work. She'd become a fantasy, which was easier in many ways, as fantasies were at least partly under my control.

The gallery opened for business on 12th April. We had a bout of strange weather that week: mild, springlike sunshine, then sudden showerings of snow. I remember sitting in the main gallery a few days after our launch party, reading the paper and basking in the heat as passers-by slid through the slush, braced against the onslaught. My first assistant, a rather earnest woman called Chloë, wasn't due to arrive for a couple of hours, and I was only really there to get myself out of the apartment. Kosovo was in the headlines again. A NATO pilot had bombed a refugee convoy, mistaking it for Yugoslav military. I hadn't particularly followed events in the Balkans, or taken a view for or against the NATO bombings. I was no wiser than anyone else about the issues and animosities. But I did think of Mergim, whenever another story reached us of atrocities and massacres; I thought of his shy smile and wary eyes. He'd been moodier than Arber, less self-assured. Wars get more visual as technology and time move on. In the First World War, cinema audiences were horrified by grainy footage of soldiers going over the top, flailing into star-shapes as they were hit. That film turned out to be a staged version of real events, but it fooled observers, who could be heard crying out in their plush seats: 'Oh God, they're dying!'
No such shocked realisation nowadays. Pictures flow into our papers, onto our screens, past our eyes and daily preoccupations, eliciting a tut, a shake of the head—broken and bloodied children, held aloft by keening parents; rows of corpses, displayed as proof of a point, their eyes still open, their jaws loosened. I would look at those faces sometimes, wondering if I might recognise Mergim and

223

recall his expression of quiet elation when Dino praised his work.

'This boy will be a craftsman', I remember Dino saying. 'He has the gift.'

On that morning in April I also thought of Arber, and on an impulse, made a call to one of my contacts at Zenada to ask whether he was still there. It took some enquiries, of course—my contacts couldn't be expected to know who the *cleaners* were—and without result. No, Arber wasn't working there any more, and nobody knew where he'd gone.

I mentioned it to Scott that evening. I said,

'I hope he doesn't turn up on one of your hunting trips. That would be a real waste. He had a skill.'

Scott's mouth shrugged.

'I doubt I'd remember him if he did. And anyway they all get to look the same way once they fall off the radar. Dirt and disease, it all chips away at the differences. Anyway …' He stretched his arms above his head and talked on through a yawn. 'I don't think I'll be taking many more hunting trips. Not round here, anyway. I'll be needing a change of scenery soon. Maybe you've set me on the right track.'

So Scott started his Balkan project, and I had no-one to blame but myself. He gave up the hunting trips, as he'd predicted, and now spent his nights reading up on the Balkan situation instead. I already had a desktop computer, and Scott was a great fan of the internet, though in those days it was rather clunky. I'd hear that strange hiss and blare of the dial-up connection, and know he was settling in for a few hours' research. (When he was out, I occasionally tried a search for Rosalyn's name, but I never found her.) Scott had become quite subdued, quite different, around this time. I put it down to the depressing nature of his studies. I tried to talk him out of going. But he didn't even hear me.

Mother and Uncle Don invited us to the villa for a farewell meal. I had to beg Scott to accept, but he *did* accept, which was a mark of the change in his behaviour. The meal was pleasant enough, and we all got a bit drunk. Don toasted 'the happy snapper' with champagne; then there was white wine with the fish, red wine with the meat, dessert wine with the pud ... and so on. I don't remember much about it, but I do have a hazy recollection of Mother grabbing Scott's hand and saying, 'Please be careful, Scottie-dog. War is the worst of everything. It breaks people, even people like you.'

I remember that because of the way Scott listened, and looked at her, without scorn or sarcasm. I had the impression he was crossing a line.

'Never thought of you as a war photographer, sunshine,' said Don, and he struggled with the word 'photographer'. I bridled a little, at this casual use of *my* nickname.

'This isn't war photography,' Scott pointed out. 'Not really. I won't be on the front line, or anything like that.' He seemed to be reassuring himself. 'This is more ... aftermath.'

'Oh, Scottie-dog,' said Mother, and my mind's eye sees her snuggling right up to him, but that may be an exaggeration of memory. 'Aftermath,' she said, 'is the worst of it.'

But still, we drank and laughed and had a good evening, and I could tell that Mother and Don were pleased at my own progress. At one stage Don clapped me on the thigh and said,

'Life goes on, eh, sunshine? Life goes on.'

'Yes,' I agreed, raising my glass, which made everyone giggle hysterically. I seemed to be speaking from under water. 'Life goes on, and Scott will come back safe and sound, and take this beautiful woman's picture!'

'Oh, Christ, Nathan, not this again,' laughed my mother, and

'Too darn right, about time,' drawled Don in his appalling American accent, and, becoming suddenly serious, Scott gazed into Mother's eyes and said,

'Yes, please. Please let me take your photograph.'

I think we were all stunned by this different version of Scott. Perhaps he was reverting to his real self, who knows? As I've said, I knew nothing about him. Where did he come from? Did he have a family, a secret love, a criminal record? No idea. He seemed to have plenty of friends and contacts, but they never actually appeared within our walls. Scott Carter, a man with no past and no future—just a witness to the present, constantly clicking away, recording scenes and events without comment, without judgement.

I was bereft, when the time came for him to go.

'How long will you be away?' I asked, for the umpteenth time.

'Nathan,' he murmured, squatting to wrestle with a strap on his suitcase, 'you'll be fine. Go to the gallery. Every day, all day, whatever the weather, however you feel. Work like a slave from dawn till dusk. Work till you're too knackered to think, about your broken heart, about the shit that happens, about man's inhumanity to man …'

And then he was on his feet, buzzing with nervous energy, checking his watch, eager to get on with it. 'You'll be fine', he said, as he left.

And I was fine, of course. I did exactly as he'd told me to do: I worked myself to a frazzle every day and sank into a torpor with my brandy and my music every night. The new millennium came and went, with its preposterous predictions and celebrations. I coped with it. The year moved on. I visited design studios, exhibitions, galleries, following my instincts, refining my core collection, finding longer and longer moments of relief from thoughts of Rosalyn in those cool, unyielding, unfeeling glass creations.

53

Now that Rosalyn and Scott had both gone, Mother and Don took me up as their project. It became their mission to 'cheer me up'. I think Mother might have had a nagging worry that, without 'Scottie-dog' to keep an eye on me, I might descend into a dangerous depression. She was wrong about that: Scott had already shown me the path out of that fog, and I doubt he'd have left me alone if he'd thought I might stray off it. Still, between them, Mother and Don contrived to fill virtually every minute of my free time with theatre visits, meals, functions and parties. When I put my foot down and insisted on some time alone, there would be a phone call to arrange the next distraction. So, yes, it's pretty clear, now, that they were on some sort of suicide watch.

Uncle Don threw me a birthday party at the villa. As usual, there was no card from Rosalyn. Even three years down the line, I found it almost beyond belief that someone who had been so sentimental about birthdays and anniversaries could have let the blade cut them off so completely. (I'd been sending birthday cards every year to Auntie Monica's address—and she must have seen them, I suppose. Every year I counted off the hours as she failed to respond to those cards. And every year I reached the end of her birthday in a frenzy of rage and self-pity, as no response came.) Because of what they had been, and what they'd become, I dreaded my birthdays, and preferred not to think about them.

'I haven't got many friends,' I pointed out. 'I'm not the partying kind.'

'No ...' Mother conceded. 'I do wonder, sometimes, whether you were swapped for someone else's baby.' She was tucked into a corner of Don's white couch, peering through her reading glasses at a notebook, where she'd already started planning the event. 'But you don't need to worry about any of that, sweetheart.

Don will provide.'

And Don did, indeed, provide—venue, catering, music and guests. It was Dad's wake all over again. When you've got the cash to splash, as Uncle Don would put it, you don't have to bother making friends. They can be hired by the hour. So I appeared at my own birthday party like a celebrity cameo, ushered in to the purple-and pink-lit villa to the cheers and whoops of total strangers. They'd gone to a lot of trouble, Mother and Don. Each area of the villa was devoted to a different activity: DJ and dancing in the lobby—coloured lights and noise bouncing off every shiny surface; a casino in the games room; a caricaturist and a magician in the garden room; movies showing end-to-end in the cinema room. The garden was strung and lit with Chinese lanterns, and tables glistened with food and drink. The place was heaving. Some of my clients and artists were there, but not many. Taff was there, of course, and gave me a book about glass—I already had it, but it was a thoughtful gift. Pippa wished me 'many happy returns, Mr Hill', as she bustled past in charge of the catering. I recognised a few of Don's employees and made the rounds, thanking them for being there, dredging up some small talk. Then Mother appeared with a couple of young women I'd never seen before. She stood dwarfed between them, one arm lightly around each slim waist.

'Nathan—Penny and Dara are *fascinated* with glass. You *must* tell them all about the gallery ...'

Penny was a green-eyed beauty with S-waves of golden-red hair and freckly skin. Dara was an American brunette, slightly shorter than Penny and vibrantly *fascinated* with absolutely everything. 'Wow!' she hollered over the party din, 'You're kidding me!' she yelled, her whole face dazzled with amazement at every word I shouted. Penny was quieter, but the green eyes were fixed on mine with assured intent. In the background, I noticed Don leaning on the specially set-up bar, drink in his hand, waving around to emphasise whatever chat-up he was delivering to another *fascinated* and attractive young woman. Penny and Dara moved closer in the crush. I could feel Dara's breast against my arm, and Penny's golden hair swished against my ear every time she spoke to me. I began to understand that these were hired guests *plus*. This was a two-for-one birthday deal, courtesy of Uncle Don and Mother, with love and kisses on your special day. It was such a long time since I'd experienced pure desire, untroubled by love, misery, anger or shame. In fact I couldn't really remember a time when I'd had a simple, self-contained physical encounter with anyone. Even in my student days, when I dated the occasional sunburnt blonde, there was always the fear that she would want more than I could offer. Now, I was presented with a transaction, nothing more or less. Dara's hand found its way to my right buttock, and Penny's lips sat neatly in my ear as she delivered her cliché:

'It's so *loud* in here … shall we find somewhere quieter?'

The following Monday, instead of going straight to the gallery, I went to sit in the swivel chair and thank Don for his generosity.

'We didn't see you for much of the evening, son …' he said, with just a touch of a leer.

'No … sorry …' I swivelled the chair out of his eyeline. I couldn't bring myself to swap nudge-wink jokes with my uncle. I heard him give a little laugh, then he said:

'Money buys sex, and sex makes money. Nothing to be ashamed of, sunshine. It's all about business, innit? Doesn't have to be about *lerve*. Take it from me, you're better off with sex, it's easier.'

I swung the chair from side to side, thinking: *that's what Mother would prefer.* She wanted me to be like Don, I decided. Sex and money. Uncomplicated, unthreatening. I swung one complete circuit, then asked, without looking at him,

'Have you ever been in love?'

There was a pause, but I didn't steer the chair back to face him. I just waited. When he finally replied, he sounded like a different man.

'Yeah, I've been in love. But only once. And that was never going to work out.' His voice expanded back into its usual cartoon bluster: 'Better off with the lovely ladies of the trade, my son. You'll get a first class service and no awkward small print.'

So that's what I did. I satisfied my physical needs with professional women— escorts, I suppose you'd call them, but I just called them by their names. They were good company, attentive in bed, and the financial side was dealt with discreetly and straightforwardly. Sometimes I just wanted company. If I felt a lonely, Rosalyn-tainted evening looming ahead, and couldn't face Don and Mother, I might call Penny or Dara—both highly intelligent and interesting women—and go out for a meal or a drink. In fact, over the years, Penny and Dara both became friends. They stopped charging, and we stopped having sex. We just went on liking each other.

One afternoon, I'd called in to see Mother before setting off to the opera. She had a heavy cold; by that time she hardly ever left the villa, anyway. We had tea, interrupted now and then by one of Mother's violent sneezes and impatient curses. 'This *fucking* cold! And what are you seeing tonight? Pass me those tissues' she croaked.

'*Cosi Fan Tutte*', I said, passing her the box.

'Oh, yes ...' she blew her nose. 'That's the one with the unconvincing disguises, isn't it? And some tiresome moral about women getting their come-uppance for having fun ... Who are you going with? Anyone I know?'

231

'She's called Fay,' I said. 'We haven't met yet, but apparently she likes opera.'
Mother smiled. Her nostrils were red and flaky and she had a little pot of
moisturiser on the arm of her chair, which she kept dabbing at and smoothing over
the sore skin.

'I'm so glad you're keeping good company these days', she said. 'It's the best way.
And thank god you can do it nowadays without all the risks ...' She ferreted
around in the tissue box for a moment, possibly aware that I might take offence,
being the result of just such a risk.

'Well,' I said half-heartedly, 'it keeps my mind off things, I suppose.'

'Yes. Yes, exactly, sweet boy. And, you know, it's so much *healthier*, now that
you've got your home to yourself ...'

'Healthier?' I was genuinely baffled. She sneezed again, and did a lot of moaning
and mopping up. 'Healthier?' I repeated. 'What do you mean?'

'Well, you know—it was getting to be such a, a ... *claustrophobic* atmosphere.
Wasn't it? The three of you, in such close proximity, and all those complex, you
know ... *involvements.*'

'Involvements?' I was shifting in my seat now. 'What sort of *involvements*?'
She tucked her tissue up her sleeve and gave me her amused look.

'You are a funnyosity, Nathan,' she said. 'With your collections of this and that,
and your doppelganger duo ...'

I knew where she was heading. 'Rosalyn and Scott were not a duo,' I snapped.

'You know very well they weren't. I mean, Rosalyn never wanted him living there.
She was just ...'

'No, no, no, I'm *quite sure* she didn't' agreed Mother, holding her hand up against
my irritation. 'I should think that's the *last* thing she wanted. Most awkward, I
should imagine. Better to keep things *separated.*'

And then she launched into a nasty, wracking cough, and I had to go and meet Fay the opera-lover, and the whole poisonous exchange ended there. I tried to dismiss it as another one of Mother's spiteful little attacks on Rosalyn—which is, of course, exactly what it was. Maybe it was a sort of belt-and-braces strategy: to make sure I never entertained the idea of a reconciliation. In a way, you could say it misfired. Because try as I might to shake it off, the poison was in my veins. From that night on, my obsession was back—but in a far fiercer, far more persistent form. From that night on, I was condemned to re-live my past, over and over again, in ever closer focus, through the distorted lens of jealousy.

54

One night I woke suddenly from a deep sleep and lay there listening, uncertain what had jolted me into consciousness. After a while I got up and went to the bathroom. As I opened the door I heard the discreet purr of the shower. I stared stupidly at the cubicle, wondering whether I'd left the water running the previous day. I slid the screen aside with a bang and reached for the switch, flinching at the water's icy sting. The water-jet vanished abruptly and there he was, curled up in a soggy heap on the floor, quaking with cold. Scott was back.

I had to haul him out by the armpits, half-drag him into the main room, where I dumped him by the fire and swamped him in towels, rubbing his sides and shoulders with urgent vigour. Eventually his eyes focused on the glowing panel of flame.
'Wall's burning up' he mumbled. Then he passed out.

I let him sleep there for a couple of hours. His mouth hung open and dry; his eyelids weren't quite closed, and a hairline of bloodshot white was visible beneath them. If it hadn't been for the jagged rise and fall of his ribcage under the towels, I might have feared the worst. When he woke I plied him with coffee. He accepted it placidly, and seemed to be recovering his wits. I sat on the floor beside him. He gave me a weakly mischievous look.
'Sorry, Nathe' he croaked. 'Should have let you know I was back.'
There didn't seem much point in asking, but I did nonetheless:
'Why were you lying in a cold shower?'
He shook his head. 'Just needed ... needed to sleep.'
'In stone-cold running water?'

'Needed … something … something going on. Noise. Feeling. I just can't sleep in silence, Nathan. Can't sleep if my head's working …'

I regarded him helplessly. I said,

'Your head's not working at all, as far as I can see.'

After a moment he announced,

'Feel a bit better now. I've been so tired, it's like … violence.'

He wouldn't say much more. I found his gear stacked up outside the apartment door, where anyone could have waltzed off with it. That alone told me what a state he was in. I brought it all inside, then told him I was taking him for breakfast. He nodded indifferently. His hair, cloudy from drying by the fire, shifted and shuddered around his head. I helped him dress, tugging and buttoning and buckling him into his clothes like a mother with her toddler; then I took him by the arm and navigated him out of doors, hoping the smack of dirty city air would liven him up. I walked him a mile and a half, and by the time we reached Astey's he was taking his own weight. I bought him a full breakfast, and he managed to eat half. I sat opposite him, arms folded, and waited until I judged him ready to speak. Then I ordered more coffee and asked:

'Tough gig, then? Tougher than you thought?'

He pricked at his food with the fork. 'No. I knew it would be ugly. I knew what to expect.'

I tried another tack.

'Did you get what you wanted?'

His eyes widened at his plate. 'Oh, plenty of good shots. Plenty. Can't fail, when people turn on each other …' He petered out and shrugged. He let the fork clang onto the plate and sat back, giving up the effort. And suddenly I didn't want any answers. I didn't want to know what he confronted on his trip into aftermath. I had no need for lessons in human nature: I knew very well what we all become, as soon

235

as we're let off the leash. I said,

'I assume you've been taking all manner of crap out there.'

He shrugged.

'They all do, when they can. Helps them cope.'

I thought for a moment, then said, 'Look. If it helps you do the work—do what you have to do. As long as you don't bring it into my home. OK?'

A sneer rucked his mouth for an instant, and he said:

'Oh, no. I wouldn't dream of sullying your innocence, Nathan.' Then he dropped the sarcasm and just sounded worn out: 'It keeps me focused. Like you and your coffee, your brandy, whatever it is you need to face the day. Just helps me get on with it. Sometimes … this time, it took a bit more help. That's all. Only …'

I waited, without pushing him. This man had been moving through my waking and sleeping thoughts for months, delivering words with varying degrees of innocence or salaciousness, depending on my mood, seducing and being seduced by the woman I'd called my wife. But there was no comparison between the two Scotts, the Scott created by my jealousy and the traumatised, exhausted man slumped opposite me at Astey's. This was the real Scott, of course: fixated on his work, preoccupied with the failings of humanity, largely indifferent to individual human beings. How could I have imagined him cooking up an intricate plot just to be near Rosalyn? I knew there would be a relapse, as soon as he was out of my sight; I knew that jealous logic would re-impose itself with all the old force. But here and now, it all seemed absurd. He seemed to have forgotten that he'd started another sentence. Eventually, I prompted him:

'Only?'

'Oh. Only, you don't have to worry about any of that, now—any of "the crap". I'm done with it. It's a different planet out there. It's a kind of hell, Nathan. It's like, all the shit on the other side of your big glass wall—and then you suddenly realise there *is* no big glass wall. Nothing between you and the shit.' He leaned forward and his eyes swung from side to side. 'I met some very scary bastards out there, Nathe. Not just the arseholes with guns and uniforms. Much worse. Men who didn't need guns. Men with quiet voices. Men who are doing business, out there. Making the shit pay.'

I paid the bill and we left Astey's and walked—nowhere in particular; I just wanted to tire him out in a more sane and normal way, so that he didn't need to sleep in a deluge. We stuck to the better part of town, and he seemed more than willing to do that. No snide comments, this time, about the shabby-chic furniture shops, or the Guardian-readers sitting over their al fresco espressos, or the abstract bronze sculptures in the art gallery window. Once, he stumbled as we walked and I slipped my arm into his. When we passed a prettily lit bookshop, I couldn't resist commenting that Rosalyn had loved that place. Then I felt ashamed, and embarrassed that I still seemed stuck in my childishly circling thoughts. So I started to waffle on about some of the new people I'd met—Penny, opera-loving Fay—but that sounded crass and impossibly shallow, compared with his experiences. In the end, as we finally turned back towards the apartment, I said: 'You probably shouldn't have gone, Scott. You're no war photographer. There's no shame in that. It's just not your thing.'

He twisted away from me, suddenly straight-backed, two red circles flowering on his cheeks.

'You're wrong,' he said, so loudly that a couple passing hastened their step. 'I *am* a war photographer,' he all but shouted. 'Shit-hot, me. I can do it. Catch the moment, frame the shot, switch off everything but the beauty of that scene. Sick, obscene, atrocious, evil—I can't help seeing the beauty.'

'Not *beauty*' I offered, pressing the air with my hand as if that would calm him

down. 'You don't have to see it as *beauty*. Dramatic—yes; significant—yes, but—'
'Wait till you see what I've got' he said. His eyes closed, but I could see them moving behind the lids. He took a long breath in through his nostrils, then reached out towards me. I linked my arm with his and we started walking again. To my amazement, a few minutes later, he said:

'No word from Rosalyn, then. While I was gone.'

'No,' I said. 'Of course not.' Then I admitted: 'I had to drive by her Auntie Monica's house a couple of weeks back. I even thought about calling in. You know, just to ask after her, just to … Anyway, I didn't.'

'That's right, mate,' said Scott. 'You hang on to your pride.'

He was just talking. That's what I realise now. Just filling space with sound. His eyes were still half shut. He was talking to escape his own private torments. But at the time, I watched him with renewed suspicion. And that night, even as I listened for the sound of the shower, I was interrogating him in my mind: *why did you ask after Rosalyn?*

55

Old men, young men, lined up dead on a kerb. Hands tied, earth on their faces, dug up and laid out like a butcher's window. An old woman in an apron, screaming at a soldier. The soldier has a gun as big as a child, but the old woman is shouting into his face, pointing at his chest, and the soldier is looking over her head, elsewhere. A little girl, sitting on the side of a road, no older than six or seven. This was the picture that drew the attention, the star shot of *Aftermath*, Scott's next exhibition, which was later turned into a glossy book with brief commentaries.

'That picture will be the making of me, Nathe,' he told me. 'That's the one. It's the look in her eyes, you know? Her home was wrecked, she saw her father beaten up, all the safe, good people in her life were suddenly out to destroy her. She's lost it all. She knows everything.'

He worked as assiduously as ever on developing the exhibition, but without the usual zeal. He mentioned the little girl several times.

'I just had to leave her there,' he said, once. 'I didn't even ask her name. Didn't want to get too *fucking involved*. So I left her there.'

'Someone must have been able to help her,' I said, trying to reassure him. He shrugged.

'Who knows? I don't know. I just take pictures.'

'Well, your pictures will ... will bring it home to people. Won't they? They'll show it like it is.'

He smiled without meeting my eye.

'That's OK, then', he said.

The lost girl's desolate gaze had made it to the mainstream press before the show: trimmed and glossed on colour supplement covers, it repeated its indictment in stalls and newsagencies all over the western world. She was probably one of the few people who would never set eyes on it.

56

Soon after the fuss about *Aftermath* had died down, Scott took his portrait of
Mother. As I've said before, Mother's age was always a moveable feast, but she
must have been 70 by this time, even by the most generous calculations. And yet,
to my eyes, she'd lost none of her vivacity or charisma. She had a good figure, if a
little squarer around the hips and shorter in the waist than had once been the case.
She had an expensive hair stylist, naturally, who cleverly blurred the line between
white and blonde, and her face was still clear-skinned and well-defined. I looked
forward to seeing what a talented man like Scott could do: I had no doubt that he
could convey what nobody else had caught: my mother's unique spark.

He'd refused a fee for the shoot, and he refused to show any of us the result.
'I'm saving it,' he said. Nothing Mother or Don said would shift him. It nearly
drove Don crazy. He'd boasted to everyone who'd listen that Scott Carter was
working at his villa 'free and gratis'. He seemed to believe it reflected on his own
canniness, that he'd secured a bargain nobody else could hope to bag. And now he
was helpless! He'd paid nothing, and he owned nothing: this picture was Scott's
property, and for the time being, Scott chose to keep it to himself.

He told me he was off 'the crap', and I believed him. He'd also stopped his hunting
trips.
'I've got one more show to get out of my system' he confided. 'There'll be hunting
shots in there. And some new ones. And then I'm changing course.' He wouldn't
go into more detail than that.

One morning, Scott came back from a run, sodden and breathless, and went to have

241

a shower. This running was something new: he'd taken it up to work off the excess energy that seemed to alternate with bouts of exhaustion. He usually slipped out very early, and would be back, washed and dressed, by the time I got up. This time, though, he was later than usual. I was preparing to go to the gallery, and needed the bathroom. An hour went by and he was still in there. Remembering that awful day of his return from Kosovo, I panicked, and started thumping on the door. He opened it wearing a towel and, oddly, his still sweaty long-sleeved T-shirt. He was scratching and kneading at his hair with one hand.

'What the hell have you been doing in there?' I squeaked.

His fingers searched his scalp.

'I can't get it out' he said. 'I can feel it in there, but I can't get hold of it …'

'Get hold of what?'

He dipped his head to show me, but all I could see was a patch of raw skin under the wet hair, where he'd been pummelling his head with hot water. His hand shot back to the same place and I grabbed his wrist.

'Stop it' I said. 'You've nearly drawn blood, for Christ's sake.'

'Can you get it out?' he pleaded. 'There's something crawling in there. I just can't get it out.'

At his insistence, I examined his bowed head. I was aching for a pee, but he wouldn't leave until I'd searched every follicle. I was like the nit nurse. I began to see things myself, crawling and creeping between the hairs. But of course there was nothing there. I said,

'Maybe you've got an allergy to the shampoo. That'll be it. Some chemical in the shampoo.'

He pretended to agree. He said,

'It's criminal, the way they sell that shit and call it "natural".'

I started buying an 'organic' shampoo, and he took to wearing a hat, a woollen hippy thing, to protect his head from his own hands. Sometimes I saw him, nevertheless, digging his fingers between the thick fibres in search of invisible bugs.

One of my prized possessions is an 18th-century cabinet, custom-made to store an engraver's tools. Unfortunately most of the original contents were missing, but I use it to store some bits and pieces of my own. I've got a tungsten glass cutter in there, which craftsmen use to coax a split into sheet glass without shattering it. There are several diamond-tipped engravers in different sizes. A shaping tool, with a razor edge, which slices hairline cuts into hot glass. I've never used them myself. As I've made clear, I haven't a knack for the creative side. But it pleases me to pull open the shallow mahogany drawers, to hear the soft rattle of their brass handles, and to see the tools of the trade set out in smart ranks, ready for service. I'm a meticulous man. I notice when my routines or arrangements are disrupted in any way. I don't make a frequent habit of checking the tools in the cabinet, but one Sunday I'd been to inspect some new acquisitions in the gallery office, and was intrigued by the decoration on a piece by Phil Seymour. He's a young Seattle artist, who usually makes exquisite dishes with intricately coloured and arranged little flowers of glass, cut from canes layered like Brighton rock. The piece that held my attention, though, was a new departure for Seymour—no buds of colour this time, but a sunburst bowl in the palest breath of gold, engraved with a series of concentric circles, each one slightly denser than the circle below, bamboozling the eye so that the whole thing seemed to spin like a top. I was transfixed by those subtle gradations of line. So when I got home I looked through my cabinet, comparing the thicknesses of engravers, and generally admiring the tools—the way each one had a specific and obscure purpose, the way they'd been moulded to the craftsman's hand and needs. When I opened the third drawer down, I was

243

immediately aware of an anomaly. It was minimal—most people wouldn't have noticed at all—but to me it was like a bum note in a chord. The shaping tool was facing the wrong way. Its blade is shaped broadly as a triangle, with a curved apex; it's offset from the handle, so that the base and the side draw into a lethally sharp corner—the tip which scores the glass. I always put it in place with that tip pointing to the right. Don't ask me why—I just do; if it points to the left, it jars. So I knew, as surely as I'd know a slap in the face, that someone— Scott—had opened the drawer and moved the shaper. I picked it up and scrutinised it, so closely that I almost pierced my own eyeball. There was a blemish, a tiny dark spot, right at the very sharpest extremity. I replaced the shaper and shut the drawer.

That night I waited until he'd gone to bed, until I was sure he'd be deeply asleep. Then I got up, crept into his room like a burglar and stood over him. His left arm was thrust across his forehead, palm up, gleaming pale in the half-light from the uncurtained window. As my eyes grew accustomed to the semi-darkness, a pattern emerged: a pattern as precise and planned as any of the designs on my gallery shelves. A double row of small, superficial cuts, a perfect herringbone motif. Each 'V' cut to an exact length and depth, and left to form a dark red scar against the white flesh of Scott's inner arm. He'd left the main artery clear, but his handiwork extended halfway up his lower arm. He must have been doing this for quite a while. I thought about the morning runs, the long-sleeved sweatshirts that never revealed more than half an inch of flesh at the wrist. Scott Carter was keeping himself 'off the crap' in his own way, and Scott Carter never did anything by halves.

57

Scott didn't have to go looking for opportunities to show his work any more. People came asking. So even as the book of *Aftermath* was in production, he was planning a new exhibition, this time at the flashy new Photographic Arts Centre, funded and heavily promoted by *Lens* Magazine and none other than good old Mendel, who made the most of the tenuous connection, with pictures from *Broken Glass* included in the expensive souvenir programme. He was more secretive than he'd ever been, during the preparations. I knew the show was called *Golden Thread*; I saw the pre-show hype, of course, along with everyone else, and its promise of 'images of life and death—from Scott Carter'. That was all I knew. Nothing else was needed, by that time: just his name was enough to draw the crowds.

Ironically, during the build-up to *Golden Thread*, even though Scott told me nothing about the work, he did give away more about himself than ever before. He was still living at the apartment. Strange, I suppose; I had to put up with some barbed comments from Uncle Don about it, though Mother seemed to have accepted the situation, perhaps because of my new, uncomplicated sex life. Scott himself made no mention of his living arrangements: he had his studio, and somewhere to eat and sleep, and that was a problem solved, from his point of view. I could have kicked him out: he could afford his own place, now. But it suited my twisted purposes to keep him close at hand. My jealousy was a work of art: I developed it, refined it, as privately as Scott went about his own work. If he was part of my daily world, I could observe, note, ask the occasional question, pick at a memory with him, and later, when he'd retreated to his room, no doubt to continue his grotesque engraving, I could review the results of our conversations, of his fleeting facial expressions, of anything and nothing at all. Yes, Scott and Rosalyn were definitely having a full-on sexual relationship. Yes, Scott and Rosalyn were attracted to each other but playing games, nothing more. Yes, Scott and Rosalyn were innocent of all charges and I'd gone a little insane. The conclusions followed in merciless succession; and tomorrow I could ask, test, monitor him all over again. Neither of us had mobile phones yet, so it was trickier to check his calls, but I did have an itemised phone bill and scrutinised that on a regular basis. (Scott never did get himself a mobile. 'It's like having a private eye on your tail', he used to say. 'Why would I want that?') If he'd moved out, how would I know who he was calling, seeing, thinking about, remembering? As long as he lived at the apartment, I could pretend to have a modicum of control.

So we often spent our evenings together, drinking, talking, listening to music, sometimes watching TV. Scott loved sport, which was a surprise to me. One November night he was lying on the floor, his head propped on two cushions, watching *Match of the Day*, and I was on the couch, reading, and he suddenly said, 'I only got into football because of Mack.'

'Mack?' I said, without looking up from my novel.

'Yeah. He supported Crystal Palace; so I did too.'

'Who's Mack?' I asked, marking my place with my thumb. I remembered the name. I'd heard him say it, almost every time our hunting trips ended up in The Cut. He didn't answer straight away—some momentum was building in the game, evidently: the commentator's voice soared, Scott's body stiffened in anticipation, his head craning up, until whatever excitement it was evaporated and the tinny voice and his body relaxed again. He showed no sign of returning to the exchange, so I said,

'I thought Mack was your dealer, or something?'

'My *dealer*?' He twisted round, with a look of ridicule that reminded me of my mother.

'Oh. It's just … you used to ask for Mack. At The Cut. And then disappear for a bit.'

'Jesus, Nathan. You wouldn't find my dealer in a shit-hole like The Cut. He drives a Merc and wears a Rolex. Anyway,' He turned his attention back to the screen, 'he's not my dealer now. We won't be crossing paths any more.' Then, after a beat, he added, 'Mack is my brother.'

I lost my place in the novel.

'Your *brother*? I didn't know you had a brother.'

He corrected himself, dully: '*Was* my brother, I mean.'

I put the novel on the floor and sat forward. His eyes were still following the match.

'Yeah …' he went on. 'I always copied him. Always copied Mack. Wanted to be like him. He was so … just, *alive*.'

He put his hands behind his head, muttered some profanity about the ref. I waited, then said,

'Older brother?'

'Younger,' he said, then gave a little humourless, soundless laugh. 'You'd never think so, though. The way I treated him. He was crazy, right from the start. My earliest memory is watching him trash the toys. There was nothing *vicious* about him,' he added quickly, turning his head briefly towards me, as if I'd made some accusation. 'He was just a tornado. Wanted to be out there, trying everything, lapping it all up, and I was so *boring*! Holed up in my room looking at old photographs and movie magazines. I couldn't be like him, but I tried. WOAH! That's a corner.'

I wanted to know so much more, but I didn't know how to ask.

'And … and he ended up …'

247

'Yeah. Like I said, crazy. Nothing was ever enough. Always went further than everyone else. I couldn't do it. I went so far, and then I lost my nerve.'

'Well ...' I ventured, '... maybe that was for the best, if he, you know ...'

'Mmm. You're probably right.' He sniffed, but didn't seem to be crying. 'I tried to get him help. He didn't want it. So ...' His chest rose and fell in a sigh. I said, 'When did he ...' (I considered the phrase 'pass on', but then considered his likely response) ' ... when did he die?'

'Just before Kosovo.'

I knew he meant his trip there.

'Is that why you went?' I said. He propped himself up on one elbow; the match had gathered pace again.

'Partly,' he said. 'Plus I'd got myself into ... PENALTY! FUCKING PENALTY! Aaaah, what a ...' He switched back to me in disgust. 'Yeah, I'd sort of got myself entangled.'

'What do you mean, *entangled*?' My heart was hammering hard. Was this going to be the confession I'd sought and dreaded?

'With a woman. Stupid move. Totally stupid. Just shouldn't have gone there, you know? Inappropriate.' He sat up eagerly, as the noise of the crowd and the commentator started to swell again.

'What woman?' I demanded. I was red in the face, now, but he saw nothing but an impending goal. 'Which woman? Someone I know? Why was it inappropriate?' My hands were shaking. The commentator was going hoarse and the crowd was roaring. He waved one hand towards me dismissively:

'No, no, no-one you—GOOOOOAL!!!'

An explosion from the TV and somehow Scott was up on his knees with his hands knotted into fists, arms locked straight up in the air, head thrust back, as if imploring the gods for mercy.

58

Golden Thread. It had the biggest hype of all Scott's exhibitions, but in some ways it was the most disappointing. The critics gave it a mixed reception. One praised its 'narrative clarity', and said it had 'more cohesion, more purpose than anything he has yet produced, even including the stunning *Aftermath.*' But another took the opposite view: 'Carter's eye for an arresting image is as keen as ever, but he is too inclined toward diegesis. He calls to mind a trendy vicar, using low-life illustrations to prove his credibility and pep up his sermon. For all his sincerity, he is still a vicar, and this is still a sermon.' Scott didn't much care what the critics said one way or another, and to most of the arts brigade he could do no wrong—he was one of the charmed circle, cool boy of the class: he could have hung his holiday snaps, and they'd be all over him with their tongues hanging out.

Just another exhibition. But for us, *Golden Thread* was a burning fuse, hurtling towards a detonation. And presently it would assume a wider significance, as Scott Carter's final show.

Don, Mother and I came to the preview together. They both loved all that— sashaying in to the steel-and-glass PAC building like movie stars at a Hollywood premier. It was heaving, of course, with Names and half-familiar faces, with an extra contingent of fake tans and hair transplants: Mendel's publicity team had done a good job excavating the moneyed bygones. A mellow jazz-classical crossover quintet was playing in one corner; champagne glasses twinkled; Names bellowed and brayed and occasionally remembered to look at the photographs. Don was kept busy back-slapping and delivering his barrow-boy wisdom with other rich businessmen; Mother chatted and joked with a couple of Russian ballet dancers and a newly famous stand-up comedian, for all the world as if they were the fans and she was the star. So it took them a while to catch up with the pictures. I was ahead of them: this was what I'd come for. Scott had maintained his secrecy right up to the wire, so I detached myself from the crush as soon as I could and started my slow journey around the walls.

A young man lying on a bed, in a room which could be a cell, but is probably in The Cut. It reminds me of a Holbein painting of Christ in his tomb. The man wears only his underpants, and every protruding rib and tendon is marked out with shadow. His arms are stretched on the bed at right angles to his body, and bent so that his forearms reach vertically into the air, his hands drooping at the wrists. The face is hollow-cheeked, a draping of skin on skull; the eyes are open but unseeing. He might be dead, the arms stiffened into place by rigor mortis—it's impossible to say. I stared at the poor wretch for a long time, wondering whether this might be Mack.

A very different scene, throbbing with life and urgency. A towpath at dusk. Possibly somewhere down behind The Navigator. A dirty glint of canal-water to the left; you can almost hear the splash of some sinister fall. Ahead, the hump of a brick bridge, and two parallel scenes playing themselves out, above and below. A group of teenagers on the parapet, caught in some act of foolery, pretending to push one of their number over the edge. And below, only just discernible in the murk, two figures carrying out a surreptitious transaction. One of them is about to turn—you can feel it. He knows we've seen him. It's the split second of realisation, the instant of thought before action, the scenting before the sighting. The danger in that photograph is palpable. Scott must have made it back to the road in the heartbeat before being spotted.

Some black-and-white shots he'd kept back from the Kosovo trip. A group of well-fed, balding men in open-collar shirts, sitting around a low table in what might be a hotel room or a private house, it's not clear. One of them has just taken a drag at a cigar; he squints suspiciously at us through a veil of smoke. Another is in the act of pouring a vodka—the light sculpts and thickens the stream of liquid, and catches a couple of drops splashing back out of the glass. One man, sitting directly opposite the camera, is smarter than the rest. He laughs a confident, natural laugh, showing his even teeth, tilting his head back a fraction so that the light fills his spectacle lenses and gives him a sinister, robotic appearance. I didn't know it at the time, but this was Viktor Gurmak, one of the ring of arms dealers subsequently jailed for money laundering, illegal sales to Islamist groups and drug-smuggling. Nothing in the photograph tells us who he or any of the others might be, or what they're discussing over their vodkas and cigars. But the whole scene is glutted with money, greed and menace.

There was an alcove in the exhibition space with only three photographs, one on each wall. As viewing these images would mean a decisive break away from the social throng, not many guests had bothered. One young woman whom I vaguely recognised but couldn't place was ahead of me as I slipped into the alcove's relative calm. She was standing at the third photograph, looking hard at a portrait whose details I couldn't yet make out. I saw her taking it all in, examining the features, then looking quickly to her right, into the crowd, and back to the picture. She did that again. My flesh began to prickle. I knew what was coming.

Meanwhile, I'd been taken aback and puzzled by the first photograph tucked away in that little space. It was from the photo shoot of Don at his villa, all those years

251

back, for that dreadful magazine *Edge*. Don as the Doer and Dealer. I remembered seeing various versions of this pose at the time: Don sitting in a white leather armchair, legs spread, the epitome of macho self-satisfaction. But this particular shot was different. This was an in-between picture, the exhalation, the offguard instant before that arrogant smirk reappeared on his handsome face. I'm sure Don had only relaxed for a sliver of a second—but Scott Carter never relaxed. He trapped it, that telling dip of expression, that fractional sinking into privacy, before Don Cutler, Self-Made Man, rocketed back to the surface. So what we see is a rich man, his body sprawled in imitation of his armchair, immaculately suited, surrounded by the sheen of wealth, and in his eyes a look of fleeting introspection, the look of a hunted animal facing its last encounter, the frightened but fatalistic look of a lost man.

I didn't know why it was there, that picture. To me, it was a jarring note, a filler. I couldn't see—or refused to see—the weave of the thread. I moved on to the second photograph. A young woman, a stranger to me. She's hard to classify. She could be one of the stick-thin catwalk models used in some of Shimmer's publicity before the backlash. Or she could be a starving refugee. Or one of the wraiths from The Cut. There's no context, so there's no way of knowing. We see her from the waist up, half turned towards us, glowering: she might be irritated at the intrusion, or confused, or assuming that defiant, rebellious chic look. She wears a sort of half-garment, almost like a dirty toga, hanging off her bony shoulders, the sleeveless armholes gaping to reveal a painfully thin torso. Her hair is cropped short, messy and sticky with dirt, maybe, or with gel. Her face looks unpainted, but could just as easily be cleverly contoured with subtle brushes and tones. It's not a black-and-white shot, but there's no colour in it.

252

By the time I reached the third photograph, the other viewer had gone, and I was alone in the alcove. I took a deep breath and stood before my mother's face. How can I explain what it was about that photograph that broke my heart? Nothing about her could be put into words—neither her loveliness, nor its loss, which Scott now presented to the world. I can't describe it because she doesn't look old in that photograph. She doesn't look haggard, or ugly; it's not what you would call an *unflattering* portrait. It neither flatters nor insults. It simply tells the truth. I stood before the lifesize portrait of my mother, eye to eye, and I saw regret, self-disgust, unfathomable sadness. I saw the rose, and the invisible worm.

I turned slowly around to watch the sway and clutch of the crowd. None of them, hardly any of them, had the faintest interest in tracing the exhibition's golden thread. But tomorrow the doors would open to the less manic, more observant paying public. How diligently would they follow the plot? And even if they did, would they see this tiny alcove as a sort of intermission, a random break in the thread? I wished I could see it that way. I was pretty sure Don and Mother wouldn't.

The preview buzzed along, and I wove my way aimlessly through the swarm of guests, all performing their parts and adding to the escalating volume. It could have been any party, anywhere: it had taken on its own character and its own momentum, and I was apart from it, a one-man audience. Shrieks of laughter, booming anecdotes, an operatic whooping and crashing of voices in every possible range, and every so often a small, brief pool of quieter conversation. A glass smashed somewhere, triggering a fanfare of cheers, groans and wisecracks. Through the forest of jewelled necks and trendy hair, I spotted Uncle Don and Mother, together but back to back, each entertaining a different group of admirers.

Had they seen the pictures in the alcove? Surely they must have sought out the portrait of Mother as soon as they had the chance. Did they see what I saw? Or was I over-thinking everything? Maybe there was nothing to see?

I wasn't sure what I was waiting for, but I was waiting. Towards midnight, the crowds started thinning out, taking their voices and poses somewhere louder and darker. I saw Scott near the door, receiving the plaudits and kisses as they left. I thought: *thank god, we got away with it*—though I didn't know exactly what I meant. I slipped away and went up to the first-floor loo. As I came back down the stairs I could hear one voice over the others. I couldn't make out the words, but I knew it was Don, and I knew this was no farewell or congratulation. I wanted to turn and run back upstairs until it was all over, but that wasn't really an option. I slowed my step and leaned over the bannister to see across the gallery floor. A few stragglers had paused mid-exit and were gawping at Uncle Don's tirade. He was towering over Scott, eyes popping, cheeks feverish with rage. I thought of that image in *Broken Glass*, of the two thugs squaring up at a demo. Scott made no response whatsoever. He didn't flinch, or avoid Don's eye, or change his posture at all. He regarded Don with something akin to boredom. I heard the word 'ponce', and the word 'cunt'—and I'd never heard Don say that word, even when raging about his incompetent staff. As if that word had flicked a switch, my mother was suddenly striding towards the two men. Without hesitation she seized Don's arm with both her hands and pulled at him. She didn't keep her voice down: in fact she projected it.

'That's enough, Don', she sang out, 'You've had quite enough pop for one evening, time to go home and sleep it off ...'

And yes, he was a bit drunk, so thankfully most of his rant had been incomprehensible. Mother apologised to the last trickling of guests, who now

254

laughed it off and went their own merry way, dismissing it all as an old man in his cups, thanks to Mother. One chivalrous young man offered to help but she waved him away. The security guard was already on hand by now. He was a foot shorter than Don but built like a tank; he took Don's arm and practically lifted him off his feet. Mother muttered some instructions and he nodded and led his charge away, Don staggering in his wake like an ungainly puppet. I was surprised not to see Mother following as they left the building and the guard hailed a car. Still at my vantage point halfway down the stairs, twisting uncomfortably for a better view, I saw her return to Scott, who was backed against the wall and watching her with an inscrutable expression. She spoke to him but her voice was low, now, rapid and urgent. I strained to hear, but only made out one word, driven at him with more emphasis than the rest: *Why?* He shook his head slightly and mumbled some reply, and then there was a pause, when they both just stood there and looked at each other. Then Mother's head dipped, as if she'd run out of all energy, and then she gathered herself again, reached up and touched Scott's face. She glanced into the gallery, and instinctively I drew back from the bannister and into the shadow of the stairwell. Seeing no one, she spoke to him again. All I could hear was the quiet stress she gave each word, and the tenderness, and the regret. When I dared to look again, the gallery door was swinging shut and Mother had gone.

59

I was weaving my own golden thread. Keeping my eye on Scott, checking his search history on my computer, re-spooling and re-imagining through the early hours, while Scott was in his own room, marking off another night's abstinence on his skin. And I saw nothing. Only now, with the distance of time and loss, I'm woken by an entirely different version of events. Is it possible? A 70-year-old woman and a man 30 years her junior? Ironically, it's quite easy to accept that my mother might have inspired infatuation and even desire—but in *Scott*? Despite all my diligently sustained suspicions about him and Rosalyn, I realise now that I could never quite believe he'd fall for *anyone*. I lie alone in my stark apartment and feel the pull of that old habit of mine, every bit as destructive and compelling as any powder or blade. Was it true? Was my mother the inappropriate love of his life? And then the same question that I heard her asking, that night of the preview, flashes like a firework through the muddle of my thoughts: *why*? Why did he include that picture, the portrait of Mother's decay? I thought I was clear of all this, the churning questions without reply, the keeling this way and that: yes, it must be true; no, it's just a small, new insanity. It's too late for all this. There's nobody left who can tell me the truth.

'It's the truth.'
That was all Scott would say at the time. I asked him, of course, as soon as we were back at the apartment.
'Why those pictures? Just explain to me. I'm not picking a fight, I just want to understand.'
There was no point accusing or criticising, I knew that. Nobody was ever going to tell Scott what he should or shouldn't do with his own work. He shrugged. He was

subdued, but otherwise apparently unmoved by the whole scene at the gallery. 'Because it's true,' he said. 'It's the truth.'

'What's true? Is it all about drugs? Are they mixed up in drugs, Uncle Don and Mother? Is it something to do with Shimmer?'

'You're asking the wrong person' he said. 'Talk to Donald Duck about it, if you have to. But my advice would be to let it go. It's not your problem.'

'It is if they're—'

He turned away from me and the rest of my sentence, and headed for his room. 'It's done,' he said, over his shoulder. 'That show is done. I'm on to the next one, now.' Just before he shut himself in he added, 'Work, Nathan— that's all that matters. Go to bed.'

60

All those clever critics. All those preening guests. All the chin-stroking punters who lingered at every frame. Not a single one of them really followed the golden thread. It was just a name, and this was just a picture show. It could be about so many things—growing old, dying, making money, selling looks. Scott didn't bother with captions and notes. He'd refused point blank to say anything about his work in the programme. 'I do pictures, not words', was all he would say. The pictures of Don and Mother might have been a glimpse behind the moneyed façade, a nod to human fragility ... you could give it any storyline you liked—which is true of most good art, I suppose.

Uncle Don's office had a particular smell. That kind of synthetic, slightly addictive smell that you get in new cars, or from some kinds of glossy print. I think of it as a manufactured smell: as far as it's possible to be from the scent of earth and leaves. Same old smell, when I was admitted to Don's sanctum; still admitted by Taff, who was well past retirement age but still as neat and quick as a bird. Same old swivelling chair, though I ignored it, that day, and sat opposite Don at his desk. As Taff was closing the door Don said,

'No calls.'

He dispensed with the sunshines and the wotchers and all the rest of the act. He folded his arms and looked me straight in the eye.

'First off', he said, 'have you had any ... flak?'

'Any what?' I was genuinely baffled.

'Any flak. Comeback. Press, gossip, whatever.'

'About the pictu—?'

'OF COURSE ABOUT THE FUCKING PICTURES.' His hands shot out onto the desk and he half rose from his seat.

'No' I said. 'Nothing. Are you expecting anything?'

He sat down again and let out his breath with a sound like a dying balloon.

'No,' he conceded. 'Not unless some maniac out there fancies being sued to a *pulp*.' He spat the word out as if it might puncture Scott Carter between the eyes. He was breathing heavily.

'I would like to know,' he said slowly, without looking at me, 'what your sick little cocksucker boyfriend thinks he's playing at.'

'Scott,' I said, 'is not my boyfriend.'

Don's head was trembling. He looked old, like the defeated man in the photograph. Very softly, making an effort to control his temper, he said,

'You listen to me. I don't give a *shit*—' another bullet-word; he paused to regain his composure—'if that little arsewipe is giving it to you, or the songbird'—my heart flipped in protest and I clutched the arms of my chair—'or the queen of fucking England, as long as he STAYS. AWAY. FROM. US.'

'So ... ' I was battling to quell the visions stirred up by his reference to Rosalyn. I had to squeeze my eyes shut to focus. 'So ... you and Mother, I know you like your fizz ...' (I kept my eyes closed to avoid the mockery I knew would pass across his angry face) '... but I didn't know you were into ... anything else.' Now I opened my eyes. 'It's no great shock to me,' I insisted. 'I work with artists. It's not exactly unusual.'

He raised one hand and pointed at my forehead.

'Shut your stupid mouth,' he said, softly. 'That talk could *finish* me.' He pressed forward into his desk, still pointing. 'Understand? Me. This firm. Your mother. *Finished*.'

I said, 'Don't be such a drama queen,' and immediately wished I hadn't. I loved Don, but I was afraid of him too. I hurried on: 'Look, I don't think it's a *good idea*.

But people like you and Mother—people like Scott—don't go to prison for snorting coke every now and again. Kids on the streets, they're the ones who get punished for it. It's not fair, but it's true. So as long as that's *all* ... ' He tilted his head, daring me to go on. I bottled out, of course. 'And anyway,' I concluded, weakly. 'They're only pictures.'

There was a long silence. His chair squeaked as he leaned back and watched me through half-closed, falcon eyes. He seemed to be figuring something out. And I was deciding I'd have been better off going to Mother. Presently he took a quick look at his watch. When he spoke, he was back in chirpy character.

'Best call it a day' he said. 'I've always got time for you, son, you know that, but time, on the other hand, is money.'

He got up and walked me to the door, then stopped and turned me by the arm, studying my face.

'I'm telling you now, sunshine' he said, 'I have never taken drugs in my life. Booze and cigars, that's all Don Cutler needs.'

'Booze and cigars can kill you too, Uncle Don,' I said primly and he laughed: 'Well, son, we've all got to go somehow.' Still gripping my arm, he reached for the door handle with his other hand. Then he let it rest there, and said,

'You should've held on to the songbird.'

I was shaken. I started to answer but to my shame I let out a feral sob instead. I reined myself in again with a long, moist sniff.

'Thought she was a bit of a waste of space at first', he admitted. 'Your mother still does. But ...' He shook his head sadly. He hadn't loosened his hold on my arm. 'Shouldn't have let that evil little bastard drive her out, Nathan, son. Shouldn't have let that happen.'

'It wasn't—' I started, but he was opening the door, now, and propelling me towards it. He delivered me back to Taff with a slap on the back and a public smile.

'Don't worry about your mother, OK? She's fine with me. Just get shot of that nasty little piece of work. Dab-hand with a camera, dead loss in every other way.' He winked at us both, and slammed the door.

61

It's a glorious evening. The wind has dropped, and from the window of my apartment I get the full effect of a stunning sunset. Half the view is sky, brushed from end to end with liquid reds and pinks and shades of grey. The lower half is a cityscape doused in its light. Scrappy tiled roofs glow like a fresh wound. The gasworks are touched with a brazen sheen. I think again of that photograph Scott took, during a break in the weather, all those years ago. *We think we cause the rain.* Scott, smiling at the rain, waiting to pounce, like a cat. I swirl the brandy in my glass to dispel the memory. This view, this hour, this sweet stillness above the city—this is all I need to be aware of, now. This and, of course, the fantasy of Rosalyn, that adds soul to everything, like music. Rosalyn in the gallery, starlit by reflected glass. Rosalyn unwrapping that dress. Rosalyn ...

My phone squawks. I'm furious until I pick it up and see the screen: *Rosalyn Calling.* I allow it a couple more cries, stoking my excitement, before pressing 'Accept'.

'Rosalyn' I say. 'How are you?'

I note the split-second of hesitation. She didn't expect such casual formality. Good. I need to maintain an element of doubt.

'Hello Nathan ... Er ... I, I'm just calling, just a quick call ...'

'Lovely to hear from you' I interject smoothly. Another pause. She may be annoyed, now.

'Bo asked me to give you a ring' she says, and rattles on about Bo's idea to hold the auction on the floor where his office is.

'What, among all those miniature buildings?' I ask, with only a touch of scorn.

'Well, we'd reorganise it, obviously', she says, quite irritably. 'He just thought there'd be more room there than in your gallery. And he ... he didn't want to inconvenience you.'

I can hear the distress, now. I take a breath and change my tone.

'Yes—yes, I think that's a good idea, actually. Yes. Please thank him for me, would you?'

'I will do' she says, calming down.

Then there's an exquisitely awkward moment of breath and static. I break the silence, bringing the phone close to my mouth.

'How are you?'

'I'm fine' she says. I hear a commotion and a voice in the background. 'Oh, there's Bo now' she adds, and then her voice recedes: 'It's Nathan. He thinks it's a good idea, about the auction.' She returns to me. 'Bo says hello … and thanks …'

'No worries. Maybe we could meet up to discuss it.' She gabbles something panicky, and I add, softly: 'Soon.'

When she's rung off I press the phone against my face. A new fantasy begins to unravel. Rosalyn, trapped between the architectural models, as their tiny populations swarm down towards her, sliding and jumping off their tables, climbing up her legs, tugging at her clothes while she writhes and squirms to their tickling limbs. And then I make my way through the labyrinthine route, around garages and hospitals and schools and car parks, and her Lilliput assailants scatter as I approach, dragging scraps of her clothes as plunder, leaving her exposed in all her round loveliness for me to hold and protect.

I abandon that narrative as one to savour later, when the sky is dark and the brandy's finished and I'm in greater need of distraction. Instead I turn my thoughts to the kingfisher, and wonder how and where I'll be able to present it to Rosalyn for her birthday. I'll have to figure out a way to get her alone, though it's not going to be easy in the hubbub of Freddie's launch. I don't want anyone else there to see her lift the lid of the box, part the layers of tissue and draw in a sharp breath as the blue is released and pours out of the glass, tinting her skin and hair. It comes to me suddenly, what I'll say to her then:

'I chose it because it's the same shade as your voice.'

Yes, that's what I'll say. It's a good line. And by lucky coinicidence, it's true.

Glass in hand, I start to pad my way around my apartment. This has become a routine, on quiet evenings: prowling the boundaries of my territory. I take my time, enjoying the order, the clean lines and perfectly placed objects. Nothing in this place is dreary to look at or shoddily made. The sunset bleeds in through my windows and deepens the warmth of rosewood and leather, oak and brick. My bare feet tread around the edges, past the photographs of Rosalyn singing, Rosalyn sulking, past the hand-pulled candlesticks encasing flames of ruby; past the long, clear twists of Suki Mezler's wall-lights ... I empty my head of everything except the pleasures of my exquisite home. This is how I have survived everything, how I crawled free of those old obsessions and calamities, how I achieved a new life of tranquillity. Beauty. Peace. Terrible and shaming, perhaps, but I made a conscious decision to bask in my wealth, to enjoy a sense of relief: relief that the brutalities of life are taking place elsewhere, out of sight. Bombs fall on other cities; cell doors slam on other lives. Torture and atrocity are a plane's-flight away from our consciousness. Scott and his dangerous truths, Don and his murky dealings, Mother's last, ravaged days—all swept away. And Rosalyn is back in my life. Why did I dread that so much? This evening, it seems to me that's where she belongs. This evening, it all seems possible and real again: the sublimity of song, the grace of glass, the world of ease, and safety, and art.

62

I had a phone call from Pippa, the maid at the villa. She sounded nervous.

'It's Mrs Hill, sir. She's—she's a little … unwell.'

I could hear Mother's calm, low voice in the background, interspersed with a strange, hacking commotion. Panic stirred in my chest.

'I'm on my way.'

When I arrived, Pippa let me in with a look I couldn't interpret: a warning? Guilt? I couldn't tell. My mother was on her feet, hovering at a distance, but I could hear her wheezing, and she seemed reluctant to move towards me.

'Is Scott with you?' she called, with some difficulty. No more *Scottie-dog,* then.

'No, why would he be? What's the matter, do you need a doctor? Why haven't you called a doctor?'

'Don't fuss, Nathan' she said, shuffling back towards the sofa. 'It's just a touch of flu.' She succumbed to a fit of coughing and sat down again. I stood over her, hands on hips.

'If it's just a touch of flu why have you summoned me here? Why didn't you call Uncle Don if you needed—'

She was stifling her cough with a tissue and waving towards poor Pippa with her free hand. Pippa approached me timidly, like a scolded pet.

'I'm sorry, Mr Hill, I did try and call Mr Cutler but he's not at his office, and I was a little bit frightened …'

'Ridiculous' spluttered my mother. 'Told her not to—'

'Mrs Hill wouldn't let me call a doctor', whispered Pippa, 'and she did seem in a bad way … she brought up some … it was black …'

My mother's coughing had finally subsided and she extended a hand to me.

'I just had a turn, that's all' she croaked. 'It's this bloody flu, I can't shake it off.'

'Have you been taking something for this?'

Mother's hand found mine and shut around it.

'Of course, stop fussing. Absolute nonsense—just Pippa overreacting. I'm sorry she frightened you.'

She lifted her face to me, and I saw the same rot caught by Scott Carter's lens. The map of her features was unchanged, but underneath—subsidence. She started to say something flippant, started to smile, but this disease, or whatever it was, caught her, wrung her face in a spasm of pain, yanked her shoulders up and forward, and kicked her into a violent convulsion. Pippa flapped and whimpered at my side. Mother was still holding my hand—hanging on to it, now, in fact, like a drowning woman. She was dragging in every breath with a terrible, blood-curdling rasp, sucking at the air as if she'd forgotten how to use it. Helplessly, I tried to support her heaving body, spoke redundant words of comfort, cast around in search of a solution. She wasn't really coughing, wasn't bringing anything up—I couldn't tell what was happening to her. Something else, some demon, had taken control.

'Call an ambulance' I ordered Pippa, who even now started to protest that Mrs Hill had told her—

'CALL IT NOW!' I roared, and she scurried towards the phone.

A key stuttered at the front door and in came Uncle Don. He saw what was happening and took four long strides to my mother's side. She immediately released my hand and hurled herself onto him, letting him carry the weight of her struggle, and he sat on the sofa with his arms around her, leaning back with the force of her fit, talking steadily to her, telling her it would all pass.

'For pity's sake', I wailed, 'she needs help. She needs hospital.'

Pippa stood uncertainly on the margin of the cavernous room, receiver in hand.

'Leave it, Pippa', Don snapped, then, less harshly, 'Nothing to worry about. It'll all be fine in a minute or two.'

I flailed around like a character in a silent comedy.

'Give *me* the phone, then,' I raged, 'I'll call it myself—'

'Settle down sunshine' said Uncle Don firmly, and I realised that my mother's breathing was already easier. 'Just leave this to me. I know what she needs. I'll make sure she's all right.'

Mother gradually regained control, and Pippa sidled away back to her duties.

'What is it?' I persisted. 'What's wrong with her?'

She'd buried her face into Don's chest. She didn't look at me at all.

'It's OK, son. It's a condition. Not serious. Won't kill her, I promise.'

'But *what is it?*'

'Look, Nathan' said Don, lowering his voice. 'This isn't helping anyone. Let your old mum get her wits together. I'll look after her.'

From the folds of his shirt came the muffled response:

'Less of the old, you bastard.'

'See?' Uncle Don winked at me. 'Right as rain. Bolshy as ever. Best to go, now. Give her some space.'

I could have defied him, couldn't I? I was a grown man, I'd run my own business and made a success of it, I commanded respect in my field. But the notion of standing up to Uncle Don, calling an ambulance despite of him, was inconceivable to me. I started my retreat. Before I'd reached the door he called after me:

'Have you kicked that little dickhead out yet? Get shot of him, sunshine, or I'll come and do it for you.'

63

I'm back in Freddie's good books. A mixed blessing, as far as I'm concerned. I'd half hoped the whole thing would die a natural death, especially now that we're gearing up in earnest for the launch. I can't pretend it's unpleasant, being involved with two attractive women, but I realise it's impractical. And besides, the more I see of Rosalyn, the less inclined I am to see Freddie.

But early this morning she turns up at the apartment, all squeaky and excited because she's had a phone call from the local press.

'They said you'd arranged a full page article about it! You clever, clever boy!'
She flings herself at me, hanging on with arms and legs like a spider that's caught its prey. To be honest I'd forgotten all about that full page—a deal I wangled with their arts correspondent, who's a pushover for a posh meal. Freddie releases her grip and springs onto her pink-pumped feet.

'They want a photo of me and some of my work' she gabbles. 'Which piece do you think I should show? They're coming to the studio, I'll have to clear it with the rest of the team, do you think she'll want to take pictures of them too? Or—' she's dancing round the apartment now, knocking against the furniture—'maybe they'd be better coming to the gallery, seeing the pieces on show, what do you think, Nathe?'

I shudder slightly at her use of the diminutive. I'm tempted to say *Mr Hill to you*. I try not to sound too flat, but that's the effect this gushing has on me.

'I can't really focus on this properly until we've had that auction I told you about' I point out. Once again, there's the immediate droop of energy and downturned mouth. She must have been a handful as a child.

'This is your *business*, though', she's kind enough to explain. 'The auction is *charity*. I mean, it's amazing, really, it's so cool that you're doing that for a good cause, but, you know, Nathan, profits are the main priority, aren't they? ...'

I fold my arms and chill her with a headmasterly look. It's as much as I can do not to clip her round the ear, sometimes. Delivering her little homilies about commerce and profits, with all the wisdom of her 23 years ... I open my mouth to note that her tinpot, two-bob launch is hardly going to fill the coffers, even with the backing of a semi-literate page of waffle in the local rag. But what's the point? It'll only lead to tantrums. So I shut my mouth again, pace towards her and take her in an avuncular embrace.

'The auction' I say gently 'is only one evening, and it's important to me. And—' as she starts another protest—'it's also terrific publicity, have you considered that? Lots of hacks milling around, an item on the local news maybe ... and if Peta Krantz is interviewed, and puts a sneaky word in for the brightest new glass artist on the block ...'

She gazes up at me and props her chin on my chest.

'Mmm... OK ...' she concedes. 'I hadn't looked at it that way.'

'Anyway' I say, to hoist her off the subject of the auction, 'what will you say in *your* interview?'

That does the trick. She launches into a lengthy and pretentious disquisition on art, inspiration, conceptualisation and all the rest of it. Pretty impressive, in fact, and just the sort of thing the arts hack will lap up.

'I thought I'd tell her' she muses, striding up and down the room, 'how I started off wanting to do sculpture, and why I switched to glass.'

'And why was that? I ask, busying myself making coffee in the kitchen area.

'Oh, you know, it's so much more weird and wonderful, glass, the way it, like, changes from liquid to solid, and you can bring in all other stuff like colour, or transparency, which is even more cool, and then it's so ... *dangerous*. You know?'

'I know' I say. She skips up to sit at the kitchen bar and drink her coffee.

'I hope this reporter takes me seriously,' she says, 'you know, as an artist. Coz, like, so many people think glass art is about making shitty little Murano doggies in coloured blobs.'

I say, 'Don't worry. This woman knows her stuff.'

But I want to tell her to hold her tongue. I want to ask her who the hell she thinks she is, sneering at men who sweat away in their cramped workshops, churning out figurines with the deftness that's a legacy of centuries, to keep body and soul together. Dino came from a family of Murano glassworkers, exiled to the island some 800 years ago with their furnaces, well away from the flammable roofs of Venice. The language of techniques Freddie uses for her high art was created by those men; all the skills of incalmo, conjoining colour and form, of twisting latticino canes into candy-bar stripes—all devised and refined at those same little *fornazi* that she sniffs at for their tacky souvenirs.

'I thought I'd suggest a picture of, like, my head, with some of my glass heads, sort of in a row ...'

'Freddie' I interrupt. She blinks in surprise. 'I've just had a thought. When the launch is over, I want you to make me a piece. Private commission.'

'Awesome' she says, a bit stunned.

'A kind of portrait, a bust,' I say, as my enthusiasm builds. 'And I think, if that works out, we could be on to a lucrative course, here.'

She's a trifle miffed, of course, when I ask her to model the piece on the photograph of Rosalyn. I get round it by explaining that it's Rosalyn's birthday soon, and I hint that it might actually be an indirect commission from Bryn. But she's still a bit moody.

'It's not really what I do,' she complains. 'I'm more, like, conceptual than, you know, representational.'

'But I don't want an exact portrait' I say, cajoling her. 'Just a, a map. An idea of the face. That's all it needs to be. A *suggestion* of her. Of the face, I mean.'

She shrugs, unconvinced, and looks from the Florence photograph to the shot of Rosalyn performing.

'That would be a better one' she points out, 'for something a bit, like, abstract.'

But it wouldn't fulfill the purpose. A face in repose, that's what I'm after; a sexless face, unmarked by individual expression. A face that could be Rosalyn or Scott. I can hardly explain that, though. Not even to myself. So I drop it, for now.

'Anyway' I say, 'let's get through the launch first. And your interview! What are you planning to wear?'

64

They told me she had pneumonia. I don't even know who I mean by 'they': voices on the end of a phone, in a hospital corridor ... the nameless people who step into your life when it all goes wrong. A smooth, official voice informing me that my mother was in a private facility, saying she'd asked that I be contacted and summoned to her side.

This was the most private clinic I'd ever seen—a faceless block among other faceless blocks, with no identifying features except a large number over the entrance. I had to key four digits I'd been given onto a security pad to be allowed in. Everything about the place was as smooth as the caller's voice. The façade of tinted windows, devoid of balconies, ridges, latches or protrusions of any other kind. The noiseless doors that blotted out all sounds of the city as they slid shut behind me. The lift that took me three floors up without apparently moving an inch. 'Third floor' said another creamy voice as the lift doors melted away. 'Please turn right.'

I turned right and announced myself to a receptionist, who was on the phone, clearly being warned of my arrival. She stretched a professional smile.

'Mr Hill, please go in. It's Room 305, just down the corridor to your left. The doctor is waiting to have a word with you.'

The doctor was just leaving Room 305 as I approached, and gave me his words of wisdom.

'A touch of pneumonia' he called it.

'Can you have *a touch* of pneumonia?' I demanded.

'Everything's under control' he assured me. 'You know, of course, about your mother's lung condition ...'

The steadiness of his eyes told me he was speaking in code. I began to understand that all this—the hospital disguised as an office block, the personal security check, the specially tailored diagnosis—all this was Uncle Don taking care of things, the Cutler way.

When I entered Mother's room the sight of her was like a blow to the chest. She was propped up, rather than sitting, and had an oxygen mask strapped over her nose and mouth. Above it, her eyes smiled a welcome. She raised a flimsy hand. As I went towards the bed a figure moved out of the corner behind me.
'I told her not to bring you here' said Uncle Don. He overtook me, and took his seat at Mother's bedside. 'But you know what she's like. Stubborn as a bloody mule.'
There was a slow, deep pulsation in the room. I thought it might be the air conditioning, and wondered vaguely why it wasn't as slick and quiet as the rest of the facility. Then I realised it was the sound of my mother breathing in and out. She pulled the mask aside and spoke like a wave through shingle:
'He needs to know.'
Don kept his eyes on her. He looked more troubled than I'd ever seen him before. Her hand flopped sideways to give him a feeble smack, and the pebbles turned again:
'Go. I need to talk to my son. It's high time.'

For the first time in my recollection, *Don* was sent away, so that Mother could spend time with *me*. I was scared. I understood that she was tying loose threads. I sat in the bedside chair and for two hours she talked to me, with difficulty and in short bursts. Every couple of sentences she had to resort to the mask again, and occasionally she signalled for a glass of water from the jug on the bedside table.

273

But this seemed to set off a terrible, endlessly rolling cough that would never clear. It simply subsided to a lower level and remained there, ebbing and flowing.

She talked about her childhood, about their life as the three musketeers, and I began to relax a little. Maybe that was all it would be, after all: a stroll down memory lane. Stories I'd already heard from Don, nothing to take me by surprise. I wanted to comfort her, to remind her of the girl she'd been. I said,

'Uncle Don told me you everyone was in love with you.'

She closed her eyes and took a few moments to store up enough breath. Then she shifted the mask aside and said,

'I was the neighbourhood slut. Should have left it at that. Should have left Keith Hill alone.'

My dad, quiet Keith, reliable Keith, looked after her, treated her as a princess.

'He was always there,' she said. 'Always. Never mind what I was up to, or who with, he was there waiting to pick up the pieces.'

It was hard to tell, through the slurry of her breath, whether my dad's persistence was touching to her, or oppressive. In any case, his shy and stubborn infatuation was eventually rewarded with what she called 'a quickie in the cloakroom at a party. I didn't even take my shoes off, darling.' She was acting, now, of course—as best she could, given the mountain she had to climb with every intake of air. I have no idea how much truth she was telling. She turned sparkling eyes towards me.

'And the result of that quickie, my boy, was you.'

The war was long past, but the country was broken and exhausted. My vivacious mother was up the duff and staring at a future of married tedium to a good but boring man. And there was her brother, Don Cutler, raking in the money, full of big plans and big talk. When Shimmer took off, Don made sure Dad was on the pay-roll.

274

'He looked after us' she said. 'He looked after *you.*'

'Well,' I pointed out, 'he paid a member of staff. There's nothing so heroic about that.' She sucked at the air supply, and I went on: 'And then he pensioned Dad off—'

A marshy spluttering from behind the mask. It took several minutes before she could reply:

'He had to, Nathan. Somebody had to look after the child.'

The child. She meant me. Had she momentarily forgotten who I was? Maybe it didn't matter. I was just the audience.

She hated married life. Hated being a wife and a mother. Hated the house, the shed, the garden and Dad's carefully tended veg. She wanted parties, music, superficial friendships, fun, and that was what Don could provide. That, and more.

'I was an addiction waiting to happen' she clattered. 'Whatever came my way, I was game.'

Pretty soon, and pretty deliberately, she was hooked on cocaine.

'Expensive habit' I commented, dryly. She wheezed into her mask, unable to speak for a moment. I waited. Eventually she answered:

'Don is a wealthy man.'

'But you had a *child*' I whined, and she raised her eyebrows in amusement at my pious tone.

'That's why there had to be …' —more wheezing, more sucking at the mask— 'a *stable presence* at home. For the … for you, Nathan. And that had to be Keith.'

So Dad was paid to bring me up safely, to shield me from my mother's excesses; and Don made sure she was sufficiently entertained to stick around.

'Otherwise' she confessed, 'who knows? I might have made a break for it, just like your gran.'

So Uncle Don wasn't necessarily lying, when he delivered his disclaimer: *I have never taken drugs in my life*. He was her guardian, her supplier—keeping her sweet, keeping her under control, seeing to it that she went home to hubby and son when the partying was over.

'Don is careful' she rumbled. 'Quality, and moderation. That's what I get from Don. He makes sure I get what I need, and don't go overboard.'

'Well', I said with an effort, 'it all sounds very civilised.'

Her hand fluttered at me, and she seemed to be nodding.

'Yes' she eventually said. 'It was. Civilised. Discreet.' She nuzzled the mask again, and there was a pause so long that I thought she might have fallen asleep. I sat there in a blank, not thinking, not speaking, just hearing the rhythmic labouring of her lungs: in … out … in … Presently she tried to say something, remembered the mask and moved it aside.

'Scott …' she said. 'Scottie-dog. … Breaks the rules.'

'Tells the truth,' I said. She moved her head. I think she was nodding. Then suddenly she had a surge of energy, started to prop herself up on her elbow. I managed to arrange her pillows and helped her sit up. There was no weight to her at all. But despite her condition, she had the old look on her face, and I knew she was about to say something provocative.

'Naughty boy' she growled, still talking about Scott. 'But more fun than the wimp.'

My colour rose. She seemed to have revived her spirits, and went on goading.

'Never understood what you saw in her.'

'That,' I pointed out, 'is none of your business.'

'True' she said. She turned her head aside on the pillow and closed her eyes for a minute. I found that I was twisting a corner of her bedclothes in my hand. Then she was back:

'Songbird' she said, and a brief convulsion might have been a laugh or a cough.

276

Then: 'An exotic bird ... with beautiful plumage ... and a sweet song ... I can understand why you might ... want to put that in a cage ...'

I went on garrotting my hand with the twisted sheet, squeezing so hard that my fingers seemed about to burst through the linen. She struggled on:

'Wouldn't approve ... no ... but I would understand.' She gestured urgently at a jug of water and a glass on her bedside table. I helped her sip a little; she took her sustenance from the mask; she carried on.

'But Nathan ... why would you cage ... a sparrow?' She looked straight at me with satisfaction. She must have been rehearsing that line. 'Boring,' she added.

'Common. House ... sparrow ...' And she started a ghastly, rumbling chant:

'Cheep ... cheep ... cheep ...'

I watched her, and was overwhelmed with nausea. She could have been spectacular. But she was just a spoilt brat. A crackhead. I said,

'You're pathetic.'

She nodded, but didn't stop.

'Cheep ... cheep ... cheep ...'

I got up. At that moment the door opened and Uncle Don rattled in with a trolley.

'Coffee' he said 'and biccies. For the prodigal son.'

'No thanks' I said. 'I'm not stopping.'

He ignored me and started fiddling with the plunger on the cafetiere.

'It's not half bad for hospital fodder' he said. He'd parked the trolley at the end of the bed, blocking my exit. I didn't want to have to battle my way out, so I waited, turning my back on my mother. After a while her gravel voice said,

'Coffee smells nice.'

Uncle Don had poured me a mugful and handed it over. I took it, despite what I'd said. I thought: he can't block my way forever.

'Want some' growled my mother.

'Is that a good idea?' said Uncle Don, but he was already pouring one for her. He sat on the other side of her bed and helped her take small sips, blowing on the liquid before each one. I said,

'I'm going now.'

Neither of them said or did anything to stop me, but Uncle Don spoke quietly to my mother:

'Told you it was a crazy idea. What is he now, your father confessor?'

She leaned her head back and he held the mug ready for her next sip. She said,

'I wanted him to know who we are.'

I put my mug on the trolley and started to manoeuvre it aside. My mother was weakly pushing Don's proffered mug aside. She spoke her last words to me with desperate determination.

'Nathan.' I stopped, but didn't look at her. 'Marrying Keith Hill' she said 'was the only wise thing I ever did.'

I left the room and closed the door without saying goodbye.

65

I've been sleeping more soundly, since that day in my office with Rosalyn.
Sleeping soundly and waking early, to the croon of the ring road, which I've grown
to love, over the past few solitary years. Apparently, our most vivid dreams occur
as we're waking. The most elaborate odysseys can unravel as clear as sunlight, in
the space of half a second. And I've been having some glorious dreams, since that
day. Not sexy, I don't mean that. They don't tend to involve Rosalyn in any
obvious way—except that the idea of her is wound into my being and drenches my
synapses to such an extent that she's never really absent. No, they're more
childlike, full of colour and definition, and they career along their random ways
with a kind of comic wonder. I sometimes wake myself laughing. The other night I
was on some kind of snowmobile, an open, primitive affair which looked
something like a coal truck; I sat in it, gripping the edges, while it steered itself at
high speed along a twisting course through snowfields of pink and blue, skidding
over precipitous glaciers, sending up showers of snow as it veered this way and
that. Snow fell onto my face and hair and tongue, and tasted sweet and fresh, as
you always imagine it will when you're a child. Watching and waving from the
balcony of a lodge were five penguins, a large cat and Peta Krantz. We sliced
perilously close to the balcony and away again. I heard Peta telling one of the
penguins: 'I am not a refugee.' They were both drinking cocktails. As my snowcart
approached, the penguin looked at me and rolled its eyes to heaven. The cart
swerved just in time to avoid the balcony, soaking the spectators in slush, and Peta
called out, either to me or to her penguin friend, 'Why are you so fucking cold?'

That dream made me laugh. It didn't surprise me that it ended with Rosalyn's
parting shot. Those words have also settled into my blood and bones. It's a relief to

279

hear them in a new context—as a jokey punchline. Everything is OK, now. Everything has come full circle. Rosalyn is back in my life. I relive that kiss, that slow, loving kiss, which I'd longed for and dreaded with equal force: a kiss that spoke of the past and the pain, and healed it all. I stretch luxuriously in my bed.

Why are you so fucking cold?

I suppose it's safe, now, to open the door to that last day of our relationship—now that I know it *wasn't* the last day, after all. It was so inane, that final argument, just the usual sort of thing. It had become the usual sort of thing, by then. And naturally I picked it clean in the years before my recovery, dissecting every phrase, every nuance of inflexion. It was a pointless exercise: examining the last symptoms of a degenerative condition. Never mind. She's back. A miracle cure!

I was hanging the Florence photograph, the shot of Rosalyn in the café. It looked perfect on that expanse of white wall, to one side of the fire, with the picture of her singing on the other side. It still does. But Rosalyn hated it.
'Can't we have something else?' she begged. 'Can't we have something *cheerful?*' (Years later, I conducted a mental investigation into her dislike of that photograph. *Why* did she hate it so much? Because Scott had taken it, and she felt guilty about Scott?)
'It's a superb picture' I told her, checking its alignment against the flanking photograph.
'Cheers' said Scott, who was monitoring my work.
'But why do all your pictures have to be so *miserable?*' insisted Rosalyn. 'And don't say *because it's the truth*'—as Scott opened his mouth to say just that, no

doubt. 'It's not the *only* truth. Is it? People are happy, too. And thoughtful, and contented, and hopeful, sometimes. Not just miserable.'

She was in one of those moods. That was all I thought, at the time. Scott and I exchanged a look and carried on with our task. Scott had a pencil in his mouth and spoke around it:

'You don't need *me* putting out the happy line. Everyone else in the universe is taking *happy* pictures.' As he got into his stride, he took the pencil from his mouth and turned towards her. 'When you go into someone's office or their house, you don't see studio shots of two people vegging in front of the telly, do you? Or screaming at each other, or at the kids? *Everyone* puts "happy" on display.'

She mulled that over. I had my back to her, but always imagined her pouting, when I re-ran that scene. Pouting, and nibbling at the loose skin by her thumbnail—a habit she never lost. Then she said,

'I don't want a bad mood on permanent display.'

In all my paranoid re-spooling and re-interpreting, I never once gave her the credit of fighting for *us*. But then, by that stage, perhaps she was just fighting for herself—for her survival. I had no idea that the clock was ticking, steadily, relentlessly, towards our zero hour. I stepped back for a better perspective. I said, 'I think it looks perfect.' Every complacent comment would resound through years of hindsight. 'It captures something *real*', I said, turning appreciatively to Scott, who nodded. Tick, tick, tick. I thought I had endless years to right wrongs, soothe feelings, say what needed to be said. There was less than an hour to go. I crashed on: 'It tells a story ...'

'Oh, for *Christ's sake*!'

We smiled at each other—Scott and I. We were laughing at her outburst. Scott mimicked her, exaggerating the slight whine that sometimes crept into her voice when she was tired, or fed up:

'People are happy, too!' he mewled, and he held up an imaginary camera, and pretended to take a picture of her, as she folded her arms and legs, hugging herself, turning her thunderous scowl away from the non-existent lens. We stood there, making fun of her. She must have felt so cornered. And like a cornered animal, she lashed out, suddenly springing from the sofa and screeching into my face:

'Why can't you take it down? Why can't you do something for me? Just for *me?* Never mind the fucking *story*—just for *me?*'

I rocked back on my heels. It was so unlike her. Hormones, I was thinking. Hysterical woman, I said to my smug self. And Scott found it all highly entertaining: he went on miming his quick-fire photography. If they'd been real shots, they would have been a perfect record of our final moments together. Rosalyn's tear-stained despair; my frosty disdain. Tick, tick, tick.

It didn't end there. Still minutes to go. Still a chance to freeze the count-down. But I didn't know. The storm abated. As ever, Rosalyn had no staying power for an argument, even in her last frustration. She subsided into an unhappy calm. Scott left the room. Rosalyn went to put the kettle on. All back to normal. She watched me sadly from the kitchen area, as I continued tweaking and perfecting the position of the photograph. Quietly, she said,

'It's always Scott.'

I was irritated. Dismissive.

'It looks *right*', I said.

What if I'd left it there? What if I'd let it all settle, relied on Rosalyn to swallow her pride, accept my decision, restore a friendly atmosphere, as she usually did? Could I have stopped the clock? Gained more time? A few days, maybe. A couple of months. But no more. The damage was long since done. And in any case, I didn't leave it there.

'Tell you what,' I said with affected heartiness, 'we could always ask Scott to take a new one, if you hate this one so much. It is a bit … *out of date*, if we're honest about it.'

I looked from the photograph to her and back again. Rosalyn wasn't a vain woman; she didn't fret about grey hairs and softening muscles. Ordinarily, she might even have laughed at her own expense. But my words crackled with deliberate cruelty. I'd hit the mark: it was clear from the wounded silence that followed. I was pleased with myself, for getting the last word. For implying that this exquisite, unique woman had been diminished by her age. I deserved every second of the suffering in store. Tick, tick, tick.

The kettle boiled and switched itself off. She was crying, softly. I ignored her. Later, I found three mugs and an empty teapot waiting on the work surface. She'd carried on making tea for all of us—*all of us*—even as she reached the end of her tether. I was collecting up bits and bobs—picture wire, ruler … and then she was there, putting on her coat, gathering her bag, still crying.

'I'm going,' she said, without anger. Not *I'm going out, I'm going for a smoke, a walk, to Auntie Monica's* … just 'I'm going'.

In the endless nights of analysis, I always heard the apology in that phrase. She had to go. She had to get out of the cage. And what did I say?

'Have fun.'

That's what I said. I didn't even look at her. I threw my vile, final line over my shoulder. *Have fun.* I heard her sob, like a jolt of shock. Then a raucous cry, so visceral and sudden that my whole body flinched:

'*Why are you so fucking cold?*'

Tick, tick—slam.

And I went on revelling in my triumph, knowing she'd be back.

66

It's unfair and deeply irrational to blame anything that happened on Rosalyn's departure from my life. I was devastated, of course, but several years passed between the slamming door and all the rest of the carnage; and there was no connection, none, however you choose to look at it. Nevertheless, that was how it sometimes felt to me. As if the magnitude of that slam sent out slow ripples of destruction, obliterating the walls of my fortress, one by one.

Three weeks after I'd flounced out of my mother's hospital room, Uncle Don called at the apartment. His face was ashen.
'Bad news, sunshine', he said.
I invited him in and poured us drinks. I must have known, in my heart of hearts, but I set my face against the truth as long as possible. I sipped my drink and listened to a few bars of the music playing through the speakers. Mozart. *Idomeneo*. Sublime. Don had dropped into a seat by the window.
'She'll be fine' I said. 'She's being well looked after.'
Don slouched forward with his head in his hands. After a few moments he raised himself with a gargantuan effort, and fixed me with a look of utter contempt.
'She's *dead*, son' he said. Then his face crumpled like an empty bag. 'It was … it was …' He started to weep—great tearless, hacking sobs that threw him forward each time. It reminded me of Mother having that fit. I drained my drink, then went into the kitchen to brew coffee.

Some time later Don came to find me. I don't know how long I'd been there, leaning against the worktop, listening to the percolator spit. He was calmer, though his face was streaked with red lines, as if someone had taken a lash to it. He said,

'You're not to feel guilty. She told me to say that.'

'Why should *I* feel guilty?'

He paused. I could hear his breathing. Eventually he said,

'She *wanted* you to see her like that, you know. In that … *mess*. She wanted you to see how she turned out. To put you off. I knew it was a stupid idea. I told her, don't let him come. Don't let him see you like this. It'll kill you.'

I turned off the percolator and selected a couple of coffee mugs. I was waiting, with a certain degree of curiosity, for some feeling, some reaction to the news of my mother's death; something suitably momentous to seize my mind and take over my actions. But nothing happened, so I carried on pouring coffee.

'She told me to keep this back for you.'

He was holding out a package, wrapped in brown paper. When he handed it to me I saw the ageing flesh above his wrist, loose and stringy. I took the package and tested its weight. I knew what it was straight away.

'The paperweight' I said.

Don nodded. A wisp of a smile almost revived his face. He said,

'Remember that day? Nah, you were only a nipper …'

'When you took me to the craft fair? Of *course* … That day changed my life.'

He looked startled. Pleased. For a moment, he puffed his chest and jutted his chin.

'Yeah, well, I s'pose it did. Kicked you off with yer knick-knacks and that … Yeah, it prob'ly did change your life. Anyway'—he patted the package, confirming the transaction—'you keep that, it's yours now. She told me to keep it back, before everything goes.'

'Goes?' I blinked at the package, perplexed. 'What do you mean, "before everything goes"?'

Don gave me blank eyes.

'Your mother's, you know, stuff. Effects. Clothes, shoes, jewellery—'

He saw my look of horror and released a short, exasperated sigh, as if he had to explain matters to a slow-witted child. 'Listen, son, there's no sense keeping it. Her dresses wouldn't suit me, even if I was the right size.' He grimaced at his own weak attempt at humour. I tightened my grasp on the package, crackling the brown paper, and said,

'Isn't it a bit … sudden? I mean, I realise you'll have to give it away eventually, but …'

'Give it away?' Suddenly the old Uncle Don was back, brash and indignant. 'What am I, the Red bloody Cross? That's all quality merchandise, that, son—I should know, I bought it. Some top-range trinkets in there. Emeralds, white gold, top-of-the-range diamonds—I never stinted on her, that's for sure.'

'*Quality merchandise?*' I repeated, slowly, my mouth warped with distaste. He took a step forward, compressing the space between us. I wasn't sure whether he wanted to hit me or embrace me. His voice dropped to a whisper.

'Listen to me, Mister Too-Posh-For-Cash. You can ponce around all you like, buying the right kind of splashback, turning your nose up at the loose change. But it all comes to the same thing, sonny-boy. It's all about the readies. That's what keeps you in fancy goods—'

'—and fancy drugs' I mumbled, and he stepped even closer, almost touching me, now.

'Yeah, that's right, Nathan. Fancy drugs, quality gear. The right deals, with the right people. You ever wonder what I was doing behind the tents while you was boggling at the furnaces in that craft fair? Private business in public places. Never touched that crap myself. But I risked my reputation, my freedom and my life to keep that woman on an even keel. So don't give me that Mr Superior goody-goody Keith Hill look, all right, matey? I risked everything for her. But now she's dead.'

We stood there in silence for a moment. His chest was heaving. I thought he might cry. But in the end he just gave me a clap on the arm, took his mug of coffee and stepped back, breaking the spell. When he spoke again he sounded kinder, and tired.

'I know it's hard, mate. But life goes on, and so does business.'

'But …' I wrapped my hands around the paperwejght, taking strength from its solidity. 'But it's not just business, is it? It's … it's belongings. When you own something, when someone you love has owned something … it's not just *goods*.'

He didn't say anything for a moment and I naively thought I'd touched a chord. But when he spoke, it was without a trace of sentiment, genuine or otherwise.

'Let me tell you something, son. When my folks were flattened by the roof of the Regency, and we set up house, the three of us together—well, I didn't know how to go on living. I mean, I *wanted* to live. Just didn't know how to do it, without my old mum and dad. Keith had his job, he was all right, but that wasn't my style. So I started selling. Sold off every last piece of anything in the house we didn't need. Anything you could pick up or move around, I flogged, to whoever wanted it. And there was plenty wanted it. Sold it all, on the street, in the market—cups and saucers, cushions, curtains, my dad's old trilby hat, my mum's best coat. Photographs—they went an' all. People who'd lost everything and everyone they had, they was willing to part with a few bob to buy someone else's memories. Certificates. Got a good price for *them*. Marriage certificate, birth certificate—'

'You sold your birth certificate?' I gawped.

'Look, mate, in them days a nice respectable piece of paper could come in very handy, even with someone else's name on it.' He took a pace away from me, smiling at a memory. 'Even found a mystery brother of our own.' He could have been recalling a childhood friend. 'Francis Cutler Harris. That's where I got 'Cutler' from. Don't know what happened to him—pegged it, prob'ly. Lots of the little ones did, round our way. Or'—he shrugged—'maybe times were harder then, and mum and dad couldn't manage. Anyway. I never told your mum about that ...'

His voice caught and he hung his head. I didn't know what to say. The paperweight grew heavier in my hands. Then he roused himself again and concluded nostalgically:

'The war was a handy thing, in some ways. People disappearing left, right, and centre—even the bloody War Ministry couldn't keep track. New names and dates—desirable items, for them as didn't want to be found.'

He stood and drank half his coffee in two great gulps. Then he put the mug down heavily, drew in a long breath and said,

'I'll let you know about the funeral.'

He turned to leave, but something in the living area caught his eye. Scott had discarded his shoes under the glass table. I was always telling him about that. Uncle Don growled like a dog.

'I told you to get rid' he said. 'If it wasn't for that little—'

A great lightning bolt of rage ripped through me.

'*Scott*?' I shouted. 'Don't blame *Scott*! You could have *helped* her. Why didn't you *help her*?'

'You listen to me, sunshine, she had the best care—'

'She was an *addict*. And you *kept* her that way.'

His hand was at my throat in an instant, bunching my shirt in his fist and twisting it into a choke. He yanked me towards him and spoke through clenched teeth.

'Your mother ...'

I made a desperate, squawking sound and clawed at his hand. He released the pressure and kept his open hand on my chest as I coughed and spat and tried to re-inflate my airpipes.

'Nathan, son,' he said at last, regaining his composure. 'Your mother was special. Most people, most people, they just ... settle. Into the undergrowth. Keep their heads down, keep to the same old routine. She was never like that. She was out there, grabbing life with both hands...'

'Bullshit!' I spluttered. 'Grabbing life with both hands? What, by crouching in the bathroom, stuffing cocaine up her nose?'

He gave my chest a hard shove, and I staggered backwards a few steps. His finger wagged admonition at me, but it took his voice a moment to catch up. Then he said, 'If you hadn't come along, she'd have been, she'd have been—'

He was faltering. He seemed to forget what he was trying to say. My temper filled the gap.

'She'd have been WHAT? Dead a lot sooner? Don't kid yourself you offered anything better than she got with my dad. What's *your* great achievement? Getting rich on selling crap?'

He was looking around him with baffled eyes. I thought I might throw up and pushed past him, retching, to the bathroom. By the time I'd cleaned myself up and re-emerged, Uncle Don had gone.

67

We stand at the back door, staring at the few square feet of overgrown land between the cottage and the woods.

'Just a small patch of ground,' I coax again. 'It wouldn't need to be much. Just enough for a few veg. That's all I'm saying.'

His face is a study of incredulity, and to be fair, I can see his point. He's weakened in body and in mind; hardly in a state to attack that wilderness of brambles, nettles, goosegrass and wild ivy with a machete. But the idea's lodged itself in my mind, and today everything seems possible.

'Look', I say, encouragingly, pushing past him to examine the cracked remains of a concrete path. 'Look, it would only take one good session to clear the worst of it. I'd help. Bit of cutting and pulling, bit of digging—you could have a decent vegetable patch by next spring, start growing your own.'

'Next spring?' His eyebrows disappear under the fringe of greasy hair. 'You think I'll still be here next spring?'

'You're safe here', I say, turning to him with a serious air. 'Nobody bothers you— do they? Nobody knows your name. We got that plumber in and it was fine, wasn't it? You were pleased with him. He did a good job, didn't he?'

I've started to treat him like a small child. I suppose that's what happens, when someone's mind begins to go. He nods with pleasure at the memory of the unblocked loo.

'Good job', he mutters. 'Did a good job …'

'Exactly', I say, in my matronly way. 'He did a good job, and everything was fine. So you might as well stay on for a bit, don't you reckon? And if you're staying on, why not make it more homely? That's all I'm saying. Grow a few runner beans, some carrots, maybe, potatoes … much better for you than the crud you're surviving on now.'

That's a mistake. His eyes grow troubled, confused: he feels he's being criticised, and doesn't know why, or how to deal with it. I've come to recognise these warning signs, and I know how to fend off his panic attacks now.

'Anyway—never mind that' I say hastily, cheerily. 'Let's have a cup of tea.' That placates him immediately.

'Cup of tea!' he agrees, back on familiar territory, and shuffles back towards the sink.

While he's mashing teabags in his two cracked mugs, I hover at the open back door, averting my face from the rank air of the cottage. I won't mention clearing the yard again, but I can't help imagining how things might turn out, how we could make this into some semblance of a home for him, Rosalyn and I. She'll be shocked, of course, when I tell her the truth; shocked by the deception, and by the way I let him live. But she'll hear me out, and she'll find a way to understand— especially if I appeal to her compassion. We can work together to make him comfortable. It'll be such a blessed relief to share the burden. It'll be our own project, creating a little rural haven out of a slum. Dig him a little garden—veggie patch, a few pots of herbs and flowers; do up the cottage together, buy him some good furniture, some mod cons, convert the loft into a proper room with a shower and an indoor loo … She'll enjoy taking care of him. He'll almost be like the child we never had.

68

Mendel have been so clever. They've bucked every downward trend, done all the right things, even when all the pundits were advising the opposite, and stayed alive and fit. They don't overreact, that's the key. They know who they are. I'm glad I sold Zenada to them, even if they did stitch me up somewhat. They've been brutal, of course—they've had to be, along the years, shedding staff, closing factories, ditching this family concern and that local employer, but only when absolutely necessary. They're not one of those asset-stripping thugs who couldn't give a toss, as long as they double their profits before they cut and run. It's been quite a masterclass, following Mendel's development over the decades. I often come up here to the mezzanine when I've woken in the early hours, enjoying the coolness of the stair-treads under my bare feet, and Google the company, noting their latest moves and their newest lines. I sit here at the computer in Don's old swivel chair, and every now and then I let my knees brush against the bannister panels, just to feel the friction of texture in the glass. Zenada is still going, still under the old name, though most of the staff were laid off soon after the sale. It's not the same as it was. They've gone for fashion above quality, which I suppose came at too high a price. So now it's repulsive chandeliers, mirrors that wouldn't look amiss in a tart's boudoir. It's a shame, but I'm sure Mendel know what they're doing. They change with the times—and that's a lesson Uncle Don would have done well to learn. But by the time it all started to unravel, his mind was unravelling too. He was far beyond learning lessons, by then.

I'd told Scott about my visit to the private facility, about Mother's condition, about our final exchange. He'd listened, without much reaction. I was full of self-righteous indignation when I told him and, of course, had no idea it *would* be a final exchange. When I broke the news about Mother's death, he said nothing at first. Didn't look at me, didn't really look at anything, but his face was shadowed with shock, in a way it never had been on those nocturnal hunting trips, when he bore witness to human suffering in all its tedium. After a while he took both my hands in his with quiet, gracious compassion, and said,

'I'm so sorry, Nathan, I'm so sorry. I know how much she meant to you.'

And then he seemed to perform a slow plié, legs easing into a diamond shape, and I stumbled forward as I found myself taking his weight. He carried on sinking until he was on his haunches, and let go of me, then, putting his hands on the floor and bowing his head. I stood there, uncertain what to do, just looking at his dark hair, streaked with grey, now, falling forward to curtain his silent grief. *What would Rosalyn do now?* I asked myself. But the thought of Rosalyn comforting Scott, maybe enveloping his prone figure in her soft arms, threatened to poison even this moment of loss. So I said what she probably *would* have said:

'I'll make us a pot of tea.'

Mother's funeral was on 12th September 2001. The previous day, Scott and I sat watching apparent Armageddon across the Atlantic, guiltily transfixed by footage of the Twin Towers dissolving into a tidal wave of dust. Reports of atrocities kept on coming. At first it seemed to be a terrible accident. Then the second plane hit. American Airlines Flight 77 crashed into the Pentagon. United Airlines Flight 93 was brought down by its own brave passengers on Shanksville grassland. We became horribly inured to the flow of news; we waited for more. And as the hours wore on we made ourselves tea and coffee, plates of snacks, took them to the TV to keep ourselves going as we watched the end of the world. I ironed a shirt to wear at Mother's funeral, bringing the ironing table into the living area so that I could listen to survivors' accounts and commentators trying to piece together the shattering events. The next day, as I set off to say my last goodbyes to Mother, people were sticking photographs to walls, hoping to trace their husbands, children, sisters; or grappling with the sudden, inexplicable rift in their lives, with the end of their own particular world.

Uncle Don had banned Scott from the funeral. He still seemed to blame him for her death. I thought it was all about that portrait, somehow, or something to do with their sorry little habit. It didn't occur to me at the time that this might be the age-old, invincible affliction: sexual jealousy. But that's the sort of emotion she could still inspire, even at the end, even, I suppose, in me.

Scott was still glued to the TV news when I got home—in his favourite position, lying on the floor with two cushions supporting his head. He was holding a bottle of beer on his stomach.
'How was it?'
'Um … ' I found a tissue in my trouser pocket and blew my nose. 'Quiet. Very short, very simple. Cremation. Not many people there. No wake …' I winced at the memory of Dad's manufactured send-off. 'I was quite relieved in a way. I thought Don might go over the top.'
Scott narrowed his eyes at the screen. 'No, not this time. He probably had to force himself to let *you* come. If it was left to him, he'd have kept her all to himself.'
I began to contradict him, but as ever, Scott was only telling the truth. I thought of Uncle Don's hunched back, at the front of the near-empty crematorium chapel. I'd gone to sit beside him and started to say something, to thank him for arranging the service. It was an olive branch, of sorts. I felt bad about our last encounter. I suppose I was just starting to understand how frail he really was. I wanted to make peace. I got no further than:

'I think Mother—'

He didn't look at me; he just muttered:

'She had a name. Valerie. For Christ's sake. Her name was Valerie.'

And that was pretty well it. The address was given and prayers invited: I saw Don's hands wringing themselves white between his knees. A button was pressed and the coffin went on its way. Presently we shook hands with the vicar, walked through the concrete memorial garden and parted ways. I saw Don aim his keyfob like a pistol at his Daimler. He swung out of the car park and drove away without a backward glance.

69

I didn't hear from Uncle Don for six months. Britain and America invaded Afghanistan on 7th October; in November the Taliban was pushed out of Kabul, and their five-year ban on photography was lifted. Scott heard rumours of astounding work by local photographers, who'd been documenting life in the city secretly and, now, openly. He talked of going over there, but he'd lost his former zeal. There'd been a change in him, which I suppose dated back to his brother's death, and to giving up his habit. He'd become gentler, a little sadder; he'd lost some of his swagger. I didn't really get the impression he'd go out to Afghanistan. The only project that made his eyes glow in the old way was an idea he'd had about buildings. He'd always insisted that human beings were at the heart of all his work, so this was a change, too. He became very interested in buildings that had changed their role: derelict spaces marked with the ghosts of their old functions and occupants; purpose-built offices and apartments that had never been sold and were gradually decaying. That sort of thing.

'What about the factories?' I suggested. He was often at that wall of window, staring at the old shoe factory and gasworks that spread over miles of scrub beyond the ring road. 'You'd need to get permission pretty quickly, though,' I pointed out. 'I hear they're going to tear them down soon and build more apartments.'

In fact, it would be another five years and several more failed attempts to sell, before they started on the heritage site.

'No point bothering with *permission*,' he mused, with a hint of the old Scott Carter. 'All that bollocks can take years. Might as well tunnel under the fence.'

I tried to persuade him to go through the proper channels, outline his project to whoever was trying to offload the old factories—I couldn't see why anyone would object. There might even be a commission in it. But Scott was too impatient, wanted to suss out the territory, as he put it, and announced after going for a reccie one evening that the place was 'easy'. He'd shinned over the padlocked gate and seen no evidence of CCTV or on-site security apart from the odd warning sign. 'It's a gem,' he told me. 'I'm going back tomorrow with my gear. Fancy coming along?'

I did go with him, but I can't say I was enthralled. I tore my chinos hoisting myself over that bloody fence, and trod in a puddle of something oily in the shoe factory yard. I could see that the buildings had a poignancy—a majesty, even, with their tall brick façades and sad, shuttered windows. We didn't make it to the gasworks buildings that day—it's a fair hike to that part of the site. They have buggies now, I understand, to take visitors around. But even from a distance I could tell that the remaining buildings were solid and handsome—nothing like the image that would generally spring to my mind, of pipes and rusting metal. I should probably pay a visit some time and find out about the place. I bet Rosalyn would like it—she always loved that kind of thing, a place with a history of its own.

Anyway, when I accompanied Scott we stuck to roaming around the shoe factory, and he took a few experimental shots of the gaping interiors. A high, unshuttered window shedding an ecclesiastical beam of light over a huddle of cans and firewood left by tramps or kids. In one long room there were still workbenches, dark with mold, and a few sewing machines in various stages of decomposition. Heaped against one wall was a great drift of shoe lasts—square toes, pointy toes, a beach of brown and turquoise feet. Scott spent a long time over that, and I annoyed him by picking up a couple of the lasts to examine them, and disturbing the scene. But there was something surreal, something touching and funny and pathetic about that bank of feet, and everything they implied about the people who worked there, who spent all their days creating shoes in all shapes and sizes and colours and styles for total strangers. Scott walked around the bizarre dune, crouched, tilted his head, squinted at the pattern of shadows, the turn of a heel, the burrowing of a toe. He kept looking up at the high ceiling, where a filthy skylight was one of the few windows with its glass still intact.

'This is *so* good' he muttered. 'But the light's not perfect …'

He took a few there, anyway—'just in case the place gets bulldozed tomorrow'—but decided to return another day, when the conditions were exactly right. 'Want to come?' he asked, packing up. 'Only if you don't mess with anything, though' he added. But I refused, anyway. Atmospheric as it was, I just couldn't summon the same thrill for an empty factory as I had for Scott's hunting trips among the half-dead and the dying.

70

Bo has brought forward the date of the auction. He's spoken directly to Peta Krantz, and she's happy with it. The piece is ready and it'll be good to get it all done, she says.

'I hope' says Bo on the phone 'you don't feel I left you out of the loop.'

'No, no, no, not at all, you must go ahead, it's your baby, after all.'

I wonder whether he's noticed the change in Rosalyn, and is keeping me out of the way.

'It's just that my old employers have suddenly twigged that they could be making money from that floor' he says. 'So we have to nip in before they rent it out.'

'What about all your models?'

'Ah, well, I expect we'll find a place for them somewhere …'

I want to feel superior and amused, but the truth is I'm dismayed at the thought of all that intricate work being cleared away to make room for a minor firm of accountants, or whoever the new tenants may be.

'Maybe a museum …' I suggest, but Bo isn't dwelling on it.

'We'll sort something out. Anyway, no need for you to worry—everything's in hand and I can take it from here. Thank you *so* much for all your help with this, and of course we'll expect you there as a guest of honour … !'

'Oh, don't you worry, Bo' I assure him. 'I'll be there.'

And I am. In fact I turn up several hours before the proceedings are due to start, eager and willing to give a helping hand with anything that needs doing: shifting tables, pouring drinks, whatever.

'You're a hero' says Bo, who's supervising a team of volunteers, all wearing T-shirts that say 'Let Anna Stay'. He's sweaty and nervous and getting under their feet.

'No problem' I say, rubbing my hands. Rosalyn's in the corner, polishing wine glasses. I haven't seen her since that day in my office. She throws a glance at my chin and lets her trendy hair fall over her face.

'Hello, Rosalyn' I say casually. 'Any tasks for me?'

'It's not like you' she says, 'to be so hands-on.'

I beam at her and she blushes so violently that even Bo notices, and says,

'Are you all right Rosie? Put your feet up for a minute, you've been doing too much.'

I take my jacket off, roll up my sleeves and pitch in. We fret about where to put the drinks table, how to position the auctioneer's podium, how many chairs to have and where to put the press. It's all tremendous fun. Without its models the room is wide and spacious, but I still find plenty of opportunities to brush against Rosalyn's back, or touch her hand as I help her re-position a chair.

'Where did they go, then?' I ask, during a quick tea break. 'All the model buildings?'

'They're in the cellar, apparently' says Rosalyn, avoiding my eye again. 'In storage, for the time being.'

Visions begin to form, of exploring the newly populated cellars with Rosalyn at my side … I direct a loaded look at her. She feels it, and leaps to her feet: 'Right! Back to work. Time is of the essence!'

We're nearly done, and Bo goes off to change. Rosalyn stays to check some final details, but unfortunately their little army of helpers is still milling around, so no chance of a quick kiss. I content myself with a matey hug, covering myself with a cry of:

'Well done, you!'—and adding, for the army's benefit: 'All of you! Great job!'

She wriggles out of my grasp and says, softly:

'I have to talk to you. After all this.'

'Yes' I say, managing not to touch her hair. 'As soon as possible.'

71

I'd had no contact with Don since Mother's funeral. I'd come to assume that we were officially estranged. So it came as a surprise when a call from Mr Cutler was put through to my office one cold March day.

'Morning, sunshine,' he said, as if we'd seen each other the day before. 'Get yourself over here, will you? And grab a copy of the *Express* on your way.'

'Why would I buy an *Express*? I never read the *Express*.'

'Just look sharp, will you, son? I've got a meeting at three thirty.'

'Well *I've* got—' I started, indignantly, but he cut me off:

'Twenty minutes. Don't forget the *Express*.'

I slammed the phone down and told myself I wasn't going anywhere. But curiosity got the better of me. I told Chloë I'd be out for a couple of hours and nipped into the nearest newsagents. It took some tracking down, but I finally saw, on the bottom half of page six, why I'd been summoned to the Cutler presence.

Taff met me outside his office door. She hugged me quickly, murmured a few words about my mother, then stepped back and raised a hand in warning.

'Let's give it a minute' she said.

We could hear him shouting at someone inside. A copy of the newspaper lay open on Taff's desk. She saw me glancing at it.

'You've seen it?' she asked.

'Uncle Don phoned me at the gallery. Told me to go and buy one.'

'In no uncertain terms, I imagine.'

I made a face.

'Good job it's not silly season' Taff remarked. 'At least it's buried by other news.'

A minor celebrity who'd been caught looking at pictures of half-dressed children; a pile-up on the M42 … all deemed worthier of interest, luckily for Don. But the page six item was bad enough. *SCARRED FOR LIFE: Beauty product made me a Beast*. A stark, full-face picture of a young woman with blisters bubbling all over her cheeks, chin and forehead. Taff reached across discreetly and shut the newspaper.

'They sprung it on us last night' she said. 'We had to come up with a holding comment while we look into it.'

I said, 'Do you think there's any truth to it?'

Taff pushed out her lower lip. 'We're still trying to get to the bottom of it. We think this woman had a very unusual reaction … But we have been using different ingredients, apparently.'

'To save money?' I suggested. Taff was inscrutable. She said,

'I just take dictation and keep the diary, Nathan, dear. Sometimes I can barely remember what it is we're selling.'

The door was flung open and Don waved me in, still shouting—at two underlings, it turned out; a man and a woman, heads bowed, each clutching various sheets of printed paper.

'Good luck' muttered Taff, and closed the door on us all. Don continued his diatribe without missing a beat.

'—moronic, screw-brained, half-arsed so-called scientists, why am I paying them a fortune, to stuff my business up the—'

The two underlings had looked up with interest as I entered the room, relieved to see someone else share the brunt.

Don was brandishing a copy of the *Express* and performing a sort of flamenco, thrusting the paper aside, spinning away, slamming it open again to torment himself with the photograph. The three of us, the underlings and I, stood silent, as if one move would send him up in flames. Finally, he half-rolled, half-crumpled the newspaper into a truncheon, thumped it into his free hand, then passed it to me as he resumed his pacing. While I unscrambled the pages, Uncle Don paraded up and down in front of his desk, swearing to himself. For something to do, the underlings slid either side of me and helped me open out the paper. We all gazed again at the blistered face.

'I think' began the female minion, and had to clear her throat before going on: 'I think it looks like some kind of allergy.'

'A fucking *allergy*!' barked Uncle Don. 'That's all we need! Who's going to buy warpaint that brings 'em out in hives?'

I could sense the woman tensing up beside me. Her colleague seized the advantage and ventured:

'It could be a scam. Couldn't it? Is she being paid to say all this? How do we know she really used Shimmer? Could be anything. She could just *look* like that.'

Uncle Don halted on the spot. The woman's grip on the paper crackled. If I hadn't been standing between them, I reckon her stiletto would have nailed her colleague's foot to the floor.

'First word of sense I've heard all day,' said Don, with a sudden, icy calm. 'Scam. That's exactly what it is. Some *shit's* got it in for me.'

His arm swept out and he pointed his index finger between my eyes. I let go of the paper and the minions were left holding it open by each end.

'You think *this*' I said, gesturing at the photograph, 'is something to do with *me*?'

There was a pause. Then Uncle Don gave a sudden, barely visible signal and the two flunkies hurried out of the office, tearing the paper in their rush. They shut the door carefully, and Don and I were left with the sealed office air and the low vibration of the city. He said nothing for a while. I could see his tie fluttering as he breathed. He looked sullenly at the closed door, and I sensed his fear. Those minions would be scuttling off to the water cooler right now, jabbering to the other staff about Don Cutler's crazy accusations, his paranoia, his loose screw. *He's really lost it*, they'd be saying. *One bad story and he's gone to pieces.* You could almost feel their confidence in him seeping out through the air-ducts.

He still hadn't spoken, so I said,
'What the hell was *that* all about? Blaming me for some load of nonsense in the gutter press?'
Don moved over to the window and leaned on it with both hands. I imagined the smoky pane detaching itself under his weight, imagined him plummeting towards the pavement, still pressed against the glass, waiting for the impact. He spoke, misting the window-pane.
'Not you, sunshine. That—that faggot, that boyfriend of yours.' I stared as he screwed his face into a pantomime of contempt. 'Thinks he can get to Don Cutler. Little crack-brained poofter like that. Buzzing round my home, my family, like a, like a—' his right hand fluttered through the air as he searched for the word—'like a sodding … *mosquito*! Yeah. A mosquito. Full of *disease*. Well—' he turned his bunched fingers towards his face and addressed them: '—think again, *sunshine*. Don Cutler will *squash—you—flat—*'
He turned suddenly and slammed the mosquito hand hard into the other. Then he stood there, grinding his hands together, his face contorted with effort and rage. I felt the heat rising through my throat, my cheeks, my scalp. Softly, I said,
'Uncle Don. What are you *talking* about? This is nothing to do with Scott, or with me. Why would we—?' I changed my mind and veered away from the question. 'This is just tabloid sensationalism' I said, measuring my words, beginning to talk to him like a nurse.
He looked at me with strange, feline eyes. His pupils seemed to have shrunk

305

almost to nothing. My skin prickled. Dear God, I thought. He really is mad. Then the spell broke. It was an almost physical sensation, the breaking of a bubble. All at once his hands detached themselves, and his expression was as sharp and sane as ever.

'Nasty business' he said. 'Some little tart thinks she can screw us for a fortune, takes her ugly mug to Fleet Street …' He rubbed his thumb and forefinger along the creases in his forehead. 'She won't get a penny, mate. Not a penny … But I got more important things to think about than that sad bitch. Bloody product recall, for one thing. Retailers practically lobbing our products out the window.'

I glanced at the torn and blistered face on the floor of the office. I said, 'Well, maybe your woman was right. Maybe it's just an allergy. That seems the likeliest explanation to me.'

Don eyed me suspiciously, then said,

'No offence, sunshine, but when have you ever been right about anything?'

He strode to his desk, picked up his phone and said,

'Taff, you can let my calls through now.'

As soon as he put it down, the ringing started. He took the first call and started to shout:

'Tell him no comment. We're looking into it. One more word and I'll sue the marrow from his bones. Yeah—no comment.' He put his hand over the receiver and jerked his head in dismissal. Then he went back to his call, barking: 'Well, don't come to me about it, *deal* with it, that's what I'm paying you for …'

I heard the next call ringing through as I shut the door.

72

Mother had pneumonia. That's the unremarkable truth. Years of drug abuse probably damaged her lungs, made her more susceptible—I don't know, and I haven't chosen to find out. Shimmer's fall from grace was due to a combination of events and circumstances. Don's unceasing search for a bargain drove him to use cheaper, lower-quality ingredients. But that was, in itself, a response to the general downward trend in Shimmer's profits. There'd been a public outcry about animal testing for cosmetics—in fact I vaguely recall Don huffing and swearing about tests being banned, but at the time I was too engrossed in my personal heartbreak to pay much attention. The fact is, Shimmer had fallen out of fashion, and Don's increasing confusion only made matters worse. Bad luck, bad management, all played their part, but in the end it was just the way the world turned. To a man like Don Cutler, though, a self-appointed Sun King, the world always turned around *him*. So if his life took a turn for the worse, it could only be because someone had it in for him. *We think we cause the rain.*

Nevertheless, I still found it hard to believe, even then, that Don was really losing his grip. I didn't believe the Shimmer farrago would be anything more than a passing blip in the share price. Don Cutler might stumble, but he would never fall. The press would find some new cadaver to worry at, and the natural order would reassert itself. I went on believing that until a couple of months later, when I heard Don lecturing his 'team', and saw the vacancy in their eyes, where their faith used to be.

I was on my way to the gallery. I passed a newspaper kiosk and nearly fell over my feet. Mugshots were ranged across a tabloid's front page.

RUINED BY ROUGE! Monster Makeup Strikes Again.

Four more blistered Shimmer customers, apparently disfigured by the cosmetic of

the stars. One of them was a minor actress who'd been in a recent TV commercial.

I bought a copy and the kiosk man said,

'Sorry state, in't they? Look like aliens, poor bints.'

I stood there on the pavement skimming through the story. It started to rain.

Somewhere on the edge of my consciousness I heard the kiosk man say to another

customer,

'Look at 'im. Wishing 'e'd never put 'is blusher on this morning!'

I looked at my watch. I could have carried on to work, shut the paper, watched

Uncle Don's downfall from the sidelines. Whether it was family loyalty or

schadenfraude that drove me, I don't know— but in any case, I folded the paper

and set off towards the Shimmer head office.

I announced myself at reception and took the lift to Don's floor. When the doors

opened Don was standing there, with four of his henchmen behind him. He hadn't

shaved.

'Seen the press, then, sunshine?' was all he said, as they filed in. The lift swooned

back down to the ground floor and I followed them across the lobby, down a

corridor and into a meeting room. He didn't send me away, so I slid into a chair at

the back of the room, which was already murmuring with lesser suits. Uncle Don

and his gang of four took their places facing the troops, and he placed his hands

imperiously on the table in front of him.

'Right' he said. 'Solutions. Don't wanna hear problems. Who's going first?'

I sat and listened as one lackey after another stood up with a tremulous clipboard

and told Don what he already knew. They'd issued a press release for damage limitation purposes. They'd consulted medical experts and company lawyers. The share price was, as one brave soul put it, 'heading down the ski-run, at the present time'. Another hireling read out a hoarse list of retailers who'd announced they were pulling the brand. I saw Uncle Don draw his hand through his hair, and thought: *he's floundering.* When someone else started citing the rules of the market, he lost his temper.

'Crap!' he yelled, slapping the table. Every well-groomed head in the room flinched as one. 'Do *not* give me "rules of the market"! Rules of the market be buggered! There is only one rule in the bloody market: *fashion.* What's in is in. And we're getting further out every second I waste listening to this bullshit, so to hell with all that bollocks and someone tell us how to save our arses here!'

A churchlike silence. A shuffling of paper. A throat cleared. One timid voice: 'I spoke to a stockbroker this morning and he—'

'*Stock. Brokers.* What in the name of the holy trinity do fucking *stock brokers* know?'

'Well…' ventured the diminishing voice, 'he's been monitoring the situation…'

'Yeah.' Don sliced a hand across the rest of the sentence. 'That's what they do. *Stock brokers.* They *monitor.* They're like all the rest of 'em. Like you lot. People who sit and watch and cream off the profits other suckers *make.* Fucking parasites, the lot of you.'

A change in the air alerted me to a stirring of rebellion. This lot of parasites, I said to myself, will soon be moving on to another host. Don leaned forward, balancing his forehead on his fingers, and seemed to berate his table:

'Stocks and shares, forecasts and trends, codes and bloody regulations—everyone wants their book of sodding rules. There's only one rule you need to know. Punters are sheep. Tell them they need something, and they all flock off to buy it. Tell them it's no good any more and off they all go, bleating in the other direction.

Fashion. Snobbery. That's what it's all about. Baaaaah...' He started bleating at the table. 'Baaaah ... baaaah...'

I thought of Mother and her death-rattle mockery—*cheep ... cheep ...* Was this some strange sibling in-joke they'd shared? Or was he just copying his beloved sister's tactic? On and on he went: 'Baaah ... baaaah ...'

The parasites looked at each other and shifted in their seats. The voice that rose from the room had more confidence, this time.

'To be fair, Mr Cutler, no-one wants to use make-up that brings them out in hives.'

The bleating stopped. Two dozen shoulders contracted, anticipating a fresh outburst. But when Don lifted his head he was eerily calm:

'Listen to me' he said, his eyes travelling across rows of jackets and ties. 'Punters will cover themselves in rat-poison, they'll cripple themselves in winkle-pickers, they'll fill their lungs and their veins with shit, if you make them believe it's the smart thing to do. Punters will do *anything*. You just got to find a way to herd them in the right direction. That's all. So get herding.'

They took their cue and began to leave, no doubt planning their job applications as they went. Don hurled one last exhortation at their backs:

'I made all this from nothing. Crawled out of a bombsite with bugger all to my name, and now I pay your wages. *I know what I'm talking about.*' And then he started bleating again, aiming at them, this time: 'Baaaaah ... baaaah ... baaaaah ...'

The last one out shut the door carefully, and Uncle Don muttered:

'Wankers, the lot of 'em.'

Then he met my eyes and we regarded each other across a room full of empty chairs.

'Come to gloat have we?' he asked. I said,

'What's it all about? These stories—do you know?'

Don leaned back in his seat, arms still braced on his table.

'Of course I know' he said, with an edge of threat. 'And so do you, sunshine.'

I shook my head helplessly. 'Uncle Don—I really don't.'

His eyes assumed that lost look again and travelled away from me, searched the walls, the ceiling. He said,

'Set me up, the little ... *mos—qui—to.*'

His fingers were drumming on the table now, faster and faster, as he continued his distracted search of the room's every blank and corporate corner. Under the starched shirt collar I could see the quiver of scrawny flesh. I sat a while longer and watched Don Cutler, king of the spivs, cock of the heap, trailing an imaginary insect's flight. He started to make a quiet buzzing noise. *Bzzzzz ... bzzzzz ....* He didn't stop, or acknowledge me in any way, when I eventually got up and left. As I walked down the corridor I could still hear the receding sound: *bzzzz ... bzzzzz ... bzzzzz.*

73

Bo has sold tickets for the auction, mainly online, and he's done well. The place is teeming within half an hour of the doors being opened. A few local journalists are guided to the front, and pride of place is given to someone who claims to be from the *Independent*. The room clangs with success: loud voices, laughter, wine poured, glasses clinked. Then Bo takes to the auctioneer's podium and asks us to put our hands together for 'the reason we're all here', and Anna emerges from his office, where he must have spirited her away during the hubbub. Everyone applauds, and Anna looks shellshocked. Bo makes a speech about the terrible life she's left behind, the opportunity she has to make a fresh start, the urgency of making her case to the Home Office, and a great spiel about his charity and how to donate to it. He rounds off with a sermon about love and kindness. He strikes a convincingly clerical tone. I wonder whether he ever considered being a vicar.

'To refuse a kindness,' he declaims. 'It sounds so trivial. But that's the beginning of it all. Cruelty isn't necessarily a calculated piece of villainy, backed with dramatic chords.' Trust him to bring in chords. 'Cruelty can be incidental. Casual. It doesn't even have to be an act at all. When you learn that you can shut your mind against the feelings of others—that's when cruelty starts.' The cameras click in a desultory way; there's a general shuffling and clearing of throats. Everyone's waiting for the bidding to kick off. 'That's the beginning,' he preaches on, 'and the culmination is "necessary force"; "just war"; "collateral damage". Turn away from one person's pain; ignore one cry for help; and you're already on the road to barbarity.'

Blimey, I think, *steady on.* At this rate he's going to have a mass exodus on his hands. No-one wants to be called a war criminal, because they didn't give away their spare change. I watch Anna, standing at his side, hands clasped over her belly.

She shows no embarrassment, or humiliation, or any emotion at all, other than endurance. She's waiting for others to decide her fate.

'Most of us' Bo goes on, and now there's an audible sigh of boredom, 'are so lucky. I'm not talking about money, or status … I'm not talking about supermarkets, hot running water, all the luxuries we forget to notice. I'm talking about what we *haven't* got. That's our real privilege. The absence, for most of us, most of the time, of stomach-churning terror. The absence of a desperate fear that dogs every normal movement of the day. The absence of crazy young men with guns like tree-trunks, telling us what to do, kicking us into line, maiming, killing our loved ones, just to show who's boss. Anna—' He gestures towards her, but she doesn't even blink at her name— 'is no different from any of us. She could be taking her kids on the school run, getting the weekly shop at Sainsbury's, expecting everything to be fine. That's all Anna wants: to be OK, to be safe. It's hardly greedy, is it?'

I think someone behind me—probably Rosalyn—has given Bo a signal; finally, he introduces Peta. She comes out of his office to a whoop of relief, bearing her glasswork with all the panache of a music hall act. At last, we're into the main event.

Bo has persuaded a professional auctioneer to give her services for nothing, and she does a fine job, teasing and coaxing the audience and peppering her patter with jokes and jibes. A girl from the local news shoulders her camera and films the whole session. When it's all over she orchestrates a replay of the tussle between the two final bidders. She interviews the winner, who turns out to be representing 'a mystery bidder'. I know who it is: a Scottish dealer who's always had a penchant for Peta's work. I don't suppose he gives a tinker's cuss about Anna's future. He'll consider this a bit of a bargain, at £8,950.

313

Everyone hangs around for a while, chattering, relaxing after the battle's climax. Money and sex—I've always thought of auctions as a nifty combination of the two. And I'm in a pleasant, wine-mellowed haze of my own as I discreetly stalk Rosalyn through the crush. I know she's aware of me, of where I am in the room; I can tell by the movements of her head. When I eventually find my way past her—a gorgeously intimate moment as we're pressed on all sides—I dip to give her a congratulatory peck on the cheek and whisper:

'Where and when?'

'I'll text you' she mutters, before lifting her voice and face to greet one of her fellow campaigners.

That's as much as I'll get this evening, so I start planning my departure. I have a word with Peta, hover near the TV reporter with no result, and begin my slow way towards the door. Before I can get there I find myself in a brief clearing, standing next to Anna. I'd more or less forgotten her, and so, I suspect, has everyone else. Even Bo and his team of volunteers are too busy celebrating the auction's success to pay her much attention. If anything, it's her presence that's cleared this space in the throng. She stands there, wearing her aura of suffering like a disease. I can't avoid speaking to her, but I have no idea what to say. How do you make small talk with someone who's lived through atrocity? What do I do—offer her a vol-au-vent? In fact that's exactly what I do, as one of the helpers passes with a tray of bites.

'Thank you' says Anna, with that camera-flash smile, and takes one.

I want to apologise—for vol-au-vents and Home Offices and living in a fluke of smug affluence—but instead I jerk my head at the room in general and say,

'Good result.'

'Yes' she says. 'It's wonderful.'

'Let's hope the money helps your … cause' I say.

She nods, without the smile, and says,

'Everyone is being very kind.'

I'm struck by the way she puts it. *Everyone is being very kind*. As if it's a transient state, that could change at any moment. Maybe it's just her punctilious use of English, which as a foreign language she handles with great care. She pops the vol-au-vent into her mouth and I calculate the distance from here to the exit. I repeat myself feebly:

'Well, I hope it's helpful in some way.'

She nods. There's not much she can say, is there? It's probably not helpful at all. They can raise funds, shout the odds, wave banners about the inhumanity and injustice of it all, but sooner or later the wheels will turn, the officials will arrive and Anna will no doubt be shackled and bundled onto an aeroplane, for having the presumption to seek a normal life. Maybe Bo will secure a sliver of airtime on The Today Programme to complain about it; and in reply some jobsworth will spout a couple of statistics, and after a bit of tutting and head-shaking, we'll all carry on as before. Coffee at Astey's. Glass at the gallery. Sex with Freddie and romance with Rosalyn Rathbone.

Thank god, I think, as I edge my way past the crowd, with a sympathetic smirk. *Thank god*, as I slip through the door and make for the stairs. 'Thank god', I say aloud to the evening traffic and the dusty trees and the broad, yellow windows of restaurants and shops. And I stride away from the office, from the bubbly-drinkers and art-bidders and most urgently of all from Anna and her sufferings, clouding the edges of our world like a rotten smell.

74

Shimmer Snuffed Out. Cosmetics Wiped Clean. Uncle Don's business was in its final death throes. I turned the paper over and read: 'Shareholders bail, as bailiffs take their share.'

I went to the Shimmer offices after work. By that time of day, the receptionist had handed over to a security guard. Or maybe the receptionist had already deserted the sinking ship, I don't know. Anyway, security waved me in without a murmur.

'Go ahead, mate' he said, 'join the club.'

When I got to Uncle Don's floor I could see what he meant: a battalion of visitors filled the corridor and the waiting area by Taff's desk, and there was poor Taff, still at her post, assuring them all that they'd be seen as soon as possible. She spotted me coming out of the lift and struggled through their protests, snapped her hand round my wrist and led me round the corner and into a ladies' loo. She backed me up against the sinks and grabbed my lapels.

'Where the hell is he?'

'Uncle Don? Isn't he in his office?'

She scrutinised me for a minute, searching for a lie, then relaxed her grip. I'd never seen this side of her. But I suppose anyone who'd worked for Don Cutler for over four decades would have to be tough as well as saintly.

'He went out three hours ago and said he'd be right back. I've got a lynch mob gathering out there. If they can't find him, they might string *me* up, just for the fun of it.'

'Who are they?' I asked, easing my back away from the basin rim.

Taff stepped away in her red stilted shoes. She whipped a length of loo paper from one of the cubicles and applied it to her nose in one swift movement.

'God knows. You name it. Press, investors, health and safety, fucking fraud squad for all I know.' *Fucking fraud squad!* Coming from Taff's immaculately lipsticked mouth! I gave a little involuntary laugh. 'Arthur downstairs has given up trying to bar the way,' she went on. 'It's a free-for-all now.'

'I noticed.'

Taff flushed the paper away and smoothed her jacket and skirt. She threw me a canny look.

'Are you all right, dear? You don't look it.'

'I'm fine. Just—you know. Worried.'

'Mmm.' Her eyes flicked away again. 'Well, at least you've got your own little empire. Good for you, boy. Don't you let him drag you down.'

I was startled. I'd never heard a disloyal word from her about Don. I said, 'What about you, though, Taff? Shouldn't you get out while the going's good?'

'Oh …' She moved to the mirrors and patted her hair. 'Don't you fret about that. I'm a long way past retirement age anyway, between you and me', she said, as if there were any doubt. 'He shouldn't have kept me on, by rights, but, you know— we're like bread-and-butter now. Inseparable.'

I watched her go through the mime of image-checking: pulling at an eyelid, mashing her lips together … After a minute I registered the cue for a compliment and said,

'You don't look old enough to retire.'

'You're very sweet' she said to her reflection. Then she straightened up, ready to face the enemy, and gave me an affectionate slap on the arm. 'If you do see him' she said, 'give me a call. Just so I know he's all right.'

I drove to the vile villa. There was no-one else outside. Either I'd beaten the journalists to it, or they'd already given up. Don's Daimler was parked in the drive. He never did replace that Daimler. Had it 40 years, and it could have been fresh from the showroom. Not that he ever took care of it himself: he paid other people to do that. But he wasn't interested in trading it in.

'Only an idiot buys something new for fashion's sake', he used to say. 'I make money out of idiots like that; I don't have to become one myself.'

Well, those idiots had taken their business elsewhere, and though the Daimler was still around, Uncle Don wasn't. It took a long time to get a response to the buzzer, and when it came the voice was timid and wary, and apparently quoting a script.

'Mr Cutler is unavailable for—'

'Pippa', I said, lunging at the speaker, 'Pippa, it's OK, it's Nathan—open the gate.'

There was a pause. The crackling stopped dead as she replaced the speakerphone. Just as I was about to walk away, there was a hum and a clunk and the iron gates began to part.

Pippa opened the front door just wide enough for me to squeeze in.

'There's nobody out there' I assured her. 'I think the press still reckon they'll catch him at the office.'

She followed me through the house. Our footsteps were hollow on the marble floor.

'Mr Cutler said I wasn't to let anyone in,' she whispered, 'no-one at all, and not to speak to anyone except what I said to you …'

I noticed that she was clutching a piece of paper. Her script.

'Well, I'm sure he didn't mean *me*' I whispered back. 'Why are we whispering?'

'I don't know …' Her eyes darted around the lobby. 'It's been so weird here, since Mrs Hill's passing. He makes me check through everything that comes into the house, everything—groceries, post … I don't even know what I'm checking for half the time. My daughter came round with flowers for my birthday last week and he made me take the whole thing apart in case it had something nasty in there …'

I stood in the middle of the vast space and looked around. The place was spotless.

Not a magazine or a stray sock or a misplaced cushion betrayed a human presence. Pippa was spending her days grooming and guarding the villa for nobody's benefit but her own. I wondered whether she was still being paid.

'Happy birthday for last week, by the way,' I said.

'Thank you, Mr Hill. Do you happen to know when Mr Cutler's planning to come home?'

When I drove away from the villa I passed the first carload of reporters. I'd advised Pippa to slip out through the back and go and stay with her daughter for a while. There was some joyless satisfaction in knowing that the press would be setting up their siege outside an empty fortress.

A couple of days later I had a phone call from Taff. Her composed, capable voice was damp with tears.

'They're saying he walked into the sea, or something' she said.

'Who are?'

'Those bloody reporters. They keep asking me if he was depressed, if he left any messages ... One of them's got a story about someone seeing him on a train to Clacton.'

'Why would he go to Clacton on the train,' I asked, 'if he wanted to kill himself?' I remembered one of Uncle Don's aphorisms: *stories are stronger than facts, sunshine.* 'Reporters will say anything,' I said to Taff, 'as long as it's a good story.' She gave a long sigh, and I went on: 'Come on, Taff. We know Don doesn't give up that easily. He's coped with crises before.'

'But they've never been like *this*' she said. There was a snuffling, and I heard her discreetly blowing her nose. 'It's never got to him this way, before. He's been so, so *odd* ... Do you know what he told me to get, the other day? In the middle of all this?'

'No, what?'

'Insecticide.' She said it again, emphasising each syllable. '*In-sect-i-cide*. What did he think he'd do, spray the press to death?'

My flesh was crawling.

'He'll turn up' I promised her. 'You know Uncle Don.'

Don was right: rumours blossomed into stories; stories matured into facts. Nameless eye-witnesses were invented. Sources close to Shimmer were cited. Within five days, speculation had become assertion, and without so much as a shoe on the beach for evidence, even the broadsheets were confident in the knowledge that Don Cutler had walked away from the carnage of his company, caught a train to the coast and waded into the horizon. The lawyers and re-possessers got to work; the office was picked clean and the few remaining employees were laid off. Taff asked me to help her clear her stuff out of the office. I think she just needed to see a familiar face. There wasn't really much to do, so we spent the afternoon perched on her desk drinking tea and watching men in overalls cart out the furniture. When a couple of them emerged from Don's office carrying the swivelling chair, Taff stopped them.

'Actually,' she said, 'that chair is mine. I bought it myself, in 1959.' The two men looked at each other doubtfully. 'I'm sure I could dig out the receipt,' she said, with impressive calm. 'If you can give me a few hours.'

'Don't worry about it, love' said one of the men, clearly anxious to get away as soon as possible. 'We'll take your word for it.'

When they'd gone Taff winked at me and said,

'It's not really mine. But I thought you should have it. You loved that chair, when you were a little mite.'

I could hardly refuse. And it does sit surprisingly well in my apartment, with its spare and perky 1950s lines.

When Don's office had been emptied, we had to abandon Taff's desk for that to be taken away.

'Will you be OK?' I asked her.

For a passing moment, she looked very old and frail. Then she smoothed her jacket and straightened her spine.

'I'll survive' she said.

75

Don Cutler was officially a missing person. I was interviewed by a soft-voiced police officer who looked too young for such an onerous task. He seemed to be following a set formula. I suppose there are guidelines for this sort of thing. Was Uncle Don's disappearance out of character? Was he vulnerable, infirm, confused? Was there any sign that he might consider suicide? Was there any reason for him to go missing? Yes, yes, yes, yes, yes. I said,

'Have you seen the papers?'

He gave me a wry smile.

'We have to keep an open mind, Mr Hill.'

I said, 'There's some story about him catching a train to Clacton. I don't know where that came from.'

The officer raised a sceptical eyebrow. 'Some journalists have a vivid imagination, sir ... Does Mr Cutler have any connection with Clacton, do you know?'

I shook my head and shrugged.

'Childhood holidays, maybe?'

I remembered the photograph of my mother spinning on a seafront, showing her knickers. My memory is well trained: I knew that wasn't Clacton.

'I think they used to go to Southend,' I said.

There were more questions. Taff and Pippa went through the same routine. Pippa was asked to check his belongings, in case he'd packed a bag. Apparently he'd left the villa very early in the morning, leaving his briefcase, complete with keys and a wallet full of cards and cash. He'd left his reading glasses on the bedside table. He'd made himself a cup of tea and left it half full in the kitchen. Next to it was the previous day's *Financial Times*, folded at the latest report of Shimmer's collapse. Don was already in a fractured state of mind. The indignity of failure on this scale would have been overwhelming. Whether he'd walked into the sea at Clacton or jumped off a pier at Southend, he'd taken control of events in the only way he had left.

The police had more urgent, living bodies to retrieve, and the press had new roadkill to set them salivating. Shimmer had vanished into the history books, though by the magic of business, some of its personnel reappeared at the helm of an online 'ethical cosmetics' outfit called Blossom. Shimmer's debts were settled with the sale of company assets, and for a couple of years Pippa stayed on in the vile villa—maybe hedging her bets, just in case Don swaggered back through the door, issuing orders, one fine day. When she eventually moved out to live nearer her daughter, it signalled a final conclusion, if such were needed. In due course, the villa, Don's other properties, and even his precious Daimler were all sold. But it took another five years before Don's death was legally declared and probate granted, and during that time the villa stood empty. I never went near the place, once Pippa had gone, but I sometimes thought of those pale marble floors and the ghostly reflections that passed over them like clouds in the night.

It's a strange business, when someone drops out of your life so completely and unexpectedly. I was never hit by grief, the way I was when Mother died. Never suffered any regrets or guilt or anger, after Don made his exit. Well, he'd already removed himself from my life, really, so his absence didn't register from day to day. But every now and then a particular inflection or accent, or a song on the radio, or the sight of that bloodred paperweight would bring a waterfall of memory crashing over me, and I would gasp for breath at the impossibility of his absence, and wonder whether he gasped for air, when it was too late and the ocean was weighing him down.

76

Even in my deepest jealousy, I never confronted Scott about my fears, and I'm glad about that, now. At the time it was part of my strategy. If I openly hounded him, he'd be on his guard—or, worse, he'd simply leave. And now I'm glad because I would have looked such a fool. Anyway, jealousy is a raging fever that passes into nothing. The more accustomed I became to life without Rosalyn, the less fiercely my jealousy burned. It became more a habit than anything else: creating a fictional narrative, picturing their assignations, secret looks, brushing fingers, became a way of soothing my mind to sleep. And then, like Uncle Don, it vanished.

So I was surprised but not suspicious when I found Scott studying the Florence photograph one morning, coffee in hand, and he remarked:
'You've never really looked for her, have you?'
I halted in my tracks.
'What do you mean? I, I looked everywhere, I called her family, I—'
I was stuttering like an unmasked murderer. He carried on examining his work, and said,
'Yeah, I know. I'm not saying you did *nothing*. But you didn't look *everywhere*, Nathe. Mainly out of the window.'
'Well, what did you expect me to do, hire a detective?'
Indignation lifted my voice an octave. He finally looked at me.
'No, no, I don't mean that. I mean … maybe part of you prefers it this way.'
It was a measure of how far I'd progressed that I didn't explode with rage, but considered his words. He was wrong, of course he was. I never wanted to lose Rosalyn. But maybe I'd started to lose the Rosalyn I loved that very first night we

spent together. Maybe she's right: she could never live up to my idea of her. I didn't answer, but I didn't storm out or shout, and after a moment Scott took a sip of his coffee and said,

'I'm thinking the next show will be about absence. I want to call it *Missing*. What do you think?'

I wasn't used to being consulted about his work. I nodded, and he looked back at the photograph.

'No people,' he said. 'Just the places where they've been, places they've created and changed, and left behind.'

He wanted to go back to the shoe factory. The nights were lengthening and he wanted to use that rich, purplish blue between daylight and darkness.

'Want to come?' he asked.

I said no. I said,

'Careful you don't get caught. *Top photographer fined for trespass* … I've had enough of the headlines for one lifetime, thanks very much.'

He laughed and put on a mysterious stage whisper.

'Don't worry, I'll be a shadow in the night …'

Those were his final words before he, too, walked out of my apartment for the last time.

I had nothing to occupy me that evening. I was debating whether to call Penny and suggest a drink, or just spend an aimless couple of hours surfing the net, maybe searching for traces of Rosalyn—Scott's comment had triggered that urge, after a long period of indifference. While I considered my options I wandered around the apartment, and over to the window. I knew Scott would take the short cut to the factory—up the grass verge, vault the garden railings, then join the footpath that leads to a pedestrian crossing at the traffic lights. I squinted through the deepening gloom, but couldn't see him—he must have put on a sprint, knowing he was in danger of losing the best of the light. I was just about to move away when the sight of something made my flesh crawl. There was a large shrub overhanging the garden railings—it was overdue its annual pruning. From the corner of my eye I'd seen its shadow quiver, extend, then detach itself completely and speed along the ground. I stared at this ragged, flapping, unearthly horror, trying to make sense of it, my heart racing. And then I knew what it was, and I ran. I crashed through the apartment and ripped the door open. I hurtled down the stairs and through the lobby. By the time I reached the verge, there was no sight of the shadow, but I knew where it was going. My lungs were rasping and my muscles were screaming—I hadn't realised how unfit I was. But I couldn't afford to stop. Somehow I made it over the railings, though it was more of a fall than a land, and now I saw that filthy creature on the far side of the ring road, flailing its way towards the factory site. I had to wait for a gap in the traffic. My legs were shaking and I was audibly fighting for breath. I nearly crumpled in a heap in the middle of the road but I staggered away from the trombone-slide of car horns and pounded heavily to the factory gate. I nearly gave up, at the prospect of climbing that gate. I couldn't breathe, let alone shout. But it's astounding, the resources we can summon when danger is real. I hauled myself up and over the gate by force of will, and stumbled towards the shoe factory. I heard the rhythmic clang of metal and knew the shadow was climbing the fire stairs to the roof.

There were two levels of roof. The highest overlooked the skylight in the workroom ceiling, about ten feet below. Scott had talked about going there to gauge possible views of the room through the skylight. He also wanted to catch that point of transition, when the building's few remaining windows, the metal details, the puddled yards, sucked in the last daylight and gave out a rich radiance. The metal fire stairs led to the first level, with the skylight. From there, a vertical ladder, fixed to the wall, gave access to the highest roof. I was catching up, by the time I dragged myself up that second ladder. I saw the shadow, close above me, flopping onto the roof. I heard its hoarse voice calling his name. I collapsed onto the flat surface of the roof just in time to see Scott's stricken face as he turned from his task, expecting to see me. I saw him take two paces backwards, then steady himself. It was getting darker all the time. My head was swimming from my exertions, there were purple spots floating across my vision, I couldn't even speak—I don't know exactly what I saw next. In my imagination, the shadow grows, fills my vision, engulfs the tiny, pale figure of Scott Carter. When I try and rid myself of that idea, which is clearly preposterous, when I try and piece together the following few seconds, there are two versions that vie for attention, each one as real and credible as the other. In one version, Scott steadied himself for only an instant, then, as the shadow advanced on him, took one instinctive backward step too many, toppled on the shallow stone edging of the roof, and overbalanced. In the other version, just as vividly, that ragged creature took three calm paces forward, lifted Scott under the armpits, dangled him like a puppet over the edge, and let go.

77

An explosion of glass—and then everything is clear. My memory is lucid again. In fact it has a hyper-real clarity: each sound rings out, and the last colours of twilight stand proud as if applied by hand.

'Oh God!'—my voice, echoing over the factory yard and the grumbling ring-road. I was looking over the roof edge, down through the hole Scott had scooped out of the skylight, an uneven oval with a dribbling trail, like a map of some new country. The ragged man stood quietly, watching me. 'Oh God ...' I said again, and then found I could move. I threw myself back down the precarious ladder, half-fell down the metal fire stairs, agitating them into a cymbal clash that was still reverberating as I shoved through the sticky wooden door into the workroom. He was sprawled on his back, haloed with glass needles, one large chunk of window at his feet. I came to a halt before reaching his body. I didn't call his name. My voice was repeating one word of its own accord—'shit ... shit ... shit ... shit ...'—like a puttering engine, to keep me going, to let me think.

I turned around and left the workroom. He'd followed me down from the roof, but slowly; he might have been calm, or dazed, it was hard to tell. I stopped saying 'shit' and said,

'Oh, Jesus ... Oh, Christ ... Uncle Don, what have you done?'

He spoke with a voice that he seemed to dredge up from his belly.

'I haven't done anything, sunshine. What have *you* done?'

He was no longer a terrifying winged shadow. He was just a crazy old tramp. I took in his appearance properly, for the first time. His once large, strong features had been pared down to a nervous sketch of bone. Above the tangled beard, his eyes were enormous, filling the sockets between cheek and brow. He was wearing several layers of indeterminate clothes, all of them, and his furrowed skin, merging into the colour of soil. I was trying to think. I'd left my mobile in the apartment. Scott had never owned one. (*It's like having a private eye on your tail. Why would I want that?*)

I said, 'We need to call someone.'

Those protruding eyes stared at me, stony, unblinking. He didn't look bewildered. The voice rasped again:

'Why do we need someone?'

I couldn't figure it out. Either he didn't understand, or he understood all too well. I said,

'I'll go and—' then changed my mind and glanced back at the workroom. I didn't want him going in there. I didn't want to take him away with me, either. I just wanted him back at the bottom of the sea. But something had to happen. Events had to move on. I said,

'Come on. We'll get the car.'

He followed me meekly enough, scaled the factory gate with startling agility. It was getting dark, and rush hour was petering out; we crossed the ring road quickly and I told him to wait while I fetched the car. I half hoped he would have disappeared again by the time I'd driven around to the road, but there he was, slipping briefly through the beam of a streetlamp and into the car. In that confined space, his odour hit me like a mallet. This wasn't the same smell that permeated The Cut; not the smell of death, but the restless whiff of life, accumulated year after festering year.

'Christ, Uncle Don!' I gagged.

Like a demon rising, the familiar voice of Don Cutler suddenly barked at me:

'All right, all right, son. We can't all soak in rosewater and lavender at the end of a busy day, can we?'

I gaped at him. He pointed a skeletal finger towards the ignition.

'Start the engine' he commanded, as if he were still in his high-rise office, bullying his staff.

OK, I thought, play along. Keep him calm. I started the engine.

'Two junctions on. Burger place,' he said. 'You can buy me dinner, sunshine.'

I was still trying to plan, trying to take charge. But my splintered mind could only cope with following his orders, for now. Should I go to a police station, a hospital, Clacton sands? I took the sliproad onto the dual carriageway and drove towards the burger place. Even murderous old tramps need to eat.

I didn't ask him where he'd been, or why he did what he did. I just opened the windows and drove. He said nothing more on the journey, but after a few moments started rifling through something—a tramp's bundle, I supposed, camouflaged against his rags. Out of the bundle came a comb, which he started stroking over the surface of his knotted hair.

We pulled in at the burger place. It was a throwback to the '70s, little more than a shack with a sign on it really, where tired lorry-drivers and bored families shambled in and chewed the cud, looking vacantly out at the car park or watching acne-torn youths shove grease around a pan. We got out of the car and I handed him some money. That was a strange and not unpleasant sensation.

'Go on, then' I said. 'I'll wait.'

A flash of the old mockery rippled across his leather face.

'Sorry, sunshine, you'll have to do the legwork here.'

So in I went to the filthy eatery, to order him a double cheeseburger with fries. By the time I came out again I could feel a layer of slime over my skin. A couple of cars had parked near ours. I saw the occupants get out, register Uncle Don's aura and swerve away quickly, finding a longer route to the entrance. One woman unrolled the collar of her jumper to cover her mouth and nose, and a boy shouted some obscenity. To my amazement, I saw Don cower under the insult, rounding his shoulders and lowering his head. He seemed to think this child was about to attack him. Maybe that sort of thing had happened, during his adventures on the road.

He made short work of the burger and chips, and I stood by the car with all the doors open. I was running through the options in my head, trying and failing to attach any meaning or decision to them. Police. Social services. Hospital. Or take him somewhere safe and leave him there, go back and deal with the rest, let him fade into mad oblivion. Salvation Army. Somewhere like that. Better not aggravate him, that was my overriding thought. Keep him onside.

When he'd licked up every last revolting globule of fat I said,
'Right, let's find you somewhere to get clean and sort yourself out.'
Through the grime and hair, I saw his face twist in alarm.
'You're not taking me nowhere, son' he said.
'It'll be fine' I insisted. 'We're just going to go and get some help to—'
His burger box clattered at my feet. He'd tried to hurl it at my head, but it was too light to gain momentum. He cabbaged the greasy wrapping in his hands and threw that at me instead. It bounced off my cheek. Sauce and grease splattered over my shoulder. For a split second we stared at each other, then he launched himself at me. The shock sent me staggering backwards, and he was all over me, a stinking mass of rags and hair, weak but overwhelming nonetheless, like a giant bat. Eventually I managed to push him off and pin him, panting, against the car.
'You're not taking me nowhere' he said again, between crumbled breaths. 'Fuck you, sunshine. Fuck you.'

His voice broke into a hideous cough. I lifted my hands from his infested shoulders and started to back away, palms up ready to fend off any further assaults. But he was in no state to do anything now, hacking and retching away. We must have been a disturbing sight in the sickly light of that car park: the wild-haired tramp, coughing his guts up; the dishevelled observer, with streaks of tomato sauce down his lapels. Still, nobody approached us. I thought of accosting someone, asking them to call for help. I had a swift, brief vision of the future that might lie ahead: investigations, accusations, expectations; and Uncle Don at the centre of it all, thrashing between sanity and insanity, doing his damnedest to pull me down with him. A wave of self-pity engulfed me. Why should I deal with all this? Let him go back to the ditch. Life had been easier with Uncle Don on the ocean floor. *Good for you, boy*, Taff had said to me. *Don't you let him drag you down.* I made a decision.

'You've had your meal' I said. 'You can have all the money I've got on me. And you can go your merry way.'

We got back into the car, and Don got back into executive mode.

'Get on the motorway. Layby on the northbound,' he instructed, 'just before junction 21. Drop me there.'

This layby was no quiet bracketing of an A-road. It was on the busiest part of the motorway, and just getting into it was a challenge, with half a dozen foreign lorries bearing down on my behind. I only just managed to swing in without losing my bumper to the front wheels of an articulated furniture truck. There were two other vehicles there: a family saloon, Dad snoozing in the driver's seat, Mum helping a toddler relieve herself in the overgrown verge; and a minibus with curtained windows and a giant daisy painted on the side. I got out of my car and tried to look as if I was just stretching my legs. There was a crash of approach through the dusty bushes. Two virtually identical, long-haired figures in grungey shirts and jeans came stepping over the fronds and branches, hand in hand, piled into the minibus and pulled away. Mum was mopping toddler up; she cast me an apologetic smile and I smiled back.

'Need a break from it sometimes, don't you?' she yelled, indicating the howling traffic.

She wrestled her struggling child into the baby-seat and Dad began to stir. A couple of minutes later, they were off, Dad leaning out of his window to seek a way in to the stampede, Mum already shouting the odds.

I opened the passenger door. My skin was already sooty from exhaust. He flopped out of the car and opened a grey palm to receive all the notes I'd had in my trouser pocket. He spirited it into his bundle, drew himself up and looked at me with tearful sentimentality.

'The boy. Did he suffer much?'

My heartbeat doubled. I watched as his chin steadied, the tears dried in his eyes and slowly, slyly, his expression changed to a vulpine, evil leer. My reply was inaudible, but he understood it:

'Go. Don't come back.'

He scurried away, bent over almost on all fours, covering the layby with unlikely speed and vanishing, with a soft splash of branches, into the undergrowth.

78

There it is—that pall of smoke, heaving to and fro above the church. In a couple of miles I'll plunge into the tunnel of trees on the corkscrew descent into the village. For the time being, I'm enjoying this straight run along the Roman Road, singing along to *Don Giovanni* at the top of my voice and taking in the wide view to either side. The weather's blustery, constantly on the move, trailing occasional showers and driving grand, sculptural banks of cloud across the sky. Around me, colours pulsate with every change—black-green, gold-green—and here and there shoulders of woodland shrug from the wind.

A fast car inflates abruptly in my rearview mirror, noses at my bumper, brays and accelerates past. I watch it diminishing ahead without swearing or fuming; I feel no malice towards anyone today. I muse for a minute about youth and its obsession with speed. That's the way I am, since kissing Rosalyn: benevolent, indulgent, curious about everyone who crosses my path. That's who I'll be, from now on.

I've been rationing my thoughts about the whole episode. I apply my mind to other matters, mull over work issues, note the weather and the scenery … and then I reward myself, returning to the beginning again: Rosalyn's voice, announcing her presence in the gallery; Rosalyn coming in and shedding that mack … and I guide myself through every subsequent moment, barely able to keep my attention on the road ahead.

I'll text you, she said, after the auction. It's been an exquisite kind of torture—the phone call, the snatched seconds of proximity at the auction … One might think it was all in my imagination, our rediscovered love, if it hadn't been for that one kiss.

So I go back to that, every time, to remind myself that this is real. She was embarrassed, that day in my office, when we finally finished the kiss. We sat at the table again, and I hung on to her hand, but she kept trying to talk about other things: Peta's design, how terrible her experiences must have been, what we should do about organising the auction … I was enchanted. I watched her profile, the way she averted her eyes, and angled her head so that her newly straightened hair formed a curtain between us. She was like a shy teenager, and I found her irresistible. Every so often I moved forward, wanting to kiss her earlobe, the curve from her neck to her shoulder, but she would pull away. Once she said, 'Nathan—no.'

'Sorry', I said, but I was smiling. Of course she felt bad about Bo—so do I. He's a nice man. He's her husband. I don't want to upset him. But they've had over 20 years of comfortable family life, and look what that did to her: silenced her voice, tamed her beauty into some comic turn as the dithering granny. When Bo sees her now, sparkling, vibrant and confident and young—well, he's no fool. Surely he'll understand that being with me can make Rosalyn *herself* again.

I almost forget to turn off the road. It's tempting to keep driving, pressing on like the Roman battalions, mile after mile after mile. But I do remember, just in time, and sneak onto the virtually invisible one-track road, soaked in shadow whatever the season or time of day, and start my slalom ride down to the hovel.

Rosalyn asked about Uncle Don. She must have reckoned it would get me talking more successfully than all that stuttering about Peta Krantz. She launched into it from nowhere—

'Wasn't it awful about Don? Did you ever find out what happened?'

—so that I couldn't avoid answering; and then she took the opportunity to snatch her hand back and start collecting her belongings to go. I fudged the reply, of course. I wasn't about to embark on all that in the afterglow of our first kiss in decades. I just wanted her to stay a little longer, to let me catch her to me again, kiss her again … so I said,

'Well, I expect you saw the papers. He just … couldn't cope, I suppose.'

She nodded, still avoiding my eye, and then the phone rang, and Gabby was tapping on the door, and before I knew it Rosalyn had made her getaway.

I'll text you. That's what she said. It won't be long until next time—and it won't be a quick clinch at the back of the gallery, I can tell you that. But I've got to be careful. She's troubled by the whole situation, naturally; she wouldn't be Rosalyn, if she took it all in her stride. If I chase her too obviously now, I'll frighten her off altogether. That's why I'm paying this unscheduled visit to the cottage: to keep me occupied, to keep me out of harm's way. I can't risk a moment's lapse of judgement. Rosalyn is no Freddie Pannage. It's not going to be that simple, and there's so much more at stake. Having said that, the principle remains the same. Let everything simmer for a while. And then she'll come to me.

79

After Uncle Don had scampered into the undergrowth and out of sight, I got back into the car. I was still functioning on a step-by-step basis. All I knew, for now, was that I had to drive back to the factory. All other doors in my mind were shut fast. What had happened, who was lying there, in the silent workroom: these were thoughts I could not follow. I suppose it was shock. I can see that it must be a useful defence mechanism, this closing down of everything except the next move. I concentrated on finding a gap in the traffic, and manoeuvring out of the layby. I drove at the speed limit, overtook with caution, observed the rules and courtesies of the road. The only clue to the horror I'd witnessed was a faint echo in the back of my mind of the sound of breaking glass.

By the time I'd parked in the apartment garage and was returning on foot to the factory, one phrase was spooling around my thoughts along with that calamitous sound: *there's been an accident*. It was the only phrase that could bring some semblance of normality, of sanity, to the evening's events. Accidents happen, don't they? All the time. They're terrible, distressing, traumatic—but we know they happen. *There's been an accident*. Scott overbalanced and fell through the skylight. Surely, that's what happened. He turned and saw a ghost, and took too many steps backwards. Nobody's fault. Just an accident.

I hurried across the dark factory yard, with my own laboured breath in my ears, overpowering the traffic. There was no other sound, no sign of activity at all. I could almost believe Uncle Don *had* been a ghost, or a figment of my imagination. I could almost believe the skylight would still be intact, and the workroom empty;

that Scott would be waiting for me at the apartment, and it would all turn out to be a dream.

But the workroom wasn't empty. He was still there, and the glass was still shattered.

80

Scott always seemed to have so many nameless friends, in so many places. This turned out to be the same as having no friends, anywhere. He was only in the 'simmering' stage of his next show, so there were no concerned calls from funders or organisers. Nobody else was involved; and apparently, he didn't cross anybody else's mind. I did speak to a colleague of his, another photographer, who called the apartment asking for him. I was a little vague about it all. I just said there'd been an accident.

'Christ, I'm sorry to hear that', she said. 'He was shit hot. Had a real eye, you know?'

I had the impression she thought I was glossing over the facts—and that she wasn't particularly surprised. Maybe she thought it was drugs. I could tell she was drawing her own conclusions. She didn't ask much about it, and after expressing her dismay and sympathy, said,

'I didn't really know him that well, to be honest. I was just after a contact number.'

I found her the number, and she said,

'So sorry for your loss' and rang off.

I forgot the colleague's name as soon as she'd finished the call. Maybe she was responsible for the short obituary that eventually appeared in one of the broadsheets; I don't know. Whoever it was had developed the conclusion in another direction, and diplomatically despatched Scott 'after a short illness'. There was a brief paragraph about his work; no mention of any family, no clue to his past. I had a kind, neatly written card from Taff through the post, and hugs from Penny and Dara, who didn't really know Scott at all. After that, nobody asked about his life or his death. I thought there might be some word from Rosalyn, but there wasn't. Someone, somewhere, must have had a connection with Scott, other than being framed within his viewfinder. But nobody ever appeared.

I shut the gallery immediately after the accident (I insisted on calling it that, even to myself), and gave my assistant two weeks off. I needed time to think, or not to think. And I had something to do.

I'd retrieved the gear Scott took to the factory. He loved the equipment as much as the photographs it produced. Nowadays people take photos as swiftly and thoughtlessly as they'll scratch an itch: snapshots of their pets, of their food, of themselves—quick flick of a phone no bigger than a hand, and yet another image floats into the overcrowded ether. But even now, I'm willing to bet he'd still be hoisting his old camera around, manipulating its complexities as deftly and lovingly as a musician playing his instrument. I turned this fascinating, mysterious machine around in my hands, admiring the sleek curves and angles, the smooth clickety-click of the dials, the diminishing circles of steel protecting the precious, impassive, all-seeing lens. He still used film, and inside this beautifully crafted machine were perhaps the best pictures Scott Carter had ever captured. What did they show? A city street? An argument? A momentary expression on a stranger's face? My heart hammered at the thought of those final patchworks of light and shade, hidden within this metal box, waiting to be conjured into life again. I shut my eyes and tightened my grip on the camera. The ring road sang its low and endless song. A child's yell ballooned from the distance. I wondered where Rosalyn was now, what she was doing, who she'd become. I needed to talk to her, about Scott, about the way life had gone awry. But she was lost to me. They were all lost.

It took me the full two weeks to destroy the camera. It was quite therapeutic, actually. It became a rite of veneration. First I removed the film and took a scissors to it—that was the easiest part. Then screw by screw, lever by lever, I dismantled the entire thing, bearing testament at every stage to the precision, art and love that had gone into its construction. I set each element aside onto a growing heap on the floor. Then I spent four days reducing everything in that heap to little more than grit. On the tenth day I knelt before the pyre of aluminium and glass shards and wept, for the last time, over my loss. I wept for myself and for my lonely future. I wept with grief and with unnamed fear. This was no skittering, surface anxiety; this was the terror that waits in the marrow of our bones and the cells of our blood, when we're finally left to ourselves.

81

After a fortnight I reopened the gallery. Gabby didn't work there in those days. After Chloë had left to have the first of a vast brood of children, I had a succession of short-term employees, most of whose names I've forgotten, but I remember who was there then: a woman called Molly, whose red-framed glasses covered half of her face. I can't summon the face itself: I recall her as a pair of specs and a stack of hay-coloured hair. I remember her name because I spent the next three weeks thanking her for blocking my calls. I wasn't quite myself yet. I forced myself to get up and get dressed in the morning with one unquestioning command: *go to work*. That's what Scott would have said, and that was as far as I could go. I'd arrive early, let myself in, go straight into the office, accept the coffee and bun Molly brought when she arrived, and spend the rest of the day sitting there, letting time pass. Molly would ask how I was; I'd say fine, just need to take it easy for a bit, and that was that. She left me in peace, dealt with everything that came along, provided food and cleared it away again, half-eaten. All I had to do was say, 'Thank you Molly.' 'Thanks for that, Molly.' 'Bless you, Molly, you're a star.'
At six she'd put her head round the door and say,
'I'll be off now then, Mr Hill', showing no sign of noticing that I hadn't budged for the past 10 hours. When she'd gone I would come out of my den, shuffle round the gallery for a while, then go home. I didn't give the displays a glance. They were just trivia, good for nothing but collecting dust.

I found it hard to believe I'd once gleaned such pleasure from the textures and objects around me. I ate and drank—mostly drank—to fuel my body; I went to the gallery to pay the bills. I tried Astey's a couple of times, but the coffee gave me the gripes. Sunlight on a wooden floor showed up the grime and traces of dogshit from

342

somebody's shoe. My furniture, my collection, the items on my shelves—so much jumble; when I'd gone it would be scattered across junk shops and boot sales, and all those webs of connection and association would be snapped clean away. The only possession that still held any meaning for me was the photograph of Rosalyn singing. I would gaze at it during the night, losing all sense of time, longing to share her serenity.

About six months later a package arrived from Italy with a letter from Dino's niece, telling me of his death and passing on Fortuna's good wishes.

'We thank you' she wrote, in a languid, sloping hand, 'for your kindness to my uncle, and we beg that you accept a small remembering of his work which made him so much proud.'

I unpacked the crystal vase and balanced its weight in the palm of my hand. It was a small piece, with space for one rose-stem and nothing more; but the workmanship was flawless. From the bowl it narrowed to caress the stem, then flared out into a thicker rim, echoing the bud that would flower above it. I thought of Dino in his heyday, his swaggering mastery of the furnace room, his scorn at my clumsy attempts to use the pipe, and his own easy grace as he dipped and turned and blew quick kisses to transform a puddle of hot liquid into art. I placed the vase on a side table, and stroked its swan-slim neck. Such a pointless thing, I told myself. Why would anyone make a vase for a single rose? One careless move as I wandered the apartment in the early hours, and it would hit the wooden floorboards and smash. Hardly worth the bother.

And yet I kept returning to that vase, to feel its silkiness under my fingers, to test the smoky thickness of its rim and dip my thumb into the mouth. I thought of a six-year-old boy, transfixed at a craft fair demonstration. That recollection had been sullied by Don's confession: we were only there so that he could pick up a fresh dose of poison for my mother. But now I reclaimed the memory. Whatever Uncle Don had been up to, I'd been there in my own right. I'd had my own, six-year-old feelings, and I'd discovered magic that day, watching the forces of fire and chaos brought under control, tamed into an artificial form.

From the streets outside came a flurry of car horns and shouts, marking some passing conflict. I moved to the window and looked at the grey sky closing over the factories. A few lamps came on to acknowledge the change of light, and my apartment appeared behind me, reflected in the darkened glass. I saw it there, apparently unconnected with me, as if for the first time. The chairs, the floor, the glass panels and tabletops—all so cool, so permanent. All created with care and skill, and all free of the taint of life or death. If Dino's vase broke—well, OK. Someone would make another one. I turned to see my possessions in their full, three-dimensional richness. I padded through the apartment to Scott's old room and, for the first time since the 'accident', I opened the door and went inside. His scent was still there, in the air. I went to the chair where a shirt of his had been discarded, who knows how many months before. I picked it up, breathed him in, then chucked it onto the floor. I opened the wardrobe and started hauling out his few clothes, flinging everything into a pile. The hangers were still chattering in my wake as I stripped the bed. All his belongings, everything that still bore a trace of him—comb, roll-on deodorant, toothbrush—all went onto that pile, then into bin bags, which I drove to a dump on the city's edge. I contemplated a charity shop, but couldn't bear to think that the life of his possessions would be prolonged, even by some stranger. Let them be burned, or buried, or whatever happens to our leavings. I drove home, retrieved the glass cutter from its place in the cabinet drawer, and soaked it in meths. No wisp of Scott Carter remained in my home, except his visions of Rosalyn. I was behaving like a murderer. In a way, that was how I felt. But when I'd finished I was more human, more equipped for daily life, than I had been for a very long time. I poured myself a brandy and thought: 'Tomorrow I really must look for some new stock.'

82

I'm approaching my front door, getting out my keys, when I see her. Rosalyn is shifting from foot to foot, grimacing at the tiny eye of my security peephole. She won't have seen it before: I only had it installed when I was left to live there alone. 'That won't work' I say, and she jumps and drops her handbag, spilling the contents.

'I thought you were in' she says, squatting to retrieve her stuff. I help her gather up the cards and keys and tissues.

'You can't see *in*, you know,' I say, leaning forward to catch the scent of her hair. 'That's for me to see *out.*'

'I know that.'

She's annoyed. I've caught her on the back foot. I get up to open the door. I'm on a high. Rosalyn has come to the apartment, unannounced, of her own accord. And my god, she's nervous.

I take her mack. She's wearing a nursery-pink cashmere jumper. The softness of the material, the plump tension of her body underneath it, carries me away. I grab her and kiss her, and she lets me, until I press her against my groin, and then she tries to pull away. I'm not going to let her go without a fight this time. We step around blindly, tussling, until finally she ducks and flails free of me, and manages to hold me off with outstretched arms, leaning her whole weight against my advance.

'*Please*, Rosalyn' I say. I sound like a drunk. This is not how I planned to come across, but I'm not in full control any more. '*Please …*'

'Wait, Nathan, wait, wait'—she sounds on the verge of tears, and then shouts, '*Don't!*' with such desperate misery that I have to snap out of it and stagger away.

My calves make contact with the couch and I double on to it. There's a moment's pause. Rosalyn is searching for something up her cashmere sleeves. She sniffs hard, and then produces a tissue and turns away to blow her nose. Her bag is open on the floor. Out of her sight, I reach in and take a tissue for myself.

'Sorry', I croak, after a while. She gives one final sniff and turns back to face me.

'I can't—' she starts. 'I just, I can't—' She tucks the tissue back up her sleeve. 'Oh, sod it,' she mutters, 'I knew *exactly* what I was going to say ...'

'My fault' I say, then, with genuine fury: 'I'm such an *idiot.*'

I feel her sympathy easing the tension between us. She speaks with kindness: 'No, don't take the blame. It's my fault, it's just ... It's just ... the situation.'

But that's not what I meant. My idiocy isn't about wanting Rosalyn, it's about playing the whole scene so badly, bringing everything to crisis point before we've even begun. I realise I may have set the whole thing back by weeks. Months, even. But I can barely lift my eyes, can barely look at her in that jumper, like a soft pink cat, without having to touch her, fill my arms with her ... I know I'm in danger of scuppering the whole damn thing. I put my head in my hands to squeeze out her presence. Then I feel her cool hand on my skull, and it's my turn to flinch away.

'If you touch me—' I warn her, and she moves quickly to the opposite chair and sits, clutching its leather arms like a lifebelt.

For a long time we both sit there, saying nothing, waiting to find out how this ends. After a while, I'm aware of her getting to her feet, and I muster the strength to look at her again. She's gazing at the photograph on the wall.

'Florence' she whispers.

I feel the tears welling again and bury my face in the tissue. This is ridiculous. I'm behaving like a teenager. I try and arrange a coherent sentence in my mind, but before I can speak she says,

'Did you keep that because Scott took it?'

I'm so nonplussed by the bitterness in her voice that I forget my self-pity and gape at her. After a couple of failed attempts to reply I manage:

'No. Because it's *you.*'

She gives me a cynical eye. I back-pedal a little.

'OK, it's a good shot ...' I concede, and she gives one triumphant nod.

'That's more like it.' Her eyes wander back to the picture. 'He was a talent, I can't deny that.'

I've recovered my senses now. This sudden rancour has been like a splash of icy water in the face. I sit up straight.

'Why would you *want* to deny it?' I demand. 'What *is* all this about Scott?'

'Nothing—' she starts, but I won't have that. We've come to this pass: may as well get it sorted. I take a deep breath and say,

'I used to think you and Scott might be ... involved.'

She stares. Blood flows and billows under her skin. The urge to touch that skin is almost unbearable. She starts to say something and I get up, waving my hands—

'*Used* to think. I got over it ... ' (and even now, the thought occurs to me: what if I was right? Should I be so ready to dismiss the idea?)

Her face is all frown. She says, quietly,

'*Me*? And *Scott*?'

'I know, I know, I was in a strange state of mind, I ...'

The sentence wilts under her thunderous consternation. We stand there for an age, facing each other across this monstrous misunderstanding. Then she speaks, in a small voice at odds with her expression:

'Your mother ...'

I hear the iciness in my own response.

'My mother—*what*?'

'She said you'd be better off—'

'Without me, yes. You said. You said she was doing you a favour, as I recall.'

I prefer this. A touch of contempt. I feel I'm regaining some measure of control.

'Yes. Without me, and *with Scott*. She said you could be yourself with him. *Just walk away*—that's how she put it. *Just walk away and let Nathan be himself.* She said I should go and have a family, be happy. She said you were never going to be a family man.'

There's a silence. We don't touch.

'Did she say we were lovers?'

She considers this.

'Well ... not in so many words. But then your mother never had to put everything into words, did she, Nathan? Her meaning was always *perfectly* clear.'

'Why didn't you ask *me*?' I ask, with a clenched jaw.

She lets out a long, tired sigh.

'I suppose ... I suppose I didn't want to. It was just another reason to go, Nathan. Not the only one.' She reaches a hand towards mine and the tips of our fingers touch. 'Let's not turn this into a tragedy. I made my own choice.'

She withdraws her hand and moves away. She starts to gather herself, to talk to me normally again.

'I have to go. Someone's coming to fix the washing machine.'

I feel very old. I say,

'She lied.' I remember my mother's rattling chant: *cheep, cheep, cheep.* 'She lied all her life. About everything. *Everything.*'

'Nathan' says Rosalyn, tenderly, 'don't hate your mother. Whatever she did, she always loved you.'

Rosalyn hasn't got a vengeful bone in her body. She is the finest, best and kindest person I have ever known. The full force of this truth hits me as she puts on her mack again, heads for that door again: the extent of my loss, of the life I could have lived …

'Don't', I say, more harshly than I mean to, 'Don't go. Not yet.'

'I've *got* to go' she says, firmly. She reaches the door, then turns and regards me with serious eyes.

'I love Bo.'

'I know—' I start, but she ignores me.

'I love Bo, and I love my children. That's my life. That's real.'

I step towards her. I say,

'I love you.'

After a long pause she says,

'No, you don't. You love the idea of me. You always did.'

'And Bo loves the *real you*?' I sneer. 'Wasn't he just a groupie who was there to catch you when you fell?'

She shakes her head. She feels sorry for me.

'Nathan, you have no idea. Bo is … we've had *children* together.'

I close my eyes. There really is no answer to that. I can't compete with the boisterous, joyful, anxious, exhausted intimacy of 20 years of parenthood. Rosalyn stands here, in my apartment, and what does she see? A lifetime of order and silence and sterility. And that, to her, is nothing. To Rosalyn love, real love, is the daily accumulation of kindness and compromise, the toleration of irritating habits, the boredom and contentment of the semi-detached, pebble-dashed home. She takes one sweeping look around my home and says:

'This isn't real.' Then, when I can't summon a reply, she adds: 'This is just … nostalgia.'

I know she's bringing our encounter to an end. But I haven't given up hope. She can give me all the earnest little speeches she likes, but Rosalyn Rathbone came to my home, and kissed me, and she's not just going to walk out of my life a second time.

'Before you leave,' I say, suddenly, 'do me one favour. Sing for me.'

She rolls her eyes, turns away, says,

'Nathaaan ...' in a way that reminds me of our first years together.

'Please', I wheedle. 'Just for old times' sake. Just to hear you again ...'

'I've got no voice' she protests. 'It's been years.' But she clears her throat, so I don't say any more. She thinks for a second, coughs again. Then softly, simply, she begins:

'Lullay, lullay, my little tiny child ...'

Not what I expected. Maybe it's all she can manage these days—a Christmas carol. She sings three verses, knows all the words. To be honest, by the last verse I'm a touch bored. It's still in there, somewhere, behind the loosened vibrato and the slightly scratchy throat. I can still make it out—the melancholy, yearning quality that used to chill my spine. But it's only a hint. It's a pleasant, light voice, now, unused and unsupported. An ageing voice.

'Thank you' I whisper, when she's finished. I kiss her tamely on the cheek. The scent and warmth of her skin, the remnants of her singing, move me profoundly, but my physical desire has subsided, for the time being. She doesn't want me—not enough. Not yet. I hold the door for her, eager, now, to be alone.

83

Rosalyn. One hundred million volts. So many years of hard work, gone to waste.

After that terrible night, the crash of glass, the fizz of shrubbery as Uncle Don spidered out of the layby, I made my choice. I dammed up all the past, and I mastered the art of living in the present. It wasn't easy. It took a lot of determined perseverance. I could have let it all plague my mind and contaminate the rest of my days. But I refused. I walked the same way to work every day. Had my regular coffee at Astey's. The barrista never needed to take my order. Another assistant left the gallery and Gabby took the job. Sometimes I thought about letting the business wind down, selling it on and looking for pastures new. But I couldn't quite bring myself to let it go. I still relished every new piece. I read about new wars, new atrocities and disasters, tutted and shook my head, and put it all away: all the foul, sick filth of it, all the wrenching, ugly grief of it, all the pain. I turned away, and filled my life with beauty. Beauty is not a soft option. It's a ruthless, cold-eyed, conscious choice. It's survival.

The gallery went from strength to strength. Peta Krantz made a splash with her first British collection; Suki Mezler was just beginning to find her form. I was gaining a reputation for taking risks with bright new talents. We entered the digital age with confidence, and planned to launch a website. That's what I was doing, one particular February day: studying the pictures we were going to upload. I was looking at a mirror by Trent Hope, as it happens. She'd indulged her usual obsession with blues and created a frame that rippled like blown water, in dazzling strips of powder blue, midnight blue, royal blue, all competing to distract the eye from its reflection. The phone rang. I let it ring for a while, thinking Gabby would answer. Maybe she was with a customer. It carried on ringing, and in the end I picked it up.

'Nathan Hill Gallery.'

'Morning, sunshine.'

I heard my own breath. I said,

'Where are you?'

It sounded defensive—not concerned. He said,

'Somewhere with a phone,' then I heard a distant thunder-roll, and realised he was laughing. I tried to picture him, but my mind flipped chaotically between images: Don in a business suit, at a desk; Don in his rags, stinking out a phone box. I said, 'What do you want? Money?'

My head throbbed at the prospect of another layby transaction. *He can't force me*, I told myself. *He can't make me do anything.* I could go to the police. I could—

'Just want to know how you're doing, son. That's all.'

'I'm OK', I said, then, automatically, 'How are you?'

'Don't worry about *me*,' said Uncle Don, in a voice like rust. 'I can cope. I can light a fire with a rock and a prayer. I can skin a rabbit. I can kip under a hedge ... '

'What do you want, Uncle Don?' I asked again.

'Nothing, sunshine. I don't want nothing. I come from nothing before, I'll do it again. I'm just biding my time.'

The phone went dead. I sat for a long time, wondering about my next step. I heard the chink of the gallery door opening. Slowly, I rose from my desk and went to the office door. As I opened it a woman's voice called,

'Hello?'

A thin, elderly woman with fragile movements and expensive clothes. Passing trade.

'Hello, there, how can I help you?'

I consigned Uncle Don to his madness for the present, and went back to business. *Work, Nathe. That's all that matters in the end.* This was the doctrine I followed and believed—until Rosalyn went bustling past, shopping trolley in tow, and brought it all flooding back like sewage, lapping against my dreams at night and my thoughts all day. It'll take a great deal of effort to restore my equilibrium. But I'll do it. I'm a tightrope-walker who's momentarily lost his balance. I'll find my centre of gravity. I did it before, and I'll do it again.

84

'Here you are' I said, without conviction. 'Everything you need'.

I dumped the carrier bags on the cottage floor, then immediately picked them up again. It didn't seem wise to let anything touch that floor. I swept a space of sorts on the draining board and started to unload the bags. A travel kettle, two mugs, a plate, fork and spoon. Cuppasoup, bread, crisps, fags. Teabags, milk, beer, chocolate. I didn't want to risk anything that needed cooking until I'd satisfied myself that the decrepit oven was fit for use. He was loitering in the only other downstairs room, examining the rubbish piled in the hearth.

'Someone's been using this' he said to himself, then raised his voice, for my benefit: 'Someone's been in here! They might come back.'

I carried on clearing the kitchen as best I could, and called cheerfully back,

'No, they won't come back. Not once they see there's someone here.'

He went bumbling round the room, muttering, exploring his new hidey-hole. When I'd done all I could do in the kitchen I went to cast an eye over his living area. Fireplace, chair, table. A wooden ladder in one corner, with a hatch leading up to the loft, where he would sleep. I said,

'I'll sort out some kind of heating for you. Shall I make us a cup of tea? Might as well use the milk before it goes off. I'll fix up a little fridge for you. Soon as the elecricity's reconnected.'

I wrestled with the tap and pressed on, delivering an inventory of the mod cons in his new bijou residence.

'Outside loo, very hygienic … quite a bit of garden out there, under all the jungle … Oh, and I've got a camping lamp in the car, one of those wind-up things, that'll do until I can get some lighting sorted out …'

'Don't want light' he snarled, shuffling up behind me. 'No light. Might be spotted.'

'You won't be spotted' I said, barely keeping my patience. 'There's nobody here to spot you. You'll be perfectly safe to light a fire, light the lamp, make yourself at home. And once the power's on you can turn on the Blackpool illuminations in here and nobody's going to notice.'

My little speech was greeted with such a protracted silence that in the end I turned to check he was still there, and was alarmed to see his face crumpling like a child about to cry.

'You'll be fine …' I said, and put a tentative arm around him. His lower lip trembled and he turned his frightened eyes to me. I sighed. 'Look, why don't you come back to the apartment? It'll be—'

'No.' His mood changed abruptly and his lip relaxed. 'This is good. This is what I want.'

'I'll come back' I said. 'I'll make sure you've got everything you need.'

When I drove away that first evening, seeing the darkness pool among the trees in my rear-view mirror, aiming my car towards the blessed lights already pearling the city's edges, I assured myself this would pass: this was just a phase. He'd soon tire of it. But he's still there.

85

Find a gap in the traffic. Manoeuvre out of the layby. Drive home. *There's been an accident.* Follow the rules of the road. Faint echo of breaking glass.

Parked my car in the apartment block garage. Walked back to the factory site in the dark. *There's been a terrible accident.* The workroom door scraped reluctantly open. He was still there, lying with the shattered glass. I took four paces and stood over his body. I said,

'He's gone.'

I looked at Scott's pale and lovely face. I saw a couple of sparks of light: tiny glass fragments on his cheek and chin. But no blood that I could see. I said again:

'He's gone. For good, this time.'

One of the lasts shifted fractionally. Then the movement spread through the whole mound of blue and brown feet, which began to undulate under Scott's weight, with a clattering that built into a tumultuous round of applause as he battled into a sitting position. He shook his head hard, like a dog, ridding his hair and skin of the few specks of glass that had landed on him. There weren't many. Glass can take you by surprise, that way.

I helped him to his feet. We went carefully, testing, but it had been fairly obvious from the moment I'd first seen him there, nested in the shoe lasts, that he wasn't seriously hurt. He grunted and groaned a bit, nursed his lower back, but there was nothing worse than bruises. Or at least, nothing that we could see.

'Maniac,' he muttered. 'Fucking maniac.'

'I wasn't sure you'd still be here,' I told him. I was holding him up by his arm, but he suddenly sat back down on the heap.

'Tried to kill me' he said. 'Actually tried to kill me. Fucking maniac.'

I squatted down in front of him.

'Did he?—I can't make sense of it. I don't know what I saw' I admitted. He shook his head, went on shaking it. I wasn't sure whether that meant *neither do I* or just general disbelief. I said again,

'I wasn't sure you'd still be here.' I noticed that my hands were shaking. The shock was starting to hit. Scott said,

'Waited for you. Scared to *move.*' His head stopped shaking but he didn't look at me. 'Waited for you. Didn't know if you'd come back.'

'Of course I came back!' I shouted, then: 'Sorry. We're both a bit ... Come on. Let's go home.'

Now he looked at me, and his eyes were peeled wide, his body quivering like a wire.

'No' he breathed. 'Not home. Not there. He was ... *waiting*, Nathan. He was *waiting for me.*'

I reached forward to take his hands.

'Don has gone' I told him, but my voice wasn't steady. 'He's just a sad old man, losing his mind, and he'll probably die in a gutter.'

'I'm not going back there,' said Scott.

'Well ... where, then? The studio? Shall I book you a room somewhere?'

I was helping him to his feet again, and he seemed to be thinking hard, his eyes following different possibilities.

'Where's the car?' he asked.

'I left it in the garage. Come on, I'll book you a room—'

'No,' he said, straightening now, regaining some confidence. 'I'll sleep in the car. On the floor, in the back. He can't see me there ...'

I stopped and studied his face.

'In the *car*? Scott, for Christ's sake, if you don't want—'

'In the car. Until I think of somewhere else. Now, quickly, before …'

He was already on the move, limping slightly, clutching my arm. It wasn't until we got to the garage that I remembered his equipment, still on the upper roof. He hadn't even mentioned it.

He was convinced that Uncle Don would come back for him, adamant that he would not return to the apartment. It occurred to me that, left to his own paranoid devices, he might resort to old habits and hide among the zombies in The Cut. So I offered to sleep in the car with him. I spent the night huddled in the front, shifting the cramp from one part of my body to another, while he fidgeted and snuffled on the floor in the back. Every so often I fell into a light sleep, busy with vivid dreams. Hour after hour I sat there, my cheek pressed against the cold window, alternating between the sallow lights of the underground car park and the carnival colours of my dreamworld, where Rosalyn sang and glass bubbles grew and burst and a horde of wild-haired, spectral creatures advanced on me in an alleyway, getting a little nearer every time I closed my eyes.

Eventually, I woke to a glottal dawn chorus of cars responding to their owners' key fobs. Hurried feet tapped across the concrete and a procession of expensive cars began to glide out of the garage. I received a couple of curious looks from passing drivers, but they probably assumed I'd had a fun night out. I reached between the front seats and prodded Scott's arm.

'Come on. Get up.'

He made a wincing sound as he sat up.

'You need to see a doctor' I croaked, easing my legs painfully from the seat.

'Check you did no damage.' My eyes were sticky with gristle.

'NO.' The sound of his voice was a shock. Guttural, ancient, nothing like his own. 'No doctor.'

I massaged the bridge of my nose and opened the window a fraction to release our night stinks.

'Scott,' I said, after a moment, 'should we call the police?' I twisted round to look at him. He was slowly hauling himself up onto the back seat. I hesitated, then added: 'Because the truth is, I don't know what I saw last night. I don't know what to tell them.'

'He tried to kill me' said Scott, as he had the night before. But he sounded more clear-headed. 'Fucking maniac tried to *kill me.*'

'Are you *absolutely sure*?' I said. 'Are you sure you didn't just fall? Sure enough to tell the police?'

He screwed his eyes shut. I thought he might lose his temper, but he seemed to be trying to remember, because presently his eyes opened, and he shook his head. 'I just know he *wanted* me to fall.'

I sighed. I gave a long but awkward stretch. I watched a Jag swim past and said, 'Well—what now? You can't spend the rest of your life in the back of my car.'

He didn't answer. When I looked back again, he had his sleeve rolled up and was stroking the scarred Vs on his arm. We'd never discussed their presence, and I didn't know what to say. I was suddenly very cold. There were no fresh scars there: it was some time since he'd needed to carve away his urges. Now Uncle Don's ghost had infected Scott with his madness. I dreaded to think what kind of treatment he might seek, or how he might resist it. I turned back and addressed the mirror.

'OK,' I said. 'What if I find you somewhere? Somewhere new, somewhere nobody could possibly know about, or even reach?' I was ad-libbing furiously, but I had his attention, and I was pretty sure my solution was possible. Anything's possible, if you can pay. I pushed on:

'I'm thinking, somewhere really remote, where nobody knows you, or me. Just for the time being. Until we can be sure he's gone.'

Scott rolled his sleeve down.

'Can you do that?' he asked, and he sounded like a child.

'Yes,' I said. 'I can do that.'

87

It's the day of the launch. Freddie has somehow managed to get her own way: Gabby and I spend the morning clearing the whole gallery to display her work. Gabby has even made a pointed comment:

'Freddie's obviously flavour of the month, then ...' —with a mischievous, fractional look. That's pretty strong stuff, coming from Gabby.

Freddie arrives at noon, jittery and clipped. No girly embraces today, no surreptitious pinches or winks. Freddie is At Work. She spends an age over the placing of each piece, changes the display a dozen times: no, the glass eyelines are too uniform; no, the angles don't work; no, the colours are too dissonant, too consonant, too this or that or the other. At 4 o'clock Gabby sinks into her chair, sweaty and tired, and says,

'We'd better eat something soon, or we'll starve to death before the hordes descend.'

Freddie glares at her own creations, turns a slow circle, turns back, heaves a defeated sigh.

'Oh, well,' she says, 'I suppose it's never going to be *perfect* ...'

'Looks fine and dandy to me,' says Gabby. 'Shall I go and get the teas?'

When she's gone I touch Freddie on the elbow and murmur:

'There's nothing to worry about, you know. They're going to *love* you.'

For the first time, the old Freddie reappears. She flings an arm round my neck and kisses me full on the mouth. But it's a theatrical kiss. Not a lover's kiss. Something has changed.

'You've been such a star' she says. 'You've been *incredible.*' There's a valedictory sound to that. She's already leaving me behind.

The first guests start arriving at 8, by which time we're all washed and brushed and at our best, handing out the buck's fizz and caviar bites. I guide the main players round the display and deposit them in front of Freddie, who's in her element, now, nodding, thanking, coming out with immaculate quotes about her method and inspiration. The glass heads watch at carefully varied angles. Disdain; interest; suspicion. They stare at the guests, and the guests stare back. The gallery fills; the voices bubble; we prop the door open and a few people spill on to the pavement to smoke. No sign of Rosalyn yet.

'I've always been intrigued' Freddie is saying to an audience of half a dozen, 'by the fission of face and, like, feeling …'

She breaks off to pose for a photographer next to one of her heads.

I move towards the door again. Ah. Here they come. Rosalyn and Bo stop-start across the road, watching for traffic. They're holding hands. Sweet.

I make my way to the back of the gallery, performing little half-dances around people, touching arms and checking names, and slip into my office. The box holding the kingfisher is on my desk, tied with a scarlet ribbon. My plan is to catch Rosalyn's eye and summon her in here, where I can watch her open it, see the progress of her emotions, say my line:

It's the colour of your voice.

Might have to dispense with that one, after hearing her sing the other day. Never mind: the gift will make my point. She'll be back, in a week, a month, a year … I can wait. Maybe the beauty of it will have immediate results, and I'll claim my reward as they're toasting Freddie's debut in the next room.

I prise the door ajar and look into the fray. Some dolt is directly in the way, telling a loud joke. I glimpse Rosalyn. She's talking to Freddie, congratulating her, all smiles and generosity. I'll have to give it a few minutes. As I'm shutting the door again,

'Nathan! What are you doing, lurking in that cubby-hole? Not hiding, are we?'

Oh, piss off, Bo.

'Bo! Good to see you! Glad you could make it!'

'Wouldn't have missed it' he says, then drops to a whisper. 'I don't suppose there's a loo back there? Old man's trouble, you know ...'

I can hardly lie; Gabby would probably give the game away. So I open the door just wide enough to let him in, and direct him through the office to the loo at the back. While I'm waiting for him someone raps on the office door; I ignore it. Bo emerges from the loo and is trotting back to the party when the box catches his eye.

'Ooh' he says. 'Looks exciting!'

'Oh, no, it's ...' Oh, sod it. 'Actually', I confess, 'it's a little something for Rosalyn. It's her birthday, isn't it? Hope that's all right ...'

'I'm sure that's *more* than all right!' he bellows. 'Let's get her in to open it!'

'Oh, no, no' ... I seize his elbow and steer him out. 'Too embarrassing. Honestly, it's only a ... Let's save it for later. She can open it at home.'

Of course, he makes a beeline for her as soon as we're out of the office, weaving between the guests, shouting over their heads.

'Rosie! Hey, birthday girl! Pressie for you, back there!'

Is this deliberate? I'm beginning to think Bo's not quite as innocent as he seems.

Rosalyn shoots me one of her looks—half pleading, half exasperated.

'Nathan, really ...'

'Oh, it's nothing', I snap. 'Really. Just something I thought you'd like ... Pick it up before you go.'

Bo ignores my petulance. He puts his hand on the small of my back and goes up on his toes to speak into my ear.

'By the way, don't know if you heard—Anna was sent back.'

'What?' I widen my eyes in horror. 'Sent back? You mean, deported?'

'Afraid so. That's how it goes, I fear. It was always a long shot. But, Nathan'—his hand presses more firmly on my spine—'don't feel your efforts were wasted. It's all about communication. Putting the message across. That's what you have to tell yourself ...'

I dip my head so that I can continue talking to Bo while keeping my eyes on Rosalyn.

'Poor Anna. What a wretched business' I say. 'So, what will you do next? Another campaign?'

Bo and Rosalyn look at each other in a sickeningly conspiratorial way.

'As a matter of fact,' says Bo, 'we're off on our travels.'

'Travels?'

The friendly pressure of his hand delivers a current of dread through my innards.

'Holidays?' I suggest, with little hope.

'Oh, dear, no. Don't think we'd fancy taking our hols in the Congo!'

'The *Congo*?'

I glare at Rosalyn openly, now, but she's studiously examining her glass of fizz.

'Yes', says Bo. 'We've been planning it for a while, but we wanted to wait until the little'un was born ...'

'But don't you want to be around to see her grow up?'

There's no disguising the rise of panic in my voice. Bo pats my back affably.

'Oh, we'll keep in touch. And we'll be popping back, from time to time, I'm sure. And, you know, Nathan, when you get to our age you have to grab your opportunities …'

Your age, I rage at him in my head; not *hers*. She's still not meeting my eye. I think: *she doesn't want to go.*

'How about you, then, Rosalyn?' I demand. 'How do you feel about this?'

She has to look up. She sees the colour in my face. I don't care any more.

'We want to do something worthwhile', she says. 'Something that *matters*.'

The backs of my eyes are stinging. I want to stand here forever. As long as we're here, in this room full of nobodies, as long as I'm looking at her, she's mine. But I'm the one who looks away in the end. I don't want to weep in public. And I can't abide the pity in her face. I steady myself and say,

'Well! Best of luck to you both!'

Bo shakes my hand and says,

'Be sure to come and see us before we go.'

And then Rosalyn says, with unbearable kindness,

'I hope you'll be happy, Nathan.'

I turn my back on them but I can't move away; the gallery's too full. So I stand there, sensing Rosalyn's presence behind me, forcing myself to smile and nod at familiar faces in the crowd. I look across at Freddie, who's finished her interviews and is waving at someone near the door. Not at me. As I watch, she battles through the gallery. Pushing his way towards her is the youth from her flat.

'Kit!' she shrieks at him. Oh, yes. That's the name.

They meet in the middle of the room and clamp like magnets. Something tells me I've served my purpose, as far as Freddie is concerned.

88

'I need a shower. So do you.'

'I'm fine,' said Scott. 'I'll wait for you here.'

It was pointless arguing. That fall, which had left his body virtually unscathed, had apparently opened a wound in his mind. I left him the car fob. I was half hoping he'd drive off, and then I'd be rid of two fucking maniacs, and could get on with my life. But he was still there, folded up on the floor, when I returned after a couple of hours, showered and fed.

'Tell you what,' I said, getting back into the driver's seat. 'We're going to the gallery. You can hide in the back, go to the loo, have a wash at the sink. Molly will get you some breakfast. And I'll go and sort things out.'

I'd decided to take a firm line: keep him informed, but shut down any argument. That seemed to work. We had to go a couple of streets from the gallery to find a parking space, and he watched the cars and pedestrians closely as we walked those few hundred yards, but he was docile enough, and said a calm hello to Molly as I ushered him into the back. I told her he was a 'friend in need':

'Could you do me a huge favour and pop out for a latte and Danish for us both? Thanks, Molly. You're a star.'

The red-framed glasses and hay-coloured hair went out in search of breakfast, and I started browsing the online estate agents. I found what I was after fairly quickly—not surprisingly, given that every spare shed and cardboard box was slapped with a price tag. I saw the words *DEVELOPMENT POTENTIAL* and a fuzzy picture of a shack in the bushes. OK, I thought. Cash down, no questions asked. The perfect place for a dead man to curl up and die again—or have a shave and a miraculous change of life. Either way, in due course, I'll have it done up and eventually flog it for a profit. Win, win.

He agreed to doss down in the gallery office until I'd completed the transaction. I brought him food when Molly had clocked off for the day, then locked him in and went home. He was nervous at first, wanted me to stay with him, but when I showed him the security system he was reassured.

'Don't go into the main gallery,' I warned him, 'or you'll set off every siren known to Man.' I was exaggerating, of course, but it was enough to calm his worst fears. He tucked himself onto my two-seater sofa with the quiet wariness of a nervous pet.

Anyway, it didn't take long to do the deal. The cottage was too remote and in too dire a state to attract buyers even in that frenetic market. The agents virtually fell at my feet in their eagerness to get shot of it.

'It'll be perfect for me,' I waffled, 'once it's habitable—a perfect artist's retreat.' I don't know why I felt the need to justify myself. Maybe paranoia really is catching. Or maybe, even in those surreal circumstances, I wanted to show off.

He sat in the back of the car and I chatted inanely as I drove, eyeing him in the mirror. I began by talking up the cottage, telling him my plans for it—how I would have it scooped and scrubbed and then start it from scratch. I described the floors I'd have laid, how the meagre kitchen could be transformed, maybe a spiral staircase up to the converted loft … He remained silent, wedged into a corner of the seat, his eyes flicking, flicking, as he monitored everyone we passed. In the end I gave up on the cottage and reverted to taxi-talk—the news, the weather, anything that surrounded us but didn't touch our lives. Then I just put the radio on. As we left the city behind, I caught a movement in the mirror and saw that he was sitting forward, relaxing. Some politician was pontificating about the invasion of Iraq. 'There's no doubt *whatsoever*,' he was saying, 'that we will find *substantial* stores

369

of weapons of mass destruction, which pose an *immediate* danger to the Western world ...'

I passed some comment, and Scott nodded.

'Yeah', he said. 'The man's a twat.' He eased his shoulders back and made himself more comfortable.

To me, the city has always been a place of safety. It's the countryside that makes me uneasy. All those incomprehensible ranked fields, the dense hedges, the woods and copses harbouring their cold, endless night. That's where I'd see my demons— lurking among the branches. But as soon as there was a distance between us and the mass of other people, Scott was functioning again. This night-hunter, this witness to suffering and conflict, had relished humanity despite it all. *There have to be people*. That's what he'd said, centuries before. *Human figures, human faces. A face*, he'd told me, *a face makes it a story*. Even after Kosovo, when his focus changed to abandoned spaces, they were all about the human lives and activities that had created them. They were *city* spaces. And now all that had changed. One deranged old man, one personal vendetta, had broken Scott's bond with humanity.

I'd seen the estate agent details, and I knew exactly how isolated the place was. But until we fought our way through the anarchic shrubbery and unlocked the front door, I hadn't really appreciated the ruined state of the cottage. Something small sped out of the unexpected daylight and under the doddery oven. Scott stood just behind me, and we both looked around. There was a smell of mold, and something unnameable. I said,

'You could get some incredible shots here.'

I was trying to be normal. To spark his interest. He didn't speak, so I turned and said again: 'You could get—'

'NO.' He was still looking at the walls, not at me. 'No shots. None of that.'

'OK.' I was learning not to argue with anything. 'Well … anyway, we can start work on it straight away. Even if we do a quick spruce-up, initially, it'll be very liveable with a new cooker, a washing ma—'

'No, no, no, no …' I heard the fear rising again. 'No people. No work.' He moved past me and peered at the foliage blinding the one small window. He said, 'This will be fine. It's good. I'll be safe here.'

So I went into the village and bought his supplies. He had his brief panic, when he saw the abandoned rubbish in the fireplace.

'Someone's been in here! They might come back.'

'No, they won't come back. Not once they see there's someone here.'

I made tea; I made casual conversation. I pointed out that he'd need a fridge. Electricity. I made the mistake of mentioning lights …

'No light. Might be spotted.'

I tried one last time to coax him back to the apartment.

'No. This is good. This is what I want.'

'I'll come back' I said. 'I'll make sure you've got everything you need.'

And as I was watching him prowl the edges of his new den, catlike, and bracing myself to hand over his key and leave, he said, quite clearly and rationally,

'I want you to get rid of everything.'

'What do you mean, *everything*?'

'Cameras. Tripods. All of it. And everything else. I want to disappear.'

I made a non-committal noise and he stopped in his tracks and looked me fiercely in the eye.

'*Promise me.*'

So I promised. And truth be told, by the time I got home, the thought of erasing

Scott Carter from my life, along with Uncle Don and Mother and Rosalyn and all the other mania, had taken on its own appeal.

89

By midnight everyone has gone. I haven't even seen Rosalyn and Bo leave. They must have sneaked away quietly soon after our exchange. Gabby starts clearing up as the last guests are leaving. She looks ready to drop. I send her home.

'No rush' I say. 'I'll come in tomorrow and get everything sorted.' She doesn't argue. Good old Gabby. Never a word of complaint. I expect she'll move on to fresher pastures and a better salary before the year is out.

Freddie and Kit are the last to go, hand in hand. Freddie is a bit drunk, mainly with the occasion. She kisses me on the cheek and says,

'Thanks, Nathan. I'll never forget this.'

'Awesome' says Kit.

As they're heading for the door, Freddie remembers something and turns back:

'Oh, Nathan, that commission, you know? The portrait bust thingy?'

'Yes?'

'It's cool, no problem, I'll get to it, but—thing is, I've had so much interest, and enquiries and stuff—'

'I know', I say, raising a hand. 'Other priorities. Don't worry, Freddie. No rush.'

She blows me a kiss. 'Nathan, you are a god.'

I lock the door after them and survey the leavings of the launch. Tomorrow. I'll deal with it tomorrow. I wander into my office, and there's the ridiculous bow-tied box full of Rosalyn's birthday present, still sitting on the desk. My heart catches. Maybe this is fate. Maybe it's my cue to take it round to their place. Get her alone, one more time, before they go off on their do-gooders' Atrocity Tour …

On an impulse I untie the bow, open the box and lift out the kingfisher. *It's the colour of your voice.* For Christ's sake. The full force of my delusion crashes over my head. Day after day, I move around my little world, seeing myself like a character on a screen—self-assured and strong, a survivor, a conqueror, observing everything and everyone in my life with the objective and superior eye of a connoisseur. And here I am, hiding alone in my tiny glass universe, with an unwanted present and an undelivered line. Just a sorry old man with a sad old obsession, and a room full of pointless knick-knacks. As if to underline my humiliation, I suddenly realise what I *should* have given Rosalyn for her birthday. Not this extravagant fanfare of curving blue. I should have brought her the fulgurite from my private collection. Lightning glass. A frozen moment. A thrill of energy and life, caught and kept. I stand there, paralysed by my stupidity, by my lost past, and my empty future. From nowhere, a memory slices through my mind. Carlotta, the receptionist, her face pebble-dashed with cuts, confiding in Rosalyn at the hospital:

All those lovely things ... I used to pick them up, and they were so lovely, I almost wanted to smash them myself ...

I lift the kingfisher in both hands and pitch it against the wall. Even as it flies, I imagine a disappointing thunk and a bounce—but no, it behaves exactly as it should, shattering completely. I have to duck to avoid the flying splinters. In my imagination, a cloud of melancholy blue flowers into the air, then evaporates.

I go back into the gallery and look around. Freddie's faces gurn at me from their shelves. There are small red 'sold' stickers under most items. It won't take long. One by one, piece by piece—all that thought and care and skill and concentration will be gone in a flash, exploding all over the floor in layers of pale colour. I'll go methodically, left to right, around the room. Finish it all. There'll be hell to pay.

374

Financial ruin, maybe, psychiatric reports, definitely—and the smug headlines, nodding knowingly to each other: *Family Curse; Riches to Rags—Part Two; The Generation Game: Meltdown and Madness.* It might even reach Rosalyn, before Bo spirits her away to nowhere. She might see, then, what she's done to me. She might have a change of heart …

I make for the first glass head. It's the experiment that turned into a distorted scream. How appropriate. As I'm reaching up for it, something catches my eye. A tiny anomaly in the gallery's clean lines. An accretion clings to the underside of the shelf. A decorative nugget of wood, exquisitely carved and tucked almost out of sight. I stoop for a closer look. No, not wood—something softer, like a clump of hair or fur … Suddenly I understand: a cocoon. Somehow—god knows how—a wriggling inch of nature has found its way into my quarantined interior, and chosen this site for its metamorphosis. Surely, it's the wrong time of year—but maybe that doesn't matter in this artificial environment. I hold my breath and examine the impossibly delicate construction. Inside that bundle, a busy process of decomposition and creation is taking place. Some crawling thing has dissolved into a soup of chemicals, and its cells are shifting, rearranging themselves into wisps of leg and antenna, preordained patterns of wing. A new memory flutters across my thoughts: my father, stooping over a shrub in the garden, beckoning to me with urgent arms. His face, warm and large and stubbled, close to mine, and his voice explaining what went on in that long knot of silk suspended from a leaf … I must have been very young. I had no sense of awe—only a vague horror.

'Does that mean the caterpillar's made its own coffin?' I asked.

As usual, he offered me a silver lining:

'In a way—but it'll come out of it flying!'

For years after that, I had a recurring nightmare of strange creatures emerging from

375

the earth, pausing to shake off clods of soil and grass and rising with a slow push of their greasy, grey wings.

Staring at this knobble of reincarnation under the shelf, I feel the ripples of that childish fear. The worst of the nightmare wasn't the monsters themselves. It was the sense of relentlessness, of everything changing, continuing, without respite. I reach out to knock the coccoon away. I could crush it, easily, in my fist. I could put a stop to the whole remorseless cycle. Right now.

A helicopter flaps overhead, then fades. Light from the street burnishes Freddie's glass faces, shadowing their features and changing their moods. A pattering against the window: it's starting to rain. The pattering quickens and merges into a steady hiss. I think about Scott, who believed that rain is only rain, and has nothing to do with our petty tragedies. Scott always told the truth. Last time I visited the cottage, I found two sheets of paper crumpled near the hearth. I crouched to chuck them in with the rest of the kindling, but noticed something that piqued my interest, and smoothed one of them out on the floor. It was a used page from an old notebook— mine, in fact; I'd left it there after making a list of jobs that need doing. Only small-scale jobs. He still won't countenance the thought of major work, and the small army of visitors that would involve. There was my writing (pretty messy, these days; I'm out of practice with paper and pen): *Paint & sealant; Clean chimney*—and so on. And over the loops and tails of biro, a stronger, richer line, drawn in thick pencil, flying over the flimsy page like a starling's dance. In fact it *was* a starling: the line swooped, turned, closed itself into a perfect, confident freehand sketch of a bird. I opened out the second sheet, and there was another version, marginally different in dimension and angle; fractionally more effective. I looked up, about to call Scott, but changed my mind. If he's starting to draw, to try something new, best to give him some space. He clearly has talent. Another view of the world, a new art, is growing from that dungheap, and I'm the only one who knows about it. There's something exciting about that. Anyway ... if I don't drive to the cottage tomorrow with fresh provisions, Scott will have nothing at all to eat. So he gives me a reason to face the day, and I return the favour, and keep him alive. It's a future, of sorts.

I leave the cocoon, and the glass faces, where they are. One face has caught a stray beam of city light, and observes my change of mind with the indifferent grace of a Greek mask.

I hope you'll be happy, Nathan.

That's what everyone is hankering after, isn't it? Happiness. The right job, the right possessions, and above all, the right partner. *Love.* What a farce that is. Everyone flailing around, desperate to connect with someone who loves them back. We play this eternal, unwinnable game of 'pairs', turning one card and another, looking for patterns and parallels, trying to make everything match. It's not going to work. I love Rosalyn; I loved having her in my life. Losing her for the second time—it could break me. But I decide it will not. I decide I *will* be happy. Survivors like Peta Krantz, even people like Anna, who *really* know what suffering is—I believe they understand what that decision means. Happiness takes practice, perseverance. It's a selfish, stubborn choice. And it's the only art I have.

I find a brush and dustpan in the storage cupboard, sweep up the kingfisher's remains and pour them into the box. I take it with me as I set the alarm, switch off the main lights and lock the gallery door. I'll dump it in a bin on the way home, and cover the cost. I reach the corner of the road, where I saw Rosalyn emerge from my past with her shopping trolley. I turn to look at the gallery. Freddie's faces are inscrutable in the faint, blue glow of the night lights. Fragile and strong.

377

Ultimately, everything will splinter, shatter, wear away into grains of sand. But as long as we're here, as long as we're human, somebody will crawl from the wreckage and start it all over again: the slow and miraculous dance of molten glass, finding its form under a careful, guiding hand.

21970120R00213

Printed in Poland
by Amazon Fulfillment
Poland Sp. z o.o., Wrocław